A Crop Farmer's Daughter:

A heartbreaking emotional page-turner based on a true story

IONI GOLDSTEIN
AND CATARINA GRANATER

Producer & International Distributor
eBookPro Publishing
www.ebook-pro.com

A CROP FARMER'S DAUGHTER
Ioni Goldstein and Catarina Granater

Copyright © 2024 Ioni Goldstein and Catarina Granater

All rights reserved; no parts of this book may be reproduced or transmitted in any form or by any means, electronic or mechanical, including photocopying, recording, taping, or by any information retrieval system, without the permission, in writing, of the author.

Translation from Hebrew: Julia Ehrenfeld
Editing: Danielle Nagler

Contact: IONI@carasso.co.il;
Catarina.granater@gmail.com

ISBN 9798328821131

Preface

Ioni

I had known Catarina for a long time and yet knew almost nothing about her past. She made cute mistakes when speaking Hebrew with a heavy Brazilian accent, and I found her joie de vivre delightful. Though our relationship was not intense, we got together from time to time. I was aware of what went on in her life and she was aware of what went on in mine. One day she blurted out, in some context or other, that what she had wanted most since she was a child was to study. She said that buying her three pencils and a notebook was all the help she had ever gotten from her parents. I was intrigued.

She was a lab technician and I knew she had attended nursing school in Brazil. Little by little, she began to talk about her life.

She spoke with hesitation, as if afraid I might judge her differently after learning of her past. She didn't reveal everything at once. Feeling her story was alien, distant, exciting, sad, yet full of resilience and optimism, I suggested she write it all down.

Catarina started off alone, then we continued together. For many years we sat together every week in the evening hours. Catarina narrated while I typed. We laughed together. We cried together. I probed, and she explained the parts I did not understand. I turned my notes into actual writing which I sent to Catarina for comments and additions. *Catarina in the Corn Fields* began to take shape, together with a friendship that has made us soulmates forever.

Catarina

My past was hidden inside me like a secret. I arrived in Israel at the age of twenty-six, with fifty dollars in my pocket, two suitcases and not a word of Hebrew. Pretty soon I realized that the life I had lived was unlike anyone else's life in my new country. I met Ioni a few months later and we immediately clicked. After several years of being acquainted, I felt I could trust her, and inadvertently, I said something about my childhood. Her response, full of curiosity and interest, reassured me. With time, I told her more, until the whole of my oppressive story rose to the surface, less burdensome and impenetrable. Once all the stories were out, I felt lighter and stronger. It seemed to me that Ioni even looked at me differently.

Ioni encouraged me to write my story. I tried, but progress was slow, until we decided to write it together. At first, we did so tentatively, but eventually the story flowed out. I had an incentive to persevere—my children. I was watching them grow up in Israel, speaking Hebrew and going through a childhood completely different from mine. I wanted them to know me—my roots and theirs. My Hebrew did not allow me to describe to them the life I had lived. This book is mainly for them and I'm grateful to them for it having been written. The whole process took time. As I read what Ioni wrote, I relived the past, remembering more details that had initially been omitted. After adding them, I would read the manuscript once again. After a while I suddenly felt a change in me. I came to terms with my life, the anger faded and the pain subsided. This was better than therapy. I was free.

Contents

Preface 3

The Village 9

The House 12

Water 16

My Friends 18

The Well 20

Once Upon a Cart 21

Corn 22

The Cattle 23

The Fair 25

Winter 28

The Guest 29

My Father 35

The Storm 40

Dita 42

School 43

The Wake 46

Happiness 48

Maria 49

The Expulsion from Jacarezinho 58

Sorocaba	63
A Pot of Soup on the Stove	65
Carlinho	68
School in Sorocaba	69
Estasio de Sá	72
Still Sorocaba	77
Leaving Home	83
The First Day	86
My Sister Dita	92
Sandra	98
The Visit to Sorocaba	101
School in São Paulo	104
Christmas	105
Holiday by the Sea	109
Winter at Claudia's	114
In Sorocaba Again	119
Manuela	123
Back to School	130
Good Days	142
Less Good Days	159
Nezinho	167
Nezinho and I	173
Mother, Dita and I	176

Weekend in Santos	179
My First Umbanda Ceremony	183
The Wedding	186
Umbanda Second Ceremony	194
The Knitting Factory	196
The Weaving Factory	198
Marijuana	200
Fear	206
Pregnancy	215
Rebeca	225
After Rebeca	232
Carlos	236
The Change	240
Santa Casa de São Paulo	245
Between Life and Death	251
Working at the Laboratory	257
Marcus	259
Prof. Rosenberg	268
The Visit	276
After the Visit	282
The Valero Family	283
End of an Era	288
Pendulum	295

Separations 301

Last Days in Brazil 311

The Trip 319

First Days in Israel 324

The Paineira Tree (The Final Chapter) 337

Glossary 353

The Village

The earliest memory I can recall clearly is of a wagon drawn by two horses, all the members of my family riding in it, and four-and-a-half-year-old me, sandwiched between my mother and Maria, my eldest sister. Father held the reins as we made our way along the dirt path until, at last, he came to a stop. All around us was an expanse of tall, yellow grass and a few eucalyptus trees. The sun was shining in the clear sky and the air was dry. Father rose from his seat, stretching above me to his full height, and with one step of his long legs, reached the corner of the vehicle.

He picked up one of the bundles—a sheet made from white sacks ripped open at the seams sewn together that held our belongings—and hurled it on the ground. Maria quickly got up too, climbed off the wagon, extended her arms out to me, and I threw myself into them. After hugging me, she carefully lowered me to the ground next to her.

"Dita, give me Aroldo," she said. Bendita, my other sister, unsympathetically picked up our three-year-old brother, and passed him to Maria, as if he were a package. Then she jumped off the wagon and looked around until her gaze came to rest on a small hut in the middle of the field.

"What? Is this our house?" she exclaimed. "It's old and looks as if it is about to fall apart!"

Studying the shack surrounded by thorns, I saw that it was indeed old and dilapidated. The wooden walls were colorless, the windows were broken, and the door swung to and fro.

After throwing down the rest of the bundles, Father helped Mother, who was holding my little sister Ivone in her arms, get off the wagon.

"It's a temporary house," he says. "I'll build another one later. But tonight, we have to stay here. And if we want to sleep like human beings, we'll all have to help fix things up. Otherwise, we'll have to sleep outside, and the snakes will eat us."

A small white dog with brown spots jumped off after Mother, and clung to her heels. After setting Ivone down under a nearby eucalyptus tree, Mother pressed a bottle of water into her small hand.

"Children, go help your father. Fia, take care of Ivone and give Tupi some water. He is thirsty," she instructed as she entered the hut.

Fia pulled the cork out of the moringa, a clay pitcher we brought with us, and poured a little water into an aluminum saucer. Mother called Maria *Fia*, a variant of Filia, which means daughter in Portuguese, so that's what we all called her. We started to work. Even Aroldo. Even Dita. Father yanked out weeds and thorns with a hoe while we gathered them and laid them in piles far away from the hut.

While Mother worked inside, I heard the occasional scraping and squeaking of rusty hinges.

"Alemão," she called my father, opening the wooden window. I saw her small, dark face wrapped in a scarf, peeking out of the opening in the wall. Suddenly, the window sash broke off and was left hanging on one hinge only. Mother quickly but carefully pulled it right back into place, before continuing, "There's a lot we need to do. It will be impossible to live here when the heavy rains start. The water is going to drip from the roof on the children." Her head disappeared back inside the house, and she went on unpacking the bundles Father had dumped outside the door to the shack.

My father's name was Gregorio, but everyone called him Alemão (German), because of his tall stature, light hair and green eyes.

After a long time we took a break. We all sat down next to Ivone under the eucalyptus tree. We slept for a while, then ate the slices of meat Mother gave us and rice from a large pot placed between us. Maria poured us all water.

Twilight clouds gradually covered the sky, and a light rain began to fall. It didn't stop us from continuing to bale up the tall grass and clearing the entire area around the cabin. In the evening, Father lit a twig and set the dry piles on fire. As the fire crackled and sent sparks flying into the gray air, we heard some rustling and whispering coming from the grass near the fire.

Small snakes slithered away and disappeared into the thicket. Ivone started to cry and Mother picked her up in her arms.

"It's time to go to sleep," she determined and headed inside. Maria washed my face and hands first, then Aroldo's, and ushered us inside.

The hut had only one room, at the end of which was a small kitchen. She made us lie down on the white mattress Mother had spread on the floor. It was made from two sheets of sack cloth sewn together and filled with dried corn leaves. Next to us lay little Ivone, whom Mother was trying to put to sleep. Someone covered me with another white sack, and after that, I don't remember anything.

That was the day we left our home in the town of Cambará in the state of Paraná[1] and moved to a small village on the outskirts of the city of Jacarezinho, in the same state. The name of the city means *Little Jacare*, a type of caiman, a relative of the crocodile. I guess the first settlers discovered that the Jacare River flowing nearby was infested with small caimans and immortalized the experience when naming the place. Paraná is a very fertile region in the south of Brazil and a significant part of Brazil's agricultural activity is concentrated there.

There, in a village near Jacarezinho, I spent the happiest years of my childhood, almost four of them, until we had to leave. That village was my private paradise. Father was a tenant farmer, who worked on land that did not belong to him, in exchange for a percentage of the crops. He was hired by a property owner named Osvaldo, and we all moved to the village with my father, to work Seu Osvaldo's land: Mother, Terezinha; Maria who was fourteen years old; Dita who was ten; I was four; Aroldo was three and Ivone was one. Each of the three elder daughters had a different father. Maria's father died when she was two. After that, Mother married Dita's father, who was killed when a tractor-drawn wagon he was driving tipped over on him and buried him under sacks of rice. Then she married my father, and in 1960 I was born, followed by Aroldo and lastly Ivone.

The next morning a small delegation came to visit us. Some of Seu Osvaldo's employees brought with them dried meat, vegetables, wooden boards and tools. In the days that followed, Father repaired the door and windows and also sealed the roof.

---

1 Brazil is a federation divided into 26 independent states and a federal region where the capital, Brasilia, is located. Paraná borders the state of São Paulo, which has the largest economy in the country. Paraná formed part of São Paulo until 1853.

On the first day, Mother sent us to collect some twigs. She tied a bunch of them together with a thin string and attached them to a straight branch she found. She then wet the floor of the hut, basically dirt, and swept it with the twig broom until it became straight and smooth. Standing in the doorway, I felt the scent of the damp earth.

The rumor that a new tenant had arrived in the area spread quickly. Within a short time, a dark-skinned stranger, wearing old clothes and a worn straw hat arrived and asked to speak to my father. He was followed by another, and another. Everyone wanted to work for a meager wage, three daily meals, and a place to live, so Father hired them. They worked during the day and slept under the eucalyptus trees at night.

The House

One day a builder arrived from the city with orders from Seu Osvaldo followed by a shipment of poles and wooden boards. With the help of the workers, my father and the builder cut down some eucalyptus trees, sawed their trunks into beams, leveled the area and built us a big house, so that we could all live in it comfortably. All the while, Aroldo and I measured with our little feet the fields around the hut, slowly stretching our playing space outwards. At first Mother or Fia would yell at us to come back whenever we were about to disappear in the tall grass, but after a few weeks we were allowed to climb the nearest hill and even reach the wide stream that flowed a few hundred paces from the cabin.

Several months later the house was ready. It was a beautiful house like no other. It had a wooden floor, walls painted white, and the windows had green shutters. It was raised above the ground to keep the water from seeping in. In the living room, near one wall, stood a large, heavy wooden table surrounded by chairs. Benches were placed against other walls. Kerosene lanterns hung along the ceiling of the hall and there were two rooms on each side of the house.

"This is your father's room and mine," Mother explained, "these two will be for the children, and there is another one my mother can stay in when she comes to visit."

The kitchen was at the end of the hallway. Aroldo and I ran through the empty rooms. When I returned to the living room, I climbed on one of the benches and tried to put my hand out through the open window, but it hit a hard, cold surface. I brought my face closer to this wonder, that was as transparent as air, but impossible to pass through. I pressed my nose until it crumpled to see everything that was happening outside. A young worker was painting the trunks of the eucalyptus trees white, and another one was putting up stilts and installing a wooden fence around the house. I heard Fia's soft steps, in sync with the rhythm of Ivone crawling on the wooden floor.

"Catarina, did you notice?" Maria said, "There is glass on the window."

Mother walked the entire length of the house, and observed cheerfully: "Alemão, what a beautiful house. Bravo, really. You are wonderful. Look, children, what a beautiful house. Well done, Father." Even Dita wasn't looking angry while walking contentedly around the house.

Father said that in a few days there would also be beds and that we should start the fire in order to have hot water. Aroldo and I helped Mother bring the pieces of wood Father had chopped in from the yard.

While Fia and Dita went to the stream with buckets with which to fetch water, Mother put the wood chips inside the oven[2]. Fia and Dita filled a tin tank with water from the stream and together lifted it and placed it on the stove. The fire hissed beneath it and the smoke that rose through the tin chimney emerged out through the ceiling. From the window, we watched the smoke rising toward the sky.

"Now this is a real house," said Mother. "A house with smoke coming out the chimney is a house with life in it."

Our old shack became a storage room. In one section, Father arranged wooden logs on the floor, on top of which he placed large white sacks of

---

2   The kitchen oven was actually a large clay cube the height of a table, with a double top. The large space inside was filled with firewood. The upper clay surface served as a stove: four circles of different sizes were cut in the clay, so that the heat from the burning coals rose to the pots placed atop.

flour and sugar, as well as brown sacks of seeds, corn kernels and beans. Next to them were golden oil cans and tools. In another part of the hut lived the workers.

Every morning we got up at five. Mother lit the fire in the stove, took water from a cast iron kettle that had been standing all night on the whispering coals and made a pot of coffee. Besides the kettle, there was always a very large oil can on the stove, whose jagged edges Father smoothed out so we wouldn't get hurt, and it was filled with hot water for any need that might come up. We used this water for cooking, washing dishes and bathing.

The farmhands stood by the kitchen door with aluminum mugs in their hands. Mother gave them a slice of the bread she baked herself and poured them coffee. Father, Maria and the hired workers went out to work in the fields. The rest of the family stayed at home with Mother. We spent most of the morning in the kitchen. Dita diced cauliflower or peeled potatoes, I brought vegetables or wood from the garden, while Mother cooked.

Whenever water ran out, she took three large, empty tin cans that once contained oil and went to the stream. Father had made a makeshift handle for each one, by inserting a rod through two holes he punched in the thin metal. Mother filled all three of them with water, and twisting a cloth into a ring on her head, she squeezed one of the containers into it. The tin swayed over her head until it became stable. With her body upright, keeping her balance, she grabbed the two remaining cans and returned home.

Toward ten in the morning, she divided the meal she had cooked into several individual aluminum bowls, stacked like a tower one on top of the other. She then bundled everything into two cloth carriers and swung one over her shoulder, while Dita carried the other. Mother tied Ivone in a sheet to her back and we all set off. We walked on the dirt road to the bridge and crossed it, seeing whole cast-off snake skins rolling on the sand. We continued past the beautiful fazenda, the farm that belonged to Seu Matias, Seu Osvaldo's partner, and strode into the fields. The tall grass was covered with morning dew, moistening our bare feet and tickling our calves. Mother said we should let Tupi run ahead of us, because he knew how to spot snakes and would warn us ahead of time. We walked for a long time across the pastures.

Cows were scattered around, munching leisurely. We crossed the barbed wire fence that marked the beginning of the cultivated fields, the ones my father had sown. Endless fields covered in corn crops stretched before us. We walked through until we reached the slope, then marched down between beanstalks toward a green area where proud palm trees grew. A small stream whose waters were cold and clear flowed between them. Mother looked out into the distance searching for Father, but he was nowhere to be seen. She pressed her hands to either side of her mouth, like a megaphone, and shouted:

"Alemão, Fia, where are you?" And we called loudly after her:

"Father, Fia, where are you?"

A distant echo answered us. We continued in its direction, while calling out loud. Mother shouted and also whistled in a high, sharp pitch. Suddenly we heard distant voices calling back to us. Several figures appeared marching toward us from among the tall corn stalks.

We sat down under a palm tree while Mother distributed the overflowing bowls. One of the workers always made sure to fill a moringa with fresh water from the river. We stayed in the fields until the afternoon. Mother and Dita worked with Father. Aroldo and I helped a little and played a lot. Sometimes Father or one of the workers climbed up a palm tree and cut out the heart for us. Mother collected the hearts of palm and took them home. She would pickle and keep them in several jars.

We returned home before Father did. Mother tidied up the house and cooked dinner. Father and the workers came back later and stored their tools in the warehouse. Taking clean clothes with them, they went to bathe down in the stream. Aroldo, Tupi and I went down with them and came back all clean, with our hair washed too. The workers handed enamel plates to Mother who was standing in the kitchen doorway. When the plates were full, they sat down to eat in the yard under a tree. The family gathered in the kitchen for dinner. Mother held Ivone on her lap to nurse her. Often Aroldo would go up to them, roll down the neckline of her dress with his small hand, press his lips to the free breast and suckle on it too. I sat close to Maria holding a piece of wood or an empty bottle in my arms, carefully wrapped in an old piece of cloth. I had a baby too.

On Sundays, Mother collected the week's laundry, and went to the river. She and Fia led the way, both slender, strong and upright, each carrying a large sack full of dirty clothes and sheets. Dita followed them with Aroldo and me right behind, both of us holding Ivone's hands. She had just learned to walk. When we arrived at the stream, Mother and my sisters knelt down by the water and washed the clothes on a washboard, with coarse soap that Mother made from cooked pork fat, *mamona* fruits and caustic soda flakes.

The freshly laundered clothes were hung on the lines of a wire fence Father had installed for that purpose on the river shore. We, the little ones, waded in the water and splashed each other. When we returned home, Mother went into the kitchen to cook and Fia cleaned the house. After scrubbing the glass windows until they became invisible, she polished the wooden floor with wax. Sometimes we went outside, where Fia dug small holes in the ground and we both scattered seeds in them. We covered them, watered them, and after two to three weeks we had tomatoes, cucumbers, watermelons and flowers growing.

Water

Summer was in full swing. It hadn't rained for a long time. Father was worried. He gazed at the sky, looked for clouds and sighed. "If it doesn't rain soon the crops will shrivel and nothing is going to grow," he said. The cracks in the hardened soil were growing wider.

One hot Sunday, Mother went into their bedroom and returned with three figurines that stood on a white cloth napkin, atop a small table against the wall. The most beautiful one was that of Nossa Senhora Aparecida.[3] She was made of black clay, with curly hair, a crown and a

---

3   Nossa Senhora Aparecida, is a version of the holy Virgin Mary as a black woman, wearing a lavish blue cloak and a gold crown on her head. Her figurines and pictures are venerated by Catholics in Brazil, who consider her their patron saint.

white puffy princess-like dress—all made of clay too. Around her neck was a blue cloak made of a stiff fabric, with its borders embroidered in gold. I thought she resembled Mother a little. The figures of the other saints were made of dark wood.

We, the children, never touched them. Sometimes my mother would light a candle at their feet, quietly whispering words like "Bless us Holy Mary and watch over our family." Or "Please, may we never lack bread on our table," and then she would cross herself.

She handed us the sculptures, instructing us to hold them carefully, because we were taking them down to the creek. We had no choice. It was the last resort and she believed it would help. Her face looked a little more worried than usual. Dita took Maria Aparecida, and Aroldo and I took the two remaining statuettes. We all went to the creek that Sunday, even Dad.

We lined up along the bank with Tupi prancing around us. Mother unloaded the contents of the laundry bags and turned to us: "Now, children, immerse the statues in the water. First take off Nossa Senhora's cloak. Like this. Yes. Dip the whole figurine in the water. Ask in your hearts for it to rain. Ask hard and believe it will happen! And now take it out of the water and put it back in. Exactly, three times... Very good."

Looking up at the blue sky, clear of clouds, she said quietly: "If you ask and truly believe with all your heart that it will rain, then it will, I am sure."

"Yes," said Father, "I really hope it will."

We were all in a happier, lighter mood.

Father left us for a few minutes, went home and came back with a large sieve Mother used to sift the beans and coffee. Rolling the hem of his pants up to his knees he waded into the stream. He taught us how to place the sieve in the water and then pull it up quickly, teeming with glittery jumping silver fish.

Then it was lunch time. The sun blazed above us but the water was cool and pleasant. Suddenly, Father stood up.

"Get out fast," he shouted, and hurried us to the bank, where Dita and Maria were hanging the laundry over the barbed wire. He pointed to the shore, not far from us. A yellow snake with a brown stripe along its body slowly crawled out and slithered into the water, before diving in and disappearing.

"Children, under no circumstances will you enter the water at lunchtime, because that's when snakes go in to get away from the heat. It is very dangerous," he explained. We frolicked around the adults, briefly touching the water and shrieking excitedly with every rustle in the grass, until the heat subsided. That Sunday we had grilled fish for lunch. A few days later, the rain came.

My Friends

One day, before dinner, we heard a sound outside the house. Looking out the window I saw a thin man, wearing worn clothes, standing outside the gate. He clapped his hands and called out:

"Hello, ode casa? Hello, is anyone home?"

His face was black and wrinkled. A fine, nearly white beard sprouted from his cheeks. The hair on his uncovered head was gray and curly. He stood hat in hand, hunched and embarrassed. As soon as Father came out of the house, he strode toward the visitor. He opened the gate for him, inviting him into the courtyard. From the window, I watched them talk.

The man's body slouched slightly forward, somewhat submissively, when speaking to my father, and most of the time he looked at the ground.

Father came back in and informed Mother that he had agreed to hire the worker for a trial period, even if he wasn't sure he would be suitable. He looked too old to him. In any case, he would take him out to the field with him the next day and observe him at work. Mother filled a plate with rice, added a slice of meat, and served it to the man.

He sat down in the shade and began to eat. Afterwards, when I looked out the window again, I saw him caressing my dog. The next day, when he returned with Father from the field, I was out in the yard watching him. When Tupi ran up to him, he asked if he was my dog. From a distance, I held his gaze but did not answer. The man smiled and continued about his business.

The old laborer became a member of the household. Even Mother liked him. Sometimes in the evenings, they sat together in the yard, smoking. He often turned to me and waved for me to come closer. "Don't waste your time, Seu Benedito. Catarina doesn't talk to people she doesn't know. She doesn't talk to those she knows either, for that matter," Mother told him. But Seu Benedito did not give up.

One evening, when he was stroking my dog, he noticed I was watching. Turning to the dog he said: "Tupi, did you know I had a dog just like you? I taught him to dig and bring me potatoes. Do you also want to learn to fetch?" I looked at him with curiosity. Seu Benedito stroked the dog some more and went on talking to him: "Whose are you anyway, Tupi? Do you belong to Catarina by any chance?"

He turned his eyes to me. I did not answer.

"Maybe you're nobody's dog. Would you like to be my dog?"

I couldn't let this go and remain silent. Tupi was my dog. Each one of us, I, my brother and sisters, was sure that Tupi was theirs.

"He is mine!" I whispered loudly.

"Catarina, did you say anything? I didn't hear you. You need to come closer. My ears are old. What did you say again? Is it mine?"

"No!" I got closer to him. "He's mine!" I protested.

"Oh, he is yours! Then why didn't you say so before! Come a little closer."

When Mother walked out of the house to join him for a cigarette a few minutes later, she was surprised to see me sitting on his lap, listening intently to a story he was telling me.

I had one girlfriend, who was my age. Her name was Neoza but everyone affectionately called her Preta (Black) maybe because she was fair, had chestnut hair, and her eyes were golden. Her parents worked for Seu Osvaldo's partner, Seu Nestor Matias, and they all lived in the backyard of his mansion.

We didn't see each other often, only at events and when our parents got together briefly, but I was fond of her. She was cheerful and smiled a lot. One of her legs was thinner, as a result of polio she had contracted as a baby. She limped, but still moved really fast, so we could walk together without me having to wait for her. We were able to play almost any game, except perhaps tag. Preta was my best real friend.

The Well

Time went by. The flowers Maria sowed grew into rose bushes and lilies. Chickens scampered around the yard pecking at the ground. The meandering stream surrounded the fields and most of our lives. We went there to bathe and wash, draw water, fish and play.

Father would clear the bank nearest us of driftwood and debris, so that the water my mother and sisters pumped would be as clean as possible. Mother would boil the water in a pot over the large opening of the coal stove, and fill a clay moringa. Once the water cooled, we could drink from it.

One evening Father announced that he planned to start digging a well the next day. We had to work so hard to get one jug of drinking water. Wasn't it better to invest a few weeks of effort in order to have water right in our yard? A long discussion took place. Where to dig? If we chose to place the well near the entrance to the house, it would indeed make pumping very convenient but we would have to dig very deep, and that could take many days. If we dug closer to the stream, water would certainly emerge much sooner, but we would have to carry it a greater distance every day. In the end it was decided that it would be better to invest a little more effort in building the well in exchange for the convenience afterwards.

The project began the next day. The workers dug a large hole a few steps from the door that led out of the kitchen. They made it deeper every day. Whenever someone was digging inside the hole, only his head and shoulders showed. Two thick poles were driven into the ground by the edge of the pit, and connected with a log, onto which a long rope was tied, with a bucket hanging on its other end. The person digging filled the bucket with earth, while another one stood on top, pulling the rope up, and then dumping the contents of the bucket over a mound of dirt that kept growing higher and higher.

After a few days the pit was so deep that when Father stood in it with Aroldo standing on his shoulders, they were still not visible from outside. On that same day all of a sudden, Father told us that water was seeping in. He and the men continued excavating for a few more days, until the water began to gush in, filling the bottom of the pit.

I was sitting on the steps at the entrance playing with Ivone, when we were startled by a shout of joy. I saw two of the workers climbing up the rope and out of the pit. Laughing out loud together with Father, they threw their hats up in the air in celebration.

"We've got water!" they shouted. Tupi ran around them in circles, barking. Mother came out of the kitchen, crossed her arms over her chest and looked at Father and the workers with satisfaction.

In the following days they built a wooden frame around the pit with a wooden cover over it. From that moment on, the bucket and rope would be used to get water. The water had to "rest" for a few days until it became clear, while the soil settled at the bottom.

The first time we brought water from the well, Mother poured some for all of us to drink. It was wonderfully cool, with only a subtle taste of mud.

Once Upon a Cart

Sunday came again and we all walked to the stream. The dirt road next to us originated in the town of Jacarezinho, passed near our house, crossed the creek on a narrow wooden bridge and continued climbing further, toward the fishponds, the magnificent mansion and the school. A horse-drawn cart loaded with goods, probably from the city, rolled past us making a rattling sound, headed in the direction of the stream. We followed it with our eyes.

The two horses pulled the cart across the bridge and then started up the steep slope beyond it. The cart was probably too heavy, and one of the horses tripped, making the cart tip to one side. The coachman yelled and tried to pull it back but failed. The vehicle overturned and fell into the water with a loud splash, dragging the horses down with it. The animals neighed desperately while we stared at the event that was unfolding. Father put down his work tools and other objects he was carrying with him, and ran toward the bridge. We all raced after him.

The driver was standing in the stream, close to the bank, in water up to his knees. His hat was dripping with mud. Grass and leaves hung on his wet clothes. He untied the horses to set them free. The wagon lay on its side in the water, with two of its wheels in the air. Sacks and boxes were scattered around and peering out of the stream. We had never seen such a strange spectacle. Father went down to help the coachman. He grabbed the bridle of one of the horses and pulled hard. The horse tried to get up on its knees but when he failed, he bucked and dragged Father into the water. Father fell to his knees, then rose and looked at us.

"You guys, come help instead of standing there and laughing!" he said.

Excited, we went down into the water and began pulling out the soaked sacks and floating jugs. After about an hour we managed to rescue the horses, the wagon and most of its cargo. The driver thanked us and continued on his way.

Ever since, every time a cart passed over the bridge, struggling to climb the slope, we secretly hoped it would tip over and fall into the water. But the smart coachmen made sure to get off the wagon, grab the bridles and lead the horses safely up the slope.

Corn

The main crop Father cultivated in the fields was corn. Every morning we walked to the fields looking for him in the brightly lit areas. After lunch Aroldo and I frolicked between the furrows. The rows of corn were as tall as we were, allowing us to hide among them. Once, while we were looking for Father, I suddenly saw a small doll on one of the stalks. She was wrapped in a green dress and had long yellow hair. She was so beautiful, I reached out and picked her. Then I saw another one with red hair. And yet another one, with brown hair this time. I picked all of them. I now had three little girls with beautiful long hair wearing green dresses with whom I spent not only the rest of the day, but also many hours in the following days.

I fed them, stroked their stringy hair and talked to them. Small cobs of corn before ripening—those were the dolls I played with then, in the countryside near Jacarezinho. They were my babies and my best friends.

The corn ripened and harvest time came. Once the crops were gathered, our parents went to the wholesale market in town to sell our share of the produce and return with other necessary supplies. Twice a year, the workers loaded sacks full of corn, beans and fruit from the orchard onto the cart.

Mother would take a long thin rope and pass by each one of us children, from eldest to youngest. First, she measured Fia's foot, and tied a small knot. She then marked the length of Dita's foot—from the previous knot to a new knot she made in the rope. That was how she noted all our shoe sizes.

Mother and Father went to the city of Jacarezinho, to return only in the evening, while I sat on Seu Benedito's lap and listened to a story, holding a corn doll in my arm. The cart they drove in was loaded with sacks of flour and sugar, cans of oil, and cardboard boxes with leather sandals for all of us.

The Cattle

I stood in the yard in my new sandals, speaking to my pink corn doll and telling her that Seu Benedito was actually my grandfather. That once, on one of the farms where he worked, a foal was born so small that he did not know how to nurse and Seu Benedito fed him from a bottle until he grew up to become the best horse around. The grateful animal followed Seu Benedito everywhere as if the kind man were his mother.

A muffled noise rose in the distance.

When I looked at the dirt road bordering the yard, I saw a cloud of dust in the horizon while feeling the ground shake beneath my feet. I got closer and climbed up the rungs of the fence to get a better view. The sounds of hooves stomping and bells ringing came and went in waves.

A large herd of cattle was galloping in the distance. Dita and Aroldo also rushed up to the fence and Tupi ran alongside it, barking the whole time. Panicking chickens squawked in the yard, scattering in all directions. The herd rushed toward us. Two men in cowboy hats with scarves wrapped around their necks, covering their mouths from the dust, rode on either side of the herd, urging the cows on with loud calls.

When they saw us, they motioned for us to move back. We were breathing dust. Mother came out of the house and yelled at us to quickly climb off the fence and back away.

"These big cows," she said, "are bulls, and they are very dangerous. They have sharp horns and you'd better not stand in their path."

The beasts continued on at a gallop, speeding past us in an unending stream. We stood with our eyes fixed on the cows that flashed in and out of sight. Two men on horseback appeared once again, flanking the herd. One of them stopped his horse and approached the fence. Removing the scarf that covered his face, he asked Mother for water in a polite tone. Days-old dusty bristles studded his face. Nodding, Mother turned toward the kitchen and came back with a clay pitcher filled with water from the well. She tilted the jug and let the water flow in a thin trickle.

The cowboy put his face under the stream and drank in loud gulps. After washing his face and neck he filled a leather pouch that hung from his belt. He then thanked Mother, spurred his horse and galloped away to catch up with his companion. The herd continued advancing past us, until abruptly, the stream of cattle stopped.

A small group of cows who had lagged behind the rest appeared, and three shepherd dogs surrounded them, urging them on with their barks. A cowboy and several dogs alongside him began to round them up. We followed all the figures with our gaze until they became invisible behind clouds of dust. We remained standing in the yard, looking at the empty road leading to the bridge over the stream, until the barking faded completely.

The Fair

Once or twice a year a fair was held in our village. The estate owners bought animals and led the herds from the city to the large corrals across the bridge. Many people attended, arriving from the city and from nearby villages. The annual fair was the most important and joyful event in the remote place where we lived.

On Saturday evening there was great commotion in our house. Father talked about the fair to be held the next day, Sunday, while Fia and Dita listened excitedly. Mother held in her arms a floral print dress she had never worn before. She placed it flat on a bench, which she dragged into the kitchen, and then sprinkled some water on the garment. She lifted the heavy iron that stood on one side, opened its lid, filled it with hot coals from the wood stove, and then closed it. Gripping the handle of the iron, she set it down on the colorful fabric. As she slowly glided the iron back and forth, the fabric stretched out, becoming smooth and beautiful.

The next morning, we went to the fair. Father left the house long before us, because he went there to work. For us it was a real outing: we were all neatly groomed and dressed in clean clothes. Mom wore her floral dress and a matching orange scarf wrapped around her head. She couldn't stand her frizzy hair and preferred to hide it under a kerchief.

We walked up the bridge, with the stream flowing below us. From the stout trunks of the Jaboticaba trees that grew along the banks hung small black fruits that I liked to pick. I would crack open their skin and suck out their contents, which resembled sweet, juicy cotton wool, and then spit out the small, glossy pits. The road, lined with eucalyptus trees on both sides, stretched out before us. To our right were small azure lagoons that shone like mirrors, with flocks of birds hovering above them. They were fishponds. To our left were sugar cane fields. Further along the way we passed through expanses of pasture until we finally arrived at the magnificent fazenda of Seu Nestor Matias. It was a two-story house, with a wide balcony on the top floor adorned by a carved wooden railing.

The manor was framed by a wide lawn, surrounded by fruit trees and flower beds. A small pond with a fountain and ornamental fish marked the center of the garden. Opposite the fazenda was the large field where the fair was being held. Cowboys rode horses and herded cows into pens. The horses neighed and tapped their hooves, the cows mooed. Three men I knew from the area were playing music under a tree. Two played the guitar and the third one, the accordion. A small crowd gathered around them and clapped their hands every time a song ended. Nearby a somewhat nervous, excited horse had been left in a fenced corral. He whinnied incessantly and sometimes broke into brief gallops along the fence. A few strange men stood around the fence examining him. They didn't look like they were locals, and Dita said they must have come from the city. One of them was holding a halter and bridle and they were talking to each other. At that moment I saw my father's tall figure, walking toward us and waving. We ran up to him and he smiled, directing us to a pen full of cows, which connected to another pen through a narrow passage with gates at both ends. A fire was burning near the fence and an iron rod had been placed over it.

"Have you ever seen how cows are marked?" he asked.

I never had. We crowded along the fence, close to Father who held the blazing rod. A worker approached one of the cows and drove her toward the gate. As she passed through, she found herself squeezed in the small passage, trapped between two fences. Father pulled the rod out of the fire and I recognized the peculiar shape at its end, the hallmark of the herds Father was responsible for tending. The metal was red hot as Father touched the pole to the cow's rump. We heard a faint whisper, like the sound of the hot iron on the damp fabric of Mother's dress, and I smelled singed hair. The cow mooed and dad opened the gate, releasing her into the second corral. She stepped forward to join the other already branded cows that stood there chewing on hay. For a long time, I looked at the beasts, one after the other, moving from pen to pen, and Dad branding them on their way through.

Hearing cheering behind me, I turned to see one of the men who had stood before watching the wild horse, now astride the animal's back, holding the bridle he had managed to put on it. The horse reared up, kicking its hind legs in the air, but the man, who must have been very experienced, did not fall.

An engine rattled in the distance. A pickup truck was rolling down the dirt road into the fairgrounds. I knew that only farm owners drove cars, so it had to be someone important.

"Here's Seu Matias' van," Mother said, and we all followed the approaching vehicle with our eyes.

Dad straightened up, left the corral, took his hat off and waited reverently. When the truck came to a stop, a very tall, handsome gentleman got out slowly. He had a well-groomed mustache and wore good clothes—a pretty fine-checkered shirt, a brand new pair of jeans, a cowboy hat and shiny boots with spurs. The door on the driver's side opened, and a boy slightly older than me got out of the car. He was the most beautiful boy I had ever seen.

He looked like a miniature version of his father, also smartly dressed, with a hat, boots and spurs, and even a plaid scarf wrapped around his neck, just like his father's. Seu Matias greeted us all with a smile, caressed the head of Ivone, whom Mother was holding in her arms, and turned to talk to Father.

I gazed at the boy, unable to take my eyes off him. He was so perfect. I didn't even notice Seu Osvaldo's Beetle pulling up next to the van. Even though every time I heard it driving down the dirt road by the house, I would run out to watch it pass by, with its blue color and the dust it raised in its wake.

When the sun was high in the sky, smoke billowed up from among the trees and the smell of roasted meat wafted through the air.

We walked toward the pit filled with swirling pieces of beef. Cobs of corn were being cooked in a large cauldron full of boiling water. Everyone ate to their heart's content. We were given metal mugs that could be filled with cold water from a clay jug. I chose to fill mine with Guarapá, the sweet nectar of squeezed sugar cane. A man standing by a special contraption took my cup and put it under the pipe. He turned the handle on the device and my cup was filled. The men drank *Pinga* and the women *Caipirinha*. Spirits were high. The musicians began to play again and a small group of couples danced under the shade of the tree.

We returned to the corral once again and Father went on branding the cows. We got home when the sun started to set. That evening father brought with him a cow he had bought for us. He put her in a fenced plot behind the house and the next day built a shed for her, where she slept. From that day on, as soon as the crowing of the roosters woke me up in the morning, I ran to the shed with an aluminum cup. Dad filled it with warm milk straight from the udders. When I brought the cup to my mouth, the aromatic foam tickled my lips, drawing on me a white mustache.

Winter

The great heat was over. The days became more pleasant and it rained every day. Summer passed and autumn arrived, ushering in the celebrations of São João. On June evenings, when it didn't rain too hard, people lit bonfires. We also lit one in the field next to the house, and from the flames we saw flickering in the distance, our neighbors did so too.

The whole family sat around the fire, together with the laborers, to have dinner outside. In the spaces between the coals, we placed potatoes, chestnuts and sweet potatoes. When the peels were charred, someone rolled them out with a stick to let them cool. We would nibble on them, blow on the steaming lumps and laugh, displaying soot-covered teeth. All this while sipping *quentão* that made us warm inside.

After the fire died down, the men held competitions to walk barefoot on the still sizzling embers.

One particularly stormy winter night, I burrowed under the covers listening to the wind howling outside. Branches creaked out in the yard, the windows whistled, leaves and twigs flew in through the gap under the door. It started to rain, and then to pour. Suddenly the sky lit up and a terrible noise shook the windowpanes.

Mother called: "Alemão, what if lightning strikes the house?" And father replied, "Everyone take your blankets and get under the dining table."

Mother urged us on as we all crawled under the table, including Father despite his height. We sat there wrapped in the white sack cloths that served as blankets, shivering with cold and fear every time we heard thunder roaring over our heads. The roof began to leak and drops of water dripped, landing noisily on the wooden floor.

Lightning flashed in the sky, followed immediately by deafening thunder. Then cracking and a crash. Father said lightning had hit a tree. We remained under the table until the storm abated. When we got back to bed it was almost dawn. We woke up to a cold, wet morning, with the yard covered in puddles. Beyond the fence that surrounded the house, the charred skeleton of a eucalyptus tree lay on the ground.

The Guest

One fine day a woman I didn't know showed up at our house. She was good looking, tall and dark skinned, her black wavy hair done up in a bun on the top of her head.

She was carrying a tied bundle on her arm—indicating she must have come from afar.

As she entered the yard, Mother looked out the kitchen window to see who had arrived. The second she noticed the stranger, she put her knife down and hurried outside. As she approached the woman, her voice sounded different than usual, a little choked:

"Hello, Mother," she said.

The woman walked up closer and hugged her.

"Hello, my daughter," she replied, looking into my mother's eyes and hugging her for a long time again. "I was at your house in Cambará and the neighbors told me you had moved here. Come, let me look at you, Terezinha. I see there's something new in the oven." Smiling, she placed her hand on Mother's belly.

All of a sudden, I noticed Mother's bulging belly that looked like she was hiding a watermelon under her dress. I was standing there, holding a blonde corn doll, already from the second season. The first round of dolls had turned black and I replaced them with new ones. Mother turned to me and said:

"Catarina, this is your grandmother, Nazare Rosa. Come, give her a hug." The stranger grinned and I saw that her face was beautiful and her black eyes were always smiling. I came closer and wrapped my arms around the waist of the grandmother who I didn't even know I had.

"Is that Catarina?" Grandmother asked, "I didn't recognize her. So grown up. What beautiful hair you have." She stroked my head and gave me a kiss on the forehead. Then she toured the yard and became reacquainted with Dita, Aroldo and Ivone.

Mother caught a chicken, as she did on festive occasions, and she and grandmother went into the kitchen for a long time. That evening we ate the most delicious chicken soup in the world, with lots of chunky meat, potatoes and carrots. Dad had two platefuls.

Grandmother sat next to Fia, stroking her cheek from time to time, and never stopped smiling. In the following days there was much commotion around the house. Grandmother prepared dishes Mother never had, and they talked a lot. Not many conversations went on at home when just Mother was with us, but now everything was different.

Father built a clay oven in the yard and made trays out of oil cans that he sawed and flattened. Mother and grandmother kneaded dough, formed loaves of soft, sweet bread and placed them on the trays. A few minutes after the trays were put in the oven the yard would be filled with the wonderful smell of fresh bread.

That was also when I tasted *pamonha* for the first time. Grandmother taught Mother how to fill the green wrappers of the corn cobs with ground corn kernels, to which milk and sugar were added.

The wraps are tied and cooked in boiling water. After cooling, they can be opened, and their doughy, sweet and very tasty contents are ready to be eaten.

All three of us were in the kitchen grinding meat. I was sitting, talking to my dolls. Grandmother asked what I was doing and Mother answered that it was a good thing that at least I talked to corn because to other people, I didn't talk. But then she added that I was a good girl, after all, and sent me off to the yard to get another piece of string. Mother went on grinding the meat, seasoning it, and stuffing the mix in pork intestines.

Grandmother asked Mother if she still worked as a *curandera*, healing babies, like she used to in Cambará. Mother replied she no longer did. "Since we moved here, I've stopped. No one knows me here and they don't know that I am a curandera. There aren't any people living nearby either. You see, Mother, how isolated we are here, with no neighbors around."

Mother cut the string into short strips and began to tie the long pork intestine tube into a chain of sausages. "Besides," she continued, "Alemão doesn't like me messing with that stuff. He doesn't believe in it at all and he needs me in the fields now. I have no time."

At that moment I vaguely remembered our former home. There were neighbors all around, even in the lots that bordered ours. On summer evenings, when we returned home from the fields and pumpkin patches, neighbors and people who had come from far away and whom I did not know, were already waiting for my mother, holding babies in their arms.

The line could sometimes get quite long. I remember one time Father grumbled: "What about dinner?" But Mother ignored his complaints and turned to what she saw as her calling. Aroldo and I stayed around, playing in the yard. "Catarina, take your finger out of your mouth," she said, and headed over to a whimpering baby. Mother asked what the problem was and the neighbor said the child had a fever. She put one hand on his forehead, supporting his head with the other. Closing her eyes, she mumbled words that sounded like a prayer. She plucked rosemary branches from a bush that grew in the yard, swept them gently over the baby's head, shaking them as if to brush the illness and pain away. She muttered a prayer, ending it with "Amen" and threw the branches over her shoulder.

She went into the kitchen and took some leaves from a medicinal plant she had, placed them in an aluminum mug and poured boiling water. I followed her, standing in the doorway and watching as she collected three small hissing coals from the stove and dropped them into the cup. Finally, she carefully poured the water from the cup into a vial and went back to the yard. She handed the vial to the baby's mother, explaining she should make the child drink a gulp of the potion three times a day, and bring him back the next day at the same time.

She moved from child to child, taking care of each one as their condition demanded. As soon as the sun began to set, my mother's role was over. The remaining crowd dispersed only to return the next day. Sometimes neighbors came with their healthy children, kissed my mother's hands and handed her a chicken, cans of oil or baskets full of eggs. And that was the only payment she received.

Another distant memory came back to me. It was a cold but sunny winter morning. We came out of our freezing house to bask in some heat. The air was still very cold and we sat down on the bench in front of the house, huddled together and wrapped up in blankets. Baby Ivone was bundled in a blanket on my mother's lap. Fia brought a hissing coal from the stove because my mother wanted to light a cigarette for herself. Without her noticing, the small ember stuck to the end of the cigarette in her mouth. She was still smoking when Ivone started crying with heartbreaking wails.

"She must be cold," said my mother, tightening the blanket around her. Ivone's bawling became louder, until finally, she cried herself to sleep. Relieved, Mother sat back on the bench. When Ivone woke up, she began to scream again and wouldn't calm down.

Mother came into the house to change her diaper.

"Dear God!" I heard her exclaim in anguish. "Alemão, come quickly. Look what happened to the girl... What have I done?" She went on, her voice breaking. "Now I understand why she cried so much ..."

We ran inside and saw the little ember on sobbing Ivone's lower back. The charcoal had fallen off the tip of the cigarette and slipped through the space between the blanket and Ivone's nape, down to her waist, where it seared the flesh and dug in. Mom treated the wound with the best potions and concoctions she knew, but Ivone was left with a bright scar she has to this day.

Of all the neighbors, I especially remembered a large, dark-skinned woman who lived in the house across the street. In my head, she was an important part of the Cambará landscape. Her bulky body, wrapped in a flowery pleated dress, swayed from side to side when she walked, because the weight made movement hard for her.

One day, when I was playing in the yard with my thumb in my mouth, she signaled for me to come to her. She sat down on a wooden chair in the garden and sat me on her broad thighs.

"Catarina, let me tell you a story," she began. "There is a man who walks around the neighborhood at night carrying a big sack on his back. Do you know what's in the sack?" I didn't know. "The sack is full of thumbs of children who sucked their fingers. The man quietly checks the thumbs of all the children, and if he finds out the child has been sucking on the thumb, he cuts it off and sticks it in the sack."

That night I had trouble falling asleep. My thumb found its way into my mouth without me realizing, but I immediately pulled it away and hid it close to my chest so no one would take it from me. Sleep, however, refused to come. I hid under the blanket and without the thumb man watching, I finger-sucked for just a few seconds, and that was it. That's how I got through one night after another, until I weaned myself off.

When Mother wasn't sending me to pick vegetables or bring her anything else she needed, I sat in the kitchen and listened. Grandmother gifted me a past. She talked about things I had forgotten, that happened before I learned to remember, and before I even existed.

At night she would tuck us in and tell us stories. We had a wide bed, built of a wooden frame and springs, on which the mattresses rested. All of us, all the grandchildren, except for Maria who helped mother in the kitchen, lay side by side. It was dark outside and only one lantern illuminated the room with a faint light.

Our Grandmother spoke and we discovered things we didn't know. For example, that Father had also once been a child, and that he had many brothers and sisters. His mother was widowed and married a second husband when father was eighteen years old. He didn't like the new father, so he left home and had not seen his family since. He met a woman older than him and lived with her for several years, until she died. That woman was also Grandmother's daughter, meaning our mother's sister. Mother was already a widow with two small babies, and she comforted Father, who was left alone.

"And as you know," Grandmother continued, "they got married and Catarina was born," she stroked my head, and added, "then Aroldo," she tickled his neck lightly before saying, "and then…"

"Ivone!" we answered, to which Grandmother said, "correct," and then also stroked Ivone's head. "And soon you will have another brother or sister."

"I know that mother is pregnant and in a few days the baby will come out of her womb," Dita said, and then asked, "What did mother's sister die of?"

Just then Mother walked in and grandmother quickly said: "You have to go to bed soon, so maybe I'll tell you just one short story and that's it." Grandmother didn't seem to want Mother to know what we were talking about.

"It's already very late. Your grandmother will tell you a story tomorrow. Good night," Mother said, turning the knob of the lantern whose flame shrunk until it turned blue, then disappeared. Grandmother quietly said good night to us and we saw her silhouette in the dark, leaving the room.

We knew she was going to sleep in the other room, which was intended for guests. Since Grandmother had come to help her, Mother had more time. They would both sit to sew tablecloths and napkins from white sack cloth. Sometimes Maria joined them too, because she loved handicrafts and wanted to learn how to do the Ajour embroidery that decorated the napkins. Grandmother showed her how to carefully draw out the weft threads, and then group and sew the warp threads to create beautiful patterns.

One morning I woke to discover Mother and Father weren't home. Grandmother said they had gone to the hospital, where the new baby was going to be born. Two days later, Mother returned with a package in her hands. We all crowded around her to look at the tiny face peeking out from between the wraps.

"He's so tiny," I whispered.

"You were even smaller when you were born," Mother said. "You were so small we could have kept you in a shoe box, and every two hours I had to feed you. Do you remember, Mother?" she asked, turning to Grandmother, "We weren't sure she would even live."

Ivone was big, two years old already, when Mother had a new baby named Nicolao. Mother was not allowed to exert herself and she had to lie down or sit a lot. Grandmother and Maria did the work for her, and she held Nicolao in her arms much of the time. Ivone sometimes climbed on the bed and nursed, while Aroldo just cuddled with mom, which she allowed him to do.

I felt that I also wanted to get into bed next to my mother, to curl up next to her and for her to hug me. As I stood in the corner of my parents' room, the distance between me and the bed seemed infinite and impassable to me. I couldn't remember the last time Mother had hugged me, and now it no longer seemed an option. I didn't even dare try. I turned and left the room, leaving Mother nursing Nicolao and Aroldo sleeping on her lap. I grabbed a corn doll and a piece of cloth in which to wrap it and went to look for Grandmother.

My Father

Grandmother stayed with us after Christmas, until late spring, then left. Having regained her strength, Mother returned to cooking, cleaning the house and helping father in the fields.

On Saturday, Father brought a bottle of pinga from the grocery store. He sat down in the kitchen, popped the cork and poured himself a glass. He drank slowly, enjoying every sip.

"What a week this has been," he said with satisfaction. "We worked hard. The farmhands worked non-stop, and we finished cleaning the entire southern area and preparing it for sowing."

Pouring himself another glass, he blinked and let out a sigh of relief.

"To a successful harvest!" he said, swinging the glass and placing it on the table with a clatter. "Like my father would say. My father knew how to drink. In Ukraine, where he came from, people know how to drink." He sipped slowly and sighed loudly. "Did you know, children, that my parents came to Brazil from the Ukraine? They arrived on a ship. Got married on the ship. There was a rabbi with them on the voyage. He performed the wedding ceremony... Do you know what a rabbi is, kids? He's the priest of the Jews. Because my parents were Jewish."

"Alemão," Mother said impatiently. "Stop drinking. You're talking too much." Dad didn't answer. After drinking in silence for a few minutes he continued. "The children need to hear about their grandparents. They wanted to reach their Holy Land, Palestine, but they faced many difficulties. The Turks ruled there, and it was easier to come to Brazil." He drank some more and sighed. "Things were good at home back then. Father, Mother, five children. We worked hard, but it was fine... until my father died."

He fell silent, but not for long. "Yes... So, Mother remarried. This man... He had children, whom I couldn't stand... And I had to leave. I was a child, alone in the world. I took odd jobs, moving from farm to farm. Then I came to the farm where your grandmother, Dona Nazare, lived. She was like the mother I never had. She cared for me, treated me right …" By that point he was talking to himself, lost in memories. "And that's how I fell in love with a girl—"

"Enough!" Mother interrupted him in an angry tone. "Stop drinking and talking nonsense!"

One evening Mother asked Father: "Alemão, where is your wristwatch? You haven't been wearing it for days now. Did anything happen to it?" Dad shrugged and said it had disappeared. He said he didn't know how or when, but he couldn't find it, and went back to chewing the Feijoada that filled his plate.

"How exactly did it disappear?" Mother asked in a voice charged with reproach. "You've owned it for so many years. Now it's gone and you're acting like nothing has happened? Not everyone has a watch like that." When he didn't answer, Mother sighed and looked at the ceiling. "God in heaven," she muttered to herself. "Just like that, you lose something so precious and don't even think you should talk about it …" and went over to soothe a crying Nicolao, who lay on a folded mattress in the corner of the kitchen.

A few days later she and I went to the grocery store, the *venda*, which wasn't too far away. After exiting the gate, we turned left to go toward the city, on foot. Mother bought sugar, yeast, and caustic soda to make soap. On our way back we ran into Amelia, a neighbor of ours. She was tall and beautiful, with a shapely figure and hair that flowed over her shoulders. Mother greeted her with a nod but did not stop to talk to her.

Mother had told us once quietly at home that Amelia, mother of children, had divorced her husband. And divorced women were not decent women. We were about to pass her and continue on our way when suddenly Mother saw something that made her stop in her tracks. She quickly turned around and said in a shrill voice: "Amelia, where did you get that watch you're wearing on your wrist?" Looking utterly surprised and confused, Amelia replied that it was hers. Mother grabbed her hand forcefully and took a close look. "I'd recognize this watch among a hundred other watches. This is my husband's watch. How did it get to you?"

Amelia tried to pull her hand away: "What do you want from me? This watch is mine. Leave me alone!"

Mother lost her cool and yelled: "Give me back the watch, you thief!" She tried to tear it off Amelia's wrist.

Amelia struggled, calling my mother crazy, all the while protesting that she had not stolen the watch.

"I'm talking about men!" Mother shouted, "About you stealing men who belong to other women. You slut!" I stood aside terrified, watching Mother and Amelia almost hit each other.

Amelia yelled back: "Aren't you ashamed? Making such a scene in front of your daughter, and in the middle of the street?"

This apparently had an effect on Mother. She let go of Amelia, who left almost running. Mother muttered to herself the whole way back home, while I followed her in silence, careful not to make any unnecessary movement and risk angering her further. What had come over my mother? She never acted that way. I couldn't understand what she was so upset about. Had Amelia really stolen Father's watch from him? Did Amelia steal men? How can you steal people? Obviously, I didn't dare to ask.

That evening, a serious argument broke out between my parents. Even then I still didn't understand why Mother was furious with Father. How was it his fault that Amelia had taken his watch?

Around that time, Dad started to buy larger quantities of pinga at the grocery store, and sometimes he would walk home with an unsteady gait. The day my parents went to town to sell the crops, Father returned completely drunk. He was unable to walk alone and Mother had to support him. He walked up the short flight of stairs that led to the front door with his arm wrapped around her shoulders, all his weight on her.

Once they entered the living room he collapsed on the floor and fell asleep. Mother looked at him helplessly and left. She said that when Maria got home, she would help her pick him up.

I stood in the corner of the living room, looking at the large body lying on the ground that was my father. I had never before seen him from that angle. And I didn't like it. I knew he wasn't sick, that he would be fine when he woke up, and that there was nothing to worry about. I had seen drunks before, but never my father. He should not be lying on the floor like that. It did not befit a tall, strong father like mine. It also looked pretty uncomfortable. Maybe something was wrong with him after all? A few glasses of pinga should not have knocked him down like that. Maybe he was never going to get up again? I was filled with sadness. Distracted, I was twirling the hair of a corn doll I held in my arms, when Mother called me from the kitchen.

"Catarina, come! Look! We brought you a present." I hurried to the kitchen, leaving Father alone on the floor. Mother handed me a plastic doll. It was the first real doll I was ever given. She had arms and legs that rotated on their axes, hair, and plastic clothing. Blue eyes and a pink mouth were painted on her face. I looked at her in amazement, thinking this was the most beautiful doll in the world, and that she was mine.

"Thank you," I whispered, my cheeks burning with excitement. Holding her tightly to my bosom, I promised that I would always love and take care of her.

Father started drinking more often. On Sundays he would go to the store and always come back drunk. I got to know the sound of his heavy, faltering steps up the stairs before he entered the house. His voice was loud and hoarse as he spoke to imaginary people he thought were near him. Sometimes he mumbled indistinctly and other times, he flew into a rage, shouting and cursing at whom I had no idea.

Once I stood in his way, by mistake. He pushed me aside with such force that my head hit the wall. I burst into tears but he didn't notice at all, unaware of his actions or his strength. On another occasion he ran into Maria, who had just finished curling her hair. Her head was covered with pink rollers, which when removed, made it puff up and flow in waves over her shoulders. Without any warning, Dad reached out, grabbed one of the rollers and yanked at it wildly. Maria's screams of pain merged with Father's hoarse, unintelligible shouting. As Mother came to her rescue, the commotion became more intense. Maria finally managed to escape, leaving a pink cylinder and a tuft of torn hair in his hand.

After this incident, I made sure to stay away from him when he was drunk. I would flee to the yard or to the bedroom, where I remained until all was quiet again and I knew for certain he was lying on the floor or in his bed, sleeping the heavy sleep of a drunkard.

One day, when I was playing with my beautiful doll in the living room, I heard Father pacing heavily in the yard, speaking in a shrill voice to no one. Quickly, I got up and ran outside. I watched him climb the stairs with difficulty, push open the front door and stumble inside. I heard him bump into a bench, cursing and blaspheming. For a while I stood outside, listening to the ruckus in the room. Then I heard murmurs and the sound of something heavy hitting the floor. I assumed he had fallen and continued to listen quietly. The next thing I heard was laughter. Father spoke while laughing to himself. The rage seemed to have passed. I began to relax and look for my doll but, to my dismay, found that I had forgotten to take it with me. I had left her in the living room. My doll! What if Father found her? What would he do to her!? I walked up the stairs, stood by the front door and peeked inside.

Father lay on his back on the floor. He was holding my dear doll in one hand, talking to her and snickering. With his other hand he grabbed the doll's leg and pulled hard. That's when I noticed that one of her hands was already missing. He tore off the leg, threw it in the air with a chuckle and grabbed the other leg. I watched the scene unfold in horror. I wanted to run and grab my doll, save her from his cruel hands, but I didn't dare. My heart was pounding, my legs couldn't hear me. I could only stand with my eyes wide open, watching in fear as the limbs of my beloved toy were torn from her one by one, and sent flying around the room.

I burst into tears out of anger and helplessness. Little by little, Father calmed down. His hands dropped to the sides of his body and the doll's carcass rolled to the floor. I waited until I heard him snoring and then slowly tiptoed in to collect the scattered remains. An arm. Another arm. And here was a leg. One leg was missing! I got down on all fours and searched under the table and benches. I pressed my cheek to the floor but saw nothing. Stifling a sob, I began to walk around the room quietly. I peeked behind the benches, in the space between them and the wall. There, behind the leg of a bench, I discovered the missing limb. I hugged it, even though it was twisted and crushed.

I dived into the mattress in our bedroom, trying to put the pieces back together, looking through a curtain of tears. I struggled for a long time until I managed to screw all the parts back into place. My doll looked almost the same as before the disaster, with only one of her legs damaged. I held her close, reassuring her that I didn't love her any less than I did before. On the contrary. I thought that now my two best friends each had a damaged leg.

That night I couldn't sleep. I hugged my doll and mourned my former father, who was gone. I once had a father who built us a house, dug a well, and kept us safe from snakes. Until he turned into a father who returned home drunk, slept on the floor, and pulled out hair, arms and legs. I want my old father, I murmured, sobbing silently in the dark.

In the days that followed, I was unable to look Father in the eye. I did everything I could to stay away from him even when he was sober. I don't think he remembered any of what had taken place or even noticed the change in my behavior. I thought deep down that he no longer felt anything for me, and that I no longer loved him either. As the weeks and months passed, my father forgot beautiful Amelia who had disappeared from the village. Gradually, his drinking diminished and he almost never came home drunk anymore. Life was back on track, but I could not forget.

The Storm

We arrived in the fields to meet Father, carrying lunch with us, like we did every day. Maria was tilling the land. A hefty ox trod leisurely in front of her, pulling the plow behind him, while my sister held the handles.

Dark red earthen clods, typical of Paraná, rolled over at her feet, forming long, straight furrows. Dita bent down to reach the sack that contained the seeds, scooped up a handful of them and filled the apron she was wearing, her budding breasts vibrating under her loose shirt. Mother looked at her with dismay and said nothing. Dita was barely ten years old, but she was plump and looked almost as mature as Maria. She strode between the furrows, her hair looking like black wool, as she scattered the seeds that sunk into the softened soil.

"Catarina, maybe you should help too?" Mother said, handing me a small cloth bag. I filled it with seeds and slung it over my shoulders, then scooping up the brown granules one fistful at a time, I let them slide between my fingers, just like Dita did.

A short while later, Father stopped working and told us to gather together. He glanced at the sky and looked troubled. On the horizon, dark clouds were merging into a swelling black pile that seemed to be approaching us. Father said the storm was early, and that there was no point in sowing further, because the water would wash all the seeds away anyhow. The family and the farmhands should collect all the tools and animals, and return home. He would stay in the fields for a while longer to tie up loose ends and finish some small jobs, Catarina would help him and then they too would hurry back. Once Mother and the workers had hurriedly loaded the equipment onto the carts drawn by horses or oxen, everyone drove off.

Father swept the field, marking down how far we had sown, checking whether anything had been forgotten - tools or other equipment. Once his mind was at ease, he said we could go. The wind had picked up in the meantime and the sky above us quickly covered with clouds. Big drops began to fall on us, even earlier than expected. Father advanced in long, fast strides and I ran after him to keep up. The wind blew in my face, pushing my body backwards. Father took my hand and pulled me after him. The rain was now heavy and dense. We had nowhere to go for shelter. All around us were open pastures. At that moment the sky lit up with zigzagging lines of light, like a root system made of white fire, and a tremendous clap of thunder made us jolt. By then, large amounts of rain were pouring down. I was soaked and my teeth were chattering. Father pulled me through the wind, knelt down so I could climb on his back, gripped my shins with his big hands and ran ahead.

"Hold on to me tight," he said, "so you don't fall off. You could get killed if you do." I wrapped my arms around his neck, and felt his strong back supporting my body, his warm hands holding my legs. I had never been so close to my father, and this unfamiliar feeling was strange and very, very pleasant. I felt welcome. I felt protected. My courageous father was watching over me, I thought. He cared about me. He didn't want me to die. He was fighting his way through that storm to save me.

A bubble of warmth blew up filling my chest, and I no longer felt the rain or the cold. I knew my father loved me. I loved him back and forgave him at last.

Dita

We were about to go out to the field in the morning, when Mother grabbed a wide strip of white cloth, and called Dita to come to the bedroom. Soon we heard screaming protests.

"Stop, you're suffocating me, I can't breathe!"

"Stand still. It isn't squeezing you that much. I will loosen it a little," Mother said impatiently, but Dita kept yelling in anger:

"I don't want it. It's uncomfortable!" And once again came Mother's firm voice:

"You won't go out to the field in just a shirt anymore! You already have breasts!"

"Maria has breasts too!" Dita argued, upset.

"Maria's are small. Yours are big for your age. You can't be around the farm hands like that," Mother declared sternly. After a moment of silence, Dita screamed again and ran out of the room, holding her shirt in her hand, the cloth wrapped around her chest.

Maria looked at our mother and said:

"Maybe we could tie it less tightly …"

"It's not that tight," Mother replied sullenly.

The next day, Dita went to work in the fields wearing the makeshift bra. She worked grudgingly and didn't stop complaining. At dinner, Mom watched Dita as she piled beans and cuts of meat on her plate.

"Some appetite you have, thank God…"

"What do you want me to do?" Dita replied fuming, "I worked hard so I have an appetite. I had a really hard time today. It was hot and I was drenched in sweat. I was bound so tight I could barely breathe. Dad kept yelling at me that I wasn't working fast enough and I could hardly move because you had me wrapped up like a sausage!" Fia looked with reproach at Mother, who in turn, looked at the floor. Dita went on: "I'm not going to go out to work anymore if you tie me up."

Father, whose patience had run out, shouted that everyone had to work, that she wasn't doing anyone any favors, that it was her duty, and that she should speak politely. Mother intervened and told father not to bully Dita, who immediately began to cry and left the table in protest.

"You shouldn't talk to the girl like that," Mother admonished him, "She's not your daughter. I have to discipline her, not you."

At that moment I truly regretted that one couldn't close one's ears as one closes one's eyes. And then Nicolao began to cry. Something was stuck in my throat and I didn't feel hungry anymore.

School

My parents were sitting on a bench, leisurely puffing on their cigarettes and sipping coffee.

"I talked to Preta's dad and he's sending her to school this year," Father said. "After all, Preta can't work in the field. So, I thought I could do without Catarina. You know, she's skinny and doesn't have much energy for work. We could send her to school too. What do you think?" I was just putting the dishes I had washed on the table and could overhear Dad through the open door. I wanted to shout for joy. I almost ran outside to hug him but instead, I just went out into the yard, stood by the door and said nothing.

I really, really wanted to go to school. I hadn't even dared to dream that one day I would be able to go, because my older sisters never did. Like our mother, they couldn't read or write.

"The school is very far away. She would have to walk alone for almost an hour. Do you think you can do that?" Mother asked, addressing me.

"She won't have to go alone the whole way. Only as far as Preta's house, and from there they can walk together," Father answered.

I nodded my head and felt my eyes sparkling.

A few days later, Dad brought me two notebooks, three pencils and an eraser from the venda. Mother gave me a *bornal*, a bag she had sewn from a sackcloth. I put the notebooks, pencils and eraser in the bag and guarded them like a treasure until the school year began. I thought about school all the time. I wanted to know how to draw letters and symbols in a notebook, like the salesperson at the venda did.

I wanted the patterns drawn on the sign hanging on the shop's door deciphered and turned into words I could understand. In the meantime, I drew circles and lines on the sand and imagined I was writing. When I lay in the field gazing at the clouds, like I always did, I still saw in them a galloping horse and a bull's head, but I also dreamed of Preta and me sitting in class by a desk and writing. I pictured myself reading a story in a book and then telling it to my dolls, or to myself, while we walked all the way back from school.

On the first day of school, I left at twelve in the afternoon toward Preta's house. The classes were supposed to start at one in the afternoon and end at five. The *bornal* hung from my shoulder with the two notebooks, three pencils and eraser inside. I walked for about twenty minutes, climbed the bridge and continued downhill running down the sloping path, and between two rows of eucalyptus trees beyond which stretched fishponds on one side and fields of sugar cane on the other. I passed the wide pastures. On the road, by the beautiful fazenda of Seu Matias, I saw Preta, her body slightly slanting toward her thinner leg, waiting for me.

We walked together, with Preta making sure not to lag behind. And then we entered the schoolyard for the first time in our lives. There were already several children of different ages there, and yet more children flowing in. After ten minutes a handsome man appeared. He was tall, his hair was combed to perfection and he wore glasses. His expression was serious and commanded respect. He approached the wooden structure, opened the door to the only classroom, and invited us to enter. He too stepped inside, opened the four windows in the room and said in a loud voice:

"I greet all the students. Choose your desks and sit down."

I looked around. It was a large room with wooden walls and thick wooden beams supporting a high tile-covered roof. I saw four columns, each with four desks, and two chairs behind each desk. I chose to sit in the front row. I didn't want to miss a single word the teacher said. Preta sat down next to me.

The tall man waited for everyone to settle down and said slowly in a serious tone:

"My name is Seu Benedito and I am your teacher. During my lessons, talking and interrupting are forbidden, and I am not going to accept any bad behavior." His gaze was tough and intimidating, and I felt a little sorry for having chosen to sit in the front row.

Seu Benedito proved himself to be a tough teacher, who punished students without mercy. He taught us reading, writing and arithmetic, and also made sure we did our homework and wrote in our notebooks. He paced between the desks, examining what we had written. He would linger a little longer when walking by his daughter, who was also in our class, and if he didn't like what he saw in her notebook, he would discreetly pinch her arm. The poor girl's arms were covered in bruises.

He carried out surprise inspections for order and cleanliness, looking the students over, checking whether their nails were clipped. Those lucky enough not to be chosen first would quickly look at their hands and bite their nails down to the acceptable length. Those caught having long fingernails were severely hit on the fingertips with a rod. We didn't dare make a sound during class. Undisciplined students were punished and sent to stand outside for hours, in the cold. For particularly serious offenses – in his view – children were forced to kneel for long periods with metal bottle caps under their knees. The serrated edges pointed upwards, cutting and lacerating the flesh. For a long time afterwards, they carried the marks of Cain on their knees—red flowers in the shape of beer caps.

Despite the harsh discipline, I loved school. I loved to study and I loved the walk to school with Preta. Sometimes it seemed to me that we were late and I would start walking faster, trying to stop myself from running. We would wait for Seu Benedito to arrive at the schoolyard, before classes began. We were expected to be there before he arrived. I thought of Seu Benedito's stern look whenever anyone entered the courtyard after he had opened the classroom door, and of the sting of the ruler striking my fingers. Preta always did her best to keep up with me, dragging her leg with great vigor. We were never late.

I loved the way back home from school. We walked leisurely to Preta's house and said our goodbyes there. I continued home alone, thinking about the homework I had to do and of what we would learn the next day. The summer days were long and when I got home there were still many hours left of daylight.

The Wake

We were having dinner when I heard sounds outside. Someone opened the gate and knocked on the living room door. Mother called them to come in. It was one of the villagers, who told us in a frightened voice that his baby was missing. They hadn't seen him since the afternoon and the people of the village were organizing a search. They asked whether Father could join.

In the fading daylight I saw through the open door a group of peasants who had gathered to help, carrying torches and lit oil lamps. Father also took a lantern and went out with them. Sitting on the steps I watched the last streak of light still on the horizon, until it disappeared. I stayed outside with Tupi, looking at the flicker of a lonely torch that appeared for a moment and then was gone, in the area across which the searchers were looking, and hearing the distant barking of dogs in the background. There was a feeling of unease and the possibility of a bad outcome hung in the air. After it became completely dark, I went inside.

We didn't go to sleep that night. Mother waited up for Father or for the news to come. Late into the night, Father returned and told us with great sadness that the boy was found in the depths of the well in a yard, because now almost every yard had a well. He had fallen in and drowned. Several hours had elapsed by the time they found him and pulled the little body out.

We walked to the house of the family that lost their little son that night. He was only two years old. By the light of lanterns, family members and neighbors sat on benches around a large wooden table. Some sighed or whispered prayers, while rolling beads between their fingers. Others wept softly. The baby lay in a small coffin. His body was covered and surrounded by wild flowers, with only his face visible. A neighbor entered through the open door, and walked up to the coffin, his head bowed. He knelt down, mumbled a muted prayer, and lit a candle. He then crossed himself, got up, and sat down on a bench. The mother and daughters were in the kitchen, frying fritters, making coffee and serving the guests.

People drank coffee and feasted on pancakes, while I sat on a bench against the wall, thinking about the baby lying dead inside the well. After all, it was water drawn from that same well that was now being used to make coffee and knead the dough. I felt nauseated. I looked in amazement at the people chewing and sipping. One of the sisters offered us a bowl full of hot fritters, which I declined politely. Obviously angry, Mother whispered to me:

"Why don't you eat anything? It's not polite to say no every time. When they serve you food again, have some."

One of the neighbors pushed a bowl in my direction and urged me to eat. I took a fritter, because Mother was glaring at me. When no one was looking, I flung it under the bench, a procedure I repeated every time the food tray came my way. Then I went outside to play with my siblings and the other children. Little by little the younger kids left to go back inside. When I entered the house, I saw them already asleep with their mouths open, resting their heads on the wall or on their mothers' laps.

Our hostess spread some blankets across her bedroom floor. Almost like sleepwalkers, the children got up, lay down on them, and fell back asleep immediately. I joined them too. I woke up at dawn and returned to the living room, to where my family was. A pale light seeped in from the windows and the room slowly got brighter. The guests got up to leave. I stole a glance at the area where I sat when we first arrived. Under the bench, on the floor next to the wall was a mound of piled up fritters.

Happiness

At dusk the heat faded and a pleasant wind began to blow. Several large tarpaulin sheets were spread out in the yard, covered with black beans or coffee beans left to dry.

Dita and I took a folded sheet just like that one from the storeroom and climbed up the hill, with Aroldo trailing behind us. Walking among the fruit trees, we chose a ripe papaya or mango, and after eating it, we licked the sweet juice off our hands and rubbed them on the grass until they were no longer sticky. Then we took the huge sheet and extended it along its entire length, with Dita holding one end and I, the other. We lifted it above our heads while Aroldo stood between us holding the center with his short arms stretched up as high as he could reach. From the top of the hill, we looked down at the waves the wind made across the patches of yellow grass.

"N ... O ... W ...!" Dita shouted, and we started to run down the slope, the wind blowing against the fabric like a sail. "We're flying!" Dita shrieked.

"We're flying!" we repeated after her, feeling the sheet becoming taut above us like a big white wing.

On clear summer evenings, Father sometimes lit a fire outside. We all sat on the ground, around the fire, watching the flames dance in the light breeze. Father grilled meat and Mother brought out bread and dishes from the kitchen. One of the farm hands made coffee.

I looked at the sparks rising from the fire and followed them with my eyes as they soared upwards, until they became invisible. The sky was full of stars, and it seemed to me they were the same sparks that had returned and reignited. As I breathed in deeply the scents of roast meat and coffee, I was filled with peace. A happy tranquility flooded my body, and it felt good.

Maria

One bright day, Seu Benedito announced that from that day on, school uniforms would become compulsory. According to his instructions, all the girls would have to wear a white dress that reached below the knee, fastened at the back, and have a white belt made of the same fabric sewn onto it and tied at the back. When I returned home on Saturday evening, I informed my mother that starting next Monday, I would have to wear a white dress to school, because the teacher said we had to. Angry at the news, Mother replied that we could not afford to buy new dresses, and returned to her occupations.

I looked at her in despair but couldn't find any words to convince her otherwise, so I didn't say anything. I felt anguish creeping up my throat. If I didn't have a dress, I wouldn't be able to go to school. What could I do? I couldn't find any way out of this predicament. No solution was coming from any direction. I felt desperate and my stomach began to hurt. At dinner, I couldn't eat anything.

"What's wrong, Catarina?" Mother asked drily. Maria looked at me with concern and felt my forehead with her hand.

"I think she has a fever," she said. Mother sent me to bed. Fia escorted me and told me not to worry.

"Everything will be fine," she said, reassuring me.

The next morning Fia took a white burlap sheet, marked my measurements on it, and then proceeded to cut and sew. A short while later she handed me a dress and asked me to try it on.

It fit exactly as I had imagined. I showed it off dancing joyfully, hugged Maria and told her she was a magician, like in Grandmother's bedtime fairy tales. Maria smiled and asked how I was feeling. Nothing hurt me anymore.

Our third summer in Jacarezinho was coming to an end and the San João holidays were upon us. Maria was seventeen, a strong, beautiful country girl, youthful and healthy. Boys were interested in her, but my parents forbade her to talk to men they didn't know.

Maria waited with excitement for the upcoming festivities. It was a rare opportunity for her to break free from the harsh, stressful routine and the close supervision of my parents. In honor of San João, my mother allowed her to buy a piece of light blue fabric with white dots and make herself a dress. Maria watched her reflection in the only mirror we had in the house, in my parents' room. The dress had a narrow cut and widened slightly toward the knees, where it ended abruptly. Frowning, Mother remarked that the dress was too short.

"This is what people wear today," Maria said in protest, irking Mother who said: "I don't care what other girls do. My daughter won't." Maria remained silent. Clearly, she was too smart to start an argument and too stubborn to give in.

When evening approached, we left together to go to the dance. We walked up the bridge and past the fishponds toward the large fairgrounds. Maria marched in her short dress, her head held high, her hair combed in waves. Mother walked beside her with Nicolao strapped to her back, giving her eldest daughter looks of displeasure. I also wore a party dress my parents brought me from the city when they sold the last crops. I had been waiting for a chance to finally wear it. My hair which I brushed until it shone, rested on my shoulders.

The big lot was teeming with people, the air filled with the familiar smells of smoke, roasted meat and boiling corn. The breeze played with the chains of colorful paper flags hanging between trees and wooden poles. Several bands performed in different corners, each surrounded by large circles of spectators and dancing couples. I wandered in the crowds looking for Preta.

The sky was getting dark. A man drove a large nail into a tree trunk and hung a burning kerosene lamp. All of a sudden, I noticed a boy in a riding suit, wearing boots with spurs and a cowboy hat. He was the son of Seu Matias. I knew his name—Nei. He was my secret love. Every time I watched him from afar, I felt a storm in my chest. For days afterwards I would make up stories in my head about how we would meet, talk and eventually become friends.

When Nei passed close to me I lowered my eyes and stole a glance at him. He stopped, looked at me and asked: "What's your name?"

My legs were shaking so badly I thought I was going to fall. Feeling my cheeks burning, I whispered with some effort: "Catarina." He didn't say anything further and neither did I. After a few seconds he continued walking, while I stood there, waiting for my heart to stop racing.

I made my way between the revelers. The night fell slowly and dozens of lamps lit up among the trees. I spotted Preta in the distance, standing in a crowd watching the dances. As I headed in her direction, I saw Maria at some distance from the crowd, standing next to an older man I didn't know. Her face aglow, she was completely absorbed with her companion and did not pay attention to me. I searched for one of my parents but didn't see them anywhere. I was surprised. One of them was always watching over Maria. In the meantime, I reached Preta and didn't think about my sister anymore.

The next day, at lunchtime on Sunday, Maria announced with flushed cheeks that she had met someone at the fair and that he should be arriving shortly. Our parents looked at her in surprise.

"How did you meet him?" Mother asked matter-of-factly. "Did he approach you on his own, without anyone introducing him to you? Do you even know who he is?"

"Isabella's husband, who works for Nestor Matias, knows him. He gets his hair cut there sometimes," answered Maria humbly. "His name is João, he owns a barber shop in Jacarezinho and he is very nice." A tense atmosphere prevailed that day in the kitchen.

Someone clapped their hands by the gate. Father got up to open the door for the guest, and Maria hurriedly joined him. I heard his footsteps crossing the path and his voice greeting my father and politely introducing himself.

When they entered the living room, they passed in front of the kitchen door. It was the same man I had seen in Maria's company at the fair, when I was looking for Preta. Dita examined him with curious eyes, grimaced and declared: "He's terribly old."

That evening, João asked my father for permission to come visit Maria on Sundays. He was twenty years older than her and had never been married before. My parents didn't see any noticeable flaw in him, and since Maria wanted him, they approved of the relationship. João returned to visit Maria on Sunday afternoon. The living room gradually emptied of other members of the household. Father went out drinking to the bar and Mother got up to tuck my younger siblings in bed.

"Dita, stay in the living room," she ordered. When Dita protested, Maria said she would rather have Catarina stay. Maria sat on a bench with her back straight against the wall, while João sat down on the bench across from her.

They spoke using the formal manner of address, the distance between them being the entire width of the room. I was playing in the corner with my dolls, completely engrossed in serving them dinner and quietly scolding an orange corn doll who refused to eat. Nei, the father and my beloved knight, had come home from work and walked into my imaginary kitchen. I whispered that he should take his place at the table, and then told him how the plastic doll had behaved so well and done all her homework.

About an hour later I had to leave my post to go to the bathroom in the yard. I knew I had to hurry back because Maria was not supposed to be left alone with João for too long. They were not married. When I returned, I found João standing next to Maria, holding her hand. When he suddenly noticed me watching, he seemed startled at having been caught. He hurried back to his place with an expression of embarrassment on his face. Maria lowered her eyes and blushed.

For almost six months, João visited Maria every Sunday afternoon until the evening hours, with me acting as a chaperone. Sometimes my sister would look at me as if making a silent request, at which I would leave and go for a short stroll in the yard. When I returned, I would deliberately make some sort of noise, stomp my feet or bump into a chair outside, lingering for a little while so as to give João time to get back to the other side of the room.

Toward December, Grandmother came to us bringing with her joy at the news of the approaching Christmas as well as a package wrapped in brown paper and tied with string. When we opened it, we found a pile of fabrics in all kinds of colors. Every evening as soon as she returned from the fields, Maria sat down to sew, so that on the holidays we each could have a new garment.

Mother no longer had time to help father in the fields as she and Grandmother spent all their time cooking out in the yard. The clay oven worked non-stop, churning out trays full of buns, sweet braided sweet bread, cakes and cookies. Father had already agreed in advance with Preta's father that we would be buying half a pig and a quarter of a cow from him. Mother had been fattening several chickens for months. My parents made sure that none of the family members or farm hands would go hungry.

On the eve of the holiday, Father placed a large wooden board over several bipods under the eucalyptus trees. This was the long table we all shared for Christmas dinner—the family, the employees and also João, Maria's suitor. After dinner he and Maria shut themselves in the living room with Father. They talked for quite some time and when they came out, they all looked displeased.

The next day, at lunch, Maria sulked and ate very little.

"What do you want?" Father chastised her, "Three more months! It's not that much. Help me with the harvest, we'll sell the crops and throw a proper wedding celebration."

Maria lowered her eyes without offering any reply. Grandmother placed the steaming pot of soup on the table and patted her head.

A week went by and João arrived as he always did. And like the other times, he sat opposite Maria, while I played in the room with the dolls. About two hours later he got up to go, and Maria walked him to the door. As soon as we sat down to eat, Maria announced that she was not feeling well and was going to rest. We heard her footsteps as she strode down the hall toward the bedroom, and ate our meal without her. After some time, we heard the door of the other room, the one Grandmother used, close.

Grandmother put us to bed, while a single kerosene lamp lit the dark room, transforming us all into dark silhouettes. Sitting on Maria's empty bed, she began to tell us our favorite story: "Many years ago, there lived in the forest a poor woodcutter with his wife and two children, a boy and a girl, named Mariazinha and Zonzinho (Hansel and Gretel). Bad times came and the woodcutter could not earn enough money to buy food for his family …"

And so the story continued with the birds that ate the bread crumbs Zonzinho had scattered in the forest, and how they reached the candy house, all the way to the happy ending, where Mariazinha shoves the witch into the burning oven. Grandmother got up from her seat, leaned by all our beds, kissed us good night, and headed for her bedroom. She first knocked on the closed door, knowing Maria was in the room. When no one answered, she opened the door only to find an empty room and the window wide open. Grandmother screamed.

My parents came running and began to search frantically through every room in the house and in the yard—Maria was gone. We all got up, went outside and called Maria's name. We were enveloped by a thick darkness. My parents raced up and down the empty street, under a moonless sky, shouting her name. After over an hour they gave up and returned home.

Mother entered the bedroom, opened Maria's drawer and was horrified to discover what she already suspected.

"She ran away!" she cried. "She took her clothes and ran away! How could she do such a thing!"

Father looked stunned for a moment, and then his face reddened.

"So reckless! She ran away with him! The bastard was waiting for her in the street! They planned everything in advance! They had too much freedom to meet. You, Terezinha, allowed them to sit together in the living room for hours, every week! This is the result!"

I felt my ears burning. Now Father would blame me for not having supervised them properly. And really, maybe I shouldn't have left the living room so many times and let them get so close to each other. It must have been my fault. But he didn't say anything to me. He was silent for a few seconds and then burst out: "I will kill him! I'm driving to his place right now and I'm going to shoot them both!" he shouted. He entered the living room with giant strides and took the shotgun off the wall where it hung.

Frightened, Mother quickly grabbed his arm.

"Alemão, calm down! What's wrong with you? Tomorrow we will go to Jacarezinho, find them and marry them, and that's it. What can we do? It's not what we had planned, but what is done, is done... Come, let's go back to sleep now. There's nothing we can do this late at night. Children," she said addressing us, "go back to bed. Father and I will get up early tomorrow and find Maria."

Grandmother urged us on, while Father sat down in the living room and lit himself a cigarette. I saw his face, ashen and tense behind the coils of smoke. I cried silently in bed, because I felt I would never see Maria again—and it was precisely in such moments of distress that I missed her so much.

The night Maria ran away was the dividing line that crossed our family's life. The days bathed in light in endless fields were gone forever, and in their place came days of hardship and strain—days of misery and struggle, of a never-ending battle for our sheer existence.

At dawn my parents hitched a horse to a cart and went to look for Maria at her fiancé's house, in order to marry them immediately. They arrived in town and quickly located João's barber shop. They married Maria off in a hasty wedding and rushed home at noon. As they approached our village, they noticed a Beetle driving up among clouds of dust.

They recognized its blue color and knew the car belonged to Seu Osvaldo, the owner of the land that my father cultivated. After pulling to a stop, he turned his round face toward them: "Is anything wrong? Why are you coming from the direction of the city at this time of the day?" he asked in surprise. "You're usually in the field by now, Alemão."

My parents told him briefly that they had gone to Maria's wedding. Osvaldo was shocked, and his face became very red: "You had Maria get married?" he cried in disbelief. "Why did you suddenly marry her? And where will they live?" he asked in an offending tone.

When he heard that she had moved to the city to follow her husband, he was struck with inexplicable rage. My parents looked at him, unable to comprehend.

He climbed out of the car and stood in front of them: "Listen carefully. Without Maria, I don't want you here! Take your things and get off my land. I'm serious! How could you do such a stupid thing and marry her off!" He returned to his car, pressed wildly on the gas and disappeared in the dust.

All the way home, my baffled parents tried to decipher his words, until they came to the only plausible conclusion: Osvaldo, who had a wife, two small children and a round belly, had set his sights on Maria.

He must have had ulterior motives and had waited patiently for her to grow up and be at some distance from her parents' watchful eyes. The unexpected wedding had ruined his fantasy. The next day Father went to work in the fields as usual. When he returned in the evening, he said that he had received a visit from Osvaldo. From atop his horse, wearing a cowboy hat, boots and a gun in his belt, he roared at him that he had meant every word and that we must leave at once. Father said that as soon as he could sell the crops and recover his expenses and wages, he would go. Osvaldo replied he didn't care about all that and that he wanted us out of his land immediately.

Despite this, Father did not give in and continued to go out to work. Then, one morning, he returned shortly after leaving for the fields, looking pale. His voice quivering, he told us that during the night Osvaldo led a herd of cows into the cornfields and turned them loose. Half a year's work was lost. All the seedlings were trampled, masses of small cobs lay on the ground. Heartache. A terrible disaster.

Father no longer went out to work, because there was no point in doing so. He went to Londrina, the big city, to inquire about his rights. He filed a lawsuit against Osvaldo for the damage suffered. Seu Matias, despite being Osvaldo's partner, sided with Father. Osvaldo became enraged when he found out that Father was willing to stand up to him and was even suing him. He came to our house but Father refused to see him. Mother went out to meet him.

"Where's your macho?" Osvaldo scoffed, "Hiding behind your skirt? Doesn't he have the guts to face me?" Controlling the tremor in her voice, Mother replied:

"You two have nothing to talk about, Seu Osvaldo. We'll see you in court."

"If he gets to go to court," Osvaldo hissed. "Tell him to be very careful with me. I'll be back." From the kitchen, where I was helping my mother, I heard the sound of his heavy boots moving away toward the Beetle that was parked in front of the gate.

Father sat on the bed in his room, unkempt and unshaven.

"He's a criminal," he said to Mother. "I've heard rumors that he tried to kill someone he had a fight with. He is capable of killing me to get rid of this lawsuit. A murderer, this Osvaldo!"

Father didn't leave the house until the trial. He sat most of the time on the bed in his room or on a bench in the living room, smoking. His green eyes turned gray and dull. No longer needed, the farm hands left. We barely had enough to cover our needs.

Even my "grandfather" Seu Benedito, said goodbye to us. He stroked my head and those of my siblings. He also petted Tupi and bowed in gratitude to my mother, who escorted him to the gate together with us. He swung his bundle over his shoulder and headed out to the dirt road. I saw him walking away, slightly bent under the weight, looking sad. We waved goodbye until his dark figure and white hair disappeared from our sight. I never saw him again.

Grandmother also left us. She went to look for a new place for us to live once we left Jacarezinho. Mother didn't allow us to be outside after dark. In the evening she looked out of the window to the top of the hill and saw a stranger standing among the fruit trees and looking toward the house.

"Wicked people!" she whispered, "Who knows what they are trying to do to us."

"They're trying to shoot me," Dad cried. "They would kill me without thinking twice!" When night fell, we saw the flickering cigarette of the mysterious stranger, lurking in the dark in the orchard.

The days and nights that followed went by pretty much the same way. One day Osvaldo appeared again, demanding to speak to Father. Mother was in the yard, plucking kernels from a dry corn cob and feeding them to the chickens. I heard her answering him. Out of the window I saw her calmly scattering more seeds, without showing any fear. What a strong mother I had!

Unable to get my father to come out or my mother to panic, he became incensed and yelled at her: "Well, well, I heard you, scum. Go, go take a bath, maybe then you'll be less black." He hit a sensitive chord, the color of her skin.

The day of the trial arrived, and my parents went to town. They warned us very sternly not to dare leave the house until they returned. In the afternoon, Seu Matias drove them back home. Father shook his hand and thanked him excitedly. Seu Matias said goodbye to us, saying he would come by at dawn to take us to the train station, and that we should be ready.

"We won the trial, children," said father. And mother added hastily:

"Hurry up. Catarina, Aroldo, bring all the chickens in from the yard. We only have until morning to get ready."

She worked all night, cooking the four remaining chickens with rice in a large pot. She went through the rooms, sorted and collected whatever we could take with us. On some sheets spread on the floor we piled clothes and bedding, then bundled them into white balls. In my bornal I packed the plastic doll and three young corn cobs, which I had picked in the evening from our vegetable garden. After midnight I sat down on one of the soft bundles, like the rest of my siblings, and drowsed off, waiting for the dawn.

The Expulsion from Jacarezinho

At four in the morning, Seu Matias' truck appeared. Mother poured coffee into three aluminum mugs and served it to him and to Father. This was the last coffee they would sip standing in the yard outside our house. Seu Matias gave the empty cup back to Mother and said we should hurry. The sky was still dark and the car lights illuminated the yard for us, so that we could load up our belongings. Over an hour later, the baggage was in the back of the van, with us children stretched out between them, while our parents sat in the front.

The sun was rising when we set off. I looked at the distant village. A summer dawn. On the burning horizon appeared the silhouettes of the house we lived in and the eucalyptus trees that surrounded it.

All of a sudden, I heard barking.

"Tupi, we forgot Tupi!" I cried and looked back at the little dog chasing after the van.

"Tupi!" Mother leaned out through the window and shouted, "Go home! Home!" The dog stopped, pricked up his ears and watched us. Seeing his figure on the path becoming blurry, receding in the early morning light, I looked at my mother with questioning eyes.

"We can't take him," she declared.

My Tupi shrank until he became a small white dot, then disappeared. The truck lurched over the small bumps in the road. I swayed from side to side, feeling great fatigue coming over me.

Now I had time to feel. The fear of the past few weeks, the stress of last night, they all left, freeing up space in my brain so I could begin to understand. We were leaving our house, my dog, and my sister Maria behind. We were going, I didn't know where, and were probably never coming back. I might never see Maria again. I thought of Nei, lost to me forever. I quickly put my hand into the *bornal* I had with me, to touch my plastic doll. The three corn dolls lying next to her tickled me with their hair.

Once we arrived at the train station, Seu Matias helped us unload the bundles. My parents thanked him repeatedly. Placing his arms around their shoulders, he wished us all good luck and that God may protect us.

I had never been to a train station before that day. I only knew the freight train that passed not far from where we lived, gray with windowless cars, so I did not expect the fancy locomotive that arrived with a loud siren and clouds of black smoke. It was red and shiny, with silvery stripes and handles made of nickel. We walked along the platform carrying our bundles until we saw an empty bench through the car window. Father climbed the metal stairs and lifted the bundles we handed to him with great effort. We sat down occupying several benches—Father, Mother and Nicolao on her lap, Dita, Aroldo, Ivone, I and the packages.

The train left the station, rattling rhythmically as it rolled away. On the bench to our left sat a man in a suit reading a newspaper. In front of him sat a woman in an elegant dress and next to her was a girl about my age who wore new blue pants and a beautiful shirt, embroidered in blue and pink. Small flowers, red and blue, decorated her sandal straps. They looked like they were going to a party.

I noticed that most people around us were well dressed, combed and groomed. My gaze wandered to the window, where the scenery traveled backwards. The extreme tiredness and the train's motion made me doze off.

I woke up when the train tooted its horn and stopped, to discover that we were at an unfamiliar station. The sign read *Maringa*. The large clock that hung on a post outside showed it was seven o'clock. People got off the wagons and others got on, carrying packages and bags. After a few minutes the train started again. I rested my head on the back of the seat, following the passing scenery through the window—green fields of corn, beans, coffee plantations, pastures, and farms surrounded by small country houses.

The sun was already shining high in the sky when Mother got up and pulled a large pot out from under the bench. She placed it between her thighs and motioned for us to come and eat. After wiping our hands with a cloth napkin she handed us, we scooped up rice or a chicken leg with our fingers and ate standing up, leaning over the pot. I was wiping my face with the back of my hand while chewing on a piece of chicken, when I suddenly noticed the eyes of the other passengers were fixed on us.

The girl with flowers on her sandals was watching me with a smile of amusement. She whispered something to her mother, giggling softly. It made me feel uncomfortable. We must have been doing something wrong. We were some sort of oddity. I dropped my gaze down toward the pot and didn't pick it up until I finished eating.

We stopped at a station again and I read out loud *Londrina*. I remembered that name. It was the city where the trial Father won had been held. My parents got up and gathered our things. We followed them down to the platform and walked on the smooth, beautiful tiles. The hanging signs were white and clear. We arrived at a large, clean plaza where crowds of people walked through on their way to and from the platforms. The voice in the loudspeaker announced that the train to São Paulo was about to arrive in five minutes.

We moved to another platform and boarded the train again. We rode for the rest of the day and all night. The next morning, we arrived in the town of São Manuel.

"Wake up," said Dita, shaking me roughly. "We're getting off."

Only a few people were on the platform at the small station. By the exit to the street was a horse-drawn carriage. The driver turned to father and asked if we needed a ride. Mother gave him her brother's address. We drove a long way, until the driver pointed to a large fazenda.

"It's here," he said.

Mother clapped her hands in front of the gate to announce our arrival. When no one came out to meet us, she walked into the courtyard and knocked on the door of the manor. A worker appeared from a corner and, after asking whom we were looking for, he directed us to a small house located in the back.

A short, thin man opened the door and greeted Mother with a pale smile.

"Terezinha, hello! Come in," he said meekly. The woman of the house was standing in the kitchen stirring the pots. She was a full head taller than our uncle with abundant curly hair and brown skin. She turned to look at us without smiling, with an angry expression on her face, and, as she approached us, wiped her hands on her apron.

"They can stay here for three days," she interjected harshly. "I can't feed five kids any longer than that." She then regained her composure and explained: "The landlord won't allow more than one family to live here."

Our parents replied that three days would be enough for them to go to *Sorocaba* and back. They both left, leaving us alone with a strange uncle and a grumpy aunt.

Our hostess doled out small portions of soup for dinner. Later, she ordered Dita to spread a sheet she handed to her, across the living room floor, and we all huddled on it and lay down to sleep. Despite being exhausted, I found it hard to fall asleep. The image of Mother closing the gate behind her and disappearing with Father stayed before my eyes the whole time.

"Are you crying, little baby?" Dita said laughing in the dark, as I blew my nose.

I didn't answer and hugged my *bornal* to my bosom.

I woke up to my aunt's shrill voice. "You're the big one, Dita, aren't you? Take care of the little ones. You, the second one, arrange the bed linen and the mattresses in the living room and then come help me in the kitchen."

I peeled many potatoes, throwing the peels like at home, in Jacarezinho, into a large bin, as slob for the pigs. I cooked according to our aunt's instructions, concentrating as much as I could on the job. I kept quiet all morning, but at lunch I couldn't hold back any longer.

"When is Mother coming back?" I asked quietly, with hesitation. Dita could not resist but seize the wonderful opportunity that suddenly appeared.

"Mother won't come back! Mother is gone for good!" she said, laughing cheerfully.

The aunt snickered.

"Yes, your mother left you here for good," she confirmed. I stared at the plate in front of me, and my lips quivered.

In the evening, our uncle returned from work and sat down at the table with us. His wife served him a small portion. "Is that it?" he asked.

"This is what is left now that your entire family has moved in with us," she answered with indignation. He fell silent, frightened, and spoke no more.

At night I secretly took out my plastic doll and whispered to her that our mother had promised she would come back after three days. There was that night and one more, and then surely she would come.

The third night came, followed by the fourth day. The evening also came, and still no sign of our mother. The aunt no longer joked about our parents leaving us with her for good. She became very irritable, screaming at everyone, even at Dita. A cold fear crept into me. Maybe they were telling the truth? Maybe Mother really wouldn't come back!? I turned on the sheet for a long time...

In the morning I woke up very early. I pulled my corn dolls out of my *bornal* to hug them for a bit, only to discover they were black and rotting. Their hair had faded and started to fall out. Young cobs live only a few days, like butterflies. I went to the large bin in the kitchen and threw my dolls in.

That afternoon the gate suddenly opened and I heard my mother's voice announcing she had arrived. A huge joy filled me. I ran out of the kitchen, straight to my mother who was walking toward me, and I hugged her. I don't remember ever hugging her before, but that day I couldn't help myself.

Father walked in behind her, accompanied by a strange man, with a slight limp, wearing strange shoes. One sole was very thick and the other was normal. Mother explained that this was her cousin who lived in Sorocaba, and he had come along to help them on the trip back to the city. They had found a house for us to live in and we would be leaving the next day.

Father brought a large *bornal* filled with goods in the kitchen, Mother took out its delicious contents—meat, sausage, bread—and prepared dinner. The whole family sat around the table. Our uncle and aunt who no longer looked grumpy, their two small children, Mother's cousin and us. We even got sweets after the meal.

Sorocaba

The next day we all took the train to Sorocaba. We rode for several hours and arrived at a large, busy station, through which we entered a wonderful world—a wide street with paved lanes for beautiful cars to drive on.

The sidewalks were lined with tall houses. I felt like I was in a dream. I was dizzy from the new sights, from the amount of traffic on the roads. The cousin led us to a corner on the sidewalk near the road and explained that there was a bus that would take us almost up to the house, and that we had to wait for it. Our parents had taken most of the packages with them earlier, and only a few clothes were left to carry with us.

The big car, which looked a bit like a train, was what they called a bus. There were not enough seats. I stood swaying from side to side, holding tightly to a metal post, between Father and the cousin. Through the windows I saw the sun sink into the horizon, and the streets became dark. Surprisingly, the glass lanterns that were hanging on poles along the street lit up all by themselves, as if by magic, without anyone lighting them with a torch. We finally arrived at the home of Mother's aunt. She was a very kind and cordial woman, who looked a little like Grandmother. She welcomed us with wide open arms and hugged us warmly.

Grandmother was also waiting for us there, and they both prepared an aromatic meal in our honor. The house we rented was on the very same street, named Benjamin dos Santos, but at the other end, near the cemetery. The landlady lived next door to us, in a spacious house. Further down the yard, across from her residence, stood the outhouse.

We entered a large room containing a double bed followed by a kitchen equipped with an oven and a small table. And that was all. I searched for the other rooms: the children's rooms, the parents' room, but there was nothing. This was our entire new home. Dita protested angrily that one couldn't live like this, that we were all in the same room. But no one paid attention to her words. We were used to her and too busy each with their own personal grief. Mother placed two mattresses that were leaning against the wall across the floor of the only room. The parents would be sleeping in the bed, the younger children on a mattress next to them, Dita and I on a mattress in the kitchen.

In the days that followed, our parents went out to look for work. Mother found a job in housekeeping, with a kind pharmacist. Father, who had worked all his life in farming, had a hard time finding a job that suited him. Most of the day he wandered outside the house, and in the evening, when he returned, he would lie down on the bed and stare at the ceiling. Slowly, we got into a routine.

Mother got up very early to go to work. Father got up a little after her or stayed in bed. Dita and I picked up the mattresses and put them against the wall to make the house look tidy. We served homemade bread and poured milk, for us and for the little ones. We spent the morning in the yard, with the children of the neighbors from the same street. Dita very quickly became friendly with the boys and girls her age, and disappeared for hours on end. The responsibility of watching the younger children fell on me alone. The possibility of me returning to school never came up.

We survived on Mother's work and the compensation money Father had received from Osvaldo, which was dwindling fast. Eventually, he managed to find a job working for a renovation contractor. He would return tired and frustrated from a job that was very difficult for him, because he was not used to it. He invested half of his first salary in pinga and got drunk. In his inebriated state he shouted at Maria, whom he blamed for all our troubles. The name Maria hit me like a knife.

All my longing for her, which I had pushed deep into the bottom of my soul, came gushing out, hurting me tremendously. I realized how much I missed her. Her pleasant personality, her caring. I closed my eyes and saw Maria walking to the stream next to the house in Jacarezinho balancing a laundry basket on her head. My Maria walked in my memory, slender and straight among the tall grasses, the wind sending waves through them, and the sky high and bright.

I opened my eyes to see a bare room with a bed, an ill-tempered father sprawled across it, and mattresses against the wall. In the kitchen there was a pot of rice and a pot of tea. No chicken every week, no corn cakes every few days, and sometimes not even enough food to go to bed with our stomachs full. What would tomorrow bring? Or next week? Was this how it would go on day after day? Was that what my life would be like from that moment and forever?

A Pot of Soup on the Stove

I loved the mornings after Mother left for work. Carrying little Nicolao on my hip, I would go out into the yard, together with Aroldo and Ivone. The rooms in the house were cool after the night and outside the temperature was pleasant. The winter sun caressed my face and thawed my frozen limbs. Nicolao crawled on the ground next to me. Little by little, the children of the neighborhood gathered, my new friends. Those who attended school went in the afternoon, from Monday to Friday. In the mornings we could play rope or catch.

Aroldo was an ace in marbles. He and his friends would make a dent in the ground and each player would put some of their own marbles in it. Each in turn shot a marble at the pile in the pit, and the marbles that jumped out belonged to them. Aroldo always earned some and walked around with bulging pockets. He taught me to play and I loved joining him and the other boys, even if I lost some of the marbles he won.

Often, I would forget time and realize suddenly that it was already afternoon, and I still hadn't tidied the house or lit the charcoal. Concerned, I would perform all the tasks quickly, before Mother came back and became angry with me for playing instead of doing the housework.

Dita disappeared early every morning. For some reason she was exempt from helping out. I think Mother was scared of her. When she came back from work and Dita was still nowhere to be seen, she would send me to look for her. I knew where to find her. I ran out and, already halfway there, I could hear the music that came from the first house at the end of the street. I entered and stood shyly by the door. Three brothers, members of the household, sat on a bench, playing guitars and an accordion. They were surrounded by young people who sang along with them or danced in the center of the room.

Dita was there too. Standing by the wall, I listened to the music, feeling my legs starting to dance on their own and almost leading me to the center of the room, where everyone was. But I made them stop because I didn't dare, and just stayed by the door, quietly tapping my foot to the beat. My body moved a little, but only sometimes, when no one was looking. When the song ended, I approached Dita and told her that Mother was calling her. Dita made an angry face, said goodbye to everyone and returned home sullen.

"How long does it take you to go bring your sister?" Mother scolded me when we arrived, "Nicolao's diaper needs to be changed. The boy is soaked up to the neck!"

Father did not last long as a renovation worker and was left without a job again. After spending his entire last salary on alcohol, he came home drunk and penniless. Mother, although aware that it was impossible to talk to him when he was drunk, couldn't restrain herself and yelled that there was almost no money left, that soon we would have nothing to eat and that the charcoal had also run out.

At that very moment, Dita entered the house. When Father saw her in the doorway he strode up to her furiously and grabbed her shoulder.

"Your daughter should go to work!" he yelled. "She's already a woman! Look at her! She's out all day who knows where. You should help out a little instead of doing stupid things."

He shook her forcefully, making Dita scream. Mother hurriedly pushed him away from her. "Don't touch her!" she shouted too. "You have no right! You are not her father!"

Dita yelled that this house was hell and ran outside again. Father lay on the bed enraged. Mother turned to Aroldo and me gloomily, and sent us to collect wood from the yard, because we had no money to buy coal and she couldn't cook dinner. She lit the wood, as she used to do in Jacarezinho, and placed a pot of soup on the stove. This house, however, had no chimney. The smoke that rose from the stove filled the space in the kitchen, and then the great room. The air became clouded and stuffy, and we all started to cough. Mother immediately turned off the stove and opened the windows.

A few minutes later, our landlady arrived looking frantic, covering her mouth with her hand.

"What happened?" she exclaimed, "What's burning?" Mother explained that she just turned on the stove so she could cook. "What do you mean?" The owner of the house tried to make sense out of what she heard, "Maybe the coals have rotted. There shouldn't be that kind of smoke."

When Mother replied that she used wood because she had run out of coal, the landlady became upset. She said she couldn't believe her ears and that we really could have caused a serious fire. She looked around at the sooty walls and told us in a tone of despair that this stove was only allowed to burn coal, and that we would have to whitewash the walls again before we left.

The move to the city was tough for all of us, but much more so for our parents who carried the burden. The pharmacist, my mother's employer, was kind and generous, and helped as best he could. When he renovated his house, he moved an old medicine cabinet to ours. It was a wonderful piece of furniture, made up of rows of tiny drawers, above which, behind two glass doors, was a hive of small compartments. He also sent us the old toys of his children, who were already adults. His eldest daughter was married and about to give birth. Mother offered the pharmacist Dita's services for his daughter, and at the same time convinced Dita to go to work several times a week.

Mother's belly also started to protrude once more. The pharmacist explained to her that in order to receive the birth grant and the social security funds when the time came, she needed to have her documents in order with the various authorities. It turned out that our parents were married in a church only and never bothered to register their marriage with the Ministry of the Interior. They decided to hold a wedding ceremony at the municipality, so they could get a civil document and change all our birth certificates, listing Father on them.

In honor of her second marriage, Mother wore a light blue dress, which suited her dark skin very well. She looked slender and feminine, with a small, round pregnancy bulge showing in the front.

A few days later we received our new birth certificates. I opened mine and looked through it. After a year at school, I could read. It said: *Catarina Granater*.

My full name was Catarina Rita Granater. Someone had accidentally left out my middle name, which I happened to like in particular, but nobody had noticed. Mother couldn't read, and Father didn't think to check. I was left with one name—the one I liked less—and no middle name.

Carlinho

Mother slammed the door in anger. She was seven months into her pregnancy, her belly bloated, and her breathing heavy with rage.
"Where is she? Where is Dita? Dita, are you here?" she called out loud. I was not used to seeing my mother so angry. Unable to find her, Mother sat down at the kitchen table and covered her face with her hands. "I will kill her," she mumbled with her voice breaking. "My daughter stole a dress." I looked at her in amazement and saw that she was crying.
When Dita got home, Mother pounced on her holding a leather belt in her hand. She whipped her mercilessly as she screamed that Dita was a thief, which is why she couldn't show her face to the pharmacist out of shame. How had she dared steal a dress from her employer, the pharmacist's daughter! Dita dodged the belt as best she could and attempted to answer. Ultimately, she lost her temper and with her thick, strong arms, shoved Mother away from her.

"I just borrowed it to wear to the party. I was going to give it back!" Dita screamed.

Mother lost her balance from the force of the push, and fell on her side. Her stomach hit the floor and she let out a cry of pain. As Dita ran out of the house, Mother moaned, barely able to get back up.

In the middle of the night, we woke up to our father's frightened voice. Mother was bleeding and he wanted to rush her to the hospital. He was at a loss. In the end, he ran to the church which was a ten-minute walk away.

A police car was regularly stationed near the church, a red and black Beetle, with a blue beacon light on the roof, which lit up and turned when the siren was activated. Dad brought the police officers to our home. When they saw Mother kneeling as if to give birth, they said they were not authorized to take on such a responsibility. They couldn't help her.

Father insisted they drive her to the hospital by car. They refused again, but he did not give up. He insisted there was no other choice, that they could not abandon her in such a dire situation, that he had no way of taking her himself. In the end they gave in and Mother went with them.

Born in the seventh month of pregnancy, Carlinho was tiny. For many years he remained small, thin, and looked younger than his age.

School in Sorocaba

A few months after we moved to the city, the school year was about to begin. Aroldo was the right age to start attending, but showed no inclination to do so. I wanted more than ever to continue with my education. I was curious and wanted to learn new things, but that was not the main reason. I knew that studying would allow me to escape poverty. If I acquired a profession, I would be able to live with dignity. I didn't want to live all my life like that, like I lived then, like my parents did.

Mother came to register me at school. That was the only time she ever set foot in the place. I was nine years old and told them I had studied for a year and a half. They accepted me into third grade.

Every day at half past twelve I prepared a bottle of milk for 7-year-old Aroldo to feed Carlinho, and then left. Sometimes Aroldo would disappear with friends and forget to return in time, forcing me to sit restlessly, waiting for him to arrive. He would show up, eventually, with his slingshot and pockets full of marbles, not realizing at all how fateful every minute was for me. The second he walked through the door I would fly out and run all the way to school.

I was in class from one to five. We received our books from the municipality and they were distributed to us at school, as was our allowance of notebooks and pencils. I was given two pencils and an eraser in the beginning of the year and they had to last. I had no way of buying another pencil, so I guarded them as if they were a treasure.

One time, when I only had one pencil left, it fell and the tip broke. I didn't have a sharpener and was too embarrassed to ask my classmates to lend me one. I looked at the overflowing pencil case of the boy sitting next to me. He had plenty of pencils, also in colors, a sharpener and two erasers. He always arrived looking neat, his clothes ironed and his hair combed. I'm pretty sure he owned several sets of the school uniform. His mother was a teacher at the school and he was one of the best students. He was arrogant and only the fact that I was good at math prevented him from treating me with complete contempt.

Everyone was copying down the teacher's notes from the board except for me. I looked in despair at the missing tip. The teacher, Dona Assada, an impressive woman of about forty, noticed. I looked at the floor in embarrassment and saw her feet approaching me. Her legs were covered in nylon stockings and her feet were tucked into black high-heeled pumps.

"Why aren't you writing, Catarina?"

As I heard her voice addressing me, my gaze climbed up to the fold in the gray skirt that clung to her waist, and from there to the pink shirt buttoned almost up to her neck. I mumbled shyly that the tip of my pencil was broken.

She instructed the boy next to me to lend me a sharpener. I turned my pencil carefully until a new tip popped out, all the while feeling the stares of all my classmates piercing my nape. When I was done, I placed the sharpener on the table, next to his pencil case, and whispered: "Thank you." The boy did not answer.

I really liked math classes and was quick to grasp the lessons. So much so that the teacher asked me to help two students who were having trouble. I would go to their house from time to time, after school, and help them with their homework, but never invited them to mine.

One day the teacher asked me if the girls had come to study at my place. With some shame, I replied that I had gone to theirs. The teacher was interested in why they never came to my house, but I just kept silent and looked down. I was timid, withdrawn, and did not make friends with other children. I was afraid that if I had a close friend, she might find her way to my house and see the conditions we lived in. I couldn't face the humiliation.

For Brazil's Independence Day, our class had to practice for a parade through the streets of Sorocaba. We were supposed to march in orderly lines, wearing our uniforms, holding a green, yellow, white and blue flag—the flag of Brazil. I was tall and Dona Assada chose me to lead the class, to walk first at the head of the columns.

On the eve of the holiday, I washed my uniform so that it would have time to dry. The next day I got up early, ironed the white shirt and the black and white checkered skirt. By then we already had an electric iron. I got dressed, put on my white knee socks and black shoes. I brushed my hair until it shone black on my shoulders. I looked with satisfaction at my image in the mirror. The skirt was a tad short, I thought with concern, soon I wouldn't be able to wear it anymore.

I arrived at school on time. The teacher arranged us in rows, gave us flags and instructed me to go out into the street, with the whole class following behind.

I marched at the head of the parade bearing the flag with pride. I was beaming! How great that unfamiliar feeling was. Everyone watched me march but not mockingly, or with pity. Their looks showed appreciation, even admiration! I knew at that moment that I was not inferior to anyone. I was a Brazilian citizen, equal among equals. I deserved the same respect as any of my fellow citizens! I would get out of the misery and the dangers I lived in. I believed in myself! I would never be disrespected again!

Estasio de Sá

The compensation Father was paid only covered the damage done to the crops, and not his broken soul. And it slowly ran out. He could not keep any job for long. When he got any money, he drank it away. He squandered most of his wages that way. We had to leave our small house and move to another small house, that was older, even more neglected, in a backyard on Estasio de Sá street.

The yard was always full of mud that stuck to our feet and soiled the floor when we entered the house. When it rained, the septic tank next to the restroom overflowed, producing a suffocating stench. The atmosphere at home was worse than usual. Mother brought up the possibility that I might not be able to go back to school next year and might have to go to work too. I was horrified, but said nothing.

The following year I was given a few more months of grace, and I went back to school.

One evening, when I came home from school, I saw a small tricycle standing in the yard. I had never ridden a bike of any kind. Unable to resist, I sat down and started pedaling. At that moment, a three-year-old girl appeared, saw that I was riding her little tricycle and began to wail hysterically.

My mother came out to see what was causing the commotion. When she realized that I had taken the vehicle without permission, she dragged me home in a rage, and whipped me with her belt while screaming at me: "My girls don't steal! You will never ever steal again. Do you hear me!" Her words stung more than the blows. The reality came out of her mouth so distorted. I had not stolen it! I just wanted to try riding, to know for once what it felt like! My soul was revolting within me, but I could not explain.

On my way back from school, I used to pass by the boulevard near the large new church, which was in its final stages of construction. The walls were painted yellow, and it was decorated with brown stripes around the roof and windows. The building ended with two high towers, still surrounded by scaffolding, where several workers were applying plaster and coating for the roofs.

That evening as I was walking home, my mind was busy with thoughts of all the assignments I had due. I felt enthusiastic, looking forward to being in a quiet corner, opening my notebook and writing down in neat letters the answers to the questions the teacher dictated in class. As I passed by the church, my gaze wandered toward the spires whose roofs were covered in densely packed brown shingles. All of a sudden, I saw a large object plummeting off the top, like an oversized bundle. I heard a scream from the same direction, followed by a thud: the object hit the pavement like a sack of potatoes.

At that moment I noticed it had a torso, arms, and legs. I realized it was a person. People rushed to the body.

"A worker fell from the scaffolding!" they yelled, "Hurry up! Call the cops!"

I stared at the scene with tears in my eyes. The body lay inert, while a widening pool of blood formed under the head. Overcome by nausea, I quickly walked away. My legs seemed unable to carry me, and I had to sit on a stone fence for a few minutes, until the faintness passed. When I got home, I found Mother cooking in the kitchen. The smell of soup made me sick. I told her what had happened, seeking to relieve myself a little of the horror I had just witnessed. She looked at me and said nothing, then turned to the pots again and went on stirring the soup.

One Sunday afternoon, she was hanging laundry outside and talking to the neighbor who lived next door. I brought out another tub I had finished washing.

"Dona Ines just told me that after mass tonight, they will be handing out bread at the church," Mother said to me. At that moment I hated the neighbor. I knew Mother would ask me to go get us bread and I definitely didn't want to do that—but of course I didn't know how to say "no" to my Mother. "Go get a few loaves," she continued. "Go now, before the prayer begins, and stay until the end."

I had been to the church only a few times. The last time was when Carlinho was christened. The place was full. Since I was alone, I found a single seat in one of the rows. The hall was dark, illuminated only by the light of many candles on the altar. I felt the tranquility of holiness surrounding me. Accompanied by the pleasantly quiet, slow organ music, the priest entered, accompanied by two boys. They wore long red and white robes, and long pants underneath. They were an attention-grabbing duo: one with very dark skin and black, curly hair, and his friend fair with blond curls, like a cherub in a painting. All three of them were on the altar, the boys standing to the right of the priest. The crowd rose to its feet, and mass began.

The priest started by mentioning the names of the dead whose families asked to be remembered in prayers. An image floated in my head that I wanted to forget: the sight of the fallen worker. I tried to drive it away and concentrate with all my might on the priest's words. He talked about what was happening in the world, in Brazil, and in our neighborhood.

He spoke emotionally about children who disappeared without a trace. He offered a prayer so that they might soon be found and asked God to protect all pure and innocent souls. He reminded parents to be very strict about safety rules and teach their children to be careful. He remarked that after the prayer, free bread would be distributed, and concluded by saying that all the brothers and sisters who wished to receive the sacramental bread were invited to line up by the cathedra in an orderly manner.

The sacramental bread was shared only from the age of twelve and I was too young. I approached the altar, following the priest with interest, as he stepped down with his two assistants to stand next to the line of worshippers. He gently picked up with his fingers a thin white wafer from the tray the angelic boy brought to him and placed it in the mouth of the woman standing in front of him. She crossed herself and returned to her pew, where she knelt and prayed in a whisper until the wafer disappeared in her mouth.

I wondered what the holy bread tasted like. What made it so special? Would something change inside me after eating it? I was looking again at the priest and at the boy carrying the tray, when I saw that his gaze rested on me and our eyes met. I quickly lowered my eyelids. His face was gentle and beautiful, truly like the face of an angel, and his eyes were blue.

The ritual was finally over. A few minutes later, the two boys appeared carrying a heavy wicker basket. An elderly woman walked next to them. They placed the basket near the altar. The woman lifted the braided lid and turned to the line that was getting longer and longer in front of her. People who had not attended the church before appeared out of nowhere and joined the line. The woman bent over the basket and handed each person who approached her the number of loaves they requested. I stood at the end of the line, thoroughly embarrassed. I prayed silently that I would not run into any acquaintances, or at least that they would not recognize me.

The worshipers left the hall through the main door, and two girls from my school, with their mothers, passed near me. One of them noticed me. I stole a glance at her and saw that she was whispering with her friend and giggling. I looked in despair at the front door, but there was no way I could return home empty-handed. My turn had come. I muttered that I needed three loaves of bread, barely raising my eyes from the floor. Adding insult to injury, I once again met the blue gaze of the boy who was assisting in the distribution. I quickly took the loaves and fled the scene. I ran all the way down the scary, dark, empty streets. The echo of my steps sounded like I was being followed. I wanted so badly to get home already.

On Saturday morning I woke up early. Mother was standing in the kitchen putting a kettle on the stove to boil water for coffee. The house in Estacio de Sá, despite its squalor, had a gas stove.

I heard her say to herself, "Oh my, that's all I needed now."

"What happened?" I asked from the mattress I was lying on. She looked at me with a tired look: "I've run out of gas," she answered. "Actually, it's all over. There is nothing at home." She spoke half to me, half to herself. "I can no longer ask the neighbor for a loan. I have not yet repaid the one she already gave me. I don't know what to do." She sat down in a chair and lit a cigarette, silently stared at the curling smoke. After a few minutes she said with decisiveness, "Come on. We're going to Leonora the hairdresser."

I pulled the blanket off me and looked at her questioningly. She kept talking while I was getting dressed. "Last week, while I was cleaning the beauty salon, I saw she was buying hair to make wigs. She has told me several times that you have very beautiful hair. She might agree to buy yours. Hurry up. We have to get there early, because today is Saturday and it gets busy later. We should get there first."

I slipped on the last sleeve, pulled my head out of the collar and looked at her in astonishment, realizing that she was dead serious. "I'm sorry," she continued, "but we have no choice. I have no other choice. You are young, and your hair will grow back."

My hair was mine. It belonged to my body. How could one sell something like that! I wiped my eyes with my hand and followed Mother. Once we arrived, she spoke to the hairdresser, but I wasn't listening. I wanted to scream, I wanted to run away. I didn't want to say goodbye to the most beautiful thing in me.

The hairdresser asked me to sit in a chair and not move. I sat frozen, my eyes downcast. I didn't want to look in the mirror and see a part of me being cut off. I felt the cold scissors touching my scalp. With each snipping sound, I felt a clump of hair fall, and it hurt to breathe. I hated Mother so much in those moments. I hated my life. I swore to myself with all the strength of the anger in me that I would not live like that when I grew up, that I would be like all normal people, who have as much food as they want, gas to cook, nice clothes, and a spacious house.

When the hairdresser was finished, I looked in the mirror in fear, my vision blurred by tears. I was horrified to discover a boy looking back at me from the mirror. On the way home, Mother bought a gas cylinder and plenty of groceries. That Saturday everyone sat down for a festive meal around the table, because there was an abundance of meat, rice and beans. Even Dita joined us. I watched my brothers eat and their enjoyment comforted me a little. After the meal, Mother boiled water in the kettle, and the fire did not go out. I looked at her sipping coffee and felt drained.

That night I touched my cropped head and silently mourned the beautiful hair I had lost. The next day, at moments I forgot, but a sensation of coolness on my scalp or a suspicious lightness on my neck would remind me of the tragedy. At night I thought about the reception the students would give me when they saw my short hair, the stares and the mockery. All night I prepared mentally, and yet it still felt terrible the next day at school, when the kids looked at me and laughed. Some teased me explicitly, saying I looked like a boy, while others whispered behind my back.

I felt my head was on fire.

Still Sorocaba

The money we got for my hair was gone. The situation at home was bad and mother's salary was barely enough for us to eke out a living. Father worked sometimes but spent all his salary at the grocery store on pinga. Eventually, Mother asked the grocer not to sell him any more liquor. That evening, Father came home raging with anger, complaining that Mother was restricting his actions and even involving a stranger. She gave in and did not prevent him from drinking anymore. Despite the quarrels between my parents, a new baby, Reginaldo, was born.

On one Sunday, Zazinho, Carlinho's godfather, who had been our neighbor when we lived on Benjamin dos Santos Street, came to visit. His heart sank when he saw the tough conditions we were living in and he proposed we move to a new house he had purchased outside the city, in a neighborhood under construction called Vila Gutierres that had not yet been connected to electricity or running water.

The neighborhood was located on a hill, on the slopes of which there was a closed institution for the mentally ill called *Techeira Lima*. The bus stop was next to the institution, and when I walked past alone, I sometimes heard the screams of the patients piercing the silence and penetrating straight into my head.

I had to stop going to school because there wasn't one in the area. Mother worked all day in the kitchen of a hostel and I filled her place. I cleaned the house, cooked on the wood stove next to an open window, like in Jacarezinho, and watched my siblings.

When we needed water, Aroldo and I would take tubs and pots and go to the neighborhood well. I was almost ten years old and responsible for the entire family while our mother was away from home. Every rustle made me jump. Despite the barbed wire fences that surrounded the hospital, I knew that the security there was lax, and cases of patients escaping were not unheard of. Whenever I left the house, I would look repeatedly right and left to make sure there was nobody lurking around. When I returned, I would sometimes have anxiety attacks. It seemed to me that one of the mad people was preparing to attack me in some dark corner. I hurried home and locked the door behind me. When I wasn't busy, I was looking out the only window, making sure I could see anyone approaching, which made me feel more at ease.

Across the road was a small orchard with a lone, hidden house. Its windows were always covered and I never saw anyone go in or out of it. I heard Mother say quietly to father: "I'm afraid the children might go near there. I hear screams in the middle of the night. This is not a place to live, across from a brothel." I would also peer at the house in the orchard with concern, and check that everything around it was quiet.

One hot night I had a hard time falling asleep. The window was open and the mosquitoes flying through it buzzed in my ears. As I was turning over in my bed, I heard knocks on the door. Someone was rapping really hard and fast, and a woman's voice shouted:

"Open up! Open quickly! He wants to kill me!" I heard running steps and banging. Suddenly it became quiet. Father whispered to Mother:

"Could she be dead?" I lay in bed with my eyes closed, unsure of whether I was awake or dreaming. Shortly after that the siren of the police car sounded and I saw the blue and red lights flashing in the window. There was talking and shouting and Dad said quietly, "This is it. The police filled the whole Beetle and took the girls away from here." That's when I knew that everything was real.

Early the next morning mother opened the door and we saw a pool of dried blood on the nearest step and a trail of red drops leading to the gate. Mother took a bucket of water, poured on the stains and scrubbed it well, until there was no trace left. She quickly dressed, said goodbye, and went to work. Father left too, I don't know where. I was left completely alone with my younger siblings.

On another morning hunger woke me up earlier than usual. We hadn't eaten any dinner, because there was nothing. I saw Mother sitting in the kitchen rolling a cigarette. After lighting it, she took a deep puff, inhaling the smoke. She then blew it out, blinking her eyes. She was immersed in thought, or perhaps the smoke just burned her eyes. I knew she was upset. When she saw me, she stood up and said to me:

"Catarina. I have to go to town. You will wait for me here, inside the house. Listen, I know there's nothing at home. No sugar, no rice, no beans. I will try to ask my employer for a loan again so I can buy some food. If everything goes well, I'll be back around ten." She took one last puff from her cigarette, put it out and continued, "If I don't come back in time don't go draw water from the well. I've filled all the pails and you have enough water to drink. I don't want you to go near the well, because you are without food and you are weak. I'm going now."

And she left. I recalled the time Mother took me with her to the hostel, because she was short an employee and she needed me to help out in the kitchen. The owner was a tall, noble woman, with kind eyes. She smiled at me kindly, treated me to an orange and a banana and told my mother that she had a nice daughter. I had a lot of fun that day. Mother was in a good mood and smiled frequently. After she finished organizing the kitchen, she went to vacuum and tidy up the guestroom, which had two sitting areas. When I went in to look for her, she was vacuuming the carpet.

A handsome man, with brown skin and a mustache, sat on one of the armchairs watching her. She turned her gaze to him from time to time and smiled. The man sat alone and did nothing but look at my mother, which I found unusual. Later, when we were alone, I asked her who he was and she said he was just one of the guests who lived in the hostel. And when she spoke of him, there was a sparkle in her eyes that I did not recognize.

Now, thinking back to the lady who ran the hostel, I trusted her kindness and had a feeling that Mother would return at the time she promised. The morning dragged by slowly. My stomach rumbled and I waited impatiently for it to be ten o'clock. The bus from the city center arrived every hour and stopped near the Techeira Lima Hospital. A few minutes before ten I could no longer stop myself and went outside. I climbed to the top of the hill, because from there you could clearly see the entire slope up to the bus stop, and I waited for my mother. The minutes went by slowly and then I saw the bus coming from afar. It stopped near the hospital and the passengers got off. Alert, I followed them with my eyes, but did not see her. Could it be that my mother did not arrive on this bus? Would I have to wait another whole hour for her to come back? My stomach grumbled. The group of passengers who got off the bus dispersed in different directions. A few of them climbed the slope toward where I was standing. That minute, mother emerged from behind a tall man, who had been hiding her from my view. I saw her dark, delicate figure walking toward me, laden with baskets.

I went down to meet her beaming with happiness and helped her carry the baskets to the house. My siblings quickly gathered around the kitchen table. We emptied the baskets and prepared a meal for all of us. Among all the delicacies was a large bunch of grapes. I picked a grape and put it in my mouth. It was taut and cool. I clenched my jaws and it exploded in my mouth filling it with the sweetest, most wonderful juice I've ever tasted. I ate another one, slowly, savoring the taste, and another. Since then, all my life, every time I eat grapes, that memory comes to me.

Mother became friends with another family in the neighborhood. They had a son about my age, who attended a distant school. His teacher picked him up every morning in her private car, until she went on maternity leave. They decided to return to the city so the boy could continue to go to school. Mother wanted to return to the center too because the isolation and sparse transportation made her life difficult.

It was decided we would look together for a big house and share it so as to save on the rent. We moved to a house with a bedroom, living room and kitchen. In the middle of the living room, we installed a curtain made of a dark fabric. The other family was entitled to use a room and half of the living room, while we got the other half of the living room, and a kitchen that faced the backyard. On the exterior wall there was an overhang under which Father built a stove so Mother could light wood and cook without the soot and smoke filling the house.

I was happy to be living in the part of the building closest to the outhouse.

The house was in an isolated spot on Alsindo Guanabara Street, near Estacio de Sá, the street we lived on before. On one side it bordered an empty lot, and on the other side, across the road, was a cemetery. When darkness fell, I would hold back for hours until I couldn't take it anymore, then run breathlessly to the small outhouse, before any ghost could appear over the wall.

Mother started working nights in a hotel, and Father found a job in construction. He even took over the adjoining property to cultivate his own vegetables. Life seemed good.

While Mother went to work, I took care of Reginaldo. I changed his diaper, slipped plastic underpants over it, and put him on the mattress next to me. Sometimes I had to leave his bottom bare because the plastic made his skin sweat, causing chafing and irritation. I sprinkled corn flour on his tender skin and let him lie half naked next to me. On such nights I often woke up at midnight completely wet and had to change my nightgown and sheets so I could go back to sleep,

I returned to school, to the same class and to the same teacher, even though I missed half a year of studies. I wore the same uniform as I did the year before, since I only had one set. Every morning I would wash my shirt and socks and iron them until they were dry. The plaid skirt was already too short for me.

One day the teacher came to class carrying three bags which she placed next to the blackboard. She addressed me in front of the whole class, saying she had brought me some clothes, that I should take them home and that next time, I should come wearing more appropriate skirts. I thought I would die of shame. I wanted to bury myself, disappear forever and never come back. I came home crying and told my mother.

"So why are you crying?" She said to me, "The teacher must love you if she gave you all those clothes." I asked myself why I even bothered telling my mother such things, when she did not understand them at all.

Father got fired from his job a few months later. Without cash with which to buy pinga at the grocery store, he ran up a tab. Mother was afraid to ask the grocer not to sell to him, because there wasn't enough privacy in the house to even fight—although the curtain between the two parts of the house couldn't block father's ramblings when he came back drunk either.

Dita had gone to São Paulo to work in housekeeping, to help make ends meet.

One rainy night. I woke up to the wind whistling in the windows. I heard the kitchen door open and Mother enter. She worked nights and returned at four in the morning. I sat up on the mattress in the kitchen, which I shared with my brother. Mother was drenched and her hair was dripping. After peeling off her wet sweater, said to herself, panting: "What a downpour! So cold!" She wiped her hair with a towel, and only then noticed me.

"The driver of the van, such a nasty man!" she said to me. "He left me on the street corner. Even on a stormy night like this he's not willing to drive me all the way home." She put the kettle on the stove and sat down. "You know what?" she continued, "When I was running home in the rain, I saw something strange... Children dressed in white, playing outside the cemetery gate. They were chasing one another, as if playing hide and seek or tag. Just like that, in the middle of the night. There was no one on the street but me... I stood at the gate watching them, and they went on playing in the rain, as if they didn't feel it." Her face looked worried and a shiver ran through her, either from the fear or the cold. She was sitting on a chair in the kitchen, still wearing her damp clothes.

"Why are you awake at this hour?" she asked me all of a sudden, "Go to sleep!"

"A sua abença mãe,"[4] I said, asking her to bless me, pulling over me the thin woolen blanket that Aroldo and Ivone had stolen from me while I was sleeping.

"Que Deus te abençoa," she answered—May God Bless You—and turned off the light.

I felt at peace. After all, Mother lay in her bed in the room next to mine.

Two weeks later they cut off the power at our house. Mother had no money to pay our share of the bill and a big fight broke out between her and the other family. Mother started to look for a new house to move to. Zazinho's mother, an elderly woman, was too frail to clean her house alone, and was looking for help. Mother offered me the job, and I accepted. I started working in housekeeping twice a week.

When Dita came home on the weekend, she gave Mother part of her salary. Mother asked her where the rest was and Dita replied aggressively that she also had expenses. She was wearing new jeans and silver hoops on her ears, which I hadn't seen before.

"My employer has a cousin who needs help around the house," she blurted out unexpectedly. "Why doesn't Catarina go to work there?" Mother hesitated for a moment.

---

4   A sua abença mãe - I ask for your blessing, Mother. This was a common way for a child to part from their parents or other adults close to them.

"She's only ten," she answered. I could see she was considering the matter.

"I will keep an eye on her. I will visit her often," Dita added.

I thought to myself that that might be my chance to leave the house. It was hard living there with Father and the overcrowding. In São Paulo I would see things I didn't know. Dita looked content. Maybe I really should do it.

"What do you think, Catarina?" Mother turned to me.

"I don't know. Maybe," I mumbled. "Will I be able to go to school in São Paulo?" I saw Dita scoff.

"Finish this school year," Mother interjected, "and then we'll see."

Leaving Home

I was a little over ten years old, after finishing fourth grade, when I agreed to leave home and go away to work. On the eve of the trip, I packed my underwear and a few dresses in a large *bornal*. It took me a long time to fall asleep. Question marks kept swirling around in my head: Who were these people I was going to work for? What would I discover in the big city? What would become of me there? Then followed exclamation marks. No matter what happened in a strange house, it couldn't be worse than watching my father unemployed and my mother going out at night to work and coming back exhausted in the mornings! I had to help them. I had to help myself, because I didn't want my life to go on like this, in such misery!

We got up early in the morning. It was still dark outside and mother placed a kettle full of water on the fire. She poured coffee into an aluminum mug for me. As I drank, I was suddenly back in Jacarezinho, by our cow, under the shed, holding a mug just like this one full of warm milk.

Dita pulled me back to reality:

"We have to hurry so we don't miss the train," she said, drinking her coffee in quick sips. Mother made us sandwiches for the road. Meanwhile everyone had woken up. My father and all the children huddled at the door to see us off.

We stepped out into the yard, while Mother stood in the doorway with Reginaldo in her arms and said: "May God watch over you." I thought of Reginaldo not sleeping next to me in bed tonight, and who knew when I would see him again. I said goodbye to the house, to my family and to my mother, without a hug or a kiss.

We took the bus to the train station. I followed Dita until she stopped by the large paved plaza and said: "Wait here. I'm going to buy the tickets." Once again, I was in the busy train station, among hordes of people rushing in all directions, with their suitcases and bags. A few years earlier I had stood in the same spot, at the same crossroads, waiting for the train that would take me to another reality, to a new life. I wished really, really hard that this time, unlike back then, the journey would have a happy ending.

We arrived at Dita's workplace. Her employer was kind. We had a big lunch and waited for Claudia, for whom I was supposed to work, to come and take me to her place. She arrived in the evening, together with her husband who looked significantly older than her, and their daughter Sandra, about my age. Claudia was short and plump, with a beautiful complexion, blue eyes and fine blond hair. She looked cheerful and determined, but her small, probing eyes made me lower my gaze uncomfortably. She squeezed Dita's hand and mine. Her husband hardly spoke, but behind his glasses he had kind eyes. I thought he was handsome and well-dressed, and later, I learned that he was a well-known fashion designer.

While Claudia was having a lively conversation with her cousin, I looked at Sandra. She was very beautiful. A girl out of a fairy tale, with blond hair, big blue eyes and perfectly drawn lips. When we were about to leave, Claudia told Dita that she could visit me anytime.

Quietly hugging my *bornal*, I sat in the back seat of the car, next to Sandra, who exuded the scent of fine soap. I examined the skin of her face, which looked like silk surrounded by golden hair. The car arrived at a large villa with well-kept trees in front. The driveway on the side led us along a wall to a covered garage. Claudia and Sandra both got out of the car, and I followed suit. We were on a wide, tiled patio, surrounded by the wall of the villa and several smaller buildings.

Claudia led me to one of them and opened the door to a beautiful room with a wooden floor, a window covered with curtains, a bed with clean sheets and a piqué cover. There was also a small closet and a table with two chairs.

"This is your room," she said. "Put your things here and I'll show you the rest." I put my bag on the bed, feeling much better.

She then opened the door to the room adjacent to mine in the same wing, and explained it was the music room. It was there because she didn't like the noise inside the house. The wooden floor was covered with a carpet and a pile of cushions and pillows of different sizes, in between which were a set of drums and a guitar. On the buffet was a stereo system with large speakers, and the shelf below it was loaded with records. The walls were covered with posters of famous Brazilian singers—Roberto Carlos, Venosa Erzamo, Carlos Wood—and also a large picture of the Beatles. Color light projectors hung from the ceiling.

Claudia said I had to clean this room twice a week, on Mondays and Thursdays. She closed the door and we moved to another building which also had two rooms. The first one was her brother's. He lived with them, she explained. It was a modest room, with a large bed, a table, chairs and a gas stove.

"You will clean this room once a week," she indicated. "And you have to clean the toilets every day, of course." She led me to a cabin with a shower and a toilet, right next door to her brother's room. "You'll be sharing these with him," she added.

The next room we entered, which Claudia called *the laundry room*, still in the same wing, was bright, very spacious and had wide glass windows. There were two machines I didn't recognize, as well as a large sink with a rough surface for washing by hand, and two tall faucets. She opened a white cabinet that housed the cleaning supplies. An array of brooms, brushes and rags was arranged neatly on its shelves. A tall pile of folded laundry was on a dresser in the corner, next to the iron. The center of the room featured a large oval table with several chairs.

"This is where you will eat your meals," Claudia said, then turned off the lights and locked the door after us. She handed me two keys, one for my room and the other for the laundry room. "It's late now," she added, "Tomorrow morning you will get to know the house better. Now you may go to sleep. Would you like something to drink?" she asked casually. I shook my head to decline in embarrassment. "There are towels in the closet in your room. Those are your towels. Shower quickly and go to sleep, because tomorrow we're getting up early. Good night."

I sat down on my bed feeling apprehensive. This big house scared me. How would I be able to cope with such a huge job? I could not disappoint Claudia. If I failed, she'd send me home, and I didn't want to go back! I had been sitting alone in the room with my sad thoughts, when I realized I still hadn't showered. I opened the closet and found a pile of folded towels, three large and two small ones. I took one out. It smelled good. When I left my room, I saw the lights in the villa were on.

I walked into the small bathroom and undressed. The water coming out of the faucet was lukewarm at first, and then it turned hot. I stood under the shower, letting the water flow over my body. Back at home I usually bathed using a cloth soaked in cold water. I wet myself, lathered up quickly and rinsed the soap off with the cloth. I had seen showers at neighbors' homes and at the house of the elderly lady where I cleaned twice a week, but I had never taken a shower myself. It was a dream come true. I enjoyed the shower for a few minutes, before turning off the taps and drying myself. It felt so good. By the time I crossed the short distance back to my room, the lights in the house were out. I hurried into bed. The sheets were soft to the touch and smelled fresh.

I prayed, asking God to help me make it in this place, and my eyes closed.

The First Day

The huge house with its mysterious rooms and all the pavilions around the courtyard weighed on my chest, suffocating me. I took a deep breath. I so wanted Claudia to be happy with me and not send me back home. I wanted to stay in this well-groomed world, full of educated, learned people. I thought of beautiful, well-mannered Sandra. I wanted so much to get to know her better, and maybe even, I dared to hope, we might become a little friendly.

When Claudia knocked on my door at seven in the morning I was already dressed and combed. As we crossed the patio toward the house, she pointed at the tiles and said that every morning I had to wash the area, and I that had to get up earlier so I'd have enough time.

The next door she opened led to a large kitchen, lined with wooden cabinets suspended above a large marble counter. In one corner was a white refrigerator with a shiny nickel handle and in the other—an oven with a shiny stove. Our entire house in Sorocaba was smaller than this kitchen, I thought. The kitchen continued into the dining area, where Claudia showed me how to set the table for breakfast. She placed five white porcelain plates decorated with delicate pink flowers on a white tablecloth. She gave me the cutlery and explained how I was to arrange it next to the plates. She then brought cups and saucers of the same white china with pink flowers. She went back to the refrigerator and told me to take out four kinds of cheese, butter, jam, and put them on the table.

Her husband appeared in the doorway carrying a paper bag that smelled of fresh bread. He hugged his wife, left the bag on the table and entered the house without looking at me. Claudia brought a cloth-lined metal basket and filled it with hot rolls. She asked me to follow her and led me to the laundry room. After unlocking the door with the key, she said: "You can iron for now, until my husband and the children leave the house."

She took a blanket that was folded over the pile of laundry and spread it on the big table, then handed me an iron and placed twenty shirts on the table. She pointed to a small wooden device, a kind of narrow board, slightly raised at the base and lined with a white cloth, the like of which I had never seen before. "You have everything you need here," she said and left.

I ironed, trying my best to smoothen the creases, thoroughly and with utmost care. About an hour later, Claudia returned bringing a plate with a slice of bread with margarine and a cup of coffee with milk. She left them on the corner of the table, saying they were for me. I took a chair and sat down next to my breakfast. Claudia glanced at the ironed shirts I had folded on the corner of the table.

"Tell me, is that all you've done so far?" she chided with audible displeasure while she checked one of the ironed shirts. I watched her face turn red with anger. She looked at me with a frightening gaze. She spoke with subdued fury and I thought she would explode from restraint any moment.

"Do you call this ironing? Look at my husband's shirts! This is a disaster! An hour and a half and you've hardly done anything. You have five minutes to eat."

She spun around seething mad, and left the room. I sat down in front of my little breakfast, which I had been looking forward to so much, barely able to swallow. After only a few minutes, I heard Claudia's footsteps approaching. She came into the room looking calm. She said she wanted me to learn to wash. She took some dirty clothes from the laundry basket and divided them into piles. She put a pile of white cotton laundry in one washing machine and a pile of colored clothes in the other one. After explaining that delicate laundry should be hand washed, she sprinkled soap flakes in the sink full of lukewarm water. She said to let the garments soak and to come back in an hour to scrub, wash, rinse, and then lay them out to dry on towels outside.

I followed Claudia into the kitchen, with my empty plate and cup. I washed the breakfast dishes that filled the sink, and at nine o'clock, made my acquaintance with the rest of the house. At the heart was a wide hall, surrounded by closed doors that led to the various rooms. By one of the walls was an antique-style table with carved wooden legs and a pink marble semi-circular surface, atop which was the telephone. Claudia took me into the living room. It was huge. Its wooden floor was covered with carpets. A white grand piano stood in the corner, and brown leather sofas surrounded a long glass table with a vase filled with flowers.

We moved on to the bedrooms. In every room a folded set of ironed sheets had been placed on the bed. Sandra's charming bedroom was fit for a princess, with pink curtains, and a large closet, some of whose drawers were also painted pink, lining an entire wall. On one side of the closet were shelves housing dozens of dolls. I immediately thought how wonderful it would be to touch and hold them. I couldn't wait to come and clean this room.

We returned to the living room and Claudia showed me how to clean. I had to vacuum the carpets and sofas, roll the carpets, vacuum the wooden floor and wipe the dust off the furniture. Finally, I would have to polish the floor and put everything back in place. When I was done, I closed the door of the spotless living room and continued to Claudia's room.

I vacuumed, rolled up the carpets, vacuumed the wooden floor, wiped the furniture and changed the linen. And then it was time for the dream room, Sandra's pink room. I opened the windows and a gust of fresh air ruffled the curtains. I cleaned the room well, with all my heart. I changed the bed linen and covered it with the pink bedspread. When I approached the shelves, Claudia appeared and emphasized that I should clean everything really well and put it all back in its place. I took the dolls down slowly, holding each one for a few seconds. They were so beautiful. Two of them in particular captured my heart—a blue-eyed porcelain doll with a silk dress the color of her eyes and decorated white muslin ribbons, and a black doll with golden earrings and the traditional attire of a girl from Bahia. I sat the blue-eyed doll on the bed and carefully ran my finger over her dress, admiring the silver buckle on her belt and the tiny lace stockings on her legs. But then I remembered that time was running out and that Claudia would soon be coming to check what I was doing, so I quickly returned to work. I heard Sandra coming into the house. I went out to the hall, caught a glimpse of her kissing her mother and returned to the room before she noticed me.

She entered the room and placed her bag on the chair. She looked at me and said, "Put everything back to the way it was before." I nodded and she left. I carefully put the dolls back, closed the window and drew the curtain. A pink light reflected on the walls of the room and on the dolls I adored. I felt like I was floating on a cloud at sunset. I closed the room as if it were a treasure box and proceeded to clean the boys' rooms. These were decorated with walnut-colored wall cabinets and beige curtains.

The smells of cooking wafted from the kitchen. The clock hanging on the wall showed it was half past two. The kitchen door was closed and the family was gathered behind it for lunch. I heard the kitchen door open and Sandra walked past me toward her room. After a few minutes she came up to me. I thought she was going to compliment me for the way I had cleaned the room and arranged the dolls in such a nice way. She asked me to come with her for a second. I followed her in the direction of the shelves.

"You didn't return the dolls the way they were," she said. "Nothing is in the same place as before. And look how you put this doll in. You wrinkled her dress. You need to smooth it out like this." She re-seated the doll and fluffed the dress around her. I said nothing. After a few seconds of silence she said, "You can leave now."

Feeling gloomy, I continued to clean the rooms of the sons—Carlos, the eldest, who studied at the university, and Franco, who was sixteen, and still in high school.

At long last I finished and went to report to Claudia. She sent me to the laundry room, where lunch was already waiting for me. By the time I sat down to eat, my head was aching from hunger. My plate had a serving of cooked meat, rice, and beans. They smelled wonderful. I scooped a bite of meat and rice with my fork and put it in my mouth. It was a delicacy. Claudia certainly knew how to cook. I ate slowly, savoring the food with pleasure, and then, through the window, I saw Claudia hanging the laundry. I quickly stuffed what was left on the plate into my mouth and returned the dishes to the kitchen. I thought I only had the bathroom left and would be done for the day.

"Wash the dishes first," instructed Claudia, "and clean all the bathrooms." By the time I finished cleaning, it was six in the evening.

I had worked for eleven hours straight and felt exhausted. I found Claudia in the laundry room holding a pile of clothes that had just been taken off the line. She ordered me to fold the laundry and come help her with dinner. While we were setting the table, she explained to me exactly how I had to clean the patio the next morning. During dinner, the family members sat in the dining area at the end of the kitchen and I washed the cooking utensils.

"What a great episode yesterday at *Selva de Pedra*. I'm already waiting for eight in the evening, to watch the sequel. They stopped in the middle of the suspense," said Sandra, referring to a popular TV show whose title meant *Jungle of Stone*.

"An excellent novela," Claudia confirmed, "such great actors! Francisco Cuoco is really good. Regina Duarte, so beautiful."

At seven thirty the family members finished their meal and moved to the living room. Claudia swiftly fried an egg for me, sprinkled it with a yellow powder instead of salt, and added rice and lettuce salad to the plate. I took my dinner to the laundry room. The egg was tasty and well-seasoned. I quickly cleaned up the kitchen.

I couldn't stop thinking of the telenovela. I no longer felt so tired. I wanted with all my heart to peek through the door and see the moving images on the screen. I saw a TV once, in a store window, and it looked like a miracle. I knew the actors from pictures in magazines. I agreed with Claudia that Regina Duarte was very beautiful, and I wanted to see her too. A few minutes after eight the kitchen had been tidied up. I went to the hall and approached the open living room door with small steps. Peeking inside, I saw the family sitting in armchairs, engrossed in the series. I stood at the door for a few minutes, following the plot. No one noticed me.

Near the door I saw a stylish chair, next to the bookcase against the wall. I sat down quietly and watched TV. The episode ended, leaving us all wondering and intrigued, until the next one.

"Oh, she is so mean," said Sandra, "how I hope she doesn't manage to break them up …" Her older brother looked at her with a smile and said with sarcasm: "What are you worried about? If the director decides she will, then she will." And the other brother added: "But don't you worry, it will take her at least ten more episodes." Sandra wrinkled her nose in dismay. She didn't find them worthy partners for conversation because they always destroyed the magic for her.

Claudia turned to her daughter with a smile and must have wanted to say something kind to her, but suddenly caught me with the corner of her eye. She turned her head and looked at me with disbelief. I got up quickly, put the chair back exactly at the angle it had been before and left the living room.

I showered and got into my soft bed. It was a little after nine, and my body ached from the continuous exertion of that day. Still, I was happy. I felt satisfaction at having accomplished everything I was asked to do, and thanked God for that day. Before I fell asleep, I remembered to set the alarm clock for a quarter to five in the morning, so that I would have time to clean the inner courtyard before breakfast, as Claudia had instructed.

My Sister Dita

When I woke up in the morning it was still dark. I quickly made my bed, got dressed and went to my bathroom. The weather was cool and pleasant before sunrise. I washed my face and gathered my hair. I took the cleaning materials from the laundry room, connected the hose to the faucet in the yard and thoroughly wet all the tiles. I sprinkled soap powder, scrubbed the entire surface with a broom-brush, rinsed it thoroughly with the hose and scooped up the water with a mop. Finally, I dried the tiles with a rag, so that there would be no mud when they stepped on them, as Claudia had specified. The floor shone in the rising morning light. I raised my head and saw the first rays of sunlight peeping through the branches of the trees. The house was still quiet. I went into the laundry room and began to iron.

I wanted Claudia to be pleased and tried to be extra careful with the pleats of the pants, though I wasn't sure I was doing it right. Claudia appeared in the laundry room half an hour later. She said, "good morning" and added nothing more. I couldn't tell if she was happy with the way I had cleaned the patio. I left the laundry room and went to the kitchen to help with breakfast.

"Today you will clean the large windows in the living room and the balcony of my bedroom. Then go to the bathroom and the kitchen, which must be cleaned every day. In the kitchen I want you to clean the middle cupboard with the plates and glasses." At that moment her husband returned with the bag of fresh bread and Claudia ordered me to bring the cleaning products and implements to wash the windows. Before I left the kitchen, I saw Sandra walk in, dressed in her school uniform, her straight blond hair perfectly framing her face like a painting. She was so beautiful. She kissed her father and I continued to the laundry room, to get a ladder and some rags.

I was on the patio, standing atop the ladder, with the wide glass doors open when Sandra exited through the gate. I waited for a little while and then quickly climbed down the steps.

Once I reached the gate I peeked outside, careful not to be seen by anyone, to watch her join a group of girls marching toward the school. How I wished I could go too! I thought back to my black and white uniform, which I used to wash every evening and iron every morning. I recalled the morning the teacher asked me to help two girls in my class study math, because I understood the material so well—she said to me. Stifling a sigh, I hurried back to the top of the ladder.

The first week crawled slowly by. I remember every minute of those long days of hard work. I tried my best to complete each task promptly and properly. I wished for a kind word or a smile of encouragement. I hoped to hear "Nice ironing, Catarina." or "Your ironing is getting better." But Claudia's face either denoted no emotion at all, or had an expression of contained displeasure. At night I would go to bed exhausted from fatigue and frustration. Remembering that Dita had promised to come see me every week, I decided I had to talk to her. I would tell her about the cold, rigid treatment I was getting and the endless hours they made me work.

On Saturday, Claudia told me at last that Dita was expected to arrive that evening. I really looked forward to her visit. I was ironing in the laundry room, the pile of clothes in front of me slowly shrinking. After carefully putting each folded shirt on the side, I glanced at the clock on the wall. Every time I looked, the big hand had moved a little, barely three minutes. And then I heard Claudia's voice saying: "Hello Dita, come in."

In all the long time I'd been here, I thought to myself, I'd never heard Claudia use such a kind tone. Excited, I went out into the yard to see Dita standing by the kitchen door, wearing an orange shirt, heeled sandals and tight black pants. To me, it now seemed she belonged to another world, to an era I had been torn out of. At that moment I found it hard to believe I had only been with Claudia for a week. It felt like I had been there for ages. I joined them and we sat down in the kitchen. Claudia smiled the whole time and said that I was adapting well and that she was sure things would be fine.

Dita said she was happy, but she looked distant. Helplessness began to take over me. I had no one to talk to. I couldn't tell Dita how I was being treated. She wouldn't believe me, nor would she care. How had I forgotten who Dita was? How had I even dared pin my hopes on her? I would have to manage on my own. As my mother always said, nobody dies from hard work. It was my decision whether I wanted to stay. I could always ask to go home, if I wanted to. And I knew I didn't.

The next day, Sunday, I had most of the day off. Besides helping set the table and wash the dishes after each meal, I was free to do my own thing. I cleaned my room and got lots of rest. The following week, Claudia taught me how to starch shirt collars and cuffs, and iron them properly. I learned the job. I learned that I hated cleaning the wooden shutters with the many slats in the master bedroom, as opposed to the shelves in Sandra's room, which I loved to dust. I loved holding the beautiful dolls in my hands, talking to them, kissing their synthetic hair and putting them back in place, in the exact position they were before.

The second week went by faster. On Friday evening, while I was helping in the kitchen, the phone rang in the hall. Claudia left to answer, leaving the door open behind her. I heard her say hello to her cousin, Dita's employer. She listened quietly for a few minutes, then burst out in anger: "I knew this would happen. I didn't like that girl. From the start she impressed me as unreliable. They're all the same! Hold on a second…" She walked toward the kitchen and closed the door. I remained alone for a long time, feeling upset. What could Dita have done? When Claudia finally returned, she said to me: "Do you know what your nice sister did? My poor cousin… Look at me when I'm talking to you!" I raised my eyes to meet her narrow gaze and reddening face. "Your sister, Dita, just took her paycheck and disappeared! She went home without giving any notice! She simply left my cousin from one moment to the next, without any help. My cousin was so kind to her. Gave her clothes and shoes in excellent condition! And Dita? Gone without even a thank you! Is that what you people do?"

Dita's actions weighed heavily on my shoulders. The family gathered for dinner and I was able to slip out to the laundry room. Claudia's look made it clear that if things were not good before, now they were going to get worse. I was all alone in this remote place. Dita probably wouldn't come to visit me anymore. Who would take care of me? What would happen to me now? The collars and sleeves of the shirts I was ironing tangled up on me and time crept by, bringing more anguish.

When Claudia brought me dinner her face was blank. I sat in front of a plate of rice and a sunny side up egg, unable to eat. I tried to swallow a small piece, but felt nauseous. I threw the meal in the trash and returned to the kitchen to clear the dishes. That evening I didn't have the courage or desire to go into the living room and watch TV with the family. As I was walking through the yard toward my room, I saw blue flashes and heard familiar voices from beyond the wall. The neighbors were watching the same telenovela, with the door open because of the heat. Peeking over the wall, I could see the characters flickering on their screen. I was too tired and sad to stay and watch, so I chose to go straight to bed.

The next few days were very difficult. All the resentment Claudia felt toward Dita, she took out on me. She found something wrong with everything I did, and showed no mercy in her remarks. At night, in my room, I was oppressed by the realization of how lonely I was. I didn't like Dita, but she was the only link I had to my family. Now that it was broken, what would become of me? I didn't even know how to get home. I felt I had been abandoned, like that time at my uncle's house in São Manuel, on the way to Sorocaba.

As the third week drew to a close, I was getting used to Claudia's acidity. I was less offended by sentences like "Where is your head?" or "Watch what you're doing!" or "How many times do I have to explain to you how to iron a shirt?" At night I thought about my family. After all, Mother eventually did return to my uncle's house in São Manuel to take us with her. I remembered how happy I felt then. Maybe she would come to see me one of these days. She would find a way. Someone would show her where I worked and she would come to check how I was doing, and under what conditions I was living. It might take some time, because I knew it wasn't easy for her, but she'd manage in the end. Maybe.

On the weekend, a faint ray of hope shone inside me. Perhaps someone would come to see me? Inquire about how I was doing? On Sunday night, that light went out.

I got used to my new routine. One of the evenings I worked up some courage, and went back to the chair by the living room door and watched the telenovela. Claudia glared at me, but said nothing. The next morning, when I was washing dishes, a glass slipped between my fingers and broke. She pounced on me right away: "You see? This is what happens when you don't sleep enough and your head isn't in your work. Last night you didn't clean the kitchen properly. You didn't sweep the floor! No, you chose to run to the living room and sit like a prima donna to watch TV!" She was getting increasingly agitated. "And where did you find the nerve to come into our living room and watch TV? Starting today, it's over! I don't want to ever see you in the living room anymore when we're there!" She turned and left the kitchen.

I picked up the broken glass in silence. My face was burning and my eyes stung. That evening after meticulously tidying up the kitchen, I went out into the yard and closed the door behind me. The air was pleasant. Through the neighbors' open door, I saw the characters played by Francisco Cuoco and Regina Duarte[5] on the screen. Leaning against the wall I sneakily peeked through the opening. Once I found a comfortable position, I watched the *novela* until the end of the episode. I did it again the next evening too. From behind the wall that separated the two properties, I slowly got used to following the telenovela even if I could not hear so well. Watching TV alone, free, in the cool air, was much more enjoyable than sitting rigidly on a chair in the living room, afraid of making the slightest sound. When the credits appeared at the end of the episode, I would run to my room, so Claudia wouldn't see me peeking into the neighbors' house or walking around the yard at such a late hour. One evening, the neighbor's daughter came out to take a garment off the clothesline, catching me by surprise. She just looked at me, saying nothing. Still overwhelmed with embarrassment, I noticed someone turned up the volume. The following evenings the door was fully open, and the actors' voices sounded louder to me.

A whole month had elapsed. Four Saturdays, and no one had come to visit me. My Mother did not suddenly appear at the door nor did Claudia give me any message from my family out there, in Sorocaba. On the fourth Sunday, Claudia's father came from Sorocaba for a visit.

---

[5] Francisco Cuoco, Regina Duarte and Dina Sfat are the names of well-known Brazilian actors who played the characters in the series.

Claudia came from a family of modest means and had married a wealthy man. Her parents were divorced. Her father lived in Sorocaba and her mother somewhere nearby. It looked like she supported the members of her family, and her attitude toward them was somewhat cold and with only the necessary politeness. Her brother lived in the pavilion in the yard, next to my room, and we shared a bathroom. Her mother sometimes came to visit, and returned with baskets full of groceries Claudia bought for her. Before her father left to return home, she called for me and said she was transferring my salary to my parents through him. A little spark of joy jumped in my heart. Maybe now that Mother would have some money, she could come see me.

Over the weekend I jumped every time I heard the front door open, but no one came. After two weeks I waited for Claudia's father to visit. Maybe he would bring me something from my parents, something that my mother asked him to give me, for me to know they were thinking of me, there, back home.

Her father came each time, took my salary with him, and brought nothing for me. A small suspicion that had been piercing at me for a long time, turned into vague feelings like smoke, and slowly crystallized into realization. In my pain I recognized what I didn't want to, but always knew: No one in my family cared about me. Basically, nobody in the world cared about me. My Mother didn't love me! She had abandoned me. Except for Maria, no one had ever loved me. I always felt deep down inside that my Mother didn't love me, but I didn't want to admit it. Now I knew for certain.

At night, in bed, the sobs tore my chest. I missed Maria, whose image was already blurring in my memory. I missed my Mother, but I chased away the longing with anger. How could a mother abandon her daughter like that? I was all alone in the world. What would happen to me in this horrible house? So tired, so lonely. I was afraid of the future. The more certain Claudia was that no one cared about me, the more evil she would become.

I turned the pillow over, put my cheek on the dry side and started talking to myself. I told myself to relax. I had to make the best of this period and learn everything I could. Claudia was mean, but she ran a proper household. When I grew up, I wanted to be like these people around me, educated and civilized, so I needed to learn how to behave like them. Slowly my sadness turned into determination.

Sandra

My only friends were Sandra's dolls. I wanted a friend who would talk back to me. Sandra would address me sometimes, but only to ask if I had seen a book or a shirt. I held on to that one sentence and developed it into a whole conversation with her in my imagination. I asked for details about the textbook, whether or not she liked the subject. I wanted to tell her that I could help her with math and even with other subjects. I was curious to know how many children were in her class, and who her friends were. One day, when I went to buy bread at the bakery, I passed by her school. I looked through the bars of the fence at the children playing.

I so wanted to be like that group of girls about my age, wearing well-ironed uniforms, their hair combed, and looking beautiful. I wanted to stand next to them, talk and laugh like them. I wanted to go into the classroom after the break, listen to the teacher and copy the lessons from the board. I wanted to learn so much! I wanted to tell Sandra all this.

I also had questions about the shirt she was looking for, such as, for example, whether her father had designed it. Being a fashion designer, Sandra's father made her lots of clothes, especially dresses. I loved ironing them and caressing the smooth fabrics. Of course, I did not dare to speak to Sandra as an equal. Claudia had made it very clear, to her and to me, that a maid like me should not make friends with a girl from the upper class. Sometimes when a friend from school came over, they would lock themselves in her room. Through the door I listened wishfully to their chatter and laughter. I followed the conversations whenever they went into the kitchen to get themselves cookies and juice. I once caught the fragments of a sentence while cleaning the pink marble table in the hall.

Sandra said: "I saw he wanted to put a note in my schoolbag but when I walked into the classroom, he pretended to be tying his shoes," and giggled. Her friend answered in a chirpy voice: "I told you he keeps glancing at you." Then I heard the refrigerator open and sounds of pouring into a glass. They took the plates and glasses into the room and closed the door. An idea started to take shape in my mind.

When Sandra came home from school, finished eating, and her mother went to take a nap, I went up to her room and whispered: "Yesterday, when I went to the grocery store, a boy came up to me and asked if I was the one who worked for Sandra." She raised her surprised eyes, looking interested and asked: "How did he know you work here?"

"He said he's seen me cleaning the patio in the morning when he passes by on his way to school," I replied.

"Did he tell you his name?" Sandra asked.

"No," I replied, "he didn't." Sandra looked intrigued and asked to know what he looked like. I described the imaginary stranger as best I could: tall, with fair hair and blue eyes. I promised that if he contacted me again, I would try to find out more details about him. In the days that followed, Sandra searched my eyes for a clue as to whether there had been any developments on the mystery boy. She waited impatiently for her mother to retire to her room, so that we could talk freely.

Those stolen conversations with Sandra were like my holiday celebrations. We shared a secret and it was a wonderful feeling. I was granted a few minutes a day to spend in the pink room without having to wash the floor or clean the windows. I waited all morning for her to come home. At last, she was interested in what I had to say. For the first few days I said I hadn't seen him again, but when I suspected she was starting to lose interest, I made up another encounter. I told her that he refused to tell me his name, but that he had revealed to me that he was in her school and he thought she was very beautiful. Sandra blushed with excitement and asked me to pay more attention, and find details that could help her identify him—the kind of school bag he had with him, his haircut. I promised I would, and asked if she wanted me to deliver anything to him on her behalf. She hesitated for a moment and said no—if he was really interested in her, he should approach her himself. "That you can say to him, actually."

As I walked away, I felt uncomfortable. I realized I was misleading her. I tricked her with a story I made up, which had captivated her. But what value did such a fake friendship have, if it was based on a fictitious story? Besides, she was not interested in me, but in the tale I had spun. How much more creative could I get? How long could I make this artificial friendship last? I wasn't sure I wanted a fake relationship at all.

Ultimately, I came to a decision. I went into her room one day and said: "Sandra, I have something to tell you. I made up the whole story with the boy. No one asked me about you. I'm so sorry." A shade of deep red flooded her face and her blue eyes blinked.

"You lied to me?" she asked angrily, her voice making it clear that she was offended. I nodded.

"I'm sorry," I said, lowering my eyes. She was silent for a moment and then asked: "But why did you do that?" I bit my lip and said nothing. I finally looked at her and gathered all the courage I had. "Because I wanted us to talk. I wanted us to be friends."

Her face remained sullen and hard. "Don't ever do that again. If you do, I'll tell my mother."

Up until that moment I hadn't considered the possibility of Sandra telling her mother. That's all I needed, to get into trouble with Claudia. Although, I thought, the chances were that Sandra wouldn't reveal anything because her mother would get angry at her for having private conversations with me. But you never knew.

In the days that followed, every time Claudia contacted me, I was afraid she would be mad and even fire me because of what happened. But as time went by, Claudia said nothing. Sandra didn't tell her, which made me feel thankful and like her more. Sandra went right back to ignoring me and treating me as if I did not exist.

The Visit to Sorocaba

It had been six months since Dita's visit, and I hadn't heard a single word from my family. On Saturday evening, Claudia informed me that the next day they were going to visit her father, and they would take me with them to see my parents and siblings. That night I could barely sleep from the excitement. Disturbing thoughts ran through my head: How was the family? How was everyone doing? Had Father found a job? Perhaps they wouldn't let me go back to São Paulo? Maybe I would stay home and it would all be over. I wouldn't come back to this damn place.

Between the questions, slivers of hope seeped in, like light through closed blinds. Maybe tomorrow I'd find out that my Mother missed me and was worried about me? She just couldn't make it all the way here, but when we met, I would see her eyes and know. I wore a clean dress and brushed my hair, to look as pretty and well-groomed as possible. I sat tensely in the car. No one spoke. I was even more excited than on the trip to São Paulo, half a year earlier.

The entrance to Sorocaba seemed both familiar and foreign to me at the same time. In the distance I recognized the huge Paineira[6] tree after which the neighborhood Grande Arvore, was named. The streets appeared before me as in a dream. It seemed like eons since I had last been here. Claudia turned to me: "Do you know that your parents moved to another place?" I remembered her father telling her on one of his visits that when he went to deliver my wages to my parents, he found an empty house. The neighbors told him my family had moved to another address, and gave it to him. Claudia continued, "I don't remember the name of the street, but I wrote it down somewhere." She opened her handbag and rummaged through for a minute, saying finally, "Here it is,"

---

6   A type of tree resembling a big Bombax Cotton Tree.

and pulled out a note in her handwriting—Joao Silva da Fereira street number 35 near the Berberio textile factory." I knew the textile factory and directed them there.

The car entered a narrow street with old houses, not unlike many other streets in Sorocaba. We started to look for the number, when I saw in a row of adjoining houses, a wide iron screen, like the ones outside closed grocery stores, with the number 35 written above it. Claudia's husband stopped the car and said: "I think it's here."

At that moment I saw Ivone emerge from a gate leading to a backyard between two houses. The sound of a car parked in front of the house is not a common event, and she came out to check who it was. She recognized me and called out thrilled: "Mother, it's Catarina!" Mother appeared after her, together with my two younger brothers, and two-year-old Reginaldo in her arms. She was wearing a kerchief, as always, but to my great dismay I noticed her belly was large and round again, the belly of a six-month pregnancy.

She looked at me with hollow, tired eyes, as if she hadn't slept all night. Claudia greeted her very kindly, took an envelope out of her bag and handed my mother my salary. Mother took the envelope gratefully and her eyes lit up for a moment. Claudia said they were leaving now and would come back to pick me up in two hours. I followed my Mother, thinking she was much happier to see the envelope than to see me. I entered a small, dark, windowless room. It was divided by a closet into two small areas. The tiny kitchen had a gas stove, a table and two chairs.

The living space was furnished with a wide bed, a sofa bed and a small bed. It was impossible to cram anything else in there. I sat down on the sofa, watching my mother who walked around with a big belly and a baby in her arms. She asked me if I wanted coffee. She placed Reginald on the floor and put a kettle on the stove.

"Why didn't you let me know you moved?" I asked, "I had a hard time finding the house." I spoke as if everything else was fine. As if for the last six months we had been in regular contact, and only this little detail had been kept from me. As if there wasn't a whole slew of other, difficult, existential questions: How come you didn't care at all what has been going on with me? How can you live in such a dump? Why the hell are you pregnant again? Why did you abandon me, your daughter? How can a mother abandon her child like this?

"Claudia's father knew where we lived," Mother tried to justify the fact. "What a nice person he is. Every month he brings us your salary and tells us how well you are there. You look great." She poured us coffee and called Aroldo. She gave him money from my salary and sent him to buy meat and come back quickly, because she wanted to have time to cook.

I sat in silence. Eventually, I got up and asked where the bathroom was. She asked Ivone to take me. Out in the backyard I saw that another family had their house there. Before going into the small structure, I asked Ivone if the toilets were shared by both families, and she said yes, and that sometimes in the morning it got terrible because you had to wait a long time for it to be free. On the way back we passed by the neighboring house. Through the open door I saw a woman sitting on a couch. She got up, approached us and smiled. Two teeth were missing on the sides of her mouth. She asked if I was the sister who lived in São Paulo and Ivone answered yes, I was Catarina.

Mother was in the middle of cooking when we entered. "How great that you are at Claudia's," she said as she cut the meat and put it in the bean stew. "Your father doesn't have a permanent job. He works as a tiler, and gets paid by the day, whenever he finds work. I work with a woman who makes pasties and *coxinha de galinha*.[7] I help her fry and then deliver what we've prepared. She doesn't pay much though," she sighed.

I was overwhelmed with frustration. How could this family subsist at all when there was constantly less money and more children? An hour later, my employers came to take me back to São Paulo. I left without regret. I sat quietly next to Sandra. She and her parents exchanged comments about their visit with her grandfather.

---

7 Coxinha de galinha - literally translated, "chicken leg." This is a crumbled chicken breast dipped in sauce. The batter is shaped into an egg, wrapped in dough and fried. With a toothpick stuck in the narrow end, like a bone, it creates the illusion of a chicken leg.

"Daddy looks good, doesn't he?" Claudia said, and her husband agreed. "What fun we had at the zoo," Sandra said cheerfully, "and how scared Grandpa got when the lion roared. How funny that was. I couldn't stop laughing."

Of course, no one addressed me or asked me about my own visit, about my family whom I hadn't seen in six months. After a while everyone fell silent. It was quiet, except for the noise of the wheels on the road. Then I heard Sandra's deep breathing and saw she had fallen asleep. She slept in angelic peace, calm and happy. Not a shadow of worry clouded her beautiful face. I thought of my mother and my poor brothers, living in a stifling dungeon. A mother who was busy every moment in a struggle for survival. How did I ever expect her to come see me, find out if I was doing well or if I was having a hard time? How naive of me.

The trip to Sorocaba changed something in me. I came back to São Paulo older and more in control. I didn't miss home anymore. I now had a small scarred corner in my heart, which no longer felt anything.

School in São Paulo

One afternoon Claudia sent me to the bakery. Holding the warm bag to my chest I crossed the road toward the school. The year had already ended and the schoolyard looked deserted. The gate was open and my legs carried me inside, of their own volition. I walked up the few stairs that led to the front door and went right through. I was in a long corridor with a high ceiling. Along the walls hung pictures, drawings made by the students. I tried to read what was on a bulletin board: a list of exam dates and a big announcement about the graduation party, before everyone left for the Christmas holidays. I was overwhelmed with reverence, being within the walls of this institution. I wanted to absorb every detail in order to feel part of the place, as if I was actually studying here.

I heard voices from the end of the corridor—three boys walking and talking among themselves. They walked past without noticing me. I continued further along the corridor, reading the signs on the doors on both sides of it: "Teacher's Room," "Secretary's Office," "Principal's Office." The latter's door was slightly ajar. I knocked gently, but no one answered. I pushed the door softly, and stayed in the doorway. An elderly woman sat by a large desk which sheafs of papers piled up on it. Her gray hair was gathered at the nape of her neck. She glanced at the papers, looked up at me and asked with a smile what I needed. Her pleasant expression encouraged me to speak.

"I would like to attend classes here at school," I answered. "Come in. Sit down," she said. She asked my name and where I lived. I told her that I lived with Claudia. She didn't understand who that was, so I explained she was the mother of Sandra, a seventh-grade student at this school. She asked me a few more questions and I told her everything. About my job, about my family in Sorocaba, about my strong desire to go back to learning. She listened attentively and finally said she needed to talk to Claudia about it.

"We're closed for the Christmas break," she added, "so there's no point in you starting now anyway, only after the holidays." I got up from my seat and thanked her. I walked slowly, wrapped in dreams of going back to school. Just then, I felt the bread was cooling off, and I broke into a sprint. I ran all the way to Claudia's house.

Christmas

At the end of November, Claudia began preparations for Christmas. She ordered me to scrub every corner of the house and polish the silverware. I remember being on my knees, scrubbing the marble floor of the hall with a brush, and shining the delicate carvings on the table's wooden legs. I worked for hours on end.

Claudia placed a fir tree in the corner of the living room and decorated it with glass balls and small light bulbs. She and Sandra went out to buy gifts for the whole family. When they returned, they arranged the packages wrapped in golden papers tied with colorful ribbons under the tree. In the evenings, Claudia lit the tree, and the house was filled with magic. Every chance I got, I passed by the entrance to the living room just to catch a glimpse of the magnificent Christmas tree glimmering in the corner.

A few days before the holiday we started cooking and baking the traditional dishes, special cakes and cookies. I watched Claudia with attention, trying to remember what kind of dried fruit she put in the *panetone* cake and how she prepared the Christmas rolls. The day before the holiday meal, the house smelled of fresh bread. The memory of those scents transported me back to the yard in Jacarezinho, to the wood oven with the bread that Grandmother taught Mother to bake. I suddenly missed my grandmother so much, with her long, flowery dresses. I wanted to be with her and feel her hand stroking my head. I pictured my siblings running after my Tupi, who was chasing the chickens in the yard, and I smiled numbly.

"Are you done with the turkey?" Claudia said, bringing me back to reality. I hastened to pour a thick, spicy sauce she had prepared on the turkey that lay in a pan, and replied that I was about to put it in the fridge. Claudia left the kitchen for a few minutes, returned with a package and handed it to me.

"This is a dress for you," she said.

"I want you to wear it tomorrow evening, when our guests come for the holiday dinner. Brush properly and gather your hair."

I thanked her quietly, and hurried to leave the package in my room.

In the evening I opened it. It was a simple but new dress, made of white fabric with small light blue flowers. A white apron was also attached. I tried the dress on excitedly. I couldn't remember the last time I had received a new outfit. The dress was too big for me, but when I wore the apron over it and cinched it around my waist I looked just fine. I was satisfied with my reflection in the mirror. Yes, I looked really beautiful.

The next morning, I woke up earlier than usual, because I had a lot of work to do. I was in a great mood and decided I wouldn't let Claudia spoil it. I worked diligently so that she'd be happy and not make any remarks. Before anyone else in the house got up, I had time to wash the patio floor, the toilet I shared with her brother, and the laundry room. I started the machines and hung the washed clothes out to dry.

Claudia was the first to wake up and called me to come to the kitchen to help her cook the holiday meal. The kids got up late, because they were on vacation, Carlos from the university and Franco from high school. While they sat down to have breakfast, Claudia ordered me to go make their beds quickly. In the afternoon we were working on the final preparations in the kitchen, and the door to the patio was open. We saw Franco enter the music room, where he spent a lot of time, and often hosted friends. This time he went in with a very beautiful girl, with blond hair and long legs. Claudia followed them with her gaze, seemingly concerned. After showing me how to set the table, she went to get dressed. I covered the table with a white hand-embroidered linen tablecloth.

The fine porcelain set was only used on festive occasions. Next to each plate I placed a folded cloth napkin, in a color matching the tablecloth, two crystal glasses, one for water and one for wine. On either end of the table stood tall candlesticks with candles. I looked in awe at the elegant table, at the beauty that surrounded me. I was proud to be a partner in this creation. I checked the turkey baking in the oven one last time. It looked brown and juicy, adorned with dried pineapple and prunes.

I crossed the patio to go to my room and dress up for the guests. Franco came out of the music room, with his arm around the beautiful girl. When we crossed each other, she looked at me and smiled. I looked down and kept walking. After a few seconds I turned back and saw them kissing, like in a telenovela.

At seven o'clock in the evening the guests began to arrive. From the kitchen I heard the sound of the front door opening again and again, followed by the respective greetings. An hour later, Claudia came and took with her a large salad bowl and a basket filled with warm bread rolls. I carried the steaming turkey and placed it carefully in the center of the table. Claudia lit the candles and invited everyone to eat. The guests flocked into the dining room and stopped to admire the fragrant decorated turkey.

The room was filled with the creaking of chairs, until everyone sat down. I recognized Claudia's parents and her brother, her husband's cousins whom I saw on one of the weekends, and other people I didn't know. The meal began. I retreated to the back of the kitchen. The large door connecting it to the dining room was wide open. Between dishes, Claudia appeared and together we cleared the dirty dishes and brought the next delicacy to the table. I washed the recurring pile of dishes and once again heard the chairs creaking and the voices of the party drifting away toward the living room.

Claudia's mother approached me and asked me if I had eaten anything. I shook my head and went on wiping the glass I was holding in my hand. She took a clean plate and filled it from the bowls on the kitchen table. She placed it on the table in the dining room and called me.

"Eat something and continue later," she said. I went to the table, picked up my plate and turned to leave.

"Where are you going?" she asked. "To the laundry room." "Why the laundry room?" she asked with surprise. "Sit here, at the table, and eat." I sat down obediently. At that moment Claudia appeared calling her. "Where are you, Mother?"

"I was just giving Catarina something to eat," the older woman replied. Claudia looked at me with a blank expression on her face, put her arm around her mother's shoulder and they both disappeared into the living room.

I sat alone at the big table, with the embroidered tablecloth and the upholstered chairs. The back of the chair was high, reaching up to the back of my neck. I had never sat at that table before. It felt so unfamiliar. The full plate in front of me was also unfamiliar to me. Without meaning to, the large iron door appeared in front of my mind's eye, behind which my family was huddled, inside a dark warehouse, without a window or ventilation opening. Seven souls slept on mattresses scattered on the floor. What were they doing on Christmas Eve? Did they have food to eat, or would they be forced to go to bed hungry? Several times I had to go to school hungry because I gave the little rice I had at home to Aroldo and Ivone. Even that was barely enough for them, and they fought over the leftovers.

With a lump in my throat, I tried not to think. I cut a small piece of the turkey on my plate. The taste was wonderful. Everything that Claudia's mother so generously served me was excellent. It was after midnight by the time I got into bed. I felt the fatigue flowing out of my body and a great wave of tranquility came over me. I closed my eyes and thanked my God that the day had gone by peacefully. I hadn't broken anything and Claudia hadn't yelled at me.

I had learned a lot: How to season a turkey; how to set a fancy table; and how to serve the diners according to the ceremonial rules. I must keep everything in my memory and never forget.

Holiday by the Sea

The Christmas break was very long. The children were home most of the time. They went out at night and got up late in the morning. When I finally could enter the boys' rooms, it took me a long time to collect the clothes strewn all over the room. The music room was filled with dirty cups and plates that had rolled off to the floor. I worked late and felt exhausted.

At dinnertime, I overheard from the back of the kitchen Claudia talking about the engagement party for Carlos, her eldest son. She planned to have it next month and was asking for the phone number of the bride-to-be's parents, so she could talk to them. She continued, saying that after the meal everyone should go pack, because the next day they were leaving for three days. They had to start early because the beach was a two-hour drive away and it was a shame to arrive late.

I was overjoyed. We were going on vacation! I really deserved some rest after the huge effort invested in the holiday dinner. I had never been to the sea! I was excited at the thought of seeing it at last. Immediately after the meal Sandra went to her room to pack. Claudia told me to leave the dishes and come with her to the laundry room. She picked two dresses and a pile of men's shirts out of the clean laundry and told me to iron them, because she had to pack them tonight. I went to the hall with the folded clothes and called her. "Dona Claudia, here are the ironed clothes." She came out of her room and took them from me.

"Tomorrow, we leave early, Catarina," she told me. "I will leave you chores to do while we are not here. The house will be closed and you will have a lot of free time. Clean the music room thoroughly, my brother's room, the bathroom, your room and the laundry room. Make sure the windows, doors and floor are perfect, as they should be. And of course, finish the washing and ironing."

What was I thinking? That Claudia actually would take me on vacation? Really? How could I fall into the trap again and again? So what if I wanted to see the sea? So what if I worked hard? I would rest at home.

The next morning the family woke up, and Claudia was cooking in the kitchen. She made a large pan with rice, meat and beans, covered it with a plate and put a few slices of bread with margarine on it.

"You have food here for three days," she informed me. "When it cools, put the pan in the fridge inside my brother's room. Divide it up in portions so that you have enough until we get back." They loaded the trunk of their new spectacular metallic green car. The whole family squeezed in and they slowly rolled out of the driveway. Claudia ordered me to lock the exit door to the street, and then they drove off.

Slowly I returned to the laundry room. It was strange to be alone in this mansion. The main house was locked, and the windows closed. It was quiet all around, and the only sound I could hear was made by the washing machine. The pan covered with the plate was on the sideboard by the wall.

I turned on the radio and started singing along while I ironed. My loneliness was gradually replaced by peace and a sense of freedom. I folded and stacked the ironed clothes and hung a load of laundry to dry. Taking a small portion from the covered pan I sat down to have lunch. The food tasted good, but it was cold.

I headed off to clean my room. I changed the sheets, polished the window, cleaned and waxed the wooden floor. When the sun began to set, I took off and put away the dry laundry.

When evening came, I approached the wall and peeked into the neighbors' house. It was dark there too. I assumed they had also gone on vacation and was sorry I could not watch TV that night.

I stayed under the hot shower for a long time. The best feature at Claudia's house was the shower, and of course my clean room and bed. I went out into the yard, all washed and polished, toward the laundry room. I was hungry and sat down to eat a slice of bread with margarine when I heard rhythmic music coming from the radio. I turned up the volume and started to dance. I danced alone, drifting into the beat. No one could see me. I was free and liberated, like a feather in the air.

I skipped and whirled for a long time, moving my body vigorously and feeling happy. I went to sleep without setting the alarm clock. I still woke up at five in the morning. I tried to snooze for a while longer, but my body was used to getting up early and I couldn't. I charged at the tasks Claudia had left for me to do, starting in the music room by collecting the empty wrappers and cups from the floor, then vacuuming, pressing, scrubbing. A pencil and several blank sheets of paper were lying on the buffet. I took them with me and locked the clean room behind me.

Hunger started to bother me and I went to have breakfast, devouring the half slice I had left from dinner on the plate in the laundry room. I continued to work non-stop until the afternoon, finishing all my assignments.

I was content, and starved. I pulled the pan out of the fridge and took half of its contents, so I'd have some food left for the next day as well. I was sitting in the laundry room eating leisurely when I suddenly heard a noise, as if someone was trying to open the front door to the patio. I froze. It was sure it was a burglar trying to break in! I heard footsteps in the yard, coming closer to me. What should I do now?! My legs became iron bars... I couldn't move. Droplets of sweat appeared above my upper lip. My heart pounded wildly. Then the laundry room door opened and Claudia's brother appeared in the doorway.

"Where's Claudia?" he asked. I replied with a tremulous voice that they were away on vacation. He looked surprised and didn't say anything. He turned and headed to his room. I remained seated, but couldn't eat anymore. After a while I heard him leave again.

I barely managed to get up and went to take a shower. The tepid water calmed me down. Back at the laundry room I saw that the pan with the rest of the food for tomorrow was still there. I had forgotten to put it in the fridge. I hurriedly put it away and ate everything left on the plate, along with a few slices of bread. The fright made me hungry.

That night fears crept into my loneliness. It was hard for me to fall asleep. I was attentive to suspicious noises and got up to make sure the front door was locked. In the last two days the radio was on continuously, and several times I listened to the news. They talked often about crime in São Paulo and violence in the streets. It was realistic to fear a thief or a burglar. I locked my room and prayed to God to watch over me.

When I woke up it was Sunday, the last day of the beach vacation—my last day off. The family was due back that night. I headed to the laundry room to eat breakfast, but found nothing on the plate. I remembered that last night I had eaten the last slice. I had to pass the time until noon. I discovered the pencil and papers I found in the music room, sat down at the table and began to draw. Then I wrote words to myself, hoping I had spelled them correctly.

Lastly, I wrote some multiplication and division exercises for myself and solved them for fun. I remembered my visit to Sandra's school. The principal apparently forgot about our meeting and didn't talk to Claudia. Luckily. I don't think Claudia would have understood what I did. She would surely have been very angry with me. I hoped the principal would not mention the incident.

I was hungry. It was already lunch time and I allowed myself to take the last portion of food from the fridge. I waited a bit for the rice and meat to be less cold, and started eating. The meat had a sour aftertaste and an unpleasant smell. I couldn't swallow much and threw most of it in the trash.

I spent some more time drawing, with the radio playing in the background. I woke up suddenly with my head resting on the drawing pages. A football game was being broadcast on the radio. I didn't feel well. My stomach rumbled and my head was heavy. I dragged myself into my room and got into bed. I woke up in the late afternoon feeling terrible, nauseous and with a mean stomachache. The taste of the rotten food was still in my mouth. I got up to drink water, but was overcome with nausea and I barely managed to reach the bathroom and throw up the water I drank. Feeling weak, I wished Claudia would come back already.

I woke up to a knock on the door. Claudia entered my room and turned on the light. I blinked, having no idea what time it was.

"I called you and you didn't answer. Why are you in bed?" she asked. I answered in a weak voice that I didn't feel well, that my stomach and my head hurt, and that I was also very hungry.

She said she'd be right back and after a few minutes I heard her quick steps approaching. She walked in with a tray, placed it next to me and helped me sit down. I ate with appetite the crackers and the slice of bread with margarine and drank the tea she brought me. She waited a bit before leaving the room. I looked at the clock and saw that it was eight in the evening, and thought it was good that I still had a lot of time to sleep. In the middle of the night, I woke up and was happy to find fresh tea and a slice of bread with margarine next to the bed. In the morning, when I opened my eyes, I was alarmed to see it was already half past five. I was too weak to get up. With great effort I got dressed and went out to wash the patio. After a while, Claudia's husband passed me, on his way to the bakery. He stopped and asked how I was. I told him I felt better.

"Good," he said and left. Claudia came outside and called me. She asked me what happened. I replied that the food had spoiled and I had nothing to eat. She was silent for a few seconds and then told me to come into the house and help her unpack the bags.

One day, a week before school started again, Claudia burst into the kitchen screaming. At first, I didn't understand what she was so angry about, and then I caught the words: "How dare you embarrass me like this! In such a terrible way! How dare you go talk to the school principal? Is that what I'm keeping you here for? Do you think your Mother will be pleased to have you back? Is that what you want, to return to your family? What will they give you there? Nothing! Is that what you want?" I bit my lip and lowered my head.

"I forbid you to go near the school, do you hear?!" I nodded silently. Her shouts no longer affected me so much. I was used to them. But at that moment I knew that I was also stuck with Claudia without any future. I couldn't stay there for long. I had to think of another way out.

Winter at Claudia's

The children returned to school and life went back to normal. At one of the dinners I gathered, from snippets of conversations I overheard, that Carlos's engagement party would be held in ten days. Claudia never told me, except for giving me a to-do list only a few days before the event. That week Claudia was insufferable. She was compulsive in her pursuit of perfection. She put in a huge amount of effort herself, while demanding increasingly more from me, and nothing was good enough for her. Only on the day of the event did everything, finally, turn out as she wished. She decorated the engagement cake humming a song to herself. On the rare occasions in which she was in a good mood she would hum some tune.

The cake was a splendid creation made with three heart-shaped cakes, which Claudia baked herself and filled with different icings, stacked one on top of the other. The entire tower was then covered in white whipped cream, decorated with pink sugar flowers and topped off with a small open jewelry box holding two golden wedding bands.

That evening, the guests arrived together with the first rain. The house was filled with family and friends of Carlos from the university—well-dressed young people. I walked among the guests with trays of small sandwiches or crispy empanadas, loving the sophistication that surrounded me. I absorbed everything with my eyes and stored it in my memory. That was how I wanted to host my friends one day, when I became a woman and had my own house.

A year had gone by since I arrived to work in São Paulo. The days became shorter. In the mornings I wore an old sweater of Claudia's over a thin dress to go out to the patio. It was a dress I brought from home. It fit me loosely and was only a little tight at the chest. It had also gotten shorter in the last few months, revealing my bony knees. My feet froze in the Havaianas I wore when I washed the courtyard tiles with water. Although the nights were cold, the neighbors still opened their doors wide so I could watch the telenovela over the wall.

The winter was very cold and it rained most of the time. Eventually, the neighbors succumbed to the weather and closed the door, so unfortunately, I didn't see the last episodes. I had to make do with Sandra's enthusiastic descriptions: She was the one who replayed at dinner the dramatic moment when Francisco Cuoco discovers his beloved Regina Duarte was imprisoned in a cave, a consequence of Dina Sfat's insane jealousy.

On cold, wet mornings, I swept the leaves in the garden wearing a raincoat. On rainy days I was exempt from washing the patio. My bare feet stung with cold and the pain climbed up my stomach. I wiped my feet dry, put on socks and shoes, but the pain in my stomach didn't go away. In the evening it got better, but I felt a strange moisture between my legs.

I finished washing the dishes and tidying the kitchen as fast as I could and went to take a shower. When I undressed, I saw with horror that my underwear was soaked in blood. I ran to my room and found an old t-shirt which I cut into strips, and went back into the shower. I stayed under the warm stream trying to organize my thoughts.

I was obviously very ill and I might even die. I kept talking to myself. I had to relax. Maybe I would get better after all. It was impossible to tell. I had to hope for the best. Of course, I had to keep it from Claudia because if she found out I was sick, she would surely send me home, to my parents, to live in a warehouse without windows. Death seemed like the better alternative.

I dried myself and lined my panties with layers of the torn t-shirt strips. Finding it very hard to fall asleep, I looked at the ceiling and prayed with all my heart: "I don't want to die. Please …" The tears flowed.

I closed my eyes and pictured my prayer rising up to the sky, a sky full of stars. The Jacarezinho sky, when the whole family sat around the fire, and Father roasted meat and potatoes. I saw the embers rising from the fire. My thoughts wandered farther, to the creek nearby, its sunny bank a picture in my memory, with children wading along. They were Dita and Aroldo, and I was also among them. We were trying to catch some fish with a large strainer.

A memory that had been completely forgotten suddenly floated up. Aroldo raised the strainer and yelled: "An eel! We caught an eel!" We helped him pull the strainer out of the water but it contained a snake coiling up inside, not an eel. We screamed and threw the strainer in the air, it fell face down into the water, causing ripples all around. Aroldo and I ran out and Dita quickly picked it up and hurled it ashore. The strainer rolled like a ring, fell to the ground and stopped, allowing us to see the bottom was empty. We carried it home squealing with laughter—chatting about how we almost caught a snake and thought it was an eel. I heard a chuckle, and quickly realized I was in bed, at Claudia's house, laughing to myself.

The next morning my stomach hurt less. I hurried to check the cloth bandages I had improvised and was happy to discover only light spots. At every opportunity I ran to the bathroom to check my condition. During the day my illness got worse again and the flow increased. All day my face was like that of a woman on death row. Even Claudia noticed my gloomy expression and asked if I was feeling alright.

With confidence, I confirmed that everything was fine. After three days of me still being alive, the spots finally started to fade. They paled until they disappeared completely. I was miraculously saved from the mysterious illness. At night, in bed, I thanked the good God for healing me.

Winter continued, with the cold and the annoying rain that fell without a pause. That's where São Paulo got its nickname from—*Terra da Garoa*—the Land of the Drizzle.

On that mid-September morning, when I opened my bedroom door, I felt the start of spring. Flowers began to bloom in the garden and their delicate scent carried in the air. The branches of the trees grew small fresh leaves. It didn't rain, and I had to wash the yard. It didn't bother me at all: I could enjoy the quiet. All the other members of the household were asleep and the garden was mine only.

The sun's rays rose and shone at me through the branches of the trees. The shingles on the roof glistened, emitting a golden light. My bliss was disrupted by Claudia's shrill voice calling me. I could tell from her tone that she hadn't woken up in a good mood.

I went in to help her serve breakfast and saw that her face looked tense and her eyes were red, as if she had been crying all night. She grumbled something about having called me but I didn't hear. She told me angrily that she had already taken out a stick of butter and why was I wasting time looking for another one.

Later, as I was cleaning the master bedroom, she appeared in the doorway and shouted in fury: "Where are you? Don't you hear I'm looking for you? Come to the kitchen!" In the kitchen, she pointed to a pale-yellow stain on the surface of the counter panel, by the cupboard. "Clean the panels. Make sure you get that stain off!" she shrieked, then turned and left.

I scrubbed the marble strip with all my energy in an attempt to remove the yellow stain, but it was too old and stubborn and it refused to go away. Claudia returned after a few minutes to examine my work: "Haven't you finished yet?" She flew into a rage. "What have you been doing until now? You haven't gotten the stain off yet?"

"I have been scrubbing it," I replied.

"Are you trying to make a fool of me?" she screamed.

"The stain won't come off anymore, Dona Claudia," I replied.

She furiously grabbed the rag from me and began rubbing the stain like a maniac.

"Here, look! This is how it's done! Do you see? Here, like this!"

I knelt close to Claudia, her face was close to mine. It was contorted with insanity and her jaws clenched with the effort when she didn't open it to yell at me. She was truly frightening me and I didn't want to be there anymore. When she turned to face me, I mustered all the determination I had. Looking her straight in the eye, I said: "I want to go home." A fierce slap landed on my cheek. I lost my balance and fell to the floor.

Claudia hit me! She threw the rag at me and left the kitchen toward the patio. With shaky legs I dragged myself to the laundry room. I heard Claudia saying loudly to her brother, at the door of his room:

"Tomorrow early in the morning you take her to Sorocaba. On the first train!" He said nothing and just walked with her a long way across the yard. Shaking his head, visibly concerned, his eyes remained fixed on her back as she stormed away from him,

All of that day I went through the usual routine. I cleaned and helped Claudia in the kitchen, without her saying a word or even glancing at me. It was a long, difficult last day, maybe almost as hard as that first day, over a year ago. In the evening, under the stream of lukewarm water in the shower, my tears dissolved into the water.

Goodbye hot shower and clean, soft bed. Goodbye room all to myself. I tried not to think about the damp warehouse I was moving to. I opened my closet and took out my few possessions: three dresses were all I owned. One dress I brought with me from home, the dress I got for Christmas, which I bundled up in a brown paper bag, and an old dress of Sandra's that Claudia gave me, and which I left on the armrest of the chair, to wear the next day.

The events of the day went through my mind like a play in a theater. Claudia's wild fury. Her crazy demands! And the way she slapped me! The shock I felt! But the real surprise was me. I finally dared to open my mouth and face Claudia. I talked back. I said I couldn't remove the stain. I said I wanted to go home! Despite the slap, I felt good about myself. I knew that at that moment something had changed in me. From that day on I would know how to stand up for myself. To say "enough" or "I disagree." At that moment I caught sight of my image in the mirror inside the open closet door, and saw a young woman. I wasn't the frightened little girl who arrived here a year ago.

I snuggled for the last time in the soft bed, which would no longer be mine. The sadness slowly waned, and was replaced by a surge of inner strength. I was no longer afraid of what would happen to me. I knew that from that day on I would control my own destiny. I was sure I could take better care of myself, and I felt serenity coming over me.

I woke up early, as usual, and immediately remembered I was going home and wasn't expected to wash the patio. I could get up and shower at leisure, for the last time. At six o'clock Claudia's brother walked into the laundry room. I was waiting there with my belongings already packed.

"Good morning," he said, "we need to leave, to catch the train."

"I'm ready," I replied.

I took a last look at the laundry room where I had spent so many hours. After locking the door, I handed him the keys. The big house was dark and silent. I crossed the yard one last time to the heavy glass door leading to the street. I walked through it and closed it behind me. The faint click of the closing door echoes in my head to this day.

We waited a few minutes for the bus, got on and rode to the train station.

Out the bus window, I watched the streets, the tall buildings, the shops I didn't know with curiosity. I tried to memorize everything. I had been at Claudia's for almost a year and a quarter, and all that time I had only known the one road leading from the house to the shopping center near the school.

We entered the bustling train station through a wide iron gate. People of all kinds and colors came and went. My head was spinning from the crowd of moving people. Claudia's brother bought two tickets and asked me to wait for him right there. Minutes later he was back with two *pingado e pão com manteiga* (coffee with a drop of milk and buttered bread rolls) for the two of us. We sat down on a bench, because we had some time to spare until the train arrived, which he used to scan the newspaper he bought. I took a bite of the bun and a sip of the coffee.

It was the best tasting coffee I'd ever had.

The train tooted, announcing its arrival at the platform. We got on right away and looked for a seat. Claudia's brother relaxed and continued reading his paper. As we left, I gazed at the rolling landscape in front of me, green fields and trees full of blossoms. The sun flickered between the branches, caressing my face through the window.

In Sorocaba Again

Claudia's brother waited politely outside while I opened the door. When he saw me, Father looked puzzled and got up from the sofa. I told him Claudia's brother was waiting for him outside. Father came out to greet him and shook his hand. The brother said that Claudia had asked him to bring me home and handed Father an envelope with my last wages. He hesitated for a moment and then added in an agitated voice:

"I may be Claudia's brother, but with all due respect, if I were Catarina's father, I would go kill my sister."

Father smiled at him looking embarrassed and helpless, without saying anything in response. Claudia's brother bid us farewell with a nod and left.

Once inside, my father asked what had happened. I told him that Claudia had hit me. He growled and lowered his eyes to the floor. He poured us both coffee and lit himself a cigarette. The house was quiet and I asked where everyone was.

He replied that the baby was sleeping and that the others were at school.

Mother arrived at noon. She did not seem surprised and just asked what happened. I told her, and, contrary to what I expected, she was not angry. She just said I needed to find a new job. I told her not to worry and that I would look for one. My brothers came back from school and I felt a welcoming warmth in their smile when they saw me. Ivone immediately went to pick up the strange baby who was my new brother, Aguinaldo. While Mother was making dinner, Father took a few Cruzeiros from my salary and left.

"Fia and her husband Joao have moved to Sorocaba," she told me. "They appeared at our doorstep a month ago and stayed here for a few days, until they found a home."

My Maria! Her memory was kept deep in the treasure box in my heart, but who knew if this was still her. Would I recognize her and she me?

"Where do they live?" I asked. "Wait," said Mother and went over to a ceramic urn on a shelf above the stove. She tilted it toward her and rummaged inside.

"Here," she said, handing me a note. An address was scrawled on it, in large, hesitant letters. Maria's place was quite some way from my parents' house, but at that moment I knew I would go visit her on the weekend and I began to feel excited.

Everyone was there for dinner. Dita came home from work. She was working at a banana stand in the market at the time. She arrived with a bunch of bananas in her arms and chewing gum in her mouth.

Father came back, not completely steady on his feet and his breath smelling of alcohol. Mother pulled out the two beds and the couch. Dita opened a cot for herself. Our parents slept in one of the beds with a six-month-old baby between them and a two-and-a-half-year-old toddler at the foot of the bed. In the second bed I slept in opposite directions with Ivone and Carlinho. Aroldo and Nicolao were on the couch.

I tossed and turned in the dark, unable to rest. I remembered with sorrow the comfortable bed at Claudia's house. I could hear the rhythmic breathing around me. Carlinho rolled over in his sleep and kicked me. I thought everyone else was asleep except for me. Suddenly I heard chewing from the direction of Dita's bed and then the blowing and popping of a bubble. Dita stopped chewing for a moment and turned to me out of the silence:

"Catarina, are you going to stay at home for a long time?" I replied that I hoped not, and pushed Ivone's foot away from my face.

I woke up early, as I was used to getting up at five. Everyone was asleep except Mother, who was boiling water on the stove in the corner of the kitchen.

I got up and she examined me intently. After making coffee for both of us she beckoned me to come closer. When I was a whisper away, she quietly asked me when I first bled. I was shocked that she knew I was sick. I stammered in embarrassment, told her it had been about six months, but that by now I was already healthy. As she looked at me, her face grew more worried than ever. "I'll take you to the doctor today," she said. A little anxiety climbed up my stomach. It was not a good sign, if mother was so worried that she decided to skip work because of me.

We took a bus to the city center, to a major branch of the INPS public health organization. The clinic was teeming with people and we sat for a long time in the waiting room until the doctor finally called us. Mother whispered something to him so I would not hear. The doctor nodded and invited me to enter the examination room and lie on a bed. He touched my stomach, pressed the sides of my neck, pulled my lower eyelids and looked into my eyes. He asked, like mother had, when I first bled. I answered again that it was six months ago but that since then I felt fine, and that I thought I had recovered completely.

"You're not sick and you never were," he said gently, his voice showing a slight surprise. "The bleeding is a normal phenomenon. Every girl around the age of twelve gets it. Sometimes at an earlier age and sometimes later. It's a sign that you're turning from a girl into a woman." He went on to explain that I was supposed to bleed every month, which is why it's called a monthly period. In the first months it was normal for the cycle to be irregular. Because I was weak and anemic, it had stopped completely. He, the doctor, would give me a treatment of vitamins and iron, and in a few months, I would return to him for a follow-up.

On the way home I sat on the bus and all the people in it seemed nice to me. I looked out the window: The old streets were actually beautiful, and I was healthy and had no deadly disease. I only had a nagging thought—how had Mother not explained anything to me and let me think for hours that I was still very sick? But that also went away immediately.

In the meantime, I waited impatiently for the weekend. When Saturday came, I got on the bus that would take me to Maria, the kind, beautiful sister from my happy childhood. I arrived at the address Mother gave me and opened the gate of a small garden. With my heart pounding, I stood before the three steps that led to the front door, and clapped my hands to announce my arrival. The door opened and at the top of the stairs was my Maria. I recognized her immediately, even though she looked a little different.

"Fia, it's me, Catarina!" I said, beaming.

"Oh my God!" she cried and ran to me.

She hugged me tightly. We looked at each other, our faces wet, and hugged again. We went inside with our arms around each other. The house was modest, almost empty of furniture, but clean and tidy. We talked a lot, about everyday facts and details. The important things we had in our hearts we said with a look, a hug or a stroke on the cheek.

"Joao will be here soon and I have to make dinner," she said. "It will be a festive meal." She looked at me with a joyful look. "Stay to eat with us and sleep over, okay?"

She moved about the kitchen cheerfully and energetically, as I remembered, but her hair was cut short and her eyes looked older. Her husband arrived too soon. He looked like an elderly person. His face was wrinkled, his back was bent and his hair was completely white. He looked at me without a smile and after a few minutes returned to the kitchen, asking angrily why the food wasn't ready yet. Maria answered in a gentle tone that she would be serving dinner in five minutes.

At the table João was tolerable, and in between bites he told me about the move to Sorocaba. While we cleaned up, he went to sleep.

Maria brought clean sheets for the couch in the living room. I stretched out in the dark on a private sofa, without any hands or feet pushing me or crushing my nose.

The next day Fia escorted me to the bus stop, and on the way, she poured her heart out to me. It was not easy for her with her husband. He was a grumpy, difficult person. He was always angry at her, insulting and blaming her for not having children.

I had been home for a little over a week when I found a new job in São Paulo. Friends of my mother's employer, new immigrants from Portugal, needed help at home and at the restaurant they owned. The couple came over for the weekend to talk to me about my working conditions. Fernando and Lucia seemed likable, and I was at ease with the prospect of working for them. I agreed with them on a salary according to my demands, and that once a month on the weekend I would go visit my family.

I was happy at my new workplace, even though I worked hard from morning to night. The couple worked alongside me and treated me like family. At five we all got up to prepare sandwiches and pasties for the restaurant in the industrial zone, where workers came for breakfast before starting their day. On the last Saturday of every month, Fernando walked me to the bus station and provided me with a letter authorizing me to travel alone. I delivered my salary to my parents myself, and at the hearty dinner it bought for them everyone was in a good mood.

Manuela

Mother told me she had met a very nice neighbor who lived down the street, Mrs. Mendes. She was a widow raising five daughters on her own. Two of them, Manuela and Marta, were close to my age and had been invited to come visit us in the afternoon to meet me. After lunch I helped Mother tidy up the house. I wanted everything to look nice in honor of my new friends. After living in isolation at Claudia's house for over a year, there was nothing in the world I wanted more than a friend my age, someone to talk to.

I sat and waited for them impatiently. Finally, I heard a gentle voice calling out from the gate and went out to greet Manuela and Marta. They were very beautiful, especially the older one, Manuela. She was tall and slender, with a heart-shaped face and large doe eyes. Her mouth was a perfect drawing, her lips dark and full, her nose small and delicate, and golden green sparkles shone in her eyes.

She hugged me and said, smiling broadly, that she had heard a lot about me and was looking forward to getting to know me. She asked me about São Paulo, about my job and how I felt, being so far from my family. Wasn't it hard for me? No one had ever asked me that. At that moment I already loved her.

I told them a little about the Portuguese family I was working for. Manuela told me about all the sisters having names that started with the letter "M"—Madalena, the eldest, was married and had two small children. She was followed by Mariana, Monica, Manuela and finally Marta, a cute nine-year-old girl. Time flew and the weekend was over. That evening I had to return to São Paulo. I said goodbye to Manuela and Marta with a hug and we promised to meet in a month from that day, when I came home again.

When I returned to Sorocaba a month later, I immediately went to find Manuela. We embraced as if we had known each other all our lives. Marta, like little sisters do, was curled up around her. But that didn't stop us from talking for hours. Manuela told me about school. She talked about her annoying, envious classmate who was always stirring up conflict; about the evil teacher; and about the boy from another class who waited at the gate to walk her home.

I told her about the exhausting children of Fernando and Lucia, about the *bauru* (sandwiches with pastrami, cheese and tomato slices fried in a pan) and the *coxinha de galinha* I learned to make. I also described my Sunday afternoons, when I joined the Portuguese family and many others like them, gathered in a large hangar, with long tables displaying an abundance of classic dishes from their homeland. A band played folk songs and couples wearing embroidered vests danced traditional folk dances, twirling around the hall to the beat of the music.

As Manuela listened to my descriptions, her eyes glistened. She told me her father also emigrated from Portugal but died when she was little, shortly after Martha was born, and she didn't remember him at all. I felt a great closeness to Manuela, much more than to my sisters, who were too distant, too young or too mean.

The next few months were happy ones. On weekends when I didn't go home, my employers took me with them. On Sundays we dined out, mostly at their relatives' home in another neighborhood, and in the afternoons, we participated in folklore gatherings.

I worked fourteen-hour days, but my bosses' fair treatment made me feel good.

While preparing the dishes in the restaurant kitchen or cleaning the family's house, I could reflect on Manuela and our conversations, which became more open and personal. Though I told her a lot about myself with her, I barely mentioned the period of my stay at Claudia's, which I would much rather forget. I was ashamed to share this dark chapter of my life with Manuela. Even at home, in Sorocaba, the situation had improved. Father found a permanent job as a maintenance man at a car dealership and Mother started working nights at a good restaurant named Churrascaria Max. When I got home that weekend, a big surprise awaited me. Grandmother came to visit. I hadn't seen her since we left Jacarezinho, and it took me a few seconds to recognize her.

She had grown older. Her hair had turned white and her face looked tired. She had wrinkles around her eyes and spots on her skin, which I remembered as being smooth and taut. I threw my arms around her. Her warm embrace enveloped me and it all was exactly as before. I knew she was living with her son in San Manuel. She said she had to help him, working hard in the fields.

"Come on, I have something to show you," Father called me, pointing to a table placed in front of the pull-out couch, with a television set on it. "We bought it with the money you earned," he told me.

After dinner, the whole family sat down solemnly in front of the screen to watch the moving black and white images. After the news, the channel began to broadcast a Western. We were all immersed in the plot—the sheriff and the townsfolk chasing the bandits—when one of the fugitives pulled out a gun and shot the sheriff. The good guys immediately retaliated. At that moment, Grandmother got up in fright and ran to hide behind the closet.

"Come here quickly!" she shouted, "They will kill you!" We, engrossed in the movie, didn't understand what she wanted, but she continued, "The man in the TV! He will kill you!" We looked at each other in bewilderment. "Grandma," I said, stifling a chuckle, "it's not real. They're just actors in a movie, and they can't jump out of the TV screen."

Mother went over to reassure her. Grandmother returned to the couch with the fear still apparent in her eyes. Our explanations had not fully convinced her, and every time there were shots, she covered her eyes with her hand. At night, when she sat next to me in bed before we went to sleep, she asked me quietly how the people got into the TV set, such a small box, and how come they never came out of it. I patiently explained that they were not people, just moving images. We saw them but they could not see us. Grandmother nodded and it seemed I had managed to put her mind at rest. I covered her hand with mine and asked for her blessing, as I always used to do:

"Bença, Grandmother …"

"Deus que te abençoa." *May God bless you*, she answered, and her words soothed me, like they had years ago.

The next day I rushed to Manuela's house. We were always thrilled to see each other. We had a long heart-to-heart conversation, mainly about boys, until Marta woke up and joined us. Changing the subject, Manuela told us about the new blouse she bought the day before.

She undressed right in front of us, without a hint of embarrassment and tried on the tight new blouse, which truly flattered her. In a completely natural manner, she asked me if I would agree to take some of the clothes that no longer fitted her. I said I was fine with that, and she immediately brought me a paper bag full of clothes. She handed it to me with a smile, as if I was the one doing her a favor. For a fleeting second, the image of three paper bags of clothes on the floor flashed in my memory, with a classroom full of children staring at me…

As soon as I got home, I emptied the contents of the bag on the sofa. There were several blouses, two skirts, a dress and a pair of pants.

I tried them all on. Everything fit and was in excellent condition. That evening I returned to São Paulo happy and well dressed.

Two months passed. When I returned home on Saturday, my mother told me Manuela had come looking for me twice and asked me to find her as soon as I arrived, because she had something important to tell me. I rushed to the Mendes family home. Going to visit Manuela always had a holiday feeling for me. I loved her warmth, her bubbly joie-de-vivre that made even everyday occurrences fascinating. She welcomed me with an eager hug.

"I have something to tell you!" she said, her eyes aglow. "You know that Madalena, my older sister, gave birth to a baby four months ago. She wants to go back to school. She is studying to become a sports teacher and is looking for a nanny. She also has a two-and-a-half-year-old toddler. We thought you might want to live with her and help out." She grabbed my hand, almost jumping up and down with enthusiasm. It felt wonderful to have such a good friend, who cared for me and wanted me close to her. After all, Madalena lived in a suburb of Sorocaba. Working at Madalena's seemed infinitely easier to me than my current job. I replied that I would be very happy to work for Madalena, but I wasn't sure whether my mother would agree.

Manuela declared firmly that her mother would help convince mine.

"Right, Mother? You will come with us to talk to Dona Teresa, won't you?" she said loudly to her mother who was cooking in the kitchen. Dona Mendes turned off the fire, covered the pot and took off her apron. "We're going to talk to her right now!" she said with a determined smile and left toward our house, while Manuela and I trailed closely behind her.

"Our mothers are good friends," Manuela reassured me, "don't worry. She'll convince her." My mother gave us her approval.

I said goodbye to Fernando and Lucia and their two tireless children and started to work for Madalena. The job there was quite reasonable. Taking care of a regular-sized house and a family with two small children was easy compared to the load I was used to. Marcino and Marcia were sweet children, and Madalena was warm and kind, like the rest of her family.

Every weekend I went to my parents' house, but I spent most of the time with Manuela. I ate at her place, slept at her place and we talked non-stop. I was very fond of her. Through her I experienced childhood. I admired the fact that she was educated: she would graduate high school next year and was planning to continue on to college.

I also admired her poise. Nothing fazed her. Once, when she was in the middle of an interesting story about a new boy she had met, she suggested I go to the bathroom with her so we could go on talking while she showered. I sat down on the toilet as Manuela undressed completely, stepped into the shower and turned on the water, still talking. I lowered my eyes so as not to intrude on her privacy. She was completely oblivious to my embarrassment. She washed, dried and got dressed so naturally.

Bathroom conversations became a habit. Manuela explained that there we could talk without anyone else overhearing. Marta didn't follow her into the shower. Gradually I got used to her free spirit and I no longer lowered my gaze. I just watched in awe as the water flowed over her naked body. I guess she knew she was perfect and that's why she felt so comfortable with her nudity. She was thin, had long legs and her breasts were small and firm. Her face was beautiful.

One Saturday, when I arrived at their place, Manuela greeted me with an aura of secrecy and adventure. She pulled me into her room and told me she had arranged to go to the movies with some boys the day after. Her mother would only allow her to go if Marta and I went too. "Will you come?" she asked, "Eduardo will be there too! You know! The one I told you about. He is so adorable! You have to come!" "Of course I will!" I promised her.

At night, in her room, we talked for a long time. I had never been to a movie theater, nor had I ever been on a date. Manuela was excited too, and we only fell asleep toward the wee hours. Already the next morning we began to try on one piece of clothing after another, until we decided what she would wear and which items she would lend me. In the afternoon the three of us left to go downtown. We were nicely dressed and our hair done.

We were supposed to meet Manuela's friends at the entrance. Sure enough, three boys were already standing outside, near the front door. Manuela whispered that Eduardo was the one in the yellow shirt. He was tall and handsome, and not a child at all. He was in a higher grade and looked almost like a young man. We got closer step by step, as if in slow motion. Manuela introduced Marta and me. The boys let us in first, as befits gentlemen, and followed us to our seats. They took the seats in between us, and I sat last in the row, with one of the boys next to me. I smiled in embarrassment. He smiled back and finally the lights went out. As the trailers were projected on the screen, the boy leaned toward me until I could feel his breath.

I was extremely nervous and started to sweat. Whispering, he asked me where I attended school. Manuela had prepared me for questions of this kind, so I answered as she instructed. I said that I had been studying in São Paulo and had missed this year.

The movie began. I fixed my gaze on the screen and sat petrified in my seat. Seconds later, I felt his hand groping in the dark for mine. I turned my head in panic to ask Manuela for help only to see her kissing her date. I was at a loss. Before I had time to recover, my suitor's lips were on mine. I felt his saliva inside my mouth. It was awful. My face was ablaze and my hands all sweaty. I just wanted to get away from there. I wished I could run to the bathroom and throw up, but of course I couldn't spoil it for Manuela. She was so into the moment, wrapped in her suitor's arms. I sat with my body twisted at an odd angle, upright and stiff as a log, staying as far as possible from the boy clinging to me. That's how I stared at the screen without taking in any of what was going on in it. That movie was the longest in my life. When it was over, I rushed out of the hall and ran to the bathroom. I rinsed my mouth with water several times, but couldn't get rid of the repulsive taste of the kiss. Manuela and Marta met me there.

On the way home I told Manuela that the cheeky boy had kissed me and that I never wanted to see him again. Manuela looked at me, amused.

"What's wrong with you, Catarina? It's just a kiss."

Back to School

The school year was over. Madalena received her teaching degree and Manuela had one more year left to finish high school. I began to worry about the future. Would Madalena still need me next year? And in general, girls my age, fifteen years old, were already finishing high school,[8] while I had barely attended school for four years. What was I going to do?

Madalena entered the nursery while I was playing with Marcino and Marcia.

"Hello, you guys!" she said cheerfully. It was her first day off after graduation. "How are you today?" She leaned over to them. They hugged her and then went back to the blocks we were using to build a dollhouse.

"Madalena, I want to talk to you for a moment," I said.

"Yes, Catarina," she said pleasantly.

"Now that you've graduated, what happens to me?" I asked. Madalena seemed puzzled.

"What do you mean?"

"Do you still want me to work for you?"

"Of course I do," she replied. "Nothing changes."

I took a long breath, without daring to look her in the eyes.

"I would like to go back to school," I said quietly.

"You can't study in the mornings, I need you during the day." she replied, somewhat apprehensive.

"I was planning to study in the evenings," I answered, "I know there are intensive courses for adults and one can get a high school diploma in two years."

---

8 In Brazil, high school is equivalent to our middle school, while grades 10 to 13 are called college.

"With evenings I have no problem." Madalena relaxed.

We smiled at each other in relief, and I was overjoyed.

That same evening, I registered for night school.

Classes lasted three hours every evening. In the first few weeks, I could barely understand what was going on. My eyes would shut from exhaustion and I couldn't write down fast enough what the teacher dictated. She was a young woman named Dalzisa. She was tall and shapely, with long, beautiful legs she accentuated with high heels. Her eyes were slightly slanted and her hair was long and straight.

I'm not sure whether it was out of kindness or because of my admiring looks, but during one of the breaks, Dalzisa approached me, holding a cup of coffee in her hand.

"How are things coming along?" she asked me.

"Okay, more or less," I replied with an embarrassed smile.

"You know you can always come to me during the breaks if anything isn't clear," she said. She sat down next to me and asked if I wanted her to explain anything I hadn't understood. With some hesitation I asked her about the material of the last lesson and she answered in great detail. From that day on she would sit with me during the breaks and tutor me while sipping her coffee. This was tremendously helpful. Though I no longer was one of the best students, as I had been in the first years of elementary school, I was making significant progress.

At the end of the year, Dalzisa loaded me with assignments for the holidays, and I accepted them willingly. I was content with my life. During the day I worked for Madalena, feeling like I was part of their little family. In the evenings I studied independently with the homework Dalzisa gave me.

My parents left the dank warehouse and moved to a bigger house. Here, too, there were close neighbors in the backyard and the bathroom was outside the house, but at least it was more pleasant to come visit. While helping my mother in the kitchen I smiled watching my siblings play outside with other children.

"It's unbelievable how fast they became friends with the neighbors, as if they had known them all their lives," I said.

Mother nodded and remarked: "We've been here for two weeks and Dita already knows half the neighborhood …"

Dita appeared shortly before dinner. A shadow seemed to flit across her eyes upon seeing me. When I asked her how she was, she nodded, mumbled something in response and went into the living room. Soon she came back to stand in the doorway to the kitchen, humming to herself. She raised her eyes to stare at some imaginary spot on the ceiling. I watched her with curiosity. Her humming got increasingly louder. She was chanting incomprehensible sentences in a voice that did not belong to her. She shook her head wildly from side to side. Her movements became frenetic, with her whole body swaying left and right, then back and forth, until ultimately she dropped to the floor.

"What's wrong with her?" I asked my mother, who put down the pots and turned to Dita. "I don't know," she said impatiently, "ever since she started going to these *Umbanda*[9] ceremonies she's been like this. I don't have time to deal with it. I have other things to do." She looked at Dita with dismay. "I don't like you doing this at home," she said to her, raising her voice. "If you want to go to Candomblé at night, go ahead. But I don't want it in the house." She went back to cooking. I also turned my back to Dita and ignored her.

Warm days passed one after another. The summer holidays were over, and February was approaching. Madalena and I were out in the yard, the children on the swing, and we were planning the carnival costumes together, when her husband came home from work, beaming. The company he was a partner in was awarded an important project in São Paulo, which would last several years, and they would have to move to the city.

---

9 Umbanda is an offshoot of the Candomblé religion, that was brought from Africa by the slaves and mixed with local Indian customs.

   Most of the worship ceremonies are held at night. A crowd comes to watch the "priests," mediums of sorts who host the "spirits" of gods in their bodies, and receive a blessing. The priests are believers who have undergone long training by the local leader, the Pai de Santo. The ceremony begins with the blessing of the leader, after which the priests dance to the sound of drums to get into the atmosphere. When the priest is "ready" he goes into a trance, receives the god into his body, and the god speaks through him to his believers. To make the god stay in the physical body, they tempt him with worldly pleasures- alcohol and cigars.

Madalena jumped up startled, not sharing her husband's enthusiasm at all.

"What do you mean moving to São Paulo!? I can't leave my mother and sisters here and live so far away!" she protested. Her husband's expression became grave.

"We have no choice," he said, "we have to take the project. We can come to Sorocaba on weekends."

They went inside and their voices became muffled. For a moment I felt I was about to panic, fearing Madalena's trip was ending my chances of continuing with school. The voice inside me said there was no way I would stop attending night school. And then I realized the two were not related at all. I recalled a conversation with Dalzisa during one of the breaks, where she asked me why I didn't look for a better job than housekeeping. At that moment I knew I was definitely capable of finding another job, and that I would stay in Sorocaba.

Within a week the family was ready to move to São Paulo. Madalena asked me if I wanted to join them. I said I was sorry but I wanted to stay and get my diploma.

That weekend, Mrs. Mendes prepared a special farewell lunch. We all sat around the table, eating, laughing and crying. Dona Mendes hugged her grandchildren sadly and I kissed Marcia with a heavy heart. I had raised her since she was four months old and I felt like she was my child in a way too. She was a chubby, cheerful one-and-a-half-year-old baby and it was hard for me to accept the fact that I would no longer be seeing her every day. Manuela escorted me to Madalena's house to help me pack my things and move them to my parents' house.

We arrived in the evening, when Mother was about to leave for work. She told me I could sleep on the couch, because Dita slept on the fold-out bed. I put my bags on the couch and walked Manuela to the bus station. On the way back I ran into Francisco, the son of the neighbors who lived in the house in the backyard. We walked home together. He was a little older than me. When we parted, he said he was going to sleep because he had to get up early the next day to look for work. It turned out that he and his sister were looking for work in the Cajuru industrial area. They wanted to arrive when the factories opened, so it was important that they leave early in the morning.

"The carnival starts in a week and then there is no one to talk to for at least ten days, you know. Everything is closed," he added. I asked if I could come along, and we agreed to meet outside at five in the morning. I got up early in the morning in complete silence, so as not to wake anyone. Dita tossed and turned in the cot and every now and then I heard her chewing gum in her sleep.

While I was boiling water for coffee, I heard Mother coming home. I opened the door for her and helped her with the bags she was carrying. She was surprised to find me awake. I updated her while we put the cooked food from the bags into the fridge. "May God help you find a job quickly," said Mother. "I wish you had a good boss like Senor Max. He himself came to the kitchen to tell my assistant and me we could take whatever was left for our children. He does it a lot. Ever since I started working there, we've lacked no food in this house. Today the restaurant was full! Unbelievable how many rich people come to eat in our churrascaria," she said with pride.

She closed the refrigerator door, took the coffee mug and her bag with her, and sat down on the couch. She set the aluminum mug on the table and rummaged through her bag for a cigarette. I stood by the door for a moment watching as she lit a cigarette, then took a deep puff. Through a thin screen of smoke, I saw my mother, in one of her rare moments of rest, relaxing on the couch with a cup of coffee. After whispering goodbye, I went out into the brightening morning. The neighbor's son and his sister were waiting for me outside.

We started walking, leaving the neighborhood behind, marching into the open fields. The industrial area was still a long way from there. We walked through tall grass and I thought I hadn't trod through the grass like that in years. Basically, ever since we left Jacarezinho.

Jacarezinho! I could see it so clearly—the endless fields with a narrow ridge winding through them, and us following the footsteps of our mother who carried the metal bowls containing our lunch tied to her back. Frightened by a snake's slough, I called Tupi who was leaping around beside us. I was six years old. I remembered my father, emerging from among the tall stalks and waving at us. I felt the taste of the corn he roasted over the fire in my mouth.

We marched for a long time. The sun rose higher in the sky and the heat began to weigh us down. I asked Francisco how much longer it would take to reach the factories and he replied that it would be roughly half an hour. I took a few sips from the water bottle I carried with me, and the cool liquid refreshed me. After walking for three and a half hours we finally arrived at the entrance to the first factory. Francisco pointed to a blackboard that hung to the right of the church gate. The letters written in chalk said:

WANTED: WELDERS - WAREHOUSE WORKER

"This is where they post job openings," Francisco explained to me. "If you find anything that suits you, you should go to the office and apply." I read the writing on the board again and shrugged.

"Wait for me here," he told his sister and me. "These aren't jobs for girls, but I'll go sign up." He disappeared and returned fifteen minutes later. "They also called me for an interview, so it took a long time. They told me to come back after the carnival."

In the second factory we reached, the board was blank. In the third factory they offered jobs as spinning machine operators. We all gave our names to the clerk at the office. She directed the three of us, in turn, to the plant manager in the next room. The manager looked at the forms and asked me where I was completing my studies. After a few minutes of conversation, he said that if I was interested in the job I should come back after the carnival.

We continued checking factory after factory. It was one o'clock in the afternoon by the time I left a second interview. Francisco and his sister were waiting for me in the yard. Groups of young people sat on benches outside—workers eating during their lunch break. They wore white clothes and caps, like nurses in a hospital.

Francisco asked me how the interview had gone. I replied it had gone fine, and that as in previous times, I was told to come back after the holiday. I looked at the white uniforms, wishing I had one like that myself.

We wandered some more, from factory to factory, until we covered all of them, then, slowly, we began to head home. In three of the factories, they told me to come back after the carnival, which filled me with satisfaction. The sun was shining and it was very hot. We stopped from time to time to rest under the shade of trees. I sipped some of the water from the bottle but it was no longer cold. I started to feel the fatigue and my sore feet. By the time we arrived home in the evening, I was limping. When I sat down on the sofa-bed and took off my shoes, I saw the blisters on my feet. Two of them had burst and the open wounds were extremely painful. I passed by my parents' room.

Through the open door I saw Mother's dress on the bed. When I got closer, I saw that mother was inside the dress, lying on her back and fast asleep, holding an extinguished cigarette butt between her fingers. The ash rolled out of it like a long, gray coil. She had dozed off again while smoking, and the cigarette had burned to the end before it went out. I returned to the living room and lay down for a moment to rest on the couch. An annoying fly first buzzed in my ear, and then sat and crawled on my forehead. I opened my eyes to see flies hovering over the dirty dinner plates my brother had left on the kitchen table. There were crumbs scattered on the table and some leftover food had fallen on the floor, which no one had bothered to pick up. I crawled out of bed and cleaned the kitchen floor. I took the dirty dishes outside and washed them in the sink in the yard.

When I returned to the living room, Mother was sitting on the couch.
"Are you back already?" she asked.
I nodded.
"Did you clean the kitchen?"
"Yes, I saw you fell asleep."
With a tiny smile in her eyes, she continued:
"So how was your job search? Did you find anything?"
I told her I had several interviews, that I had filled out forms and that I had been told to come back after carnival. She sighed. "Well, it's great that you know how to read and write."

A few days later carnival arrived. On Friday at noon, the first day of the holiday, I went to the Mendes family's house. I knew Madalena would be visiting and I missed the children very much.

The streets were crowded. Bands of musicians played fast beats everywhere. They were dressed in traditional carnival attire—tight-fitting clothes that flared out from the knees and elbows into colorful ruffles. The midsummer air was hot and humid. A group of children gathered not far from me and I heard them shouting and laughing. Suddenly, two boys turned to me, holding large plastic bottles,[10] and I felt a cold splash. I shouted in surprise and they ran away cheering gleefully. I was dripping wet, but didn't care at all. It was refreshing, pleasant, and I was in a wonderful mood.

When I arrived at Manuela's house I was greeted with joy and enthusiasm. Marcino and Marcia jumped into my arms, and we hugged for a long time. Then I kissed Madalena, Manuela, Mrs. Mendes and the rest of the family, who were already a little mine. I stayed with them until the next day at noon. I joined Madalena, her husband, the children, Manuela and Marta and we went to the events in the main square.

Everything was decorated with lanterns and colorful pennants. We went to one of the clubs, which was holding an event for children. The hall was decked with colorful curled paper snakes and a huge poster of a clown hung on the wall in front of the door. Joy was erupting from all directions—from children celebrating in their costumes, from the streamers in the ceiling, from the music playing from the speakers. We spent almost an hour with the little ones and then informed Madalena that we were moving to the nearby basketball arena, where Manuela and Marta's classmates were. We bought three tickets and entered the hall. The place was packed with young people. There was barely any place to move. Paper ribbons dangled from all sides and small, paper flakes lined the wooden floor, sometimes swirling between the dancers' legs. The musicians on stage wore carnival costumes and shook the walls with their beat and the sounds of the tropical drums.

We too joined in the steps of the dancing crowd filling the venue. I recognized among the musician's an impressive looking young black man whom I had seen the day before playing on the street. He was fit and muscular, and the skin of his arms shone in the spotlight. He wore a red headband around a puffy afro, and small round sunglasses. His beautiful face featured a wide white grin, a feature which made him impossible to ignore. Manuela was also looking him over, shooting glances at him to try and draw his attention.

---

10 During the carnival period, children usually splash water from bottles with punctured caps. When you press the bottle, the stream comes out thin and strong. Plastic bags and balloons filled with water are also thrown at passers-by.

After two hours of raving, the band stopped for a break. The three of us looked for an empty piece of floor and threw ourselves on it, tired and sweaty. Martha and I went to buy drinks. When we came back, we saw the handsome guy smiling at Manuela, getting off the stage and approaching her. Manuela returned her most charming smile to him and he sat down next to her. We approached, handing Manuela the bottle we got for her. She thanked us with a nod while keeping her gaze and her full attention focused on the boy. We did not disturb them. They talked and laughed for a long time. Ultimately, he got up and said with a wink that he hoped to see her again the next day.

Manuela spent the entire evening floating in a cloud of bliss. At eight o'clock the party ended and we left for home. With eyes that sparkled with excitement, Manuela avowed that there was no way she would miss the event the next day. I wasn't sure. I told her I couldn't come with her, because I had to be at home for a bit to help my mother. Manuela insisted: "You have to come with me! Tomorrow is the last day of the carnival! You must come!" She walked me home and pleaded with my mother to let me go with her the next day, and Mother agreed.

The next day we arrived at the arena at four. A restless Manuela made her way through the crowd toward the stage, her eyes searching for her black Apollo. Suddenly she froze, shocked. Near the stage stood the ebony idol with a beautiful girl in his arms. Manuela's mood was ruined in an instant. Her beautiful eyes lost all their luster. She moved to stand on the sideline, looking sad, and refused to dance with us. All evening she looked sullen, barely speaking. We returned to her house almost without exchanging a word.

I hugged and kissed her family goodbye and turned to go home. Manuela stopped me and asked to walk me part of the way. Slowly she began to let it all out. "What was he thinking?" she said angrily. "The nerve! To tell me we'd see each other again and then ignore me completely. Such an idiot. He thinks he can do as he pleases! What do I care about him anyway... But what he did it's still annoying. It's really wrong!" She rambled on and on, with variations on the same theme. I was glad she was talking again. After I had been listening to her in silence for a few minutes she asked:

"Why don't you say anything?"

"I was letting you vent," I replied.

"Say something."

"Well then... I think you were too quick to jump in. You don't even know him. Why would you even create expectations? You spoke with him for a few minutes and you already thought he'd remember you? That's all I have to say ..."

Manuela did not answer. We walked in silence. Her gloom was contagious. After a few moments she said she was going home, I said "goodbye" and that was it.

When I got home, I saw two figures sitting on the low fence in front of my house. I recognized Dita with another girl, a friend of hers. Looking at me she whispered something in her friend's ear, and they both giggled. I looked away from them, opened the gate and went inside. My father was lying on the sofa that served as my bed. He must have heard me, because he turned toward me, muttering something. He tried to sit up but fell back on the sofa, lay down and went to sleep.

Why had I even gone back, I wondered, when I could have stayed at Manuela's house. I didn't belong in that house and I didn't miss anyone. In the children's room they were all asleep, huddled together in one bed, two at the head and two at the feet, without any spare little space left for me. I peeked into my parents' room. Aguinaldo and Reginaldo were sleeping in the wide bed. Mother was at work and I was all alone. I returned to the living room and called my father gently a few times, but he didn't move.

At that moment the front door opened with a bang. Dita stormed in, grabbed her bag from the kitchen and left. I sat down by the table in the living room, not knowing what to do. It was late and I was tired. I put my arms on the table and my head between them, and closed my eyes. I woke up to my mother's angry voice. "Alemão, go to your bed," she shook him. He got up and staggered to the bedroom. Mother went outside, leaving the door open. It was still dark outside. I heard the sound of water running in the sink. She came back inside, wiping her face dry. She looked at me and grumbled:

"Let the carnival be over so we can get back to normal. It's impossible like this, with all the drunkards on the streets. And Dita isn't home yet! Where is that girl?" Meanwhile I took a sheet and a blanket and lay down on the sofa. She sighed. "Well, go to sleep, it's really late."

She turned off the light, and silence descended on the house. I kept turning on the couch, too tired to sleep. I also wanted the carnival to be over so I could find out if I had a job at one of the factories.

Ultimately my eyelids became heavy, and I closed my eyes. I woke up to the wonderful smell of coffee, the kind that only Father knew how to make. He was standing by the table pouring boiling water into a strainer full of coffee. I sat up on the couch and said good morning to him. He answered in his usual tone, as if he hadn't fallen asleep drunk on my couch last night. We sat next to each other, sipping quietly, without speaking. I looked into my cup and he looked out, through the open door, as if searching for something.

"Do you know that today is Ash Wednesday? That people go to church tonight to ask for forgiveness?" he said after a while. "I know. Do you go to church?"

I wanted to help us break the silence, but he didn't answer. He stood up, left the empty mug on the table and walked toward the door. His tall silhouette appeared in the yellow morning light. He left and disappeared.

The atmosphere that day was heavy. Mother was irritated. She spoke little and only occasionally uttered some angry sentences at Father. He, on the other hand, was quiet and collected, as he usually was the day after he got drunk. The day dragged on until the evening. She was just about to go to work when Dita appeared in the doorway.

"Where were you, out so late?" Mother asked her angrily. With a defiant look and a mocking tone she replied: "What do you care? Why are you asking me where I went? Better ask where I didn't go …" She blew a pink bubble which exploded loudly over her lips.

"You're lucky I'm in a rush to get to work," Mother yelled. "I don't have time to have a fight with you! You should know that the neighbors are already talking about you! And not saying good things. Soon everyone will know that you aren't sleeping at home. No one will want to marry you. I'm warning you."

Ignoring her words, Dita entered the kitchen and put a kettle on the stove. Mother took her bag and left. I sat down next to Father and stared at the TV, watching cowboys riding across the American prairies inside the screen.

Francisco's sister, our neighbor, appeared at the open door. During the day the doors in all our homes were open, and friends and neighbors popped in without an invitation. They were only locked at night, when we went to bed. She was on her way to Dona Maria, and asked if I wanted to go with her. At that particular moment I was willing to go anywhere with her, yet I asked who Dona Maria was. She explained to me that she was Pedro's mother.

"Who is Pedro? I don't know Pedro," I said.

"What does it matter to you?" she answered, "Are you coming?"

We walked together to the end of the street. Francisco's sister entered through one of the open doors and I followed her.

"Hello there," Dona Maria greeted us cheerfully. "Who is your new friend?" Francisco's sister introduced me:

"This is Catarina Granater, Dita's younger sister."

"Welcome, Catarina... Come right in. Meet my kids," Dona Maria exclaimed with a smile. She examined me and then noted with satisfaction, "You don't look alike, you and Dita."

The house was full of boys and girls of all ages. Many of them were family members, and the rest were friends. They introduced themselves and I tried to remember who was who, though it was pretty confusing. We stayed at Dona Maria's for about two hours. On the way back home, I asked Francisco's sister if she wanted to come with me the next day to the factories in the industrial area, to check if we'd been hired anywhere. She replied that she had not yet decided if she would go that morning.

"I'm going out there early anyway," I told her. "Let me know if you decide to come."

I returned to a quiet house, chose the clothes I would wear the next day and ironed them swiftly, because I wanted to have time to sleep and look fresh when I presented myself as a job candidate. I woke up early, to the sound of rustling bags. In the darkness I saw only my mother's face, illuminated by the light of the small refrigerator bulb. She was putting away the leftover food from the churrascaria.

"What time is it?" I asked her, rising from the couch.

"I don't know exactly. Around half past four, I think," she replied.

I turned to go outside to the sink so I could wash my face.

"Why are you up so early?"

"I'm going to the industrial zone. I want to get there early to see if any factory is going to hire me."

Mother straightened up and looked at me for a moment. She took her bag from the table and pulled out a small bundle wrapped in a handkerchief. After untying the knot, she picked out a few Cruzeiros and handed them to me. "Here's the bus fare," she said, "so that you don't have to leave so early. Go back to sleep." She turned to the refrigerator and went back to stacking up food containers.

Good Days

I left home when the sun was already shining. I spent the bus ride deliberating with which factory to start my round. My heart was drawn to *Ardon Plast*, the one where employees wore the white uniforms and hats, so I chose to go there first. The yard outside the plant was empty and quiet. The guard emerged from the small wooden booth by the gate and asked what I was looking for. I said I needed to get to the office. After examining me briefly, he opened the gate for me. Through glass windows I saw the production floor. Dozens of employees in white, like scientists in a laboratory, worked quietly and with concentration. I rushed to the office and addressed the secretary who was sitting behind a desk looking through papers. She raised her head and looked at me questioningly. I explained that I was expecting an answer regarding my job application.

"Why did you come today?" she said with surprise, "Not many workers showed up today. I'm not sure there is an answer for you yet. Wait a minute, I'll check." The secretary went to the room next door and reappeared a few minutes later, instructing me to enter. Behind the desk in the office sat a middle-aged man reading the forms I had filled out before the carnival. He motioned for me to sit in the chair in front of him and turned to me.

"I see you haven't had any experience in a regular job before. The work here is not easy, it's based on production quotas, and sometimes there is a lot of pressure. I'm not sure you can handle that."

A flush of resentment flooded my face. I really wanted the job and I felt it slipping away from me. "It's true that I don't have experience," I said with passion, "but I can withstand pressure. I'm used to working hard and I really, really need this job."

I looked straight into his eyes, necessity forcing me out of my natural timidity. Looking at me he hesitated for a moment, and finally made his decision: "Okay. You're lucky you came today. You're the first candidate to apply for the job. I'll put you on a ninety-day trial period. You have until the end of the week to arrange the documents required for the employee registry. Next Monday you will be here at seven ready to start work. The secretary will explain to you what you need to bring as well as the route of our employee shuttle bus."

After thanking him profusely, from the bottom of my heart, I returned to the secretary's room. When I left the factory, the world seemed more beautiful to me. The sky was very blue and the birds were singing. It was a wonderful morning. I got off the bus on the street where I lived and bumped into Dona Maria walking home.

"Hello Catarina. You look happy..." she said, smiling at me.

"I found a job in a factory!" I said, "In Ardon Plast."

"Well done. Good luck! Come to our place tonight. There will be many young people. You deserve to celebrate today!"

As I neared my house, Dita was just heading out and passed me by without even glancing at me. Mother shouted after her, looking more furious than ever. Upon seeing me, she burst out: "Why did you have to leave Madalena! Now you have no job and all the load is on my shoulders! The best was when you worked for Claudia. Your salary came straight to me every month and it was easier for me to cope! How long can we go on like this... Everything always falls on me!"

"Next month you will get my salary," I retorted. "I got hired and I start next Monday."

Mother calmed down. She may not have seemed happy, but at least she stopped yelling. In the evening I took out clean clothes and ironed them properly to go to Dona Maria. My spirits were still high. Mother couldn't ruin this for me.

I walked through the open door and Dona Maria welcomed me cordially, as she did last time, as she welcomed everyone. She announced that I had been hired at a factory named Ardon Plast.

Her older son, Pedro, said he had heard about it—a new company that manufactured hospital supplies. I wanted to find out if he knew more details, but at that moment his friends arrived and he turned to receive them. I heard their greetings:

"Hello"

"Hi"

"What's up? No studying today?"

I glanced toward the entrance, to check out the new arrivals. Two boys entered the house. At first, I didn't recognize them, but a second later my gaze met a pair of blue eyes I had never forgotten. Those were the eyes that looked at me from the pulpit in the church, at the end of the Sunday mass. I was breathless. My eyes shifted to the other boy. He was the boy with the brown skin who had been standing next to the angel with the blond curls back then too. The altar boys who helped out the day I was sent to the bread line, materialized that evening. They had grown up but hadn't changed too much. My eyes wandered back to the angel, who was still staring at me, searing my heart like a blazing cattle-branding rod. The room and its occupants were no longer there. Only he and his blue gaze existed for me.

Pedro's voice brought me back to reality.

"Do you know each other?" he asked.

"No," the angelic assistant to the priest immediately replied. Our host introduced us:

"Catarina. Rafael."

I knew he remembered me as well as I remembered him. I knew he wasn't telling the truth, so as not to raise unnecessary questions, and I felt grateful. Rafael shook my hand and said that he was very pleased to make my acquaintance. That evening we didn't talk anymore. I felt his gaze resting on me often, but he only spoke with his friends and did not approach me.

As I walked back home the air felt cool on my face, which made me realize my skin was hot. The whole way I replayed in my head the wonderful encounter Rafael and I had shared that evening. He was so beautiful to me, like a Greek god. He had grown taller and his shoulders wider. His curls were darker but the eyes remained the same. Had he guessed what I felt when we met? How did he feel about me? Did he know how much he meant to me back then? That he was a piece of blue sky within all the humiliation of the bread line?

That night, in my bed, Rafael's face floated in front of my closed eyelids. I woke up early, hoping to have time to have my picture taken and make it to the Ministry of the Interior as soon as it opened, and save the bus fare at least. Among the boring procedures and red tape requirements, a joy named Rafael was hovering in the air for me. I managed to obtain all the necessary documents for the employee registry and returned home by sunset. In the evening I went outside and stood by the gate for a long time, looking down the street, in the direction of Dona Maria's house, hoping I might see him pass by on his way to them. When my legs got tired from standing, I went home but found no rest. I sat down in front of the TV, next to Father, and tried to relax.

"I heard you went to arrange the documents you need to start working," Father said suddenly.

"That's right," I replied.

"And how will you get to work every morning? It's a long way to go," he continued. I explained that there was a shuttle. We then fell silent until he got up and headed for the bedroom. I remained seated on the couch, knowing I wouldn't be able to fall asleep easily that night either.

The next day I tried to pass the time again. All day I had a lump in my chest. I wasn't hungry and my temples throbbed. I helped my mother with the housework and then went to visit Manuela. She was back to being jubilant and had completely forgotten the handsome mulatto from the carnival festivities. We exchanged news. She told me a lot while I said very little. I kept the encounter with Rafael to myself—I didn't want to share it with anyone yet. On my way back, as I passed Dona Maria's house I peeked in through the open door, but all was quiet. There was no one inside.

My first day at work arrived at last. I handed over the documents at the office. The secretary directed me to the foreman, a pleasant man in his sixties, and instructed me to return to her during the break. The foreman took me to a large wooden table in the center of the room on top of which were several large bundles of thin plastic tubes.

He took a package of tubes to a nearby wooden table. "This is your table," he explained. "Take this knife and saw off all the tubes in the pack here, in two, right through the middle, where the marking is."

He grabbed a large, sharp knife and pressed it hard against the plastic stems. Leaning against it he began sawing until the blade sliced through the tube. "You have to do it at an angle, like this," he continued to explain, "so that it's easier to insert the tube into the piece that connects it to the IV bag."

He moved the two resulting bundles over to another wooden table and instructed me to try it myself. Each pack had fifty tubes. I had to lean with all my weight on the knife for it to penetrate the plastic. I began working through the whole pack with some effort. It took me a while to cut all the tubes. It was hard physical work, and my forehead was damp.

The foreman looked critically at the two resulting heaps. "You need to be more precise with the sawing angle, but it's not bad for the first time," he said and left me alone.

I picked another pack and worked on it for a long time. The other girls in the department managed to finish a few packs before I was able to place the halved bundle on the corresponding table. When I tried to take a new pile, I saw that the table was empty. The other girls had set some packs aside for themselves, leaving no work for me to do. They ignored me blatantly, making me feel lonely and ostracized. I had to lie in ambush when the next batch was delivered so I could grab a few bundles to keep me busy.

During the lunch break I went to the office again. The secretary handed me my new employee registration booklet and wished me good luck. She asked me how it had gone so far and I answered unenthusiastically that it had gone okay. She nodded understandingly and told me that was how it was with new employees. The veterans feared they would lose their jobs because the young earned less and sometimes produced more. They didn't always receive the new hires well, but I had to be patient and polite, and in the end it would all work out.

At the end of the working day, I boarded the shuttle bus and took an aisle seat. I thought about the secretary's words, knowing she was right. Already at the line for lunch, the girl standing next to me started talking to me. She was also relatively new and had only worked for three months in the same department I was assigned to.

I opened my bag and drew out my new employee booklet. I got acquainted with it, page by page. The first one contained the details of the fund to which my pension payments would be transferred. This was the first time I had social benefits and was properly registered in some official institution. I felt that I belonged to a large group called *workers* that would stand behind me like a supporting wall. On the second page my hourly salary was recorded. I remember it was 2.24 Cruzeiros, the minimum wage at the time, and still much higher than what I got working in housekeeping.

I arrived home around seven in the evening. Mother was already at the door, on her way to work.

"You finally arrived!" she said. "Why so late? Is it going to be like this every day?"

I took a quick shower, grabbed my books and notebooks and raced to night school. It was the first day after the carnival holiday. During the break I approached my teacher and told her happily that I had been hired to work at a factory, as per her advice. Dalzisa was interested in exactly what kind of job I had been assigned and where. Her eyes showed she was proud of me and I was overjoyed. When classes were over, I collected my things, left the classroom, crossed the front door of the school and started down the stairs leading to the street.

Suddenly, as in my dreams, I saw Rafael standing on the first step. I didn't know what to do or what to say, so I continued to descend slowly, my face burning with currents of heat. When I reached the first step and stopped, the whole world stopped with me. We looked at each other and the silence lasted what seemed like an eternity, until Rafael spoke: "I'm sorry if I surprised you. I was hoping for an opportunity to meet you but it didn't turn up."

"How did you know I was going to school here?" I stammered. "Dona Maria talked about you after you left. She said you studied in the evenings, and I was listening." I nodded awkwardly, unable to find anything to say. I knew he was just as nervous, and I was striving to find something to say. My thoughts floated like clouds in my head and I couldn't collect them.

"How was your first day at work?" He came to the rescue.

We started to walk in the direction of my house. I told him I liked the workplace but was worried that I might not be able to pass the three-month trial. He reassured me, saying he was confident I would be hired and that I had nothing to worry about. Then he told me about his job.

He had started to work the year before at a relative's workshop that made plaster ceiling decorations. He worked in the mornings and attended college in the evenings.[11] He asked me if I knew what decorative plaster was. I told him I did, remembering Claudia's house.

The guest room had a sculpted strip around the ceiling, elegantly joining it to the walls. The other rooms also had similar but more modest strips. I examined their forms sometimes, but had never stopped to think about what they were made of. We reached my street and were close to my house. I stopped and said that I would prefer that he not walk me home because my parents would not approve of me walking down the street with a strange man. I was afraid Dita would see us and tell Mother, adding all sorts of distortions and mean embellishments.

"Okay," he said, paused for a moment, then continued, "Catarina. Can I wait for you sometimes after school?"

"Yes," I said.

"Tomorrow I cannot come, but I will some other time," he said. He looked at me warmly and added, "You haven't changed much. I was very happy to see you again."

"I'm happy too," I answered, feeling myself blush.

"Good night," he said.

"Good night," I replied, and we remained standing across from each other.

Finally, I took a small step back and said good night again.

He smiled, and started walking away. I turned toward my house, but after two steps I looked back and saw him looking at me. I waved goodbye to him and he waved back. We both laughed awkwardly, then we both turned around and kept walking. I levitated home. My feet barely touched the pavement.

The house looked quiet and dark. The door was unlocked but when I pushed it open, I met resistance with a chair that was blocking it from the inside. I did my best to push slowly and avoid making noise or waking anyone. I made my way in the dark to the table in the middle of the room. I reached for the switch attached to a cable dangling from the ceiling, and clicked on the light.

---

11   In colleges and universities of Brazil it used to be customary to allow evening studies so that the students could work during the day.

Dita was on the folding bed. As I started to make my bed on the sofa, I heard a gum bubble pop. Dita was staring at me with wide open eyes and pink gum smeared around her lips. She slowly peeled it off her cheek and put it back in her mouth. "I heard you started working," she said while she chewed. "You won't last long there."

I turned off the light and went to bed. I closed my eyes and saw Rafael before me. I tried to fall asleep but couldn't. I lay awake in the dark, going over all the little we said and all the things we didn't.

The next few days were very busy. I got up early to catch the shuttle bus. At work I did my best to learn and do what was required of me without mistakes. I really wanted to prove to myself and to the manager who hired me on trial that I could do it.

At five we finished work and left to wait for the shuttle back. The bus drove slowly, circling through endless stops. Sometimes I got home so late that I couldn't get to school on time. I would wash my face, grab the books and run to school. During the breaks, Dalzisa helped me make up what I missed. The pace was crazy. I barely had any time to eat. I would leave exhausted after class, impatient to get into bed and close my eyes.

And yet, amidst this dense fatigue, I felt a small pang of disappointment every time I saw the bottom step was empty and no one was waiting for me there. In every free moment I had, my thoughts focused on Rafael. One night, on the way home, I ran into him. He was walking down the street, not far from Dona Maria's house, with his usual friend. When he saw me, he left him waiting and crossed the road to greet me.

"Catarina, I'm sorry I haven't been in touch with you this week," he began, "I've been busy and had a lot of exams these past few days."

"It's fine," I answered immediately, "I've been very busy myself…" And I thought how wonderful it was that he was more beautiful than in my dreams, and that I must be important to him if he felt the need to explain.

"I really want to see you on Saturday," he said. "Are you free?"

"Yes," I said.

"Can I come pick you up at half past seven?"

"Rafael," I said hesitantly, "my parents won't let me go out with someone they don't know."

"No problem, I'll talk to them when I get there. I will ask them for permission to meet with you," he said simply.

I asked him to be there by seven, before my mother left for work, so he could meet her. He stretched his arms out and placed his hands around mine.

"Okay, I'll be on time. Good night. Don't worry. I'll talk to your parents," he said, and I stopped worrying.

The next day I woke up before five. Father made coffee and Mother was getting ready to go to bed. I got up and poured from the hot kettle for all of us.

"I wanted to talk to you both before Mother goes to bed, so I got up earlier," I said. My parents looked at me in silence. "On Saturday evening, Rafael will come to ask you for permission to meet with me," I said quietly, trying not to show how excited I was. Mother looked surprised.

"Who is Rafael?" she asked in a harsh tone. "Are you dating boys? Soon you will come home to me with a big belly!" Her mouth twisted in displeasure. "How did you meet this guy?"

How could she turn something so beautiful like my relationship with Rafael into something cheap and despicable! I heard myself screaming inside. I answered with restraint that I had met him at Dona Maria's and that he wanted to come talk to her. "What do I have to talk to him about?" she spat out at me. I got up, said I had to get ready for work so as not to be late, and went to the sink outside to wash my face.

I never managed to understand what I had to do to make my mother happy. She treated me with disdain, and judged me unfairly. She had fixed ideas in her mind and did not consider the facts at all. Everything I did seemed wrong in her eyes. She actually didn't see me at all, didn't know me. I was a stranger in this family. I didn't have a family. I was alone in the world, and luckily, heaven had sent me Rafael. As long as Mother didn't spoil it for me.

I waited impatiently for Saturday to arrive, yet the week went by quickly—it was so busy. On Saturday I got up very early in order to finish my chores and prepare for the event that was going to take place at seven in the evening. I washed the clothes that had accumulated from the whole week. I dusted earnestly, put the furniture up so I could sweep the rooms, poured a bucket of water on the floor and scrubbed until it shone. I continued to the outhouse in the backyard. From there I moved on to watering the vegetable bed in front of the house.

Dad was proud of his little garden, which included a flower bed and two fruit trees, a lemon and a papaya. I looked up and discovered three papayas hanging on the high branches. I also splashed water on the small patch of ground between the gate and the front door, to eliminate the dust, and went over it with a broom of twigs to smooth it out. It was already after two, and I was satisfied with how the day was progressing.

I was willing to clean a few more houses just so that time would go by faster and evening would come. After quickly eating some of the food Mother made for lunch, I collected the dirty dishes and washed them in the yard. When I came back, I saw she had dozed off on the couch. She was fast asleep and I was debating whether to wake her up so she would go to her bed. In the end I decided in favor. I wanted the house to look tidy. She got up with her eyes almost closed and walked sleepily to her room. I spread a blanket on the table, and a sheet on top of it. I turned on the iron and took the dry clothes off the line.

While I was ironing, I thought about what I could wear for Rafael. I remembered a white denim dress that Manuela had given me, and it seemed appropriate. Since I had met the Mendes girls, my life had changed. I had a wardrobe to choose from. When would I meet Manuela and finally tell her what was going on in my life? My thoughts were interrupted when I saw my father standing by the doorway, dressed in clean, freshly ironed clothes.

"Are you leaving?" I asked with concern.

"Yes," he answered curtly.

"But Father! Rafael is coming this evening," I protested.

"I'll be back in time," he said and disappeared.

I wonder in what condition he'll return, I thought bitterly. After hanging the ironed clothes in the closet, I returned the iron and the table covers to their place. I looked at the gleaming house with satisfaction. It had the peaceful aura of a Saturday.

All members of the family were away (except for mother who was fast asleep), and everything was in order. I loved the house during those hours. I didn't care that it was humble and austere. When it was clean and tidy it looked almost festive. On weekdays it was upside down and messy, like my family's life.

Mother woke up around five, went straight to the coffee pot and poured herself a cup. She sat down, lit a cigarette and asked me where everyone was. I replied that I didn't know and continued to roll my hair in buns. She took a sip of her coffee and asked again: "Where's your Father?" I replied that he was out. "As if his drinking were not enough, he also started playing cards every Saturday…" she said angrily.

Father came back at half past six, staggering and smelling of alcohol. I was already dressed and groomed, checking the mirror every minute, arranging a curl or a tuft, reapplying the light red lipstick Manuela had given me. Mother looked at Father in despair and said: "I told you not to drink today! You know the girl is waiting for a boy! You should be ashamed of yourself. I have to leave soon…"

Father grumbled in protest: "Then go. What do you want from me? I'm not drunk. Leave me be."

"Someone's calling Catarina at the gate!" Nicolao announced standing by the door.

All week I had been waiting for this moment, and here it was. I'd been preparing for it all day and now, when it was really happening, I didn't know what to do. A Father sitting drunk on the couch was not at all the setting I had planned. I looked at my mother helplessly. "Wait with Rafael outside," she commanded, "I'll be right out to meet him."

I rushed out with great relief. My voice was almost steady as I greeted him. He looked into my eyes and smiled. I felt my legs melting. He kept looking at me, as if waiting for something. "My mother asks that you wait for her. She's coming out to talk to you." He nodded and came closer to me. He cupped my face in his palms and held it as if it were a precious and fragile object that he was afraid to drop.

"Is everything fine?" he asked quietly. The warmth of his hands on my face climbed up to the roots of my hair and crept down my spine. I looked at him against the backdrop of the falling evening, thinking that must be love. That was exactly what love looked like.

Suddenly we heard my mother's footsteps approaching. He let go of my face and moved away from me a little. Mother came up to us and said hello. I made very polite introductions. She said she didn't have much time because she was in a hurry to get to work. I noticed she fell ill at ease, not knowing exactly what to say.

Rafael made the first move and said casually: "Dona Teresa, I want to ask for your permission to meet with Catarina."

Mother replied that she had no objection, but that she did not want us to meet on the street, in all kinds of corners, and for people to see us and talk. She wasn't going to tolerate hearing gossip from the neighbors. And we should not be back late. Rafael said in a calm voice that she had nothing to worry about, that he would take good care of me. Mother hurried to say goodbye to us. I said: "A sua abença mãe."

Rafael wished her a good night and a pleasant time at work. Mother left, and we were finally alone. We walked together to the stop to catch the bus that would take us to the city center. We talked the whole way. He told me about himself, about his family. I felt he was so close to me that I could tell him everything. I talked about Jacarezinho, about our escape and the first years in Sorocaba, when we first saw each other in the church. I told him about the difficult days and even about Claudia. I was even able to admit to him that I didn't invite him in because my father came back drunk. I knew I had never been as happy as I was at that moment.

The words gently peeled away, layer by layer, the little strangeness that was still left between us. We sat in the square and ate ice cream in a cup, like a real couple. We returned home at about ten at night. The street was deserted and the house was dark. We sat down on the fence next to the gate, held hands and said nothing. The silence was dense and I found it a little hard to breathe. Gently, he put his arm around me. After a moment of dizziness, I relaxed and rested my head on his shoulder. We remained in our embrace for a long time without saying a word. I don't remember who got up first, but when we stood facing each other, he wrapped his other arm around me as well and hugged me tightly. I hugged him back. I raised my head to him and looked at him. He again wrapped my face in his warm hands. He brought his lips closer to mine and kissed me on the mouth.

We stayed close in the kiss for a long time. I heard his breathing as if they were coming from me. My body was shaking, and so was his. When our lips drew apart, we hugged for a moment longer. We let go slowly and he spoke to me. His voice was hoarse.

"I want to see you tomorrow. Is it okay if I come at three?" I nodded. "I will wait until you are inside," he added.

"Good night," I said, smiling at him.

I reached the front door and pushed it slowly, to prevent the chair blocking the door from making noise. I looked back one last time to see him standing by the gate. I waved goodbye to him, went inside and closed the door. I stood in the dark, still feeling his lips on mine. The taste of it was in my mouth and I didn't want it to go away. The room was empty. Dita wasn't home yet. I spread the sheet on the couch and undressed slowly. His scent stuck to my clothes. In bed I replayed our kiss over and over again. It had been nothing like that pathetic kiss back then, in the movie theater. Tonight's was my first real kiss, a kiss of love.

The days that followed were wonderful. I saw Rafael on Sunday at noon, and when Monday came, I went to work happily, because nothing seemed hard to me now. I arrived at the factory, entered the locker room and put on work clothes—white pants, a white coat and a matching hat. I felt at peace.

I found myself talking easily with the girls from my department, and already during the lunch break I made friends with several of them. We took our trays outside and sat down to eat on a bench. On the other side of the fence, fruit trees grew and beyond them stretched green fields. We were surrounded by space, sky, and clean air. At the end of the work day, while we were waiting for the bus, I had some free time to roam in the yard, and sometimes I would go to the fence and pick a mango or two for the road from one of the trees beyond it.

A month passed, and I received my first salary. At the end of the last day of the month, I stood in line with everyone in front of the office, until my name was called. I entered the room where the secretary and the accountant were sitting and they handed me a pay slip and an envelope with the money in it. I held the envelope tight until I got on the bus. Once seated, I opened it carefully and counted the bills that were in it. I had never received that much money at once. I put the bills back in the envelope, the envelope in the bag, the bag pressed to my chest and I felt rich. I thought that maybe on Saturday I would go to town to look for fabric to make me a new dress. I had never had a dress I liked sewn before, and now that I had money, I had earned myself, I believed I was allowed to do so. A series of dresses in different shapes, paraded through my mind, and I was debating which pattern to choose.

In the meantime, the bus arrived at the station closest to my house. I got off. Mother approached and walked toward me, on her way to work. She was surprised to see me arrive so late and I explained to her that the distribution of salaries took a long time. I handed her the envelope with the money and ran home in time to get my books. As I rushed to school in long strides it occurred to me that I shouldn't have given Mother my entire salary, but rather should have kept some for myself, for the dress.

Now I would have to ask her, in hopes she would agree to give me some. We met at home the next morning, as usual, while I was getting dressed to go out and she was coming back from a long night shift.

"Your salary is better than what you got at Madalena's," she said with satisfaction.

She seemed pleased, which gave me the courage to ask if I could have some money. She asked what I needed it for, and I explained that I wanted to buy fabric for a dress and pay the seamstress.

Mother opened her bag, took out the envelope and opened it slowly. "You know you were not working for a long time, and I gave you money, once for the bus fare and once for the photos and papers you needed to get the employee registration card," she said and continued, "I have to buy some things for the house."

"Mother, I'm not asking for much," I insisted. "I will buy cheap fabric." She pulled out a few bills and handed them to me. "Take good care of this money," she warned me.

I thanked her and left immediately. While on the bus I made calculations in my head, realizing I'd have to find an economical cut, because I wouldn't be able to buy a whole lot of fabric.

I'd have to flip through magazines and catalogs and look for something beautiful.

On Saturday I arrived in the city early, even before the shops opened to the public. In the inner courtyards, where the warehouses were located, the shopkeepers carried rolls of cloth for display through the back doors. I walked back and forth along the sidewalks, trying to catch a glimpse of the rolled fabrics and see if any of them would do.

It was opening time, at last. The rolls of fabric that were on sale or clearance were placed in front of the store facing the square. I was trying to find red fabric among them, which would be great for the jumper dress I dreamed of sewing. They were all too expensive for my budget. I moved to the next store and the one after that. I went through almost all the stores in the area and was about to lose hope, when suddenly I saw a fabric in a color similar to the one I wanted. I checked the price, and it was reasonable.

I asked the salesperson how much fabric he thought I needed to sew a jumper. He measured me with his eyes and said that the color would be very flattering. He measured one and a half meters, folded the cloth he had cut and handed it to me. I thanked him, feeling happy, and continued to an accessory store where I bought a buckle for the belt and a hair pin. I was trying to imagine what Rafael would say when he saw my new look. I had enough money left to have the dress sewn and even for the bus ride.

I showed the seamstress a crumpled page I had found in a fashion magazine. The model in the picture was wearing a red jumper, exactly what I asked her to sew for me. She said it would be ready that coming Friday, and that I would have to come in for a fitting once before then.

At last, I put the finished dress on a hanger, over the string that was stretched across for this purpose in the children's room, in a prominent spot so I could admire it when I was home. Mother was about to leave for work just as I was getting dressed to meet Rafael. She looked at me and seemed pleased. "Is that the dress you had made? Good seamstress," she determined.

Soon I heard clapping at the gate. Rafael was leaning on the wooden fence, waiting for me to come out. I appeared in the doorway in full glory and felt his blue gaze looking me over.

"Wow, meu Deus do céu, que bonita!"[12] he said. He walked up to me, closing me in. "New dress? Lovely! When did you buy it?"

"Rafael, you're embarrassing me," I mumbled, feeling my cheeks becoming the color of the jumper.

Time went by. I finished the trial period at the factory and was hired as a full-fledged employee. Rafael and I were officially a couple. We got together every weekend and went downtown, to the zoo or to meet friends at one of the houses. He never took me to his place but some-

---

12 Meu Deus do céu, que bonita - God in heaven, how beautiful.

times we visited his aunt, who had a daughter my age. Marta was a kind, outgoing girl, and usually there were other friends at her place. Someone would play a record and we would dance, or just sit and listen. It was a wonderful year.

But Dita, consumed by jealousy, was quick to make up lies. "A friend said she saw Catarina and Rafael on a bench in a dark garden. When they saw her in the distance they ran away, Catarina buttoning up her shirt quickly while she ran. That's what she said," Dita proclaimed on Saturday night, before Mother left for work.

Mother's face turned reddish-brown and she screamed at me: "Catarina, I'm going to kill you. You won't see that boy again if you act like that!"

"But Mother, it's not true!" I protested, "Dita is just making that up."

"Dio de céu! These girls will bury me. Tomorrow morning, young lady, we will talk," she warned me. "You know I have to go now, but it's not over yet. We'll have a talk tomorrow." I looked at her helplessly, having nothing to add in my defense.

On another occasion, Dita said she heard some neighbors whispering that I must have already slept with Rafael and eventually would have a baby in my belly, bringing great shame upon the family. I protested vehemently that it wasn't true and that Rafael respected me and acted impeccably, but Mother just looked at me with skepticism, and I felt her lack of trust piercing me.

A year and a half had elapsed since I began to study, and the course was about to end. We had to pass the final exams in order to get a diploma. I had a very difficult few weeks, studying at every free moment: during the lunch break at work, on the bus and at home, after work. The most productive hours were at night, when all members of my family were fast asleep and the house was quiet, the only time I could concentrate. The next day, however, I could hardly drag myself off the couch having so few hours of sleep left. In the last week before the finals, I didn't even meet with Rafael on Saturday and Sunday.

I took exams every evening. When I went to take the last one, I looked around me in the classroom. These people, who were diligently solving math equations, had been a part of my life for a year and a half, and when this test was over, we would part ways forever. I looked at Dalzisa, our teacher, walking between the desks to make sure everything was clear to everyone. How would I say goodbye to her forever? I would miss her. But I had to banish those thoughts, I told myself. Concentrate, Catarina, concentrate, you've got to make it.

I started reading the questions written on the page. Time was running out fast. I barely managed to finish the last question when Dalzisa asked us to hand the pages over to her. "In exactly one week we will meet here and you will receive the results, and of course a diploma will be granted to those who earn it," she announced with a pleasant smile.

The end of the month fell on a Friday. When the work shift was over, we were asked to gather in front of the secretary's office. When she appeared, she said how terribly sorry she was to announce that the money had not arrived from the bank and we would only be paid on Monday. Dejected, we all got on the shuttle bus. Someone said he had heard that the company's situation wasn't good, which was worrisome. I wondered what would happen to me if there were cuts. The newest ones were usually the first to be laid off.

I would have to wander again between the factories looking for work. When I got home, my mother asked me where the salary was. I replied that we would receive money only on Monday. "I was counting on your salary!" she cried. "There's nothing here. I wanted to buy groceries. What will I do now!? I'll have to ask for an advance at work again."

I said nothing. I didn't mention our concerns about the factory being in trouble. I had no strength left to hear her complaints and I didn't want to add to her load, which she insisted on sharing with me.

On Saturday I woke up early, out of habit. Mother asked if I could go shopping with her. She probably got the advance. We walked through the awakening streets toward the market.

"When do you get your diploma?" she asked. I replied that they were expected next Wednesday and we continued to walk in silence.

"I think you will get married before Dita," she said suddenly, "Rafael seems like a good guy to me. He is studying too." After a moment of silence she asked, "Have you already met his mother?" I said that I hadn't yet. She thought for a short while and said, "You're studying too. You work and study."

I looked at her and saw pride in her tired eyes. My mother had shown interest in my and Rafael's studies! On the way back, as we were carrying the full baskets, I said to her: "You know you can learn too. At night school there is a class for older people, your age. One can learn at any age."

She smiled shyly and said quietly, "I would love to know how to write my name. Whenever I have to sign a paper, they smear my finger with ink and I leave a fingerprint."

"Learning to write your name is not a problem," I said, "anyone can teach you."

"Never mind," she sighed, "I can't grasp anything anymore. And if they find out about it at home, they'll laugh at me."

We put the groceries away in the refrigerator together. She retired to sleep and I cleaned the house.

Rafael arrived in the early evening, after two weeks of not seeing each other. I ran into his arms and we kissed. In his embrace, when he whispered to me how much he missed me and how much he loved me, I thought no one in the world was happier than me. He asked me how the tests had gone and what happened since we had last met. I told him and then asked him how he was. A shadow crossed his eyes and he said he had had a hard time, but did not elaborate. I wanted to ask more, but I let it go.

Less Good Days

The atmosphere at work became tense. We didn't know if we would get paid or if we would still be employed the week after. On Monday at four in the afternoon they called us to the office. We received our money and could breathe again. The week went by quickly, and on Wednesday I arrived at school to receive the test results.

Dalzisa was cheerful and smiling. From her look I gathered I had passed the exams and was graduating. When it was my turn, she handed me the diploma and hugged me. She wished me good luck in my future endeavors. I thanked her, thinking I managed to pass to a great extent thanks to her. She made me believe that I could achieve any goal I set my eyes on. I left school with a diploma, but had no one with whom to share my joy.

Rafael did not show up and my mother was at work. As I passed by Dona Maria's house, I saw that the lights were on and heard voices coming from inside. I walked in with a huge smile and announced that I had just got my diploma.

Dona Maria wished me good luck and all the best and asked where Rafael was.

"I told you he wouldn't come," said Pedro, her son, suddenly, "his mother won't let him."

"What do you mean his mother won't let him?" I felt scared. "What's wrong?"

Dona Maria's face clouded and she shouted: "Pedro, why did you have to open your big mouth? Why do you interfere?"

But I insisted, "Pedro, what do you mean? If you know something, speak up. You can't hide things from me."

And he did. Rafael's mother wanted him to marry a rich girl, and after finishing college she intended to send him to study at a university in the big city. I felt that someone had snatched my heart and was wringing it hard, like a rag used to mop a floor. I ran home and threw my diploma on the table. It no longer seemed so important to me.

I put the sheets on the sofa, covered myself with a blanket up to my neck and covered my face with a pillow. I wasn't good enough for Rafael's mother. She wanted to keep us apart. If our love ended now, what would I do with myself?

In the morning I got up with puffy eyes and went to work. At ten they summoned the workers to an emergency meeting in the dining room. The production manager opened his speech with the news that the situation was not good. The factory was in financial distress and the quality of the production was far from satisfactory. A few days earlier an entire shipment was returned due to poor quality.

He made an appeal for the workers to pay attention to the quality of the work, and added that in order to produce the returned goods again, everyone would have to put in extra hours at their own expense, because the factory had no funds to pay them. The management would try to avoid firing employees, despite the difficulties.

In the evening I sat down in front of the TV, so as not to think. Suddenly I heard Raphael calling my name from outside. I went out to him, surprised. He was standing by the gate. He apologized for not having come to the school the night before to celebrate with me.

"It's fine, I understand you've been busy," I answered calmly and walked through the gate toward him. He stood close and looked at me. "I know you've been told all kinds of stories," he said.

"What stories? It's true, isn't it?" I interjected. "Why didn't you tell me that your mother does not approve of our relationship? Must I hear that from other people?" He wrapped his arms around me and held me close.

"I'm sorry," he said quietly. He hugged me tightly and spoke close to me. "Listen carefully. No one will keep us apart. I love you. I'll handle my mother."

"But Rafael," I murmured from his chest, "she wants you to marry someone else."

"It won't happen," he said firmly, pressing me against his body. We kissed like we had the very first time. I felt that in his arms I was safe, that nothing bad could happen to me. I loved him so much.

Valentine's Day was approaching. I had been saving the allowance my mother gave me for a long time, so I could get a nice gift for Rafael. I went to town and walked around the shops. After considering the matter for a long time, I decided to buy him a shirt. I saw dozens of them and in the end chose a white dress shirt, with thin light blue stripes, like his eyes. Valentine's Day fell in the middle of the week. Rafael came to see me in the evening only for a little while, because he had to go back to school. We exchanged gifts, and I received from him a record with French songs. When he opened the package I handed him, he said with admiration that the shirt was very beautiful.

On Saturday we met as usual. A smiling Rafael was wearing the shirt I bought him.

"It really suits you, Rafael," I said, thinking he looked wonderful.

He asked if I had listened to the record and I told him that of course, every day, and the most beautiful song, *Je T'aime... Moi Non Plus*[13] I heard maybe a hundred times.

---

13 Je T'aime... Moi Non Plus... is a song written by Serge Gainsbourg in the late sixties. It was banned for broadcast shortly after it was recorded, and was not played for years. The song describes an intimate situation between a man and a woman. The woman sighs and whispers, "I love you..." And the man replies, "Me too. I move inside you..." I was too young and inexperienced to understand what it was about.

Rafael told me the song was banned from being played on the radio and it was no longer available in record stores either. From that moment we became partners in a tiny, secret sin, and I felt a shiver go through my body.

The main city square was filled with loving couples like us, celebrating the holiday on the weekend. The cafes were crowded. We walked with our arms around each other. He treated me to pizza and then ice cream. We walked hand in hand on the way back. He always walked on the side closest to the road so I would be on the safer side, away from the cars. We climbed onto the bridge over the Sorocaba River, leaned on the railing and looked down at the water flowing below us. I don't like looking down from high places, it makes my fingertips ache. But on that wonderful day nothing scared me. We walked and talked the whole way. I told him everything I was going through, about the financial issues at the factory and how I missed my teacher Dalzisa since I had finished school. He asked me what I was planning to do now that I had graduated. I replied that I wanted to continue studying and was thinking of enrolling in nursing school. He hugged me and said it was a very good idea.

The next day I told my mother about my plans to become a nurse.

She didn't say anything. Dita, who was home that morning and even awake, burst out: "What, Mother, do you agree? It's just an excuse for her to leave the house in the evening to meet her snobbish boyfriend. You let her do anything she wants!"

I didn't even answer. Her outbursts of jealousy were so familiar. The next day, when I was taking the linen off the couch before leaving for work, I found strange colored candles under the pillow—red, green, brown. The black candle was the scariest.

"What are these doing here?" I asked and showed them to my mother. She looked annoyed. "It must be Dita and her Umbanda! Don't worry, nothing's going to happen to you. You can go to work in peace. I'll talk to her when she wakes up." I tried to relax, but Dita's hatred filled me with fear. Who knows what could befall me because of her. She was into sorcery. You never know how evil a witch can be.

I started attending nursing school. It was a six-month basic course. I was disappointed with the low level of the studies, but it was better than nothing. I continued to meet with Rafael on weekends. He sometimes wasn't in the mood to go out so we would sit in the yard without going anywhere. Dita sensed the stagnation in our relationship and took advantage of the situation to interfere with my life. When we were with our Mother she would say, looking at me: "There, Mother, you see! He is no longer as enthusiastic about her as he used to be. I told you this guy is no good. Now that he got what he wanted, he'll leave her." And Mother, despite knowing Dita well, would still lose her good judgment and admonish me.

I was fed up with Dita's hatred, with the effect she had on our Mother. I wanted so badly to leave home, but the only way was to get married. I couldn't talk about it with Rafael. The status of our relationship was unclear.

One Saturday afternoon I dressed up and waited for him. Mother left for work, Father still hadn't come back and Dita was out. Rafael, who always arrived by seven, did not appear. I sat at home alone and waited. An hour and then another half hour went by. By half past eight I realized he wasn't going to come. I turned on the TV and tried to relax. Among the voices in the movie, I heard him calling my name. I got up, lowered the volume and realized that Rafael was calling me from outside.

"What happened? Why are you so late?" I cried, my nerves on edge.

"I'm sorry," he replied.

"You're sorry? Is that all you have to say? Are you aware that I've been waiting for two hours? Do you even care how I feel?"

Right at that moment my father came home, walking unsteadily and muttering to himself. He glanced at Rafael and said: "You're a good guy, a good guy…" and went inside.

Ashamed, I remained silent, but after a few minutes I continued. "I hardly see you. You used to come in the middle of the week. Not anymore. Even on Sundays you hardly come by. Today I waited for over two hours!"

He looked at me apologetically. "I have a problem," he said. "My mom is driving me crazy… I'm afraid something will happen to her. She is so… taking this to heart …"

"You know what?" I snapped, "Go to your mother! Don't come back!" My voice was choking. "You lied to me. You promised that no one would separate us, but you almost stopped coming. Just leave! I don't want to see you anymore!"

I spun around and walked into the house. My father stared at me from the couch, then got up and went to the bedroom. I put the sheets on the sofa and got in. I was drained of all willpower. I had no energy left for anything. I cried for hours until I fell asleep.

On Sunday morning I woke up with burning eyes and a throbbing headache. I finished the laundry as fast as I could and left to see Manuela. I needed her. As soon as she saw the expression on my face, she took me to her room. My sobs barely allowed me to speak. Manuela hugged me and listened to me patiently. Finally, she said: "Enough, enough. You shouldn't cry. After all, you just had a fight. In a week or two you'll be back together, I'm sure."

"Do you really think so?" "Sure!" she said laughing, "You'll see!" I laughed too and felt better. "I'm so sick of living in my house," I continued, "I can't take Dita's bullying and lies anymore. Now that I'm so distressed, she'll probably become even more abusive." Manuela agreed with me. "She must be satisfied now, the witch. This is exactly what she wanted to happen."

The next few days were tough. We were required to work every day until seven in the evening. With each passing day I knew more and more that Rafael and I would never get back together. I felt sick with pain. The longing bothered me all the time. I dreaded the despair of the weekend.

On Saturday, my mother asked me if I could come and help her that night at the restaurant, because her assistant was sick. I thought that working all night long was better than lying awake in bed thinking.

Mother introduced me to Mr. Max, the owner, and explained that I had come to help instead of Dona Bastiana, who had fallen ill. He smiled at me and seemed very nice. I peeled potatoes, garlic and onions. At ten o'clock the restaurant started to fill up. Orders poured into the kitchen. Mother couldn't read written orders, so they read them out for her: "Table of fifteen, Russian salad, rice and chips" or "Table of twenty—rice, vegetable salad and agrião salad."

Mother remembered everything by heart. She moved with great speed around the kitchen, swiftly preparing all the orders, and then served the dishes one by one, without getting confused. The pressure only eased at two in the morning, when all the patrons left the restaurant.

Mother prepared a plate for me and said I should help her wash the dishes once I finished eating. She barely ate anything herself. At half past four we finished and were about to go home. I was drained. Mr. Max approached me, took out some bills from his wallet and handed them to me. I looked at him questioningly and did not take the money.

"You worked hard tonight," he said, his hand still stretched in front of him. "I came to help my Mother," I said, "I wasn't working for the money."

"You worked for me and you deserve to be paid," he insisted. I looked at Mother and she nodded her head. I took the bills and thanked him. We reached our home early in the morning. Father was already awake and sitting on my sofa. I found a corner in one of the beds and fell asleep immediately. Mother woke me up at noon to eat.

In the afternoon I was sitting on the couch while Mother dozed off next to me. Someone was clapping by the gate. I rose with difficulty to see who had arrived. Outside were Marta, Rafael's cousin, and Pedro. I walked in their direction. Marta looked at Pedro hesitantly and then turned to me: "Catarina, I know you and Rafael are no longer together. Two days ago, they took him to the hospital. He is there now undergoing some tests. We are going to visit him. Do you want to come with us?"

"What does he have?" I asked. "He has a severe headache and a high fever. His condition is serious and we don't know what's wrong with him." "I'm very sorry," I said, "but I'm not coming with you. Is his mother there?" "Yes," said Martha. "I don't want to meet that woman," I said, "that's why we broke up. I don't want to see her."

My anger surged again. They left me feeling disturbed. Surely, he didn't have anything dangerous, I told myself. He would be out of the hospital in a few days. The next day, when I woke up, I was tormented by thoughts. Maybe I should have visited him the day before after all? On the bus, everyone talked about their plans for the weekend, and I missed Rafael. That day I got off at the stop in a hurry to get home and get my textbooks.

Mother came to meet me, walking with quick steps, looking at me strangely. There was a kind of tenderness in her I had never known before, as if she wanted to hug me. She grabbed my arm gently and said: "I came back early so I could talk to you before someone else tells you."

"What happened?" I asked, "What do you want to tell me?" "Rafael," she said. "What about Rafael?" I was scared. She spoke in a whisper that was barely audible: "He passed away this morning."

I didn't really understand what she said. I just felt my heart bursting. Darkness descended upon me. My brain exploded and thoughts scattered in my head in complete chaos. I pushed my mother's hand away and dashed toward the house. I had to make it to the course, I thought, and then I would take a bus ride to the hospital. I had to see Rafael... And then it dawned on me—Rafael was dead. My mother said he was dead. I heard screams. I looked around and saw Dita, Ivone, Aroldo and Father watching me, while I stood in the middle of the living room at home screaming. Then I came back to reality.

Father told me gently that Marta had come by and said that Rafael's coffin would be in the church tomorrow, and that the funeral would leave at half past three for the De Consolsão, the Cemetery of Consolation. "I heard he used to assist the priest when he was a child. Is that true?" he asked. I couldn't answer.

That evening no one turned on the TV, and everyone was quiet. I woke up at sunrise, and put on clean, freshly ironed clothes. It helped me feel stronger. I arrived at the church alone. From the doorway I saw the hall was already full of people. In the middle of the aisle was a white coffin, with four candles burning on each side. Knowing that Rafael lay inside I was unable to go near it.

I walked past it slowly, as if dragging lead bullets on my feet. I didn't want to see my beloved's body cold and lifeless. I wanted to remember him alive and smiling at me, his blue gaze searing my soul. I would take with me the warm hugs, the kisses, the endless conversations, our love, and they would give me the strength to go on living.

Someone grabbed my arm and pulled me toward the pews. Pedro seated me between him and his mother. Dona Maria hugged me tightly and put her hand on mine. On the pew closest to the coffin sat Rafael's family members, his best friend and the priest. People poured in nonstop. Manuela was there too. There, at the church, I was told that Rafael died of meningitis.

In the afternoon after school, all the students flocked into the church. It seemed like the entire town turned out for the funeral. Everyone present approached the coffin and prayed for the ascension of Rafael's soul, except for me. I saw his mother. She turned her head in my direction and our eyes met. Her face was pale and her eyes very sad.

The procession left for the cemetery. I was walking next to Dona Maria, far behind the head of the column, when all of a sudden Marta, Rafael's cousin, approached me and pulled me by the hand to his mother. We stood facing each other, and for the second time in our lives we looked at each other. She reached out her arms and hugged me. "I'm sorry I made you break up," she said between sobs. "Now neither one of us has him. I've lost him too." I burst into tears.

Nezinho

It had been two months since Rafael's passing. The void in my heart was just as big as on the day of the funeral. His death resolved all our differences. I loved him like I did back then, when he sneaked out of college during the breaks and came running to tell me how much he missed me.

At the end of the working week, I left the factory early and headed to the cemetery. A small cart loaded with flowers, propelled by a bicycle stood by the gate. The vendor flashed an almost toothless smile at me. "What would the lady like today?" he asked. After debating between three red roses and five pink carnations, I opted for the latter and counted the coins into his bony hand.

The absolute silence was broken only by the sound of my footsteps on the narrow concrete paths. I strode past family graves of neighbors and acquaintances.[14] I arrived at a tomb covered in blue ceramic tiles, which was my guiding sign from afar. I looked at the colorful painting of Nossa Senhora Aparecida, made of a mosaic of porcelain tiles, on the tombstone. The most common image in the cemetery was the Black Maria, the personal saint of Brazilians with African roots. Two graves away was the grave of Rafael's family. The tombstone was paved with light brown tiles, and from the picture above it a saint with a golden halo aura looked at me. Rafael joined his paternal grandmother too soon. I picked up a glass jar that contained the remains of dried lilies. Rafael's mother must have brought them a few days ago. I wiped the tiles clean with the paper the carnations came wrapped in.

I went to a nearby faucet and washed my face and neck. It was late summer, still hot. I took a few sips of water and filled the jar. I put it back in its place and arranged the pink flowers inside it. Leaning over the grave I ran my fingers along the porcelain surface.

"Rafael," I whispered, "I miss you so much. I don't know if you can hear me. I hope so. I hope you are well wherever you are. And that you forgave me... for not wanting to forgive you... I'm sorry I didn't come to the hospital when they told me you were sick... It was because I was angry. You hurt me because I loved you so much…" I wiped away a tear that had formed in the corner of my eye. "I'll never forget you," I continued quietly, "I'll come every week and tell you what's going on with me." I was silent for a moment and continued, "I finished studying this week, you know? Next week I have an exam and if I pass, I will be a certified nurse. The factory has some problems. There are rumors that due to the difficult situation, two girls have already been fired. I'm afraid they will

---

14 In Brazil's Catholic cemeteries, most graves are for families, with each one housing six, ten and even twelve family members. Some are buried in the pit below the ground while others lie inside the box-like structure above it. Each box has a metal handle in the front, so it can be pulled out and the newly deceased can be added to the family circle. The grave is lined with ceramic tiles of a solid color, and on the wall of the tombstone there is usually a colored picture, one of a permanent selection of pictures, which is also made up of ceramic tiles. The painting depicts a saint or other figure from local mythology. Sometimes the names of the deceased and dates of birth and death appear, and sometimes also their portraits.

make further cuts …" In silence, I took a handkerchief out of my bag and pressed it to my eyes, then blew my nose. The glare of the light reflected in the bright ceramic tiles dazzled me. Seeing a stain on one of the metal handles in the facade, I took the crumpled paper from the flowers and rubbed the stain off. Suddenly I saw a shadow of a man extending over the tombstone in front of me. Someone was standing behind me without me noticing. I turned and raised my head. A tall, dark figure stood beside me, blocking the sun, a man I did not recognize.

"Hi," he said, in a voice that sounded familiar. He leaned toward me, bringing his face closer to mine, until I realized who he was. "Hi, Adalberto," I answered. I didn't know him well. I'd seen him several times at Dona Maria's. He was hard to ignore, as he was tall, dark-skinned and very handsome. He was part of the group of Dita's friends too, and I knew he was also active in the Umbanda ceremonies.

"Nezinho," he said, "all my friends call me Nezinho." He smiled, revealing very white teeth. "I'm sorry about Rafael. I know you were friends, even though we never spoke, you and I." "Thank you," I said. A complete stranger had suddenly broken his way into my private journey, into my personal memories—a man with whom I had never exchanged a word until that moment. It was eerie. "Am I disturbing you?" he asked. "No, no. I was already leaving," I said, as I got up, blew my nose and began walking next to him in silence. He had the poise and lithe gait of a dancer.

"Rafael was a great guy," Nezinho said, "no wonder you're still so attached to him." I nodded, holding the handkerchief to my eyes, while we walked quietly. Only my sobs momentarily disturbed the silence. "There, there…" Nezinho comforted me with kindness in his voice. "You have to try to come out of it. You can't remain a grieving widow all your life. You need to go out and hang with others, meet people. Would you like to come to Dona Maria tonight? We always gather there on Saturdays, remember? I haven't seen you there in a long time. Afterwards I can take you dancing. Would you like to? You should. You'll see it'll do wonders for your mood."

I replied that I wasn't that much into dancing, but that I would come to Dona Maria. I tried to smile and stop sobbing. His voice was so soothing and he looked so handsome.

That evening I arrived at Dona Maria's. My friends welcomed me cheerfully. I hadn't met them since Rafael's death. Nezinho went out of his way for me. He filled a plate with snacks and served them to me with a glass of juice. He asked more than once if I needed anything and again asked me to go dancing with him. I accepted his invitation to go with him next Saturday. That week he showed up several times, while I was on my way home from work. When he heard that I had passed the nursing exam, he suggested we go out to celebrate together. "Thanks," I smiled, "we'll wait for Saturday, as we said." That week I felt less sad. One day I suddenly realized that I hadn't thought about Rafael for several hours straight.

On Saturday at noon, I went up to Rafael's grave and laid flowers, but I hardly cried. After that I stopped by Manuela and told her I was going out with Nezinho that evening. I told her it wasn't serious, that we were just friends, but I asked her advice about what to wear. The black dress was flattering, but maybe a little too formal. Besides, Marina the seamstress had finished it two months earlier and I had already worn it a few times. The green dress was brand new. Marina had finished it only the day before, but maybe it was too summery, and it was getting chilly at night.

I had to endure more interrogation from Manuela's regarding Nezinho, but I explained to her that he used to hang out with Dita and her friends, and that she seemed to be interested in him. He was just nice to me because he saw me sad, and I didn't think there was anything beyond that.

We finally settled on the green dress, and Manuela lent me a light-colored shawl to put on my shoulders in case I was cold. It was the first time I set foot in the dance club Nezinho frequented. He was waiting for me at the entrance, as we'd agreed. He was wearing a t-shirt and jeans that were tight at the hips and flared from the knees down. I smiled at him. He pressed his hand lightly against my back and led me inside. We entered a dark, stuffy space, shrouded in purple smoke. The music thundered and the floor throbbed to the beat of the bass drums. On the ceiling, above the dance floor, hung a rotating ball of colored lights, scattering spots of light on the densely packed heads.

We made our way through the crowd around the dance floor. People stopped Nezinho, asking him what he was up to, patting him on the back. Everyone seemed to know him. He pulled me gently by the shoulders toward a small group who were standing, chatting to each other. Two men and one girl were holding glasses of liquor, the other two girls were smoking and moving their bodies to the music. One of them, shapely and short, waved her hand when she saw him and danced her way up to where we stood. Nezinho knew her. Her name was Neuza. She was very dark, and even in the dim light, her face looked scarred with old sores, perhaps caused by smallpox. Neuza nodded at me with indifference then clung to Nezinho in a pleading gesture, trying to drag him toward the dance floor. He stopped her and turned to me: "Want to dance?" I replied nicely that maybe later, and watched him follow her with an apologetic expression.

Their well synched steps indicated they danced together often. Nezinho moved to face me, flashing me a smile. Neuza spun him around in the opposite direction, blocking him from view with her body. She danced vigorously between him and me, and it seemed to me that her movements were intentional, so all his attention would stay focused on her.

I agreed to one dance with Nezinho. I was shy and reserved, feeling embarrassed in front of these professionals. Neuza didn't stop looking at me with disdain. When the song ended, we left the floor. Neuza firmly took Nezinho's hand and led him back to join the other dancers. We started to head home after about two hours. My parents didn't allow me to be out too late. In the dark streets he placed his arm lightly over my shoulders, and when we got home, he said goodbye, brushing a kiss on my cheek.

The next morning, after tidying the house and washing my clothes and those of the rest of the family. I was in the kitchen helping my mother prepare lunch, when suddenly I heard the entrance gate slam loudly.

Within seconds, Dita appeared at the kitchen doorway. She leaned with one hand on the frame, while the other one rested on her round waist. I looked up from the rice I was picking and met her angry gaze. I wonder where she just came back from, I thought. Her bed was folded when I woke up. Had she slept at home that night and was ready to go out, or had she just come back now? Her black eyes narrowed, piercing me like pins.

"I heard you're dating Nezinho," she barked without preamble. Ever since she'd started caring about her waistline, she was hungry most of the time and her mood was worse than usual. I was caught off guard.

"I'm not dating him," I answered. "We're just friends. There's nothing going on between us." Her nostrils flared and she huffed. "They saw you!" she said with scorn. "So don't lie to me. He's been telling everyone you're together now!"

I tried to keep calm. "I don't know what they're saying. I'm telling you we're just friends."

"Liar …" She hissed, then lashed out: "I wanted him before you did. You're so depraved. Stealing him away from me. You have no shame! Go to hell. I wish you'd die!" she screamed.

"I won't accept this kind of talk at home," Mother interjected, raising her voice.

Dita glared at both of us with hatred, mumbled something unintelligible and ran out of the house.

My Mother looked at me scowling. I didn't say anything and went back to sifting the rice. In the afternoon I headed to Manuela's house to tell her everything that happened and also return the scarf. Nezinho was sitting on a fence at the end of the street, talking with friends. As soon as he noticed me, he left the group and approached me.

He wore a black t-shirt and jeans flared at the ankles. Thinking to myself how great he looked, I wondered if he'd been waiting for me, and if he'd been standing on the street for several hours until I arrived, or was I just flattering myself and it was all just a coincidence. I was blushing. He smiled at me. "How are you, beautiful? Did you enjoy yourself yesterday?"

"Yes, thank you," I answered politely and then continued hesitantly, becoming increasingly embarrassed, "Nezinho, listen, I don't want to come between you and Dita. She was terribly angry and hurt. I understand you are close. So maybe you and I shouldn't… I mean, be together. It really bothers her and she's my sister, you know." I stared down at my hands, scratching invisible dirt around my nails.

Nezinho remained silent. I glanced at him and saw his face was very grave and intent, as if considering very seriously his next words. We walked a bit in silence and then he stopped in a shady corner and turned to face me. "Listen," he said slowly. "There is nothing between Dita and me. Never was and never will be. I don't know what she has been imagining, but there's no way I'd ever want her. If you haven't figured it out on your own yet, it's you I want."

His words seeped into me like warm milk with honey. He wanted me. How wonderful to hear that someone was interested in me. I looked at him, feeling I was beet red. He took my hand and looked straight into my eyes. I immediately lowered them to the tips of my dusty shoes and noticed that I had forgotten to wipe them.

"I'll say it today in front of Dita, so you know. I have nothing to hide. OK?" he asked. I nodded. He walked me to Manuela's house and we arranged to meet in the evening.

With long strides I reached the front door. I had a lot to tell her. That same evening, Nezinho came to our house. He asked Dita to go outside to the yard with him and talked to her for a long time. When he called me to come out, she was no longer there, and he told me he had set the record straight with her.

Nezinho and I

Nezinho and I became a couple. My mother forbade me to go out with him alone. If we wanted to meet privately, we had to stay in our yard. We sat together on wooden chairs that I brought out of the house, not too close to each other. My dad or one of my brothers might show up and see us holding hands, which could get awkward. Nezinho made sure not to stay too late, so as not to anger my parents. We met mainly on weekends, as on weekdays it was not possible for us to do so. I worked during the day, and Nezinho had his own pursuits in the evenings. As far as I knew, he worked with his uncle, who owned a small typewriter sales and repair business. He had a sister and two older brothers and still lived with his parents. I recognized them by sight, because their house was nearby. His father was tall and dark-skinned and his mother was of Italian descent. I knew that after we met on Saturday nights he would go dancing with girls in clubs, and it didn't bother me.

One Saturday evening I was cleaning up the kitchen after making dinner for my younger siblings, with Ivone helping me. My mother had left for her night shift and my father was not home either. Hearing the gate slam I thought it was Nezinho. I waited for him to knock on the door and come in, as he always did. He was not shy and felt comfortable sitting at home in the company of my father and brothers. I remembered how Rafael would call my name, so I would go meet him in the yard, and never enter my house.

The door opened but it wasn't Nezinho. It was my father returning. Swaying unsteadily, he talked to himself or to some invisible interlocutors, and walked right past me. "Let them all go to hell!" he cursed, his breath smelling of alcohol.

I knew that Nezinho would arrive any minute and though I hated for him to see my father in such a state, there was nothing I could do. My father was uncontrollable when he was drunk. I would have tried to put him to bed, but with one push from him I might have been splattered on the wall. I had to make sure I stayed out of his reach. I prayed with all my heart that he would collapse soon, as he usually did at some point, but that night he was rather energetic. He walked around the living room muttering indistinct phrases to himself. Sometimes he would get excited, shout words I didn't understand and swing his hands wildly.

When Nezinho entered, father waved his hands screaming: "You wretched whores!" I smiled awkwardly at him and dragged two chairs from the kitchen out into the yard. Nezinho didn't even flinch. He took the chairs from me and I went back to get a pitcher of water and two glasses. Whenever Rafael came to pick me up on a Saturday and my father was in that state, it made me want to bury myself in shame. With Nezinho it was easier. He lived in our neighborhood too and knew all about drunkards. He was one of us.

After about an hour, the voices coming from the house quieted down. Father must have stumbled on some corner and fallen asleep. My siblings dispersed: The little ones went to bed and the older ones went out to have fun. Nezinho and I were left alone in the yard. It was after eleven, and we were still sitting next to each other, talking. A light wind began to blow, and it got colder. It was so quiet. I heard the leaves dancing in the wind and a dog barking in the distance. A shiver went through my body and I wrapped my arms around myself. Nezinho came closer to me and put his arm around me.

"Are you cold?" he asked.

"A little..." I nodded.

He moved closer to me.

"What if someone comes?" I said, worried.

"We will hear them before they see us. It's dark in here," he said.

I relaxed and let him embrace me. He stroked my shoulders and ran his fingers through my hair. I rested my head on his shoulder, which was firm and muscular. It smelled fresh and pleasant, of soap or deodorant. I closed my eyes, concentrating on his delicate scent, his shoulder muscle contracting under my cheek, the cool wind on my face. He kissed me softly on the lips. I wrapped my arms around his neck and pressed my lips to his. We kissed for a long time. Thinking I heard footsteps, I broke away from him abruptly. When silence returned, we decided he'd better go. We hugged briefly and Nezinho quietly slipped away, closing the gate noiselessly after him.

All morning the next day, Sunday, I felt like I was floating. I carried the large weekly pile of family laundry and put it down in the yard next to the tub. My hands rubbed on the soap, scrubbed, dipped the garments in the hot water and wrung them, but I myself was on the bench in the dark yard, in Nezinho's arms.

Ever since I started seeing him, Dita hadn't spoken to me. She completely ignored me. One day, when I was returning from the factory, I heard her arguing loudly with mother or with Ivone. As soon as she saw me, she launched a tirade: "Here comes the princess, with her matchstick legs." My face must have revealed my astonishment.

"Why are you surprised? Because I called you a princess? What do you even do all day long? You come home as if you'd been at a café, with your fancy dresses. Who do you think you are? You went to school for a bit and that makes you think you are better than the rest of us? Spending the whole day in front of the mirror. Trying to turn men's heads. You even manage to do it sometimes." Then, even more loudly, she said: "You Whore! Do you think you'll get away with this? With what you did? You really think so! Wait and see what happens to you! Don't say I didn't warn you!" She closed her eyes and started humming incomprehensible words. Her voice changed and her face contorted. "You will regret it!" Her voice was deep, not her own. Her shaved head was tilted to the side at an odd angle. She had cut her hair short because she hated that it was so frizzy.

Mother erupted from the kitchen. "Dita!" she shouted angrily, "Stop it right now! We already agreed on that I won't allow that nonsense in the house. I don't want to see anything like this anymore!" Dita opened her eyes and ran out into the yard.

"Stop provoking her!" Mother yelled at me. What did she want from me, I thought, but then quickly reminded myself—she was always that way. What did I expect, anyway?

In the middle of the night, while I was sleeping, on the living room couch as usual, I woke up without knowing why. I opened my eyes and a small scream escaped my mouth. Close up in front of me I saw an ashen, demonic face lit by candlelight. The lips formed quiet, unintelligible words. When the face saw me almost pass out with fright, it started to laugh an ugly laugh. I recognized Dita's voice. "Go away, you psycho!" I whispered loudly. She growled at me, contorting her face in strange grimaces, then blew out the candle and disappeared.

Mother, Dita and I

As I stood in the factory production floor, attaching valves to plastic pipes, I remembered how Nezinho and I had slipped behind the house the night before. We hid among the trees in the yard and kissed. His hand caressed my head and played with my hair. Then it slid down my back, sending a shiver down my spine. I glanced around to see if any of my co-workers noticed I was blushing.

Nezinho invited me to go away with him for a weekend to Santos, by the beach. His married sister had a summer house there, and she told him he could come and stay there any time he wanted. I had never been to the sea. I wanted so badly to go with him, but doubted my parents would allow it. There was no way my mother would agree for me to spend a night away from home in the company of a man who was not my husband.

I opened a new bag of valves and emptied it into a box. I took a valve and pushed a thin plastic tube into the designated opening. Maybe if we were engaged, Mother would agree. Did I want to become engaged to Nezinho? Was I ready to be his wife? I tried to think of my feelings for him. Did I love him like I loved Rafael? Whenever I thought of Rafael, my heart crumpled with tenderness and longing. My Rafael was pure, and transparent, like his blue eyes. I would have wanted to share my life with Rafael. He went to college and knew things. I admired him and wanted a life like his.

My thoughts shifted to Nezinho, and my heart did not flutter. I liked him, that part was true. I had a strong attachment to him and felt comfortable in his company. I loved when he kissed and caressed me. I believed he loved me and was willing to marry me. But what did he do in life, after all? He worked very little, lived with his parents, got up late, attended Umbanda ceremonies in the evenings and danced at night in clubs. There were rumors that one of his brothers was involved in drugs, that the same brother had once been in prison and that he was wanted by the police again. What was I actually doing with him? Life with Nezinho would not be exactly the life I had dreamed of.

I returned home to a heated argument. My mother, wearing a brown house dress, was yelling at Dita. She looked angry and her arms moved expressively. The dress glided over her narrow body, still slim and shapely even after nine births. She vowed that she was not going to allow Dita to go out if she did not come back at night. She knew she hadn't slept at home the night before! What would people say? What kind of a reputation would she earn?

Dita held her ground, poised for battle, her voluptuous breasts pushing out of a tight t-shirt, her dark hands resting on her hips. Her legs, enclosed in tight jeans, were slightly apart. She was wearing make-up, her lips painted a dark red, and had probably been on her way out. She yelled back at my mom not to interfere. She was sleeping at a friend's and didn't have to report all the time. When she saw me, an evil glint lit up in her eyes.

"What do you want from me anyway!" she shrieked. "The whole world knows that Catarina is sleeping with Nezinho. Everyone's talking about it." My mother paled. Her jaws tightened and I saw the muscles stretching along them. She let go of Dita and turned to me: "What is this? What's going on with you and Nezinho?"

"She's lying!" I screamed, quickly stepping away from her. "You know she's just making that up. I'm not doing anything with Nezinho."

"I really hope she's just rambling," Mother hissed at me, "because if not, you're not my daughter anymore. I don't want a promiscuous woman in my house. You should be very careful."

I was red with fury and humiliation. Even though I had gone through a similar ordeal when I was seeing Rafael, I still hadn't gotten used to it. Dita was nowhere to be seen. My mother turned on her heel and returned to the kitchen muttering: "My God, these girls are going to kill me one day."

That night I lay in bed with my eyes closed, trying to dissipate the anger that had built up in my chest. *I have to get out of here*, I thought. I didn't want to live in that house anymore. Maybe I really would end up marrying Nezinho just to free myself from this horrible family. I felt he could be my lifeline. I would leave this house for a different, better life. If I stayed there, I might end up like my mother, working myself to the end of my strength in order barely to bring food to my family. I would stay that way, at the bottom, with no studies, without making any progress. That wasn't a life. Nezinho was a gamble.

I didn't know what I was going to find, but it was well worth a try. When I got up in the morning, I found a black and a white candle under my pillow. I knew those were the colors of Satan's candles, which Dita used in her rituals. I felt a chill. I threw the candles by the folding bed where Dita was sleeping, and went to wash my face.

Nezinho kept begging me to go with him to Santos. Dita was sometimes absent at night and my mother seemed to be coming to terms with her behavior. One Sunday, when my parents were in a good mood, I told them that I was invited to spend the weekend with Nezinho's sister, who had a house by the sea in Santos. My parents hesitated and then agreed. Suddenly my mother asked suspiciously if his sister would also be there. I tried to answer without stuttering and said I wasn't sure. My mother frowned. My heart sank. The trip was almost within my reach, and now that it was being taken away from me, I wanted it very much.

"Maybe Ivone can join us? We've never seen the sea! When will we get another chance like this? If Ivone comes, I won't be alone with Nezinho …" I begged. Mother reluctantly agreed and allowed us to go.

Weekend in Santos

Ivone came with us and we took a bus to Santos. I sat on the back bench, between Nezinho and Ivone, and he discreetly put his hand by mine. A song by Roberto Carlos[15] played in my head: *Las Curvas da Estrada de Santos*. "The windings of the road to Santos make me forget my lost love and they disappear in the distance of the rearview mirror..." the words said, while I reflected on the twists and turns of my life. In another era, many years ago, I was a seven-year-old girl, sitting on a bench in the living room, holding my doll with the broken leg. Maria and her fiancé, seated on opposite sides of the room, looked at each other with enamored eyes. History was repeating itself, only the roles had changed. As the bus turned to descend toward Santos, it began to drizzle. Nezinho said it usually rained in the fall but that it didn't matter, one could still go in the water.

The summer house was neat, comfortable and pleasantly cool, with two bedrooms and a living room. Nezinho decided that Ivone and I would have a bedroom, each, and he would sleep in the living room. Mine was the master bedroom. I sat down on the double bed, hearing the welcome squeak of springs. I was in a great mood. I threw myself on the comfortable mattress, feeling free. I was wearing a yellow bathing suit I borrowed from Manuela, with a sundress over it. I took the sandwiches I had made at home for all of us in a plastic bag, so we could have a picnic at the beach. Ivone came out of her room in shorts and a sleeveless shirt. I enjoyed looking at her, almost as if I were her mother. I took care of her until she was five, when I was sent to São Paulo, and now she was eleven years old, slim and beautiful.

---

15 Roberto Carlos was the most popular singer in Brazil in the 1970s and was called the "Prince of Romance." In his well-known song "On the Road to Santos" he compares the love and pain of his complicated life to the twists and turns of the road to Santos.

Nezinho was waiting for us in the living room wearing swimming trunks and a taut t-shirt stretched across his chest. He was holding a bag swelling with a bottle of juice and towels sticking out. We left for the beach, the three of us.

For the first time in my life, I saw the sea. It was infinite. I knew it from pictures, but seeing it with my own eyes was different. Noontime. Cloudy. A gray sea full of movement. Waves rose, sweeping to shore, then breaking into white foam. Our feet sank into the sand. Nezinho took off his rubber Havaianas thongs and held them in his hand. We did as he did and walked barefoot. Our toes digging into the cool sand was a bit like walking in a dream, when you want to hurry but can't.

Nezinho laid down a large towel near the water. We sat down to eat by the sea, mesmerized by the ceaseless swaying of the waves. After a while he suggested we go into the water. The sun was a patch of light behind a layer of clouds and light gusts of wind chilled our arms. I said it was too cold to go in.

"Well," Nezinho said, "I'm going for a dip."

He took off his shirt and entered the water. I watched him going in deeper. A wave lunged at him and Nezinho jumped over it. He emerged to the surface and again dove over another wave. He did so several times. He had his back to me so I couldn't see clearly, but I saw him waving his arms and making strange movements. The sea was rough, so he occasionally disappeared behind the waves, which scared me. When he finally came out, I asked why he had gone so far in. "I was worried."

"I had to," he replied. "I had to ask the gods for permission, because today is the first time in a long while that I have come to the sea." I did not understand. "I am a *Filho de Santo*," he explained. Seeing my bewilderment, he continued, "This is a kind of priest, a medium, in Umbanda. Eventually you can even become a *Pai de Santo*."

I knew he was a member of the Umbanda religion, like Dita, but I didn't know the rest of the terms he was using. He continued to speak and I slowly learned that he was not new in Umbanda, and after years of study he was a kind of mediator between the gods and the believers. His body opened up to receive another being. During the ceremony he invited an incarnation of a god or good spirit to enter him and use his body and voice to speak to the faithful. The problem was that when his body was open, evil creatures could also enter—even sinful, dangerous souls. He needed to be on good terms with the gods in order to be protected.

When going to the sea for the first time, he had to ask the sea gods for permission because this was their territory. He hoped they would accept his request and give him their blessing. That way he would be safe from spirits and demons, in case they tried to enter him. While he spoke, his gaze was fixed on some point in space. I felt like a shadow passed over us, and a shiver went through my body. We were both sitting on the beach towel while the sun slowly set in the sea, behind the clouds.

Ivone splashed around in the shallow water. Every time there was a wave, she ran away to the dry sand with shrieks of laughter.

"How does a spirit get into your body? I don't understand... How does it happen?"

"It's impossible to explain," he said, looking at me again. "I think we're born with it. Even before I met Pai de Santo, the leader, I felt like I knew things before they happened. When I told him about it, he said that I had the ability to be a psychic and suggested I donate my body to the gods and spirits, to help other people. It took me a while to learn and now I'm Filho de Santo. You should come see. Do you want me to take you to a ceremony sometime?" I hesitated, afraid, then nodded.

When the tide began to lick the ends of the towel, we got up and headed back home. Ivone was as cheerful as a bird. I was overwhelmed by sea, stories of gods and a night in a strange bed, in an unfamiliar house, just steps from where Nezinho was going to sleep. We dispersed to our respective rooms quite early. Nezinho said he was very tired and made his bed on the couch in the living room. Ivone yelled good night to me from the room next to mine and I answered her.

I lay down in the comfortable bed, pulled the cozy blanket over me, and closed my eyes. The sea inside me moved up and down while the waves crashed inside my head. Nezinho's silhouette jumped over the waves and landed on the couch in the living room, so close to me. Suddenly I felt the mattress next to me sinking, and my body rolling down the resulting slope. I woke up in a panic. A faint light came in from the window. Nezinho lay on his side, in my bed, gazing at me.

I raised myself on my elbows, surprised. He reached out and stroked my hair.

"Don't worry," he whispered, "I missed you. I just want to be close to you and feel you a little bit." He continued to stroke my hair and comb through it with his fingers. "What beautiful hair you have," he said quietly. He caressed my shoulder and assured me that Ivone was sound asleep and couldn't hear anything. I glanced at the door and saw he had closed it behind him. I moved closer and clung to him. I wanted to feel the body I had seen bare for the first time that day in the sea. At the same time, I knew I was doing something forbidden. My heart pounded with excitement and fear, as I buried my face in his chest. The stiffness of his body and his smell intoxicated me. I felt real, intense passion for the first time in my life. Within the dizziness in my head, I heard my mother's voice talking to me:

"What are you doing, you slut! How can you allow a man to touch you like that?" I agreed with her and said to myself, "You have to stop. Now!" But I couldn't.

We kissed and he caressed me all over. The voices inside my head became silent and all thoughts were gone... I felt myself becoming wet, and had no idea why. Nezinho whispered to me that I was beautiful and pleasant to touch, and that I could relax because he wouldn't do anything I didn't want him to do. I felt the blood throbbing in my temples and I wanted to get closer to him, to unite with him, to be a part of him. He rolled me on my back, and climbed on top of me, pressing his body against mine. We rubbed against each other and I heard his excited breathing. Suddenly my nightgown became moist. Nezinho relaxed and rolled off me.

When I touched the fabric, my hand felt a smooth, sticky liquid.

"What happened?" I asked in a panic, sitting up abruptly to examine the stain on the cloth. Nezinho lay limp on the bed, caressing my legs casually. My understanding of the facts of life was minimal, but I knew that men had a fluid that made babies.

"Nezinho," I cried, "what have you done?" I rubbed my forehead in desperation, feeling anxiety rising in my throat. "What happens if I get pregnant? What's going to happen to me? My mother will kill me."

Nezinho sat up, taken aback. He hugged me, his tender voice revealing a smile as if he were speaking to a child. "There's no way Catarina, sweetie. You won't become pregnant. You can't get pregnant like that.

Nothing happened. You are not a woman yet. You remain as you were. There's nothing for you to be concerned about."

He gathered me in his arms and we lay together, close, my head on his chest. He ran his fingers through my hair in soothing motions and I thought he was laughing to himself. After he left the room, I was left alone with my despair and fears. I felt that I had done something that should not be done and woe and behold if anyone found out. I opened the closet door to check in the mirror whether I looked different. I rolled the nightgown into a ball and hid it at the bottom of my bag, then I put on a t-shirt and got into bed. I tossed and turned, greatly disturbed, until I fell asleep at last.

My First Umbanda Ceremony

We had only one night in Santos, one that created a stressful, awkward intimacy between us. The fear that someone would find out or that Nezinho would tell anyone didn't let go of me. A few days later he asked if I would go with him to the Umbanda ceremony.

We met in the evening on a street corner, not far from the church, near the home of the local leader, Pai de Santo. Nezinho wore a white dress shirt with long sleeves, slim white pants and a white cloth belt tied around his waist. We arrived at a long, one-story train-like building, consisting of a row of townhouses, like many other buildings in Sorocaba. Nezinho headed to one of the houses and opened the door. We entered the living room and walked across to the kitchen. To me it looked like any other house I knew. The door at the other end of the kitchen seemed to lead to the courtyard. When we stepped through it, we found ourselves in a dark space, lit only by candlelight, the air impregnated with the smell of incense. Once my eyes became accustomed to the darkness, I saw we were inside a large room. Along the wall in front of me were several tiered wooden stands, holding statues of gods, with more statues and lit candles on in the spaces between them.

There were maybe thirty statues of different heights: small ones that didn't even reach my knees, and others that reached above my waist. The characters were familiar, the ones I might have encountered at our neighbors, in parades or in folklore celebrations, and also in stores catering to the followers of the faith. I recognized the better-known gods, such as the God of Children with lighter colored candles, probably pink, at his feet, and the Goddess of the Sea and Love, the beautiful Yemanjá, in a blue dress which floated over her body. In one of the corners a bongo drum, a conga, and some pandeiro drums were lying on the floor.

There were rows of benches against the wall, partially filled with people. The center of the room was empty. The leader of the group approached us and greeted us with a smile. After introducing him to me, Nezinho quietly told me to go sit with the other guests. A thin stream of people continued to appear at the door. Nezinho was standing in the corner of the room, close to the statues, talking to a group of people who were dressed like him, except their belts were of different colors. I assumed they were priests, Filhos de Santo, like him.

When the seats were filled, the leader walked to the center of the room and signaled with his arms that the ceremony was about to begin. The audience fell silent. The leader greeted those present and called the drummers to approach the instruments. Four men sat down next to the drums and started to play a soft rhythm.

"Today, we are hosting the gods of the sea, and Marcelo will be the one to receive them," the leader announced, and pointed to one of the men and his group of followers. Marcelo walked to the center of the room and began to sing and sway to the beat of the drums. He was followed by Louisa, who received the God of Children.

Nezinho, in turn, also joined the widening circle of dancers in the center of the room. He would receive the *Preto-Velho*, the 'Black Old Man.' I knew the character of this god, a kind, dark-skinned elder. I had special feelings for him because he reminded me of my grandfather from Jacarezinho, *Seu Benedito*.

The volume of the drums increased and the priests chanted louder and faster. The faithful sang along with them. Many knew the words to the songs that invited the gods inside, into the room, into the hosts' bodies. The priests danced to the rhythm and their gaze was lowered or glazed, as if they could not see what was around them. Gradually their movements became more intense. They leaned forward and shook their heads, or straightened up with their eyes closed, throwing their heads back. One of them moved her body frenetically, her voice growing louder.

Suddenly her face contorted and froze in a bizarre expression while her body stood at an odd angle leaning to the side. That was exactly the way Dita acted when she attempted to scare me. From the corner next to the statues emerged a man holding a lit cigar over a tobacco leaf and handed it to her. She held it between her lips as red flashes rose from its end. She blew out the smoke and retired to a secluded area, close to the wall. Several women got up from the benches and strode in her direction. A woman sitting closest approached her first, and the others sat back in their place. The priestess made several movements with her hands and body, and they seemed to be conversing. It was hard to see in the dark through the thickening smoke screen. Nezinho left the circle, twisting his body and his facial expression out of their natural shape. I overcame my embarrassment, got up from my seat and approached him. Another person was already standing next to him. I receded to a polite distance, but I managed to hear Nezinho speaking in a voice I didn't recognize: very deep and slow, different from his usual tone.

After a few minutes, Nezinho and the person in front of him bowed to each other, and parted ways. I took a step toward Nezinho. He beckoned me to come closer and said softly, in his other voice:

"Come, my Daughter, come closer." When I was within touching distance, he grabbed my hand, leaned toward me and pressed his right shoulder to my right shoulder. He repeated the movement with his left shoulder. I tried to do the same. He straightened up and spoke to me slowly: "Are you the partner of the man whose body I am inside?"

That was weird. I didn't know how to relate to the figure standing in front of me. Was it Nezinho? Or maybe not? Was there someone else inside it, perhaps a representative of Preto-Velho, and if so, how did that representative know who I was or anything else about me? I also felt some doubt seeping in… Maybe it was all just trickery?

"Yes," I nodded, "I'm Nezinho's girlfriend."

"How can I help you, my Daughter?" he asked.

I whispered that I wanted to be stronger, less tired, and to continue to have a job. I heard myself answer, but my thoughts were busy with the mystery. Who was this crouching man with a twitching face, talking about Nezinho in the third person? Was he really some entity residing in my boyfriend's body? Or maybe it was all just a show?

Nezinho took a drag from the cigar and blew the smoke at my body, first to one side and then to the other. He said he was cleansing me of all evil influences and protecting me from demons and pests. He spoke to me in his deep voice, commanded me to light a candle every night for a week, and blessed me with abundant health and a good livelihood. I thanked him and we parted with a shoulder-to-shoulder bow. I waited for another half hour on the bench in the dark air, saturated with the smell of incense and wax, until the cigar smoke burned my eyes and throat. I went outside and waited for another endless hour outside until the stream of people leaving dwindled and Nezinho finally appeared.

He asked me if everything was okay, if I felt good about the experience I had. I said yes and that it had been very interesting. All of a sudden, it seemed like I hardly knew him. He had hidden corners in his soul that I would never be able to penetrate. I felt some distance between us, and perhaps some fear mixed with reverence.

The Wedding

Nezinho asked for my hand. After the trip to Santos, I found myself constantly pushing him away from me behind the screen of the awning in the laundry area. Every weekend, when we sat in the yard, he would take my hand and pull me after him to our private hideout, so we could embrace and kiss. I was frightened by the slightest rustle and wouldn't allow his caresses to get too bold. We had no privacy, after all.

I agreed to marry him, and Nezinho also received my father's consent. Deep down inside I had doubts about my love for him, but I quickly concluded on my own that living with his followers was a much better prospect than a miserable life devoid of love and respect among my family members. As soon as I got married, I would be free from my parents' authority. If things with Nezinho didn't work out and we got divorced, I would already be considered an independent adult, and no one would have the right to order me around and tell me what to do.

Nezinho's grandmother lived on Alcindo Guanabara street, near the cemetery. She had a small living unit in her yard, and that's where we were going to make our home. From the courtyard gate, a narrow path that ran along the wall of the house led to the door of a small kitchen. The bathroom, adjacent to the kitchen, had a shower. Then came the guest room followed by the bedroom. These accommodations were given to us for free, which made our future life together much easier.

I enthusiastically engaged in the wedding preparations. I bought white fabric and Marina sewed a wedding dress for me. We got the household organized, Nezinho, some friends and I. My mother increased my allowance so I could buy some essential furniture and accessories. My choice for our wedding night was a white lacy nightgown. I remembered with longing the night in Santos, and a shiver of excitement ran through me. I would no longer have to stop myself and be afraid. After we were married everything was allowed.

Nezinho's family gave us a gift of fine cotton sheets and towels. Everything was in order and ready for our arrival that night, after the wedding party. I made the double bed and excitedly lay out my beautiful nightgown on it. The party was planned to take place in the evening, after the wedding ceremony at the church, in the yard outside my parents' house. I remembered Claudia's son's engagement party and especially the beautiful cake. I knew I wouldn't be able to throw a party that came even close to that event, but I put all my efforts into designing the cake. My friends and I baked a tall, beautiful cake, covered it with pink and white icing, and decorated it with silver beaded candy and miniature bride and groom figures. On the morning of the wedding day, we registered at the municipality in the presence of our families and a handful of friends. Maria arrived alone and said that her husband would come in the afternoon for the ceremony. Manuela stayed home with me to help me get dressed and wait for her sister Madalena and her husband Alcides, who were going to drive us to the church in their car. My dress was simple, made of a white see-through fabric and a satin lining underneath. The veil was fastened to my hair with a bunch of white silk flowers. Manuela arranged the tulle around my face and gown, and told me I looked lovely.

My family and the guests were waiting for me at the church. I was sitting in the back seat of the car, next to Manuela. Alcides stopped the vehicle and said that my father did not feel able to walk me down the aisle, and asked if it was okay for him to do so. Was my father too drunk to walk beside me without stumbling? I banished that disturbing thought and said with a smile that I would be happy to have him walk me. I stepped out of the car holding the hem of my bridal gown and climbed the marble steps. Manuela and Madalena went inside and I waited with Alcides by the door. A young assistant priest approached the wide wooden door to announce that we were welcome to enter. We stepped inside into the cool, dimly lit space, and the voices of those present died away. In the silence I could hear whispers: "How beautiful she is." "What a gorgeous bride."

At that moment, the sounds of the organ rose, permeating the space while the walls echoed the melody. The choir joined in, singing *Ave Maria*, which I liked and had chosen together with Nezinho for the wedding ceremony. The holiness filled me with emotion. We walked slowly, majestically, down the long aisle that led from the front door to the chancel. One by one I recognized the guests sitting in rows on the wooden pews, on both sides. The backs of the seats were decorated in white with a rose and a satin butterfly. I nodded, smiled at the people I knew and kept walking.

I hadn't been to church in many years. My family didn't go on Sundays. Although I had been there a few days earlier, for the rehearsal I was too busy to notice how full of majesty the place was. I looked up and saw arched windows with colorful stained glass, where angels hovered and saints were surrounded by halos. Rays of sun penetrated through them casting spots of light of all shades on the walls and floor tiles. The heels of my shoes tapped softly on the marble tiles.

On the chancel at the end of the aisle, a few steps up, stood the priest, with two altar boys behind him. In the background, in one of the corners was the choir, and below them the organist. White flowers and candles decorated the space. At the foot of the platform, on one side, stood my mother, Maria and the Mendes family. The daughters of the Mendes family looked very elegant in their long dresses. My mother wore a more modest but festive dress. On the other side was Nezinho, with the members of his family next to him. He was wearing a white suit, his shoulders looked broad and his skin was more tanned than ever. In the first row I saw my father sitting with my brother and sister Ivone. Dita was not there. She had gone to Santos a few days earlier because she didn't want to be present at my wedding. My father, wearing a white shirt and gray pants, looked as good and sober as ever. I remembered that he didn't have a suit and assumed that was why he felt uncomfortable walking beside me down the aisle. Now I could make out my mother's features. She had a worried expression, as always.

Nezinho took a few steps toward me. He gave me a slight, teasing smile, looking even more handsome up close, with his navy blue satin tie. At long last, we stood next to each other, and the priest extended his arms to us, inviting us to come closer to him. We climbed the stairs and knelt on the top step. One of the boys stood next to the priest holding a brass censer that hung from a chain, whose ornate links glittered in the candlelight. I gazed at the boy carrying the incense, looking for someone else in him, but he was just a young boy with black eyes and an ordinary face. My heart shrunk with longing.

Once the ceremony ended, Nezinho and I left for my parents' house, as husband and wife. While the guests gathered in the courtyard, my father and brother grilled meat on the fire, my mother and sisters arranged platters of sandwiches and vegetables on the tables. My friends carefully took out the cake and presented it with a flourish. It was so pretty, no one really minded the taste, which was rather mediocre. The party lasted until almost eleven.

Alcides drove us and the many packages containing presents and useful items for our new home. After Alcides said goodbye to us, Nezinho hastened to take the clothes and utensils we had brought with us into the house, while I waited by the door. He then came back for me and carried me in his arms. I wrapped my arms around his neck feeling the pinga in his breath. He carried me easily, crossed the kitchen and the living room and threw me, laughing, on the double bed. He then threw himself on top of me and started kissing me forcefully.

"Just a minute, Nezinho," I said giggling, "I need to take my dress off." He helped me sit up, opened the zipper along my back and took off my wedding dress. He dropped it quickly, on a chair, then rushed back to me pinning me to the bed again with his weight. I could hardly breathe. He grabbed my shoulders with a force that hurt me, and squeezed my neck hard.

"Nezinho," I groaned, "you're hurting me…" But apparently, he was not with me at all. His movements became bolder, without restraint. The creature lying on top of me was not Nezinho. Not the same Nezinho who had caused such a stir in me that night in Santos. He took off his clothes and the rest of my clothes, all the while kneading and pinching the flesh of my arms and biting my neck. His naked body rubbed against me, and suddenly I felt a terrible pain in my loins. I choked and screamed, but Nezinho didn't hear. He continued to thrust at me like a madman, unaware of the suffering I was going through, buried beneath him. After endless minutes, he relaxed and rolled over. I lay motionless for some time, waiting for the terrible pain in my body to subside.

I sat up slowly, aching all over. My mind began to take in the sequence of events. Next to me lay the man I had married, who suddenly had become a monster and turned me into a doll, an emotionless object to serve as an outlet for his passion. I looked at my naked body. A warm trickle flowed from my groin and I saw a dark red stain spreading on the sheet. I was overcome with nausea. My head hurt and so did my neck, shoulders and stomach, inside and out. I started to cry, at first quietly and then in loud sobs.

Nezinho woke up from his stupor, stood up and looked at me as if he was seeing me for the first time. He reached for me, but I recoiled in disgust, feeling outright hatred. I turned away from him to avoid looking at him. The stain below me was growing wider. Panic didn't let me breathe.

"I want you to take me to the hospital," I sobbed. "I don't feel well." He did not answer. I had no choice but to look at him. He seemed worried.

"What hospital now?" he said. "You don't need any hospital. I'll help you get to the shower. Come on. Get up. Slowly." He supported me as I tried to get up, but my legs wouldn't obey.

"Bring me a towel," I asked, "because I'm making a mess." I wrapped myself in the towel he handed me, trying to soil it as little as possible.

To me, it was such a shame to ruin the gifts we had received like this, before we even used them at all. I was especially sorry about the sheet.

Inch by inch I crossed the living room on my weak legs, leaving a trail of red drops behind me. After Nezinho helped me get to the shower I asked him to leave me there alone.

I sat down on the floor letting the gentle, lukewarm stream wash over me. I had dark red marks, from having been squeezed on my shoulders and arms, on my stomach and even on my chest. I felt beaten and bruised, and my face was still burning. Up to that moment I didn't know that an act of love was supposed to hurt so much. And maybe it didn't have to. Perhaps it was Nezinho's fault, and it all could also have been very different. And this was my husband now. I didn't want such a husband. I would have to leave him at some point. I would not stay with him for long. One day I would be strong enough, and then I would get up and leave.

I sat in the shower with my forehead resting on my bent knees. The water flowing over me moved in a pink stream toward the drain and disappeared.

"Catarina, are you okay?"

Nezinho's voice brought me back to reality, and I felt sick again. I got up with difficulty and turned off the water. I wrapped myself in a clean towel and took a sanitary pad with me from the bathroom cabinet. Limping out I replied that I thought we should go to the hospital anyway.

"How will we get to the hospital now?" Nezinho said in a worried tone. "It's a long walk, and now it's the middle of the night. There is a bus once an hour. Go back to bed, rest, and we'll see how you feel tomorrow."

He wasn't worried about me, I realized. He was afraid to take me to the hospital to confirm what he had done to me. What an idiot I was, thinking he cared about me. So dumb. He tried to grab my arm but I pulled it away and walked cautiously into the bedroom, leaning against the wall. Once in the room, I put on some underwear and my white embroidered nightgown. I wore it only for me, for myself, and not for anyone else.

I saw that Nezinho had removed the stained sheet and carelessly laid out another one. I called out to him that the sheet should be soaked in cold water for the stain to come off. I curled up on the edge of the bed, with my back to the middle, and tried to fall asleep. I heard the bed creaking as Nezinho sat down on it, on the edge opposite from me.

"I'm sorry," he said quietly, "but it's not my fault. Someone put a curse on us, I'm sure." He paused and continued, "When we entered the room, I saw a light falling on the sides of the bed, right where you are lying now. It's a sign. I didn't want to say anything so you wouldn't panic. I think it's Dita, she must have cast a spell on us. You know how mean she is and how much she hated that we were together." He raised his voice angrily, "I never imagined that she would reach so low, such wickedness! To do such a thing on our wedding day!" I lay there without speaking. I didn't know how to respond to such a statement. It was not at all what I expected to hear. I shut my eyes tight and said nothing.

The rays of the sun coming through the window warmed the room and woke me up. I got up with a blurry headache. My body hurt less. I looked at my shoulders and arms and saw that the marks left by the pressure of his fingers had turned blue. I looked at the body sleeping by my side, with its back to me, covered with a blanket up to the head. I felt disgust mixed with indifference. It was still hard for me to walk, but I was getting better. I had fallen asleep, and for a long time. I went to the bathroom only to see the sheet soaking in the sink. I moved it to a bucket so I could wash it in the yard outside, and was happy to see that the stain had faded.

I took a bath and saw my face in the mirror, a sad face with puffy eyes. I washed my eyes with cold water and decided that I needed to recover. I chose a short-sleeved shirt instead of a tank top, to cover my bruised shoulders. I made some black coffee and drank it alone in the kitchen, because Nezinho was still asleep. I was feeling better.

When I opened the windows in the living room to air the house, a strong smell of citrus blossoms wafted from the orange tree growing in the yard. I saw the trail of blackened drops leading from the bedroom to the bathroom. I took the sheet out to the laundry tank in the yard, scrubbed it with soap and left it to soak some more. I returned inside with the bucket, grabbed a rag and scrubbed the path of drops. With each black spot that disappeared, I felt the disaster of the night before drift farther away from me, while I got stronger.

Nezinho woke up around noon. He asked how I was feeling. I said better. I thought about what tasks I could busy myself with in order to get away from him and avoid talking. At that very moment I heard the courtyard gate open. I looked out of the living room window and saw a short, plump figure enter, with dark hair gathered into a bun rolled on top of her head. Auzira, Nezinho's mother, walked briskly toward the front door with a large gift-wrapped package in her hands. I went to the kitchen to greet her. She entered and set the package down on the table in the living room.

"I brought you one of the presents left by Catarina's parents," she said. "Dad and I took some home. Come eat with us and take the rest of them. I made pasta." She smiled with her honey eyes. I squeezed her plump arms while her ample chest pressed against me. After planting a kiss on each of her cheeks, I went to open the package, tearing the paper off a large carton full of pots. As I extended my arm to reach the other side, my sleeve slid up. Auzira came closer and examined my arm:

"What is this?" she asked. "What happened to you?"

The purplish-black marks peeking out from under the sleeve were now visible to her. She reached out and stroked the spots. Trying to sound cheerful, I said: "I'm perfectly fine, Dona Auzira. Sit down for a little. I'll just change clothes and then we can go." Nezinho came closer and hugged his mother. She looked at him with a slanted look: "What did you do to the girl?" He remained silent.

"He didn't do anything to me," I said lightly. "I'll take with us some salads and meat that we brought yesterday from my parents' house, and we'll be at your place right away." For a moment I was horrified by the scenario of him being accused of abusing me, and me having to return home. I'd put up with anything just to avoid returning home to my parents. I'd get along with Nezinho. Auzira didn't need to know anything.

Umbanda Second Ceremony

I got used to the new routine. Every morning I got up and went to work, leaving Nezinho asleep, usually. He was still working for his uncle, but left the house later than I did. In the afternoons I got home first and prepared dinner. For a few days, we didn't talk during our meals. At night I did my best to stay away from him and did not allow him to touch me. All the while Nezinho was very kind, making an effort to soften me up. After a week I thawed and allowed him to hold me. He suggested that we do another wedding ceremony, according to the Umbanda religion, officiated by the Pai de Santo. He believed that this way we would be blessed by the gods, all curses would be removed and our marriage would finally be blessed.

The Pai de Santo was such a warm, pleasant man, I thought, his presence would only do us good. What could be wrong with having a ceremony honoring Nezinho and me? On the contrary, it might even be nice. What did I have to lose, really? Besides, I had married Nezinho of my own free will and I had to give our marriage a chance. I said yes.

Nezinho explained that I had to wear a Yemanjá dress to the ceremony. I bought a shiny light blue fabric and Marina sewed me a dress that fell down to my feet, with long, wide sleeves. It cinched in at the waist and had a wide neckline that exposed my shoulders. A cape attached to the back also reached almost to the floor.

When I tried the dress on, I felt like a princess, and felt happy again. On the evening of the event, we arrived at the leader's house. Nezihho was wearing well ironed white clothes and I donned my Yemanjá dress. The hall was prepared in our honor and lit with a great number of candles.

Yemanjá, the Goddess of the sea and love, was displayed at the center, in a dress similar to mine, in front of the other gods. Each one of the candles burning at her feet was framed by a wreath of flowers. The now familiar smell of incense and melting wax invaded my nostrils. The leader welcomed us with a wide grin, shook our hands warmly, and led us to the center of the hall. The drummers sat down by their instruments and began to play a quiet African beat. The priests, who were already present, formed a circle around us and one of them placed a beautiful crown of flowers on my head.

The leader addressed the audience seated on benches, and signaling that the ceremony was to begin immediately, he announced: "Today I have the pleasure of marrying Catarina and Adalberto. I invite the representatives of Yemanjá and the other sea gods to come and bless the young couple with love and happiness." The leader then introduced the priests who were to host the spirits of the gods, and the celebration began.

This time Nezinho was by my side, and was not one of the hosts. The drumming intensified, the priests moved in a circle, sang and became the hosts of a visiting entity, each one in their turn. They received a cigar and formed a circle around us, chanting, stomping their feet in unison to the beat of the drums. They inhaled the smoke from the cigar held between their lips and blew it in our direction, a gesture meant to give us good luck and protection against curses and witchcraft. I stood in the center and everyone orbited around me, showering me with blessings and attention. Beside me stood Nezinho, his large hand holding mine.

At the end of the wedding ceremony, we were invited to sit on the first bench, closest to the aisle. The guests passed us on their way out, shook our hands tightly and wished us the best of luck. We stayed until the entire crowd dispersed.

We returned home, with Nezinho's arm around my shoulders. A sweet fragrance rose from the pink clusters hanging from the trees, and warm currents of citrus blossoms blew toward us. Summer was approaching. My long dress danced with every step I took, swaying from side to side, like blue waves.

When we lay down to sleep, Nezinho moved closer to me. I cringed in fear. Gently, he turned me around to face him. Though the bestiality of our wedding night was no longer in him, the memory was still pretty much alive in me. I didn't push him away, because I knew I had no choice as long as I was married to him. He didn't hurt me but neither did he show any particular interest in what I was feeling. I didn't suffer. I didn't enjoy it. The experience left me indifferent. My body was simply there, but my thoughts were elsewhere.

The Knitting Factory

One morning I arrived at work and the production manager called me into his office. He informed me that unfortunately the factory would be closing down at the end of the month, which meant I had two weeks left to work there. He reminded me to bring my labor registration booklet on my last day, so that the clerk could record my employment period on it, as required by law. He wished me success in the future and said he was sure I would find a new job. Bad news always comes as a surprise, even when you already feared it and prepared for it for many months. I came home dejected.

A few days later, Nezinho told me that Neuza, who sometimes danced with him at the club, worked in a knitting factory that was looking for female workers. I said goodbye to the plastics plant and the next day showed up at the knitting factory. They accepted me for a three-month trial and asked me to start a week later.

Nezinho went to work and I was left alone in our little house. I was glad to have some time to sort things out at ease. I planned the curtains I would sew for the living room. I pushed the table close to the window, then dragged it back to the center, where it was in the first place. After covering it with a white tablecloth embroidered with yellow flowers, a wedding gift from my sister Maria, I placed on it a glass vase that was just out of the box. I rushed to my florist friend at the cemetery and bought a small bouquet of daisies, which perfectly matched the fabric. Then I made dinner, like I did every day, and waited for Nezinho. When he came home, he gave me a hug. Then, in the living room, he noticed the tablecloth and flowers.

"It's obvious you were home today. The house looks different," he hugged me again as we sat down to eat. "Didn't you make meat in the oven with potatoes today?" he asked suddenly.

"I only prepare meat in the oven on Sundays," I replied in bewilderment. "Don't you like steak in the frying pan?"

"That's fine," he replied, "but I thought that since you were home all day and weren't too busy, you might make it. It doesn't matter. The steak tastes great."

Nezinho got up, leaving the dirty dishes on the table, and retired to rest. At that moment I knew for sure that I could never, ever, be just a housewife. A few days later I started working at the knitting factory. The foreman led me to my station and instructed me on how to use the knitting machine.

I adjusted the settings of the machine to the required measurements, and shifted the handle to one end, then to the other, and the small loops of wool joined each other, row by row, forming a sleeve, front or back of a sweater.

Neuza's workstation was in a far corner of the hall. She ignored my presence, even though I was sure she could see me. Her job was to receive the parts of the sweater, iron them and pass them on to the seamstress, so that they could be put together and become a garment.

I worked diligently and by the end of the day I had almost completely mastered the quirks of the knitting machine. None of the workers acknowledged or spoke to me. In the following days I worked in solitude and with concentration. During my lunch break I tried to strike up a conversation with a girl who worked on a machine near me. She answered me briefly and then I saw her whispering with Neuza, who continued to ignore me. At the end of a week, the supervisor called me and showed me one of the front pieces that I had knitted that day. She explained that one part of the collar was too wide to be attached to the back of the sweater. She asked me to pay more attention to the measurements. I went back to work and didn't quite understand where I had gone wrong. Two weeks later the manager called me again and reprimanded me, saying one of the sleeves was too long. I looked at the sleeve carefully and it seemed tighter than the other sleeves I had knitted. The yarn's eyes seemed slightly spaced apart.

I went to where Neuza was and looked at her. That day it was her turn to iron again. She looked smug as she continued her work. A quiet month elapsed, until the manager remarked to me that the collar on the back of the sweater I had knitted did not fit. I approached Neuza and whispered to her: "I know you iron my pieces at a higher temperature and ruin them on purpose. Why are you doing that?"

She looked at me with indifference, said she had no idea what I was talking about, and that I should learn the job before blaming others. The girls next to her glared at me, and I knew the battle was lost. After another month, right before the end of the trial period, the supervisor called me to announce that I was not up to the job and that I was fired.

The Weaving Factory

I was out of work again. And I was also well aware that I had to avoid staying at home for too long, lest Nezinho get used to having a personal maid to serve him. And, in addition, he would also be convinced that I was the one who should feel grateful, because he was the breadwinner. I kept reminding myself that I must stay independent, working for a living, because one day I would surely get up and leave.

I asked neighbors and friends if they knew of any place that was looking for workers. The answers were similar: This factory was closed. That factory was downsizing and had laid off some workers. Shops were not recruiting because business was weak. So, I set out to find a job on my own. I got up early and dressed carefully in a narrow light green skirt and a striped green and white shirt. I added faux pearl earrings to an outfit that I knew flattered me. I looked modest, and yet my good figure showed. After combing my hair, I dabbed a little blush on my cheekbones, as Manuela had taught me, and applied a light eyeshadow.

I headed to the industrial area not far from where we lived. I crossed the railroad tracks and walked on dirty sidewalks along the low buildings that housed small factories and workshops. *Alberto Furniture-Carpenter,*

Aonso-Seamstress. The job offers were written on the blackboards next to the names. Next to a low building with the inscription *Mario Textile* the board said: "Weaving machine operator wanted." In the rattling sound that came through the open door, I discerned dozens of rhythmic ticks-tocks. When I peeked inside, I saw women wearing white gowns and caps, standing along two rows of machines. The place looked well run and inviting. I walked in and found myself in a large and noisy hall. The light that penetrated through the tall narrow windows fell on clouds of cotton dust floating in the air. I took a few steps forward. The stairs to my right led to a small office with large glass windows. The door opened and a man in his thirties who looked Japanese, came down to me and said something.

"I'm sorry, I can't hear you," I answered. He came closer.

"Can I help you?" he said kindly. His face seemed pleasant and through his glasses I could see a kind look. He pointed to the office and invited me in. When he closed the door the noise of the machines died away.

"It's about the job," I said, trying to sound confident. "I used to work in a knitting factory. And, oh… My name is Catarina."

As the man sized me up, I saw appreciation in his eyes. I smiled awkwardly, and immediately lowered my gaze. He smiled at me and said: "How can you say no to dimples like those?"

He then introduced himself. His name was Mario and he owned the place. He was interested in my previous work and I answered briefly that I had been fired because of difficulties. He asked if I was married, if I had children, and when I would be able to start the trial period. I answered that immediately. He nodded with satisfaction and suggested I join one of his more experienced workers for two hours, and if the job suited me, I could start tomorrow. He led me to the exit door from the office and said: "Wait a minute." He opened a closet near the door and handed me a white robe. "It's a shame for your clothes to get dirty." He fixed his stare on me, making me blush. I didn't know what to do with myself. "Good. Come with me," he said at last.

We left the room and headed toward one of the machines. A young woman raised her head as we approached and put down her work. She had friendly blue eyes and was even taller than me.

"This is Helena, one of my best workers. Helena, this is Catarina. She intends to join us. Will you please show her the job?" Helena extended her hand, took mine warmly and squeezed it. She then proceeded to demonstrate to me how to operate the loom. Her movements were skillful and confident. She explained to me that the factory only produced natural fabrics, which were then sent for dyeing, and therefore all the spools of thread were the same color, a yellowish white, only of different thickness. She very patiently showed me how to place the spools of yarn on the loom, how to adjust the settings to get the desired pattern, and how to weave. Afterwards, she let me try it myself. She praised me for grasping it all quickly and assured me I would fit in easily. The factory was a good workplace and its employees were treated fairly and with consideration.

That's how I started working at Mario's factory. Helena stayed close to me on the first days and became my friend. We grew attached and she was like a big sister. The fact that I worked in the weaving factory near Helena improved my mood and made me feel empowered. I went back to believing in myself and in the possibility that maybe the day would come when I would be strong enough to leave, finally to become independent.

Marijuana

On that day I got home early to an empty house, with Nezinho nowhere to be seen. I washed the dirty dishes he left in the sink. I finally felt I had the energy and strength, and that it was time to tidy up the bedroom closet, where I had put away the wedding gifts. I'd been planning to do it for a few weeks but kept putting it off. I grabbed a rag and tied a handkerchief to my head, declaring to myself that on that day I would start and finish the task and be done with it.

I opened the closet doors wide and emptied its contents onto a sheet on the floor. I dusted the inside of the closet so as to return each item neatly back inside. I began opening the packages, one by one, put aside a pair of towels from the neighbors, and pulled a large white package from the pile. I knew it contained a woolen blanket from my mother's employer. When I opened the wrapping paper and shook off the blanket in order to refold it, a fat brown rectangular package fell out. Curious, I picked it up only to discover it was softer and lighter than I expected. Peeking inside, I saw it was full of dry leaves. I held a few of them to my nose. They smelled strongly of marijuana. My stomach clenched. I never smoked drugs, but I knew the smell. I also knew they were bad and that trading in them was very dangerous and immoral.

I was aware that Nezinho smoked sometimes, but I never, ever would have guessed that he was also a dealer! A chilling fear crept up my spine. At that moment I heard footsteps outside. Maybe it was the police! Nezinho's brother was on their wanted list and no one knew where he was. Perhaps that very second the officers would break into our house and find me holding the huge package. How would I explain to them that it was not mine, that I didn't even know it was there? I could already feel the handcuffs on my wrists. I was furious at Nezinho for putting me at such terrible risk.

I sat down on the sheet, trying to think of what to do. I had no idea when Nezinho was coming back. Then I heard footsteps outside again. They didn't sound like my husband's. Nezinho had a light, nimble gait. Those were the heavy steps of thick leather soles, like the ones policemen wore. I froze in place. The footsteps receded until they blended in with the sounds of the street.

I ran to the kitchen, took an empty paper bag, put the package of marijuana in it and dashed outside. I quickly passed a few houses along the street, turned into a neighboring street and crossed the road toward the cemetery. After circling around it, I arrived at an empty lot with a large puddle that extended all the way to the dense bushes growing in one of its corners. Beneath the vegetation, in and around the puddle rolled cans, bottles and small piles of waste. I hurled the package into the bushes and ran home.

I closed the door behind me and threw myself on the sheet still on the floor, steadying my breathing. My forehead felt damp, and when

I wiped the sweat off, my hand was shaking. I arranged all the presents with my vision blurry. Tears wouldn't help! I folded the old sheet, placed it on the shelf where it had been before, and shut the closet doors. I plopped down on the bed, with my head heavy and empty of thoughts.

An hour went by, maybe two. I lost track of time. I may have dozed off. I heard Nezinho enter the house. As was his habit, he called: "Catarina, are you at home?" I remained silent, pretending to be asleep. He turned on the light in the living room. I heard his steps closer to the room where the cursed closet was, and then its doors being opened. I knew that soft squeak well.

For a few seconds there was silence, then he shouted in a panic: "Catarina, Catarina!" I raised my head to see his tall silhouette against the pale background of the living room. The light of the street lamps that came through the window was reflected in the white of his eyes, which seemed unusually wide to me. "I see you tidied up the closet. Did you see a large package wrapped in brown paper?" He spoke quickly, clearly worried. I pressed the blanket to my chest, stayed silent for a second, and then I exploded. "Yes, I did! How dare you keep such a thing at home? You're not allowed to!"

"Where is it? Where is the package?" he bellowed.

"I threw it away!" I screamed back. "I threw it far away from here. I'm not willing to have things like that in my house!"

He was silent for a moment and then turned on the lights. "What house are you talking about?" he yelled again, "This is my grandmother's house. Do you hear me? If you don't like it here, you can go back to your family!" His face looked ashen. "You dumped it. You can't be serious…" He added quietly, his voice subdued. I nodded.

"I threw it in the garbage!"

"You are crazy!" he shouted again. "How could you do that! I only had to keep it for two days. Today I was supposed to pass it on! Do you know how much money it's worth? Do you have any idea of what you've done? Stupid girl! Where will I get the money to pay for it?" The color returned to his face, turning it dark red.

"Where did you throw it?" he roared. I shrugged.

"I don't know. Far away."

"Stop the nonsense. What do you want now, for them to come and destroy our house? To beat me up? To kill me? I'll have to pay for it. Will you tell me where you dumped it?"

I hesitated for a moment.

"In the empty lot, near the cemetery, where the puddle was. Among the bushes. I don't think you'll find it in the dark. And I don't care. You should have thought about that before bringing that stuff into the house. You put me at risk too!"

Without waiting for me to finish, he ran out of the house, slamming the door behind him. I was left alone. Alone at home, alone in the world. Maybe I shouldn't have thrown away the drugs? What would happen now, if he didn't find the package? What then? What future did I even have, with a man like that as my partner? I had to leave. But where would I go? I was drained. I was tired of struggling. I was tired. So tired. Tired of life. A huge sob rose in my chest and came gushing out. I buried my face in the pillow.

When I calmed down, my eyes and nose were swollen, and I could hardly breathe. My head was being pounded by hammers. I thought I would have loved to fall asleep and stop all thoughts. I got up on weak legs and went to the kitchen. After filling a glass with pinga, I dragged myself to the bathroom and turned on the light. The reflection of my flushed face was in the mirror, my hair a mess, my nose red and runny, and my eyes burning in their sockets.

The pitiful sight made me cry again. I opened the medicine cabinet and found a box of headache pills. I opened it and emptied all of its contents onto the palm of my hand. There were three pills. Only three? Whatever. Maybe combined with the pinga they might work. I wanted to sleep and never wake up again.

I popped the pills into my mouth and swallowed them with a big gulp of the liquor. Leaning on the sink I waited for the pills to go down. How long would it take? I closed the cabinet door, careful to avoid looking at my image in the mirror. I turned off the bathroom light and walked slowly toward the bedroom, sipping the rest of the pinga. By the time I entered the room, I was nauseous. Taking a deep breath didn't help. I felt the pinga and the pills crawling back up my esophagus, refusing to continue on their way down to my stomach. I ran to the bathroom and threw up in the sink. Everything came out: the pinga, the pills, and the unidentified mush I had for lunch with Helena. That day it had been my turn to bring lunch.

I was still alive.

Nezinho did not come home that night. In the morning I got dressed and drank hot black coffee. With my eyes still puffy, I tried applying eyeshadow to conceal the red blotches around them. I did my best. I set out for work on foot, like I did every day. On the way I made calculations in my head, trying to estimate how much money I would need to save before I could leave Nezinho once and for all.

When I arrived at work, Mario looked at me questioningly but said nothing. I rushed to the wardrobe, hung up my thin coat and put on the robe. Helena was standing by the mirror, tucking her light curls into the white cap.

Her reflection chuckled at me and waved me hello. I looked at her and our eyes met. Helena spun around in surprise and came closer to me.

"Catarina, what happened?" I wanted to answer, but my voice choked. She held my hand and didn't let go. Her worried expression moved me. I sat down on the bench next to the coats. Helena put her arm around me and I told her in bits and pieces, little by little, about the night before—about the drugs, about the argument with Nezinho, and about the fact that he hadn't come back all night. I told her that I was unhappy and that I wanted to leave him. Helena stroked my head and shoulders. She told me in her comforting voice that I was still young, that we were newlyweds, and that all beginnings are difficult. She went on to say that she was sure that Nezinho loved me and that in time we would get closer to each other. Drugs were very serious and a matter for concern, but maybe it had been a one-off thing.

She told me that it had been hard for her too at first, when she got married eleven years earlier, but now she and her husband had a ten-year-old girl and she was happy. In the end I felt relieved. That day I tried to concentrate on work as best I could. The loom did not respond to me and the threads got tangled under my fingers. Mario approached me and asked me to come into his office. I followed him apprehensively, ready to apologize for my low productivity, but he asked me gently to sit down and said he just wanted to know what happened to me, because he felt I was upset today. I told him the main points. I said that I was not happy at home, that I did not trust my husband and that I was thinking of leaving him.

Mario looked at me so intently that I felt embarrassed. He said calmly that I should decide what was best for me, and that if I left my husband, he would help me. I thanked him profusely and hurried back to my workstation. I tried hard, in my personal struggle with the loom, until finally one of the handles got stuck and I couldn't work at all. I called out to Helena in desperation. She checked the machine and said she thought a technician should be called. I was completely distressed. I apologized from the bottom of my heart to Mario but he told me not to worry. He said there were days like that, and that I should just calm down. Nothing terrible had happened and maybe I should go on a lunch break.

Helena joined me. She took the mishap lightly, mimicking my troubled face and ruffling my hair until she made me laugh. She pulled the pan she had brought from home out of a bag and served us both steak with beans. We talked a lot. I told her how I had met Nezinho and why I decided to marry him. I told her about the Umbanda ceremony I had experienced. That day the real friendship between Helena and me began. I felt that I could trust her and that we had a real emotional connection.

When I came home from work, I found the house exactly as I had left it in the morning. Nezinho had not returned. I changed clothes and went into the kitchen to place a pot of oil on the stove. While it was heating up, I sliced some vegetables for a salad. I peeled potatoes and cut them into thin strips. I threw them into the pot when bubbles began to appear in the oil. At that moment the door opened. Nezinho entered and I frowned.

"Hi," he said. The nonchalance with which he walked in, and the light indifference with which he conducted himself, made my anger rise.

He strode right through the kitchen and headed for the bathroom. The dishes clanged loudly while I scrubbed them. The oil was boiling and the potatoes had taken on a golden hue. I scooped out the fried strips with a skimmer spoon and placed them in a colander for the oil to drain out. When I turned off the flame, the storm in the oil subsided, but not in me. I heard Nezinho's steps behind me.

"Where did you spend last night?" My voice sliced through the space, shrill and irritated.

He did not answer and I could no longer control myself. "Were you with Neuza?" I yelled. "Then why did you come back!? You can stay with her if you want to. Go to her!"

Nezinho calmly went to the kitchen shelf and reached for a glass which he then filled with tap water. In a fit of rage, I picked up the pot of oil and emptied it into the sink, aiming to hurt his hand. Thick steam and sizzling sounds rose from the sink as the boiling stream hit the cold porcelain. Nezinho quickly pulled his hand away, and the hot spout missed it.

"You're insane!" he screamed. I looked at him intently, my face burning.

Furious, he raised his hand menacingly, and I thought he would hit my face. "Yes, hit me! That's the only thing you know how to do!" I screamed, even though he had never hit me before. His eyes flared but his arm remained frozen in the air. He turned on his heel and left the kitchen. His footsteps receded into the living room and the bedroom door slammed behind him. I sat down on a kitchen chair, rested my arms on the table, cradling my head with my arms, and let the tears flow. An hour later I left behind a clean kitchen and cold fries in a colander.

Again, days of silence between Nezinho and me ensued. In my heart I felt that I was drifting apart from him. Chances of ever really loving him one day seemed to me highly unlikely. Even after he appeased me with caresses, and I responded to him as a faithful wife must, the distance between us did not decrease. I didn't even ask him if he had found the drug package, even though I wanted to know, and he never told me.

Fear

I returned home late one evening, and found Nezinho in bed. When I asked him why he was back so early, he replied that things with his uncle were not working out and that he had stopped working with him. A week later, Nezinho was still unemployed. I would find him in bed, dirty dishes scattered in the kitchen.

"Nezinho," I said firmly, striding into the bedroom, "You can't stay at home like this doing nothing. You should be out looking for a job during the day." He looked away from me without replying. "At least tidy up the house while I'm at work."

"Do you want to come with me today to the ceremony at the Pai de Santo?" He asked changing the subject. "I went with you last week," I answered and headed for the kitchen. Nezinho followed me.

"Today there is a different kind of ceremony. I've never taken you with me on a Friday. It's called Kimbanda, and it's only held once a month." He spoke softly. "It's a different ceremony from Umbanda, a bit scary, but it's fine for you to come. I'll make sure nothing happens to you."

The large room in Pai de Santo's house was lit by dozens of candles, most of them black and some red. The smell of wax was stronger and sharper than ever. At the center of the stage stood a large, red statue of a god, or a demon, actually, with horns and a black cloak, surrounded by other smaller statues, all red and black. In the light of the flames dancing on their faces, their expressions changed constantly, making them look alive.

Nezinho escorted me to the bench and whispered to me not to worry. He left me to join the group of priests who were standing on one side, dressed in normal clothes rather than in white, as in the ceremonies I was familiar with. The priestesses wore colorful clothes and heavy makeup. Several women occupied the seats next to me. In fact, most of the audience was made up of women. The Pai de Santo announced that today the gods Eshu, Pomba Zira, his partner, and their band of demons would be the guests.

The drummers began their ritual and the priests joined the circle one by one. The gentle drumming gradually increased until it became louder and faster than ever. The dancers who were humming raised their voices to a shout, and occasionally whispered like snakes in a thicket.

One by one they bowed in front of the statues, twisting their bodies and talking to the gods out loud, in words I did not understand. They each froze in turn, and were flung violently to the ground when the entity entered their bodies. The spirit within them, or perhaps they themselves, took a cigar and a bottle of whiskey each, ready to receive the believers.

Women got up from the benches and approached the gods. They looked weary, downtrodden, and bitter. The atmosphere was oppressive and the thick cigar smoke burned my throat. My eyes searched for Nezinho, who was busy with one of the believers in the corner of the room. A small burning candle went out with a hiss, releasing a white rising spiral. A wooden god looked at me from behind it. He was black, wore a red cloak, and flashed me an evil smile. After two hours the ceremony was finally over.

We walked home in silence.

"How was it?" Nezinho asked me.

"Scary." I replied.

Nezinho laughed quietly and put his arm around my shoulders.

"What can you even ask Eshu and all these demons for?" I asked.

Nezinho explained that usually you'd seek revenge on your enemies and people who had done you wrong. Some women, for example, might have a boyfriend who was in love with another woman or even married, and they wanted him for themselves.

They could request that this man leave his wife or stop loving their rival and marry them.

"And would that really happen?" I asked, amazed.

"It depends on whether they do exactly as their representatives tell them to do, then it often works." We continued walking down the quiet streets. Nezinho asked me if I remembered the north junction that led to the cemetery. I nodded.

"Believers who have requests for the god Eshu must go to this intersection," he said. "They must make an *oferenda*, an offering to the gods. In the middle of the night, they should bring a roasted chicken, whiskey, and then light candles. They have to make certain motions with their hands and retreat walking backwards, without turning their back."

Nezinho spread his arms in front of him, crossing his hands one over the other, like scissors. "The rules say you should walk a few steps away without turning around and leave everything you brought to the gods, they listen and help you," he said.

I knew the intersection next to the cemetery, the place where people left their oferendas. Abandoned pots and buckets of extinguished candles sometimes rolled off to the side of the road. They always gave me an unpleasant chill, and I hurried to cross over to the opposite sidewalk to get as far away from the remains of the offerings as possible.

A few days later I discovered a new addition to our home. Above the closet in the bedroom, two statues of gods made of black wood appeared. One was Preto-Velho, which I loved. The second one had an undefined face, a small beard and an angry look, and he made me uncomfortable.

One day, when I came home from work and again found the house turned upside down and my husband wrapped in a blanket up to his head, I sighed a sigh of despair.

At the sink, while I was washing dishes, I heard footsteps behind me. Nezinho stood in the doorway of the kitchen with a strange expression on his face. He started to hum and his body trembled, making me shiver. My attention went back to the sink and I went on soaping the plate in my hand.

Suddenly I heard the thud of a heavy body hitting the floor. I shouted in panic. Nezinho lay on the floor writhing. As he sat up slowly, he began to whimper in the voice of a little girl. I had no idea what to do. I wanted to help him but didn't know how. I wanted to run away, but the crying baby touched my heart. She sounded distressed. Someone had taken something away from her, candy I think, and she was miserable, asking in a pitiful voice that the stolen candy be returned. Although I couldn't see her, the little girl, I felt her there, surrounded by invisible children who were teasing her, and my heart went out to her. She raised her face to me, and with closed eyes called out still crying: "Aunty, tell him to give me back my candy." I wanted to take her in my arms and comfort her. I approached her a little, with caution, and asked quietly: "Who are you?"

At that moment she stopped crying and Nezinho's body fell back and continued to convulse on the floor, until he gradually calmed down. He then lay still for a few seconds with his eyes closed until eventually he opened them, sat up on the floor, looked around in confusion and asked where he was.

"You are at home, in the living room. What happened to you? You were acting very strangely."

He got up with difficulty, sat down in a chair and said he had no idea what had happened to him. He asked me to describe what I saw. I told him slowly, with some effort. He listened intently and nodded. At the end he said: "Apparently the spirit of a baby girl entered my body. I told you that my body is open and that's a problem. Good thing it was just a baby. You never know who will turn up. It can be dangerous, especially when we live so close to the cemetery. I need to consult Pai de Santo." He rubbed his forehead and asked me to pour him a glass of water.

"Dangerous?" I asked, handing him the glass. He sipped slowly and replied: "Well, I hope the gods protect me, as I already explained to you. But still, there is some chance that an evil spirit will enter me, say a criminal or even a murderer." He looked at me. "You needn't be so afraid," he continued, "I really hope not, but you can never be sure." He got up and walked slowly to the bedroom, as if something had squeezed all the energy out of him.

I stayed alone in the kitchen leaning over the table to calm down. I didn't care that Nezinho had gone back to bed. I didn't mind doing the dishes myself. After dinner, while I was tidying up the kitchen, it was dark outside. With every rustle, every creak of a branch, I imagined a spirit hovering over the cemetery, flying toward our little house and making its way in through the windowpane.

I was happy to leave the house the next morning, thanking God for the job I had. But that bit of luck also ran out.

One day Mario called me to the office and sadly informed me that the factory was undergoing some difficulties and that he had to cut the number of employees. He emphasized again that he was very sorry but I would have to leave, because he had no choice. At the end of the day, I said goodbye with a sorrowful hug to all my friends. Helena held me tightly to her bosom and we promised each other that we would stay in touch.

Finding Nezinho at home, I told him that I'd been laid off and that I was very worried, since we were both out of work. He took my hand and said he would make more of an effort to find something. The next day, after we had breakfast together, I went job hunting again. Nezinho promised he would leave soon after I did. I wandered for hours between workshops and factories, but there were no vacancies posted on the boards by the front doors. When I returned, Nezinho was not there, and I was glad that he was out searching. In the corner of the living room I found the large statue of a god whose name I did not know, and which had not been there before.

A week went by, and neither one of us had been able to find anything. Nezinho went back to lying in bed for hours on end and I asked around among friends whether anyone knew of a job. I didn't like my life. I dreamed of leaving Nezinho, but I had not yet gathered enough courage or confidence.

Whenever I got home in the evenings to find the house upside down and Nezinho lying in bed, I would lose my patience. He would not respond, but it seemed to me that my anger had made him weaker, more open to other beings. From time to time, he would wander around the house swaying, then collapse and speak in a different voice. I knew he couldn't help it, so I would leave the house until he was himself again.

By then, there were already five statues of gods in the house, two of them with horns. Every time I passed by them, I did my best to avoid looking at them, yet they seemed to be following me with their gaze. Sometimes I would stand in front of the sink, with a whole series of empty rooms behind me, and beyond the bedroom, the cemetery. I would suddenly feel a startling certainty that someone was behind me. That a black figure would creep up behind me and reach for my neck. I didn't dare turn around for fear. I only tried to calm the throbbing in my temples and steady my shaking hands. I was aware that I was alone in the kitchen and that he was alone in the living room or the bedroom. The fear would leave me slowly, with my legs barely able to hold me.

I returned home at noon, after another full morning of wandering between factories and finding nothing. I announced my arrival loudly to Nezinho. He answered me from the living room, asking how I was and whether I had found anything. I said that I had seen many closed factories and had not found any job yet. "I haven't found anything either," he replied, taking a sip of his coffee. "I passed by a meat shop," I said on my way back to the kitchen. "Got us steaks for dinner. I will cook rice too."

Nezinho said nothing, but after a few moments he crossed the kitchen headed for the bathroom holding a pipe in his hand. "I bought a face mask," he said. "I'll rub it on while you cook. My skin is terribly dry."

He reappeared moments later with his face all plastered in white. I peeked through the door and watched him sit down on a chair and close his eyes.

Going back to the stove I called to him:

"How would you like your steak this time? Well done or rare?" At that moment I heard a scream and a thud. I rushed to the living room and found him lying on the floor, his body jittering from side to side, while he growled like an animal. With his white face and dark holes instead of eyes he looked like a ghost, a non-human being. I stood watching him from the doorway, afraid to go near him, not knowing what to do.

All of a sudden, I smelled something burning. I rushed to the pot only to discover the rice and steak were completely charred. I turned off the gas and went back to check on Nezinho who was sitting up on the floor with his eyes closed.

"All my food is burnt," I blurted out in distress. "Why are you letting these spirits enter your body and take over you!? I can't live like this anymore. I'm afraid to be near you. Since I was in that Kimbanda I am afraid to even be at home. Everywhere I go, I bump into statues of terrifying gods!" I stood there for a moment, trembling, and yelled again, "Look at yourself! You look like a demon, with that mask on your face! Now, of all times, you had to let them enter your body?"

"You mustn't talk about them like that," he said.

"Why shouldn't I? They are ruining my life!" I shouted. "They're everywhere. You've put statues even in my room. I live with them twenty-four hours a day, and you're telling me I'm not allowed to talk this way?"

At night, I was accosted by nightmares. I didn't remember what they were about but I woke up covered in sweat, with my heart pounding. I remember one of them. I was in a field lit up by the fire of torches and candles. A group of unfamiliar people were standing there with their heads bowed, swaying from side to side in a dance. Sometimes the light shone on their faces, but I couldn't recognize anyone. I didn't understand where I was or what I was doing there. Unexpectedly, a tall figure appeared and approached me. He looked like a human being, but from the waist up he had dark gray fur and his head was large, hairy and with two horns. The people in the field approached him slowly and formed a circle around him. As he spun in the center, he turned to look at me with his big red eyes. At that moment I was filled with terrible fear, because I knew the monster was Nezinho.

I was startled by a loud noise like a storm wind. I climbed out of the depths of the dream through vague layers of consciousness, until it was all over. I lay still, curled up inside myself, waiting for my pulse to stop racing. I rolled over on my stomach but my chest hurt, and I had to roll over and lie on my side again. I could find no rest.

The next day I slept late, not feeling my best. I was nauseous. The restless sleep had probably affected me. Nezinho was no longer at home. The nightmare was still spinning in my head and I wanted to drive it out of my mind. I got dressed, and was sorry to find that the pullover I had received from Manuela a few months ago had shrunk and become tight in the chest. I put on a wider shirt and started tidying up the house.

As I stood by the sink with my back to the rooms, I again felt someone standing behind me, someone with a dark fur and red eyes. I left the kitchen and wandered around the house with unease. The gods looked at me from their pedestal above the closet. I felt like I had to talk to someone, or I would lose my mind. Who could I talk to about this? I remembered the strong, authoritative figure of the Pai de Santo.

Yes, he was the best person to talk to about such matters. As I got off the bus, I bumped into Suali, the wife of a friend of Nezinho's. We greeted each other and my eyes rested on the round belly bulging out from under her dress. She smiled proudly.

"I'm already in the seventh month," she said. "And what about you? Nothing new?"

"Not yet," I replied with a shrug.

"So, when?" she insisted.

"I don't know," I said, smiling awkwardly.

"What are you doing in our neighborhood?" she asked. "Want to come over to my place?"

For a moment I thought that Suali was very nice, and she seemed to like me. Maybe I could talk to her, open up my heart and tell her everything I was going through. No, I thought, she wouldn't understand. She'd think I was weird or mentally unstable. It was better not to say anything. "Thanks, Suali. I need to sort out some stuff. Come to us on Saturday, okay? It's been a long time since we last saw each other."

I knocked on the door of Pai de Santo's house and his daughter opened without even a trace of a smile on her face. I asked if her father was there. She said yes, and that she would call him. Barely looking at me, she disappeared while I waited by the door. After a long time, he suddenly appeared. He did not seem distant or mysterious as he had in the gloom of the ceremonies. He was tall. His skin was a light chocolate shade, and he was smiling. After inviting me in he asked what the matter was and how he could help.

I searched for the right words to explain but couldn't find any, so I started to cry. He didn't stop me. He went to the kitchen and brought me a glass of water. He was a kind, humane person who knew how to listen.

I began to talk. I told him about the spirits entering his disciples' bodies, about the statues of the gods at home and in our bedroom. I told him about my bad dreams at night and my fears during the day, about the feeling that someone was trying to kill me. I poured my heart out about Nezinho being out of work. The Pai de Santo listened to me without interrupting. When I finally finished speaking, he looked at me, seeming upset.

"Adalberto isn't allowed to have gods in the house. He is not ready yet. This is not a game." He didn't call him Nezinho, but referred to him by his official name. "Tonight, at the ceremony, I will talk to him." He got up, and I followed him. "You did the right thing in coming to tell me," he added. "Don't worry, my daughter," he said affectionately. "Go home now, and everything will be alright."

Nezinho returned at night. I woke up when he lay down next to me. "You've been sleeping a lot lately," he said. "When I left in the morning you were still asleep." I said it was true, that I really was more tired than usual.

"I heard you talked to the Pai de Santo," he said softly. "He will try to help me." He caressed my hair and then my shoulders and arms. When he pulled me to him, I complied, but asked him to be careful when he touched my breasts. "Don't press hard, because for some reason it's very sensitive there." Nezinho replied that he really thought my breasts had swelled a little, and that he would try to be careful.

A few days later, I woke up late in the morning overcome with nausea. I dragged myself to the bathroom and despite my exhaustion I was relieved that the statues had finally left our home and that Nezinho's seizures had stopped. I silently thanked the Pai de Santos for making Nezinho stronger.

I undressed and turned on the water in the shower. I looked in the mirror, turning my sideways and examining my breasts, which had grown significantly. I concluded that they were beautiful anyway. I opened the closet to take out a clean towel and came across the sanitary napkins right next to the towels. The thought hit me that I hadn't needed them in a long time, and the sudden realization that I should have already had my period flashed through my mind. I was nauseous, and more tired than ever. Perhaps I was pregnant. I began to recall and calculate when the last time I had used a sanitary napkin was. I came to the conclusion that I was a whole month late.

Pregnancy

Concerned, I went to the hospital to take a pregnancy test. It came out positive. On the bus ride home, I sat paralyzed, thinking of the baby growing in my belly and shutting for me all the doors to freedom. I now had to get used to living with Nezinho. I would have to give up the dream of walking away one day, because it was not going to happen anymore. I tried to console myself with the thought that maybe my husband would change over the years. Maybe we would eventually be able to achieve a dignified, distress-free life together. I knew, however, that I was deceiving myself. I didn't have much time to grieve. I had more pressing things to worry about than the far future, with or without Nezinho.

We were both unemployed. It had been a month since I stopped working, which meant that within five months I would lose my healthcare benefits. If I didn't find a job for at least three months until the end of the pregnancy, I would have to give birth at home, because no hospital would take me. Who would employ me now, in my condition?

Back at home, while serving dinner, I announced to Nezinho: "I was at the hospital today and had some tests done. I'm pregnant." He looked up at me surprised and said nothing. Then he smiled, showing his white teeth, got up and came closer to me. He hugged me and said: "I can't believe we're going to have a baby." He stroked my hair and kissed my head. I forced a smile too, wondering angrily how on earth he didn't seem worried at all. He left all the worrying to me, and remained his light, carefree self.

The next evening, I went to see Manuela. She had finished her studies and had started to work. I was confined to a married life and we couldn't be as close as we were before. But that day I really needed her. After her initial excitement at the news of me having a baby, we brainstormed about how to find me a job.

"Maybe I'll be able to get you something," she said. "My boss likes me and maybe he'll agree to hire you. I won't tell him you're pregnant, because then you have no chance. No one at work must know." And I could see her point.

We agreed I would come by the next day and she would let me know if the answer was positive. Manuela's beauty and charisma worked like a charm in convincing the company manager to give me a job as a seamstress. She was a secretary in a small fashion clothing factory.

Manuela came down to meet me during the lunch break. Since I began working at the sewing factory, we could see each other every day.

"How do you feel?" she asked quietly.

"Very well," I said, then whispered so that no one would hear, "last night I felt the baby moving …"

"Wow, that's awesome!" she said, all excited. "That's why you're glowing." She squeezed my hand cheerfully.

"Aren't you going to get into trouble for coming down to see me?" I asked.

She once told me the boss had warned her against visiting me because it was not acceptable for office employees to socialize with factory workers. She shrugged, laughing: "What trouble? I really don't care if he doesn't like it. Stupid rules." I could only admire her composure. She was so confident of the power she had over men.

We went out into the inner courtyard and sat down on a bench. Workers put plates with food they brought from home on the tables by the benches, or pulled sandwiches out of their bags. Manuela shared the latest news about Madalena and the children. I told her about Nezinho's mother, who was ill and was admitted to the hospital for tests. Nezinho's uncle intended to sell the house of the grandmother, who moved to a care institution a few months earlier, and that included our house, built on the same plot. This meant we would have to look for another apartment soon.

We heard Manuela's boss calling her from inside the building. She glanced at the clock. "The break is over. How time flies when I'm with you." She kissed me on the cheek and hurried toward the stairs.

In the evening, as I walked home, I again felt a slight movement in my belly. I wore loose clothes so no one would notice I was pregnant, but I had begun to digest the thought. I resigned myself to the idea that I was trapped, and thought that having a baby of my own would make up for it. I remembered Marcia, who was already three years old, her small sticky hands wrapped around my neck, her wet kisses. In a few months I'd have my private little Marcia or maybe a Marcino, who knew, and that would be wonderful. It was also a huge responsibility. What kind of a mother would I be? Would I be able to take care of the child properly? It was a heavy burden! Nezinho would have to support us. Would he be up to the task?

The months of pregnancy flew by while I oscillated between anticipation and anxiety. Sometimes I couldn't sleep because of many scary thoughts about the birth itself. I didn't know much about the subject, except that it hurt and carried some risk. I had no one to ask. Of course, I couldn't talk about such things with my mother, and I hardly even saw her anyway. Maybe I'd ask my mother-in-law, Dona Auzira. How would I even know when I was due to give birth? No way. She would laugh at me. It was better if she didn't know how ignorant I was. Besides, she had enough problems with her own health. It was suspected she might have a bad disease. Nezinho was fast asleep next to me, and I tossed from side to side, unable to find rest.

One day Manuela came to see me during the lunch break with a somber face. She sat down next to me and said quietly: "My boss knows you're pregnant. He asked me and I had to admit it. I'm so sorry. You'll probably get fired." She patted my arm, looking sad. I held her hand and said:

"There's nothing we can do. We knew it would happen eventually. Don't be sorry. I'm so grateful because thanks to you I found this job. I got all my health insurance back, I can give birth in the hospital, and that's what matters." I stroked my round little belly under the bulky dress. "I'm surprised it took them so long…" I smiled. "Soon I'll be in my sixth month, so it'll really show. I don't mind leaving. There is a lot of work here and I almost always have to work overtime. My legs are swollen and achy because I spent so much time sitting down." At the end of the working day, the manager called me to inform me that I was fired.

When I opened my eyes, the sunlight lit the room through the window, and Nezinho was gazing at me.

"What time is it?" I asked in a panic.

"Just after nine," he said with a smile. He was lying on his side, resting his head on his hand. He reached out his other hand and pushed a strand of hair off my face. "You're not going to work today, remember?" He played with my hair, letting it flow between his fingers. His caress was pleasant and I smiled back.

"True. But I have to go look for a new job. It won't be easy for me to find something, in my condition," I said, stretching a bit. "It suits you. Pregnancy becomes you. It's nice to wake up together like this sometimes, without rushing to work." He said, taking a curl and pulling it gently forward to fall next to my forehead. He styled the ends, then looked at me intently and said, "Let's get up, have breakfast and then I'll do your hair. I'll cut it and do some highlights." He then ruffled my hair playfully. He liked doing my hair every now and then.

A week later, I found a temporary job as a sales agent for water purification devices. I went from house to house, clapping at the gates, and presenting each device in the catalog I carried with me. People received me kindly. My pregnancy made potential customers more attentive, and already in the first days I made two sales. I much preferred walking along the street from house to house than sitting for hours by the sewing machine, with the blood barely climbing up my swollen legs. In the evening I came home tired, after hours of walking.

One evening, when I found dirty dishes scattered on the table again, I grumbled to myself that things could not stay this way. The situation could not continue. Nezinho hung at home all day, didn't work and didn't help me with any of the chores either. I put a knife and two nearly empty mugs on a plate full of crumbs. There were cigarette butts floating in what was left of the black liquid. The nauseating smell of coffee and wet ashes rose up to my nostrils. Between half a slice of bread and mango peels I saw a small package. Inside were three marijuana leaves.

He must have smoked a few. I lost my temper. Grabbing the package, I screamed out loud: "Nezinho, what is this package doing here!? I told you I don't want drugs in the house!"

Nezinho appeared from the bedroom. "What are you yelling about?" he groaned.

"What am I yelling about?" I cried, throwing the package out the window into the yard. Nezinho lunged at me like a madman. I have never seen such rage in his face. He pushed me wildly and I fell to the floor. He grabbed me by the hair and started dragging me toward the front door, while I screamed in pain and fear. I felt like my scalp was being ripped off and I was terrified for the baby inside me, thinking it might get hurt. Nezinho ignored my screams. At that moment he wasn't sane. Perhaps he was even still under the effect of the drugs. He led me to the yard, to where the package had landed.

"Now pick it up and bring it home!" he roared.

I put the package on the table and collected the dishes. I didn't say a word. I cried softly with the phrase "My husband beat me" running through my head. "For the first time in my life, my husband hit me."

Suddenly I was accosted by concern that something bad might happen to my baby and I hoped with all my heart for a little movement, to signal to me that everything was fine. I finished cleaning the kitchen and my baby had not stirred.

I retreated into myself. All evening I didn't look at Nezinho. I didn't talk to him. When I got into the shower, I heard the kitchen door slam. Nezinho had gone out. I got into bed with my body all shriveled up, worried that I still did not feel any sign of life. Unable to sleep, I pressed the sides of my stomach to shake the baby a little—maybe she was just asleep. I got no response.

I closed my eyes and pleaded fervently: "I want my child to be alive and well. Please, God, make sure nothing bad happens to her." Suddenly I felt a light movement inside me, like a small wave, and then a kick in the sides of my pelvis. "Thank you, God," I thought, rubbing my belly with this new being inside.

The next day I didn't sell anything. It was difficult to promote a new kind of device that no one knew yet. I worked less than usual and headed to my parents' house. I had a strong desire to vent about all of yesterday's events, and when my mother woke up, I would be able to talk to her for a little while. She wouldn't justify Nezinho after he hit me.

I found her awake and upset. "What's wrong?" I asked. "Fia has left her husband," she announced angrily. "My daughters never cease to embarrass me. What does she think, that you can just get up and leave home like that? What will she do now alone? Poor Joao."

I wondered if he had done to her what Nezinho had done to me, and thought how great it was that she had the strength to leave him. Good for her. Obviously, there was no point in sharing with my mother what had happened to me. In the following days, Nezinho and I hardly exchanged a word.

In the meantime, I managed to sell another water purification device.

I was in the kitchen cooking for the weekend when Nezinho addressed me:

"My mother's condition is getting worse. I'm going to visit her at my sister's tomorrow. Do you want to come along?" Feeling a stab of sadness at the thought of Dona Auzira slowly fading away and leaving us, I agreed to go with him.

Nezinho's sister welcomed us with a hug and led us to her mother's room. Auzira was in bed, her skin hanging loosely around her face. She was very thin and had yellow circles around her eyes.

"Catarina and Nezinho have come to see you, mother," Nezinho's sister said to her, slowly and clearly. Auzira smiled weakly and motioned for us to approach. Nezinho kissed his mother's forehead and hand, and she caressed his face. With a soft pat on the sheet, she invited me to come sit by her side, and then put her hand on my lap.

"Catarina, my daughter," she said in a feeble voice, "I am so happy you're having a baby. I feel in my heart that you will have a baby girl. A few days ago, I dreamed you were having a daughter... She was silent for a moment, because speech was difficult for her. She took a deep breath and then continued. "I want you to name her Rebeca."

It was not a common name and I didn't know anyone named Rebeca.

"Why Rebeca?" I asked in bewilderment.

"It's a biblical name," she replied quietly. "Once on Sunday mass the priest told us about her. She was a strong woman, who knew what she wanted. She determined the fate of her sons, even if she had to break the rules." She paused for a moment and I rubbed her cold hand. "It's a good name for a woman," she whispered. "Call her Rebeca." A few days before the visit I was thinking of names for my child and decided that if I had a daughter, I would call her Fabiana. Fabiana is such a beautiful name.

"Well, Dona Auzira," I said softly. "I promise that if I have a daughter, I will name her Rebeca." That was the last time I saw her. She died a few days later.

After her death, Nezinio's uncle informed us that the house was sold, and that we had to find another apartment fast. Nezinho managed to find a cheap house, far from where we lived. The area we moved to, Villa Aro, was next to Villa Gutierres, where the madhouse was located, and those horrifying memories of my childhood lived. Around the time of the move, Nezinho found a job in the warehouse of a prestigious houseware and jewelry chain. I continued to sell water purification devices in the more respectable areas of Sorocaba. I didn't like being alone in our remote home, and preferred to be out all day, selling devices door to door. I exceeded my quota and received an extra bonus on top of my salary. Nezinho started to get back home later each day. He didn't even bother to come by the house before going out with friends, since we lived so far away. He just rode the bus straight from work to friends, card games, Umbanda ceremonies or the dance club.

By the beginning of the ninth month, my belly was already big and heavy. It was hard for me to run around in the summer heat of January and I stopped working. I began to prepare everything for the baby's arrival. I bought tiny knit tops and pants. I chose a soft woolen blanket with clouds in white, pastel pink and blue. I also bought baby soap and oil. Suali came to visit me with her cute six-month-old son, and a bag full of hand-me-downs.

Over the next few days, I washed and ironed the little garments, folded them and put them away in our bedroom closet. Another day had gone by. The house was clean, dinner was cooked, everything was ready for the new baby, and I was home alone, without a living soul to talk to. Thoughts about giving birth came back to disturb me.

I was afraid of not being able to bear the pain. I prayed that my baby would be born healthy and that I would survive. I turned on the record player in the living room and put on a Roberto Carlos record. I sat down on the floor and listened to music. Leaning against the wall, I closed my eyes and let peace come over me. In the middle of the night, I was awakened by the light that Nezinho turned on.

That morning the sky was cloudy. Strong winds were blowing, and it looked like it was about to rain. Nezinho went to work and I was alone. My stomach hurt, and I went back to bed. The gray sky peered through the window and branches swayed in the wind. The glare of the sun sometimes peered through the clouds, so I got up to shut the blinds and I lay down again. I closed my eyes and tried to rest, but the pain only intensified. The hours crawled slowly by. I wished Nezinho would be back already. Suddenly I heard the gate outside creak. Maybe he was early?

The clock showed only four in the afternoon. It was unlikely that Nezinho had already finished working. The pain was so strong I had trouble getting out of bed. I cried out that I was in the bedroom. After a minute someone tapped on the shutter from outside. I asked who it was. A child's voice answered me: "It's me, Ivone. Open the door."

I gathered all my strength and got up. Ivone almost never visited us, and on that particular day she was sent to me from heaven, like a gift. I slowly advanced toward the kitchen, supported by the furniture and walls, and opened the door for her.

"What's wrong with you, Catarina?" she asked, concerned.

"I don't feel well," I answered, "my stomach hurts a lot. Can you call Nezinho from the grocery store? Tell him he should take me to a hospital. Maybe something's the matter with the baby, because I'm in a lot of pain."

I explained to her where the money was in the kitchen cupboard and wrote his phone number on a piece of paper. Ivone ran out and returned ten minutes later. She told me Nezinho was already on his way. He arrived after what seemed to me a very long time. He asked a taxi driver to wait for us outside and came into the house to pick me up.

After sending Ivone home with a hug, I got into the *Beetle* next to Nezinho. On the way to the hospital the pain was so intense that I started to cry. He held me, stroked my hair and assured me everything would be fine. After the driver dropped us off at the entrance to the hospital, Nezinho helped me get out of the taxi and walk a few steps to the stairs. I climbed up slowly, and the moment I walked through the front door of the admissions department, I felt a warm stream running down my thighs, with a puddle forming at my feet. I didn't understand how I was urinating without feeling I was. I tried to hold back, but that didn't help stop the flow.

A nurse came quickly to tell me I would soon be transferred to the delivery room, and that I should not worry. She picked up the phone at the desk and within a minute an orderly appeared with a bed on wheels and helped me lie down on it. I was rolled down a corridor to a long room, separated into sections by curtain partitions. The orderly placed the bed behind one of the curtains, next to an outer wall. Through the window I could see the rain coming down hard. The nurse who had escorted us told another nurse who was in the room that my water had already broken and that my husband was dealing with the registration procedure at the reception. She stroked my forehead and said that the midwife would be examining me right away. I realized that the lukewarm water that came out of me was a normal phenomenon. The midwife arrived and asked me how I was feeling. I answered that the pain was getting stronger.

She checked me and said I didn't have an opening yet and that the birth would take some more time. An hour went by, followed by another one. The contractions were strong and came in waves. I stifled a sigh and the midwife came over to examine me again. She announced I had a four-finger opening but that labor could begin because my baby was small. She rolled my stretcher into the next room. It was a large one without windows, a high ceiling and a bed at the center. The midwife held my arms while I transferred to the bed. I lay on my back and she lifted my legs onto the stirrups for support. She examined me once again and determined it was time for me to push. I pushed as hard as I could but nothing happened. On the wall in front of me hung a crucifix. I looked at Jesus through the beads of sweat that trickled into my eyes, praying for him to deliver me from my agony.

"Is a contraction starting?" the nurse asked when she saw my face twitch. "So, push now, hard. Breathe, breathe," she said to me and wiped my forehead.

"Where is my husband?" I asked.

"He'll be back later. Now you have to push harder," instructed the midwife.

"I can't go on anymore," I whispered.

"What do you mean you can't go on?" she reprimanded me. "You want to have that baby, don't you? That's it, now it's coming. Hard!" She didn't think I was trying hard enough. "We're not making any progress like this," she said, losing her patience. In the next round I could no longer push at all. I was exhausted. "Don't let go now," she said firmly, "you have to try harder." A new wave rushed toward me, filling me with anxiety. At that moment the nurse leaned over my stomach with all her weight. I screamed, certain I was about to pass out, when all of a sudden, I heard a baby crying, and I don't remember anything more.

I woke up in the morning in a room with several beds, and a window on the wall next to me. The sky was clear and blue. Nothing hurt anymore. A ray of sunlight filtered through the window into the room illuminating the white sheets. A figure appeared against the sun, surrounded by a halo of light. She handed me a package and said: "Here is your daughter. You have a healthy baby girl. She was born weighing 2.3 kg. Take her in your arms. I'll help you nurse her."

As my newborn daughter's mouth latched onto my nipple, the nurse asked what I was planning to name her. "Rebeca Fabiana Nunes," I answered without hesitation. And so, on February 10, 1979, at the age of eighteen and three and a half months, I became a mother. I looked at the small face close to my breast. Her lips did not hold the nipple properly and her head moved restlessly from side to side. The nurse leaned over and pinched my breast.

"Not much milk is coming out yet. This happens sometimes in the first few days," she explained. "Keep trying to breastfeed every few hours. It will probably work out with time." The baby struggled for a few more minutes for the milk that didn't come out. She emitted a small bleat like a calf's. I tried to calm her down. I caressed her head, her cheek, pressed my swollen breast until a few transparent drops dripped down from it. Finally, Rebeca got tired and fell asleep. In the evening, Nezinho came to take us both home. We didn't have a crib, but I got a small mattress from a neighbor. Bringing two chairs closer to our bed, I pushed them together and put the mattress on them. The backrests acted as a railing so it wouldn't slide off.

I laid Rebeca on her new bed. Exhausted from her efforts to nurse she fell asleep after crying for an hour. She woke up several times during the night and cried for a long time. The milk that filled my breasts failed to come out, and I didn't know how to satisfy her hunger.

Rebeca

I went out into the yard to hang laundry leaving the windows and door open so I could hear Rebeca if she woke up. In the portico next to the house across from ours, sat a large, dark-skinned woman, with a small baby close to her chest. She stood up and approached our gate.

"Good morning," she greeted me, smiling, "and congratulations. Is it a boy or a girl?"

"A girl," I replied, returning her smile and walked toward her. The baby didn't stop nursing, nothing seemed to bother him.

"When did you get home?"

"Three days ago."

"Does she have colic?" she asked with a look of been-there-done-that.

"She cries a lot. I don't think I have enough milk," I said apologetically. "I feed her, and a minute later she starts to cry."

After a few seconds of silence, the woman said: "When she wakes up, come to me for coffee. My name is Aparecida. Cida for short."

"I'm Catarina."

Dona Cida opened the door for me. She was a woman of impressive size, with an ample figure, and was half a head taller than me. She wore a bright wide dress attached to which was a two-year-old toddler holding on to the fabric so as not to fall. His brown belly protruded above the shorts, the only piece of clothing he was wearing. He looked at me suspiciously, sucking his thumb. Clearly, he didn't want to share his mother with me. Dona Aparecida smiled broadly and invited me to come in and sit down in the living room. There were three other children in the house. As soon as I sat down, Rebeca started to cry.

"May I hold her?" Dona Aparecida asked. I handed her Rebeca and she sent her older daughter to make me coffee. She looked at my sobbing baby, then at me and said: "I nursed my son fifteen minutes ago and I still have milk left. Can I give it to Rebeca?"

Suddenly, the great onus I had felt since we returned from the hospital, disappeared. Could Dona Aparecida be my salvation? She opened the two top buttons of her dress, revealing a large, plump breast, with a nipple that looked like it had nourished five children. Rebeca caught it in her mouth and within a few seconds stopped whimpering. All I could hear were rhythmic sucking sounds. I was so jealous of Dona Aparecida's abundant motherhood, which oozed out of her with such ease. I felt ashamed of myself. But very quickly my envy and shame were replaced by enormous gratitude.

Meanwhile, Rebeca fell asleep. She was breathing peacefully with the nipple inside her open mouth. Dona Cida handed me my daughter and tucked the large breast back in, behind the two buttons. As soon as the spot became free, the toddler climbed back up her lap to hug her, and she enveloped him in her warm bosom.

"Bring her over whenever you need to," she told me. "Keep trying to breastfeed her so that your milk starts to flow, but if she stays hungry, bring her over." I nodded and thanked her profusely. That day I brought Rebeca to her at noon and in the evening again. When I was about to leave, she handed me a bottle with milk that she had pumped out, so that I would have it for the night. That evening, Rebeca was satisfied and calm. After giving her a bath, I put her on my bed. I wrapped her well with a *faixa de umbigo*[16] and dressed her in a tank top and a cotton diaper. Over that I tied another, wider belt. Lastly, I wrapped her up in a large sheet. She lay calm, like a package, on the mattress between the two chairs. Her tiny face was framed by black hair and her eyes were fixed on me.

---

16 The faixa de umbigo - umbilical band was a fine cotton band attached to the baby's body so that the outer, thicker cord (faixa) would not hurt her. The purpose of the ligaments was to fix the spine in place. At the time, it was believed that it was not good for the baby's body to be bent.

I continued to watch her even after she fell asleep. She slept for several hours straight, and so did I.

One morning I woke up and immediately turned to the chairs next to me, to see how she was doing. The chairs were empty. I jumped up in a panic, to find her lying on the mattress which had fallen to the floor when the two chairs slid away from each other during the night. With my face close to her I could feel her breath. She was sleeping peacefully. I thanked God that she was fine.

When Rebeca was two months old, I found a part-time job as a traffic inspector. I worked for a company that provided contracting services to the municipality. For four hours every day I sold parking stubs and gave out tickets to vehicles parked without stubs in city parking lots. During those hours I left Rebeca with another neighbor, who had a baby of her own and wished to care for another child.

After work I would run to the sitter's home and take my daughter back. We walked home at leisure, with her in my arms, close to my heart. She was small and light and did not weigh me down at all. I didn't even care that we went back to an empty house every day. I bathed her and made her a bottle of baby formula. She ate little. I learned to let her rest before feeding her again. The nurse at the clinic thought she needed to eat more, because she was too slow in gaining weight. I put the bottle aside and held her up in front of me.

"My darling filha," I said to her, "you know you have to eat so you can grow, don't you?" I kissed her nose and she wrinkled it with a grin. I hugged her and kissed the top of her head. Her black hair tickled my face and I thought she was way better than a corn doll with yellow hairs. We spent the afternoons together. I talked to her a lot and with time, she started to answer. After dinner and a bath, I would place her on the two chairs. She moved restlessly on the mattress until she fell asleep. Only then could I clean the house and cook.

Eventually, I went to sleep in the bed next to her, usually alone. When she was a little older, she switched to eating porridge made with cow's milk. Every morning of the week, the milkman came by with a horse-drawn cart and left two bottles of milk by the door. That Sunday I wanted to prepare Rebeca's dinner, and I discovered that all the milk I had left had gone sour. There was no money at home to buy new milk. Nezinho, as usual, was not there.

The sun was setting and a strong wind was blowing. Having no other choice, I wrapped Rebeca in a blanket and left on foot to my parents' house. I walked for about an hour with Rebeca in my arms. Every time the wind picked up, I pressed her face to my chest and covered her head with the blanket. I knew my dad had a job at the time and that my parents would be able to help. I arrived home out of breath. Father was lying in bed in his room and Mother was sitting in the kitchen. She received me unenthusiastically. I sat down next to her with Rebeca on my lap.

"Mother," I said, "the milk I had at home has gone bad. I have nothing to feed the baby tonight."

"You know we don't keep milk in the house," replied my mother.

"I can't leave Rebeca without food," I said, "I'm sorry to be asking, but I need some money to buy milk. I know Father got paid this week. Could you lend me the money? I promise to pay you back next week."

My mother looked at me coldly. "I won't give it to you. Take the girl and go away."

I will remember that moment for the rest of my life. It drilled its way down into the dustbin of my memories, joining the cold scissors that cut my hair close to the scalp, and the endless weekends at Claudia's where I waited in vain for my mother to come visit me. Her icy words, "Take the girl and go away" landed on top of the pile of debris with a loud clang, and on their way down, they tore the last emotional thread that connected me to my mother. I took the girl and left.

Suali lived a few blocks away. I knocked on her door and she opened. With all her heart, she gave me half a bottle of milk for free.

At seven months of age, Rebeca was small and thin, with a tiny face and big black eyes. We came home from the sitter and I made her a bottle, but she refused to drink. I held her, talked to her tenderly, and tried to feed her again. She took a few sips and then threw up the little she had swallowed. When I changed her diaper before bed and there was only urine in it, I thought I should check with the woman who took care of her if she'd had any bowel movements that day. She confirmed that Rebeca had not had any on that or on the previous day. Even when I picked her up at noon, she said that there had been no news on the matter, that she had no appetite and that she was fussy, as if something were bothering her.

The doctor who examined her at the clinic instructed me to give her a laxative if her digestion did not improve. In the evening I gave her the medication. Rebeca woke up crying several times that night. In the morning there was still no improvement and she refused to eat. Nezinho couldn't be bothered and went to work at the usual time.

I got on the bus and took my daughter to the hospital. Following an initial examination, they connected her to an IV line, because she was weak from lack of nutrition. They ran a series of tests and the doctor explained to me that her digestive system was not functioning properly, it was not clear why. There was no real treatment for her illness, so there was no point in keeping her in the hospital.

All they could do was to ease the bowels temporarily and make her a little stronger, nothing more.

The doctor told me to come back to the hospital if she stopped eating again. In the following months I was less and less able to work. Rebeca usually threw up most of what I fed her. Sometimes she would strain until her face turned red and then start crying. I hurried to check, but the diaper was still clean.

I eased the constipation with the means at my disposal. When the situation worsened, we would go to the hospital, where they would feed her via IV, give her a bowel washout to relieve her, and examine her without finding anything new.

It was always just the two of us alone, without Nezinho. Just Rebeca and I. I would sign the hospitalization consent form according to the procedure and return home, because the parents were not allowed to spend the night there. The next day I would go to the hospital again to be with her, until they released her home.

One morning there was a knock on the door and a photographer was standing outside, as was customary at the time, offering to take a family portrait. Politely, I almost refused. A professional photo was a luxury I could not afford. I looked at Rebeca and she was so small and pale, almost transparent. Without actually realizing why, I felt I needed a picture of her, to tattoo her into reality, before she disappeared. I told the photographer he was welcome to come in. I chose a red and white gingham dress with a ruffled hem and dressed her in it. She posed quietly and seriously while the photographer took her picture. She didn't object when I changed her clothes to a white, knitted woolen outfit.

The photographer returned after a month and a half with the photos. By then Rebeca was already very sick, and I was exhausted and desperate. Since I didn't have money to buy them, he left with the pictures. I sat at home heartbroken, wanting the pictures so badly.

Back home from the hospital I looked at the small package wrapped in a blanket on my lap. She looked back at me with black eyes that covered most of her face. Through the thin hair I saw two rows of needle marks along the veins, on both sides of the skull. Her head had been pierced for the IV line and she was fading away.

The next time, I went to a different hospital, Santa Casa in the city center, far from where I lived. They didn't know what the problem was either, and only treated the symptoms.

At the age of one she became very weak. For her birthday I bought her a new dress and we celebrated at my parents' house. Nezinho held her in his arms—a tiny baby in a white dress embroidered with pink and blue flowers.

A few days later her digestive system stopped functioning completely, and nothing I did helped. I gave her a bath, laid her next to me in bed and caressed her little body. Her intestines were swollen and their contour became visible under the thin skin. She gazed at me with sad intentness, her tiny hand reaching out to touch my cheek. I held her close to me, helpless to do anything. In the morning I took her to the hospital again. The doctors examined her and looked concerned. I had to sign for hospitalization as usual, and as always, I was alone.

I had a feeling that this was probably going to be the last time, that I would not take her out of there anymore. I couldn't bring myself to sign, as though I was giving up on her. I tried to postpone the end. I said I would come back later with the father, and we would both sign. The doctors would not allow me to leave her there without signing and they also objected to me taking her home, because she would not survive without treatment. I signed.

I got home before noon. I hadn't gotten any sleep the night before so I went to bed. In my agitated sleep, I saw an operating room and Rebeca lying in the corner. I knew she was dead.

I woke up with my heart pounding. It was five in the afternoon. Nezinho had just entered the house with a friend and arranged for a card game. I got up trembling, and told him what I saw in my dream. I wanted us to go to the hospital. It was stormy outside and rain was pouring down. Nezinho said I was imagining things and that I should relax. He was sure everything was fine. If I didn't want to play cards with them, I could go back to sleep. One couldn't go to the hospital in such weather. I burrowed under the blanket and tried to fall asleep, not to think, not to be afraid and not to feel.

I woke up early in the morning. Through vague consciousness I heard voices and knew they were policemen. They knocked on the neighbors' door and asked for my address. I knew why they were looking for us. Rebeca had died on the operating table. She had to have surgery, and the doctors had no way to locate us to get our approval.

Nezinho went to the hospital to get the little body in the coffin. I gave him the dress embroidered with blue and pink flowers. Before the funeral, I saw Rebeca for the last time. I stroked her face and arms. I lifted the dress to say goodbye to the small body I knew so well. On the left side of her chest, just below the heart, there was a large bruise from an unsuccessful CPR attempt.

My mother did not attend the funeral. She went to work. Neither did Dita. My father, my brother and Ivone did. After the funeral we went to my parents' home. When my mother got home, she sat down with all of us. I saw she was crying. Dita also arrived. Unexpectedly, she approached me.

"I'm sorry, Catarina," she said and began to cry. I did not understand what she meant. "It's all my fault." She broke down in tears and fell to her knees. "I'm so sorry. I cast a spell and cursed Rebeca, because I was jealous of you. I'm so sorry."

The day of the funeral was as rainy and stormy as the day of the birth. I returned home lonelier than ever, heavy with grief and guilt. To this day I don't know if I was a good enough mother. Maybe I could have done more. Maybe I should have taken her to a big city, to São Paulo for example, to the most advanced hospitals. Maybe they could have helped.

It's been almost thirty years and I still cry when I remember.

After Rebeca

A month and a half after Rebeca's death, the photographer came by and knocked on our door. I still had no money to buy the pictures. This time I couldn't hold back and I burst into tears. Surprised, he asked me what the matter was. Between sobs I told him that my little girl had passed away. He offered his condolences, gave me the photos as a gift, and left.

After the day of the funeral, my mother never mentioned Rebeca again.

Brazil's traditional carnival began the next day. Nezinho disappeared and returned only three days later. He arrived at night, got into bed and pressed his body against mine. His passion disgusted me. I pushed him away from me and told him I didn't want him to touch me anymore. We lost the last thing we had in common and I feel no connection to him. My outburst must have touched him. He realized he had crossed a line. When I told him that I couldn't live in that place anymore because everything reminded me of Rebeca, he agreed I should look for a new place. A week after the funeral, I dreamed about my baby again. It was a hard, blurry dream. I saw her body rotting and disintegrating until nothing was left of it.

I soon found another house, not far from my parents, and we moved in. I took with me all of Rebeca's belongings, the bathtub and the chest of drawers containing the clothes, bottles and pacifiers. I couldn't give any of that up. I set out to find a job in my new neighborhood.

I combed the streets looking for ads at the entrance to businesses. A sign on one of the doors of the buildings caught my attention: *Intern needed at the Physical Therapy Clinic*. That was exactly what I had been praying for. It brought me closer to my dream, to practicing the profession I had studied. I knocked on the door and entered. The secretary asked me to wait for the director to become available to see me.

Finally, a beautiful young woman with wavy black hair and slightly slanted eyes came out of one of the rooms. She wore a white coat over white pants, smiled warmly, and introduced herself as Takako. I expressed my interest in the position advertised outside. She asked about my studies and previous experience and said with reservation that I had no real training. A nursing course was not enough to work as a physiotherapist.

"I will learn!" I pleaded. "I must find a job! And I want this one so badly!" I poured my heart out to her and told her I had lost my daughter, that I wanted to start a new life without my husband and that I had to stand on my feet financially. "I will stay after work hours and study on my own time!" I promise. Takako looked at me hesitantly. She would consult with the owner and I was welcome to wait a few moments. After speaking briefly on the phone inside the office she announced:

"We're taking you for a month's trial. Here are some brochures and several articles. You will have to learn the theory and also do some practical work. It's not going to be easy. At the end of the month, we will make our decision."

I worked hard, arriving early in the morning before work hours. I asked Takako, who was already there, to explain to me whatever I didn't understand in the brochures. I learned a lot from her. I spent time with the other therapists, watching them work. In the evening I delved into the written material again. After a month I was hired. On Saturdays we worked half a day and I watched how Takako handled the complicated cases. We became friends, and sometimes I went along with her to shopping malls.

Under the white coat she usually wore a light silk shirt, with prints in delicate patterns, which went very well with her white trousers. I enjoyed looking at her. I loved going into expensive fashion stores with her, the ones I never dared to visit alone, and admiring the elegant store designs, the finely made items hanging in rows on hangers. That evening I arrived home after being out with Takako. The house was empty but traces of Nezinho's presence were clearly visible—dirty dishes left in the sink, the kitchen table covered in crumbs and ashes, coffee cups scattered around the house.

Why did I have to live like that? Why did I stay with him? What bound me to a person who contributed nothing to my life? The last thing that connected us was taken from me forever. The tears burned my throat. Nezinho came home late. I greeted him with an indifferent "Hello," but he was in high spirits and lay down next to me on the bed. He tried caressing my hair and bringing his body closer to mine.

"Leave me alone," I hissed. He tried to press his lips to my neck. "I don't want you to touch me."

"What's going on, Catarina? We haven't been together in a long time. You are always tired. You're my wife, aren't you?"

"I don't want to be your wife!" I finally snapped. "You don't have a job. You don't do any of the housework. What do I need you for anyway? Nothing is holding us together anymore!"

Nezinho was speechless for a moment and then asked quietly: "Don't you want me anymore?"

"No," I said decisively. "I don't want you anymore."

Following another silent pause, he got out of bed and left the room. I heard him moving around the house, opening and closing cupboards and drawers. Then I heard him go out into the garden, and before I fell asleep, I saw the flickering of a fire in the yard and smelled burning papers. In the morning he was asleep in the bed next to me, but when I came back from work, I found a note saying that he was leaving me and going back to his parents' house, to live with his father and brother.

The cupboards were empty of his belongings. He probably burned in the yard the things he no longer needed, which seemed like a strange thing to do. I had waited so long for that moment, and it arrived without a warning. He must have thought I would go looking for him. It didn't make sense for him to give up so easily.

My first thoughts were about what he would do without me. I knew it wouldn't be easy for him alone, without a home, without an anchor in life. But I immediately curbed my compassion. He deserved what he got and I had to think about myself. I had to seize the opportunity with both hands, before he regretted it. I found a lawyer who quickly drafted a separation agreement and sent it to him. According to the Brazilian laws of 1980, the divorce becomes official three years after the separation of the couple.

I left the house which was too big and expensive for me, and found a small room. I put the bed in place and unpacked a few necessary items. The rest remained in boxes piled up against the wall.

I dedicated most of my time to working at the institute. I signed up for an evening course in biology and physiology and studied once a week. As the economic situation worsened, the institute was forced to reduce personnel and I was laid off once more. I immediately found a job as a physical therapist at the Santa Casa Hospital, where Rebeca was born and died. The physical therapy room was in a separate building, and I was careful not to approach the corridors of the maternity or pediatric wards.

A little before noon on Sunday, I went to visit my parents. Father made coffee and Mother just woke up. She sat across from me in the kitchen and lit a cigarette.

"When are you going to bring your husband back home?" she asked. I was silent for a moment and then replied that I had initiated proceedings for a divorce. Mother blew out smoke and narrowed her eyes.

"You can't get a divorce," she interrupted. "My daughter will not be a divorced woman who everyone talks about behind her back. You need to bring your husband home and resolve the issues between you. What do you think, that you are the only one who has problems? Everyone has, and solves them. Divorce is not a solution."

I bit my lower lip and answered while keeping my cool. "My problems with Nezinho cannot be solved. I don't want to be his wife anymore."

"If you get divorced, you will no longer be my daughter."

I did not answer. I could only think about how she still managed to surprise me. I looked at Father, but he buried his face in his coffee cup, saying nothing. After a few minutes of silence, I got up and left through the open door. I walked along the quiet streets, feeling completely alone. I hadn't really had a mother for a long time, and now I didn't have a family either.

I swallowed tears of anger and loneliness and kept walking. I entered my small, cramped home and looked around. Nothing was keeping me there, dammit. Why did I have to stay buried in that forgotten neighborhood? I didn't have anyone there anyway. I need to think about what to do with myself.

Two weeks after being cut off from my family, Ivone came to visit me. It was wonderful to see her. I hugged her tightly. I made dinner and we ate together, talking and laughing. A few days later she knocked on the door again. She looked sad and guilty. She told me that Mother found out she had been with me and got very angry with her. She forbade her to see me again. That night I had a dream. I saw my Rebeca dressed in white. She was smiling and looking happy. Knowing she was well where she was, I woke up filled with peace.

A year after Rebeca passed away, I could finally start saying goodbye. I told my friends at the hospital that I was looking for a place to live, and that a modest room would be enough for me. Dona Ana, one of the nurses, said there was an empty storage room in the backyard of the house where she lived, and the owner might agree to rent it to me. The next day she arrived with good news and already that evening I went to see the room. It was shabby but cheap, and in the center of the city—far from all the places that reminded me of all the houses I wanted to forget: The house where I lived with Nezinho, my parents' house, the cemetery. I gave all of Rebeca's belongings to a poor neighbor who had three children. I sold the furniture I had, including the double nuptial bed, and bought a narrow one that fitted in the small room.

I only went home to sleep. I worked five days a week until half past seven in the evening. The biology course I signed up for was every Saturday from two to seven in the evening.

Carlos

One day, on my way home from school, a car pulled up next to me. A man stuck his head out the window. He didn't look very young, maybe fifty. He had a full head of hair peppered with white, and a pleasant face. He smiled at me and I smiled back. He asked where I was in such a hurry to go and if he could take me there. I replied that I was rushing home and thanked him, but that I was not in the habit of getting into strangers' cars.

"Is your husband waiting for you at home, that you have to get there so early?" Thinking to myself that actually no one was waiting for me in my dark room, I shook my head. "So maybe you'd like to join me for a drink. I need a cup of coffee before I drive any further. If you don't wish to get into my car, we can walk."

I remembered my modest room, in which I couldn't even make a cup of coffee, and smiled awkwardly. He got out of the car and came to greet me. He looked impressive. He was of average height, and I was a couple of inches taller, but his body was well built and his face handsome. He had a trustworthy look and a captivating smile.

I liked him.

We walked together to a nearby cafe. I ordered Guaraná[17] and he ordered a glass of beer and *linguiça calabresa*,[18] topped with onion rings and fries.

"I love Brazil," he said, sitting back in his chair. "There are people of all nationalities and cultures here, and I can feel at home." I had noticed a heavy, non-local accent. The waiter placed our order on the table. A pungent smell rose from his plate. He cut a piece of calabresa and chewed on it with pleasure.

He was married and had three children, he told me. He left Portugal with his family a few years earlier, went to Mozambique, took part in the construction of a beer factory, and then moved to Brazil.

I also told him about my life, about Rebeca and the divorce. At the end of the evening, he gazed at me warmly and said he was looking forward to seeing me again. I didn't have a phone number to give him but he handed me a business card. I preferred that he not escort me home, and we parted there.

The card said:

Carlos Sosa Machado
Electrical and Electronics Engineer

On the bottom was a phone number. I walked slowly through the quiet streets, pinning the card to my heart.

There was magic in that evening, and a happiness I hadn't felt in a long time. I kept the card in my wallet until I got to my room. Once in

---

17   A Brazilian soft drink made from berries.
18   A Portuguese dish similar to smoked sausage.

bed I read it again. Carlos, Electrical and Electronics Engineer. His peculiar accent played in my head. He was educated, interesting and very charming but... married. I don't want to be the lover of a married man. Sighing, I returned the card to my wallet. I closed my eyes and relived the memories of the evening in my head again, because I decided that was the first and last time we saw each other, and I would never call him.

During the week images of Carlos getting out of the car or Carlos chewing calabresa popped up before my eyes. I thought I could smell the sausage and the onions. Then, on Thursday, when I left work, a metallic green car was parked in front of the hospital gate. It looked familiar to me. I immediately recognized the graying mane of hair and my heart danced with joy. This time I got into the car without fear. We spent about an hour together in a cafe. After that he drove me home and I got off at the corner of the street.

A few days later I called him, and from that day on, once a week, he waited for me near work. Sometimes we also saw each other on Saturdays. Our meetings were not long. An hour in a cafe and then he returned to his wife and three children, who were waiting for him at home. His eldest daughter, it turned out, was my age.

A month went by, and one evening he invited me to dinner at a restaurant. He led me chivalrously to the entrance and opened the door for me. The space inside was dimly lit, with a pianist playing a slow love song. The tables were covered with tablecloths, set with glass goblets and a lighted candle. I felt like I was in a dream when he pushed my chair closer to the table after I sat down. He ordered a bottle of wine. A few sips later I was giddy and giggling a lot.

"Carlos, thank you very much. It was really delicious. I enjoyed it so much," I said to him as we stepped out into the cool air and walked outside, arm in arm. He walked me to the car door and closed it for me once I was inside. He sat down in the driver's seat and looked at me for a long time.

"I really enjoyed it too," he said. He reached out and stroked my hair gently. Then he leaned over to me, and since I didn't flinch, he kissed me on the lips. His kiss was soft and warm and I didn't want it to end.

After a few trysts where we kissed in the car in dark parking lots or on some hidden bench, Carlos invited me to have breakfast on Saturday.

He picked me up from the street corner and asked if I wanted to eat at a motel. "That way I can hold you and be close to you without you jumping in panic every time you think you hear footsteps," he said, smiling at me. With my heart pounding, I agreed.

We left the city and Carlos stopped at a countryside motel. We entered a well-kept garden in full bloom, its lawn stretching out to the edge of a small lake, with white swans swimming in it. Carlos asked me to wait a moment while he went to the reception. When he came back, he took my arm and opened one of the doors that faced the garden. The room was beautiful and bright. A round table for two in one of the corners was covered with a long tablecloth that reached the floor. On it was a basket full of bread rolls, a tropical fruit platter, and cheeses of various kinds.

The porcelain cups matched the plates and the coffee pot. He poured me some and asked me how my week had gone. We drank, ate a little and talked. Slowly my discomfort disappeared. When he put his arms around me, I felt very close to him, like there was no one but us in the universe. He gently pulled me to the bed with him and lay down next to me. We held each other tightly, and remained like that for a few minutes. He began to caress me slowly, starting with my hair, my neck. He then unbuttoned my shirt and said in a hoarse voice:

"You are the most beautiful woman I have ever known." He kissed me. He kissed every inch of my body. We made love, and it was unlike anything that had ever happened with Nezinho. It was the first time I could call it *making love*. Nothing hurt and the feeling of elation only increased. Suddenly I felt such great pleasure that I erupted in tears. Stunned, Carlos asked if he had hurt me and if so, he apologized. I laughed through my tears and told him that, on the contrary, I had never felt that good and that it was the most beautiful thing I had experienced in my life. He pressed my body tighter to his and kissed away my tears. We stayed that way, in a long embrace.

The Change

Three months after I started my job at the Santa Casa de Sorocaba Hospital, just before I was eligible for tenure, I was fired. I found a job at a dental laboratory as a clerk, a boring job I hated, and I was relieved when I was let go after a few months. Carlos and I kept in touch. I wanted nothing from him, only his friendship and love. He knew how to give and I finally found great love in my life.

In 1980, when the first mall opened in Sorocaba, I found a job as a salesperson in a large store for baby accessories and clothing. Toward the end of the season, the apparel stores in the mall decided to have an independent fashion show, and they asked me to model.

I told Carlos and he came. As I walked the runway, almost like a professional model, I recognized him in the crowd, watching me in admiration. The next time we met he hugged me, told me I was wonderful, and handed me a small package wrapped in beautiful paper. The gift was a fine porcelain figurine of a dog sitting on its hind legs with its front paws gracefully bent. It looked at me with green glass eyes that penetrated my heart.

As my room had no refrigerator or stove, I could not prepare anything to eat. I ate at work or at Dona Ana's. Sometimes I would spend weekends with the Mendes family, who substituted for my family. We sat in Manuela's room chatting like we used to, like sisters. On her dresser I saw a book by Sidney Sheldon titled *The Other Side of Midnight*. I picked it up and flipped through.

"Catarina," Manuela said, "you must read this book. I just finished it and it is fascinating. I couldn't put it down. Take it." That evening I went to bed with the book and read all night long under the pale light of the lamp hanging from the ceiling. Early in the morning I fell asleep for a few hours, and at work I waited for the time to pass so I could return to my book. Even when I went to Dona Ana for dinner, I took it with me to read there. She looked at me with an amused look and asked what was so interesting that I couldn't put the book down. I continued reading at night in bed and finished the book early in the morning.

On the way to work I stopped at a newsstand and bought a local newspaper from São Paulo. That morning I was Noelle,[19] empowered and experienced, who would not let anything stand in her way. I opened the job section and scanned through it. I caught a message that was addressed to me personally—a physical therapist needed in Largo Do Arouche.[20] At dinner I took out the ad I had clipped and showed it to Dona Ana.

"I'm going to São Paulo," I announced to her. She looked at the ad with curiosity, then at me, and shrugged.

"Do you have money for the trip?" she asked.

"I'll be fine," I replied.

The next day I called Carlos and asked him to meet me. We arranged for him to pick me up from work. He was waiting for me by his green car and opened the door for me. For the first time since we met, I asked him for a loan—twenty-eight Cruzeiros, to get to São Paulo and back.

I took a day off and went to São Paulo, with the ad in my bag. I got out of the bus station and an elderly lady directed me to Largo Do Arouche. I walked for twenty minutes, until I arrived at a magnificent high-rise building with a doorman at the entrance who told me to take the elevator to the institute on the tenth floor. I entered the waiting room and sat down. Two girls wearing heavy make-up, dressed in miniskirts and boots, sat on a couch next to me. They didn't look anything like the physiotherapists at the hospital. They were called into the office, stayed for a few minutes and left the place, one by one.

I walked in, and the man sitting behind the desk looked at me questioningly. I said I had come in response to the ad. Eying me in an odd way he said:

"Young lady, this position would not suit you."

"I'm experienced, really," I insisted. "Here, look."

---

19 The heroine of Sheldon's story. A girl from a French town runs away to Paris and after a severe crisis she toughens up and builds herself a glorious career.
20 Largo Do Arouche - an area of São Paulo.

I showed him my work registration booklet.

"I came from Sorocaba just for this job interview," I said, almost begging.

He looked at me with pity and explained that the job was not really about physical therapy...

In the elevator going down I cried for my naivete and for the money I had wasted traveling to São Paulo. I was walking down the street still in tears when I saw a sign on a lamppost, directing to the *Santa Casa de São Paulo Hospital* on the left. This name, I thought, resurfaced in all the important moments of my life, moments of joy and moments of sorrow. This was fate signaling me. I decided to follow the sign. I arrived at an ancient building surrounded by a wall made of burnt bricks, with a huge iron gate.

Once I passed through the gate, I was in a fairy tale, in a large, shaded garden, with a path winding between trees planted on the lawns. The road led to a structure similar to a cathedral, with three wings. The red brick walls were decorated with moldings, and so were the tall, arched windows. Its turrets looked like watchtowers, with pointed dark slate roofs. It was the most beautiful and majestic building I had ever seen.

I chose randomly and headed to the one on the right. At the top of the stairs, near the front door, I saw the figure of a nun dressed in white. I walked up and approached her. I simply told her that I had come from Sorocaba to look for a job, that I finished nursing school and that I had experience in physical therapy. She examined me and said:

"Go to the building on the far left. That is the oncology institute, for cancer. Look for a gentleman named Guido. He will know about a job for you."

I thanked her and followed her instructions. I had a kind of strange feeling, like she was an angel sent to me, to point my life in the right direction. At that moment I realized I should have asked her name, so that I could tell Guido who sent me to him. But when I turned back, she was gone.

At the entrance to the oncology building, I asked a guard dressed in an eggplant-colored uniform where I could find Mr. Guido. To my surprise he answered that it was him, and indeed I saw the name next to the letters IAVC[21] on the white label pinned to his robe. I told him that a nun from the first building on the right had suggested I talk to him.

"A nun?" he said, looking at me with curiosity. "Nuns haven't worked here in many years."

I was silent for a moment, embarrassed, then I said: "I'm looking for a job."

He nodded and said, "Come with me to the office and fill out the forms." I followed him along a corridor with chairs against the walls, and several closed doors in between. He stopped next to one of them and told me to sit and wait for the manager to invite me in. After a few minutes, a bespectacled Japanese man appeared in the doorway. He greeted me and handed me some forms to fill out, and a cheap pen. I put my bag on my lap and the sheets of paper on it so I could write. The man came back just as I finished, took the forms and looked them through.

"Do you have your registration booklet with you?" he asked. I said I did and handed it to him. He opened the notebook and leafed through it.

"We don't need a physical therapist. The only position we have is as a nurse in the operating room. I see you have no experience in the field."

"I can learn!" I retorted immediately. He examined me, adjusting the glasses on his nose.

"Yes, you can," he said. "Your job will be to assist the nurse who hands the instruments to the surgeon, that is to say you will arrange the tools and organize everything as needed."

"I'm fine with that."

He took the forms and disappeared into his office for ten very long minutes.

"Come here," he said when he returned, gesturing to me to sit down across the desk from him. He pulled out a printed page from one of the drawers and asked: "Can you start on Monday?"

I made a quick calculation. Four days to get all my affairs in Sorocaba in order should suffice. When I nodded, he seemed satisfied, and handed me the list.

---

21 IAVC - the initials of Institute Arnaldo Vierra de Carvalho, the name of the oncology institute within the hospital.

"Please bring the documents listed here, and also two photos," he said, pointing to the last line.

"So is the job mine for certain?" I asked, making sure I had not misunderstood. After all, this entailed leaving the room I lived in and my workplace, and moving to another city.

"You'll start with a three-month trial period, and then we'll see. I suppose you'll be needing a place to live?" he said. "There is a boarding house for girls on Veridiana Street, right across from the hospital. Tell the landlord you're starting to work here, and he'll find you a room."

"Thank you very much," I said with real emotion, "I'm truly grateful." He smiled briefly and held out his hand for a shake.

"See you on Monday at seven o'clock in the morning. Good luck, Catarina."

As soon as the manager shut the door to his office, I erupted into leaps along the corridor, all the way to the front door. "Mr. Guido! They hired me, they hired me!" I cried and gave him a big hug. He shook my hand with a look of surprise and wished me success.

I floated down the street and without noticing, found myself at the bus stop. During the trip back, my mind was already going down the checklist of all the things I had to do. I had to notify my employer, tell my friends and Carlos, get rid of the little furniture I had and pack up the rest.

Thanks to the book, I was about to start a new life. I managed to sell a chest of drawers and a closet that filled my small room to cover my travel expenses to São Paulo. I gave away the rest of the furniture. I resigned from the baby supply store.

Although Carlos was happy for me, there was a trace of sadness in his eyes. I realized we would no longer be seeing each other so often.

Santa Casa de São Paulo

On Sunday I got on the bus to São Paulo carrying three bags. From the central station I took a taxi to the address of the boarding house for women. The landlord said he had a room available but demanded payment in advance. I explained to him that I was going to receive my first salary in two weeks' time and in the meantime, I could give him everything I had, including my ID card as a guarantee, and he agreed. I was penniless, unable to even buy myself food.

On Monday I got up early. Hunger is an excellent alarm clock. I walked to the hospital thinking about the breakfast they served there. I showed up at seven at the office with all the necessary documents. A nurse was waiting for me and introduced herself as Odette. "I will be your guide until you learn the job and can do it on your own. Let's go eat and then I'll show you what you need to do."

In fifteen minutes, we ate a bun with butter and jam, and drank coffee with milk. I followed Odette through the long corridors to the elevator. When it arrived, I followed her in, and Odette closed the accordion-shaped lattice door. We went up to the third and last floor in front of a wide door.

Odette pressed a button on the wall and buzzed the door open. There we were, in the Holy of Holies—the surgery department. In the women's changing room, a young doctor in a hospital uniform hung the clothes she had taken off a few minutes before on a hanger. She spoke to another doctor around the same age about her recommendations for prolonged chemotherapy treatments. The significance of this made me shiver. Here I was, Catarina, from the slums of Sorocaba, having fought for each one of the six years of schooling I was rewarded with, in the company of such important, educated people.

Odette ordered me to take off all my clothes, keep my underwear and bra, and put on the sterile white shirt and pants she handed me. I wrapped my shoes in cloth covers and stuffed all my hair into a cap, also white. At the entrance to the operating room was a large sink with a tub full of antiseptic in one corner. We washed our hands, dipped them in a tub and slipped on gloves. The moment of truth had come. My knees were shaking. Odette looked at me with curiosity and I whispered to her that this was my first time in an operating room. She took my hand, held it between her rubber gloves and told me not to worry. She would help me and everything would be fine.

She pulled out of a closet a large metal case wrapped in cloth and opened it.

"These are the instruments the surgeon will need today," she explained to me. She picked out several steel scalpels and showed me how to arrange them by the operating table.

"This case came out of the autoclave, a kind of sterilization oven," she continued. She then opened a drawer, picked out some threads and needles, and handed them to me. "Here are the sutures for sewing up the internal organs. You see, they are extremely thin and are absorbed into the tissue after some time. And here are the thicker sutures, for external stitches. They are removed after about ten days. Now place them here. No, turn them the other way, yes, like this." I arranged the sewing instruments next to the scalpels as instructed. I tried to remember everything, file it in my head and not get it mixed up.

We laid sheets on the bed, and then arranged more folded sheets wrapped in paper, whose purpose was to cover the patient, on the table. They had an opening at the chest, where the surgeon would be performing the incisions. We opened the paper wrapper without touching the sheet. "Today's operation is a very complicated one," Odette said. "Lung surgery. You know, the most important thing in an operating room is to keep quiet. It is always very important to be quiet during surgery, but today it's even more so."

Soon, a male nurse wheeled the patient in through the open door. He was followed by the anesthesiologist, a good-looking woman with slanted eyes. She asked the patient how he was feeling, and he answered in a weak voice. She made sure he knew what procedure he was about to undergo—lung surgery to remove a tumor, and he nodded. She gently connected the IV tube to his arm and in less than ten seconds he was asleep.

She continued to prepare the sleeping patient. She inserted a probe into his mouth and oxygen tubes into his nostrils, as my eyes followed each one of the steps, all new to me. A slight commotion announced the arrival of the surgeons in the operating room. They strode toward the large sinks where the head of the department, followed by his five assistants, scrubbed and disinfected their hands. A senior nurse who arrived after them quickly handed them sterile towels. She wiped the surgeon's hands and gloved them. The doctor and his entourage walked up to the operating bed.

The round lamp hanging above illuminated the sheet-covered body. The nurse tied a mask over the surgeon's mouth and nose, so that only his eyes were visible. All the others, including Odette and I, wore masks. The surgeon bared the patient's chest, took a special marker that Odette had prepared in advance on the tray and drew lines on the sleeping body, like a tailor drawing a pattern on a fabric. In the process, he explained in an authoritative voice using long professional terms what they were going to do.

The nurse in charge pulled the sheet off the patient and replaced it with the special sheet, leaving only the chest showing through the opening, then handed the doctor a scalpel. He began the incision and I stole apprehensive glances in his direction. Suddenly a jet of blood came spurting out. The senior nurse immediately handed him a large gauze pad and he covered the cut with it to soak up the blood. I quickly turned my head away, feeling my legs getting weaker. What was I doing there anyway? What kind of nightmare was I in? The doctor went on cutting and apparently opened the lungs. A terrible odor of decay pervaded the room. The doctor clicked his tongue.

"It's too late," he said, "there isn't much we can do here anymore."

I felt dizzy, sickened by the stench. Odette asked me in a whisper if everything was ok with me. The doctors drained some watery substance into a bucket that Odette had told me to place there before the surgery, which filled up with a cloudy, smelly liquid. My meager breakfast rose up to my diaphragm more than once. The surgery dragged on, until the afternoon. When everything possible was done, the surgeon exited the room, leaving his staff to sew the patient up, according to his instructions.

All of a sudden, one of the devices began to beep and the anesthesiologist announced in a panic that the heart rate was dropping. She turned in our direction and uttered the name of some substance. Odette pointed to a syringe and vial and I quickly handed them to the doctor, who skillfully injected the liquid into the IV line. One of the doctors dragged a device from the corner of the room. Another one attached to the body lying on the operating table two electric cables with paddles at the ends. Someone pressed a button making the still body rise like a wave and fall back onto the bed. The doctor pressed the button again, and the body shuddered for a second time. The beeping device showed flat, dense peaks on the screen, while the anesthesiologist took action, clearly worried. The team worked under all that pressure, but in full coordination. Everyone knew what their role was. I felt that I fitted in without losing my composure.

The loudspeaker called repeatedly for the surgeon to urgently come to room three. Within a few minutes he appeared by the patient's bed and leaned over him. He then ordered another round of CPR, but the pulse remained fast and weak. Gradually, the beeping became sharper and longer, until a lifeless, endless flat line stretched across the screen. The doctors straightened up helplessly, and removed their masks. The head nurse turned off the devices and there was silence in the room. Dead silence.

The surgeon pronounced the patient dead. One by one the doctors left the room. The anesthesiologist sat down at a desk in the corner to fill out her report. Odette and I collected the used surgical tools into the sink in the hallway. We removed the soiled sheets and covered the body with a fresh white one. I looked toward the tall, rounded windows in the room. The beautiful garden of the hospital was visible through the glass. The sun, which had already begun its westward descent, illuminated the centuries-old red brick walls. I was tired but also at peace. The day was finally over and I had survived. A male nurse came in and took away the deceased, while we poured disinfectant on the floor and left the room to the cleaning staff. Odette was in a rush to get home to her children.

"But you, go eat. You can go alone, can't you?"

She tried to convince me.

"The truth is I have no appetite," I said. We both got into the elevator, and I closed the lattice door behind us. On the way out I met Mr. Guido, who greeted me with a smile.

"I heard you had a rough day," he said.

"Not too bad," I replied "Tomorrow is a new day. See you tomorrow, Mr. Guido."

I walked home in the spring wind. I arrived in my small room, which I shared with two girls. After a long shower, I went to bed early, on an empty stomach. I hadn't eaten anything since that morning. My first working day in São Paulo was over.

During the week I ate two meals a day at the hospital and went to bed without dinner, but on Sundays I didn't even have a crumb to put in my mouth. One more week, I told myself, and then I'll go to Sorocaba to get the salary due to me, and I'd finally be able to buy myself food.

That afternoon, as the hunger pangs got worse, I took a book and a bottle of water and went to the square to keep myself busy. I sat down on a bench and started reading, sipping the water from time to time.

Out of the corner of my eye I noticed a man approaching me.

"May I sit down?" he asked. I didn't respond and continued with my reading. He sat down and asked again:

"Is that an interesting book?" Interesting enough to pass the time, I said to myself. I put the book aside and turned to him: "Yes, quite interesting."

"Sorry to bother you," he smiled politely and held out his hand. "My name is André. He asked if I was new in São Paulo and what I was doing. We started a conversation, and I was happy for the minutes that went by.

He suggested I have a drink with him, and after a slight hesitation, I agreed. I didn't have much of a choice, as I was very hungry. We walked into a modest bar-restaurant nearby. He asked if I wanted to eat and I ordered something light. After that we had beer, and he paid for everything. When we got up to go, he invited me to come to his place. He was demanding the reward he believed he deserved. I told him with a smile that I was sorry but I had a shift at the hospital and I was already almost late, but I'd love to meet him the next day. I left him a phone number, told him to call me, and we said goodbye. I never met him again. The phone number was fake, of course. I had to survive somehow.

A week later it was the end of the month, and I was entitled to a salary for the days I worked at the store in Sorocaba. At the hospital they only paid on the tenth of the month, and I had no money for the bus fare. The only person I knew and who was willing to help me was Mr. Guido. I debated whether to ask him for a loan. When I left for home that day, he asked how I was, as usual. I was frank. I told him that I was fine, but I had a problem getting to Sorocaba to collect the salary that was waiting for me there, because I had no money for the trip.

"That's not a problem," he told me, "I'll lend you the money. He took some bills out of his pocket and handed them to me. "Is that enough for you to get there?"

The amount was higher than what Carlos had given me.

"Mr. Guido, this is too much. I don't need all this. Thank you very much, really," I said. He insisted that I take the entire amount, so that I could return if God forbid something went wrong and I didn't get the money. "When you have it, you'll give it back to me," he insisted. I thanked him profusely and headed straight to the central station, to get to Sorocaba as quickly as possible, collect my salary and repay the debt.

On the bus to Sorocaba, I remembered Carlos. The last two weeks had been so busy and I had been so focused on surviving that I had hardly thought about him.

I thought I'd call him after I finished my errands. The baby supply store handed me an envelope that definitively sealed that chapter of my life. That's it, I thought, at last nothing tied me to Sorocaba anymore. I was free from everything that bound me to the place, and free to start over. What a relief. I met Carlos at a coffee shop in the central station of Sorocaba. I wanted to pay back the money he had loaned me, but he refused to accept it. He asked how I was doing. He listened to every word I said about my new life, and told he would come to São Paulo in two weeks.

Before I got on the bus we gave each other a hug, and I saw him standing on the platform, following me with his eyes, until he disappeared. What future did we have together, I thought to myself on the way to São Paulo. Now that I had moved to another city and Carlos was far away, what was the point of meeting him once every fortnight or a month? Was that really what I wanted? I was overcome by sadness, and I felt that was the start of our breaking up.

The next day I returned the money to Mr. Guido and was finally able to pay the rent, get my ID back and buy myself dinner. Carlos arrived in São Paulo two weeks later. We sat in an Italian restaurant holding hands. As our encounter came to an end, I said out loud what we both felt: We were important to each other but it would be impossible to maintain a long-distance relationship. We had always known that one day our story would end.

That was probably going to be our final tryst. We kissed for the last time. Our lips touched for a long time, because we both knew that when we broke up it would be forever.

I never saw him again.

Between Life and Death

One of my roommates worked as a night nurse. Her name was Aparecida. We got along great and decided to move to a rental together. We found a small two-room apartment, on the twelfth floor of a building near the Estação da Luz train station—an old, neglected area where prostitutes lined the side of the road at night.

It was the only place with affordable rent that wasn't too far from the hospital. The apartment had one bedroom with two single beds, a living room and a kitchenette. Most of the week we sort of took turns living there because Aparecida went on duty when I arrived home. Only on weekends did we meet and go hang out together. Aparecida, or Cida for short, loved to dance, and one evening she suggested we go to a dance club.

That was the first time I set foot in a São Paulo club. It reminded me of the ones in Sorocaba, only bigger, more crowded. Cida walked in with her long legs and slim figure. She was a true Brazilian, about my age, tall and shapely, and men turned their heads whenever she passed them. We sat down at a small table and ordered gin and tonic from the waitress. Cida danced even while sitting down, shaking her shoulders to the beat of the music.

Before we even got our drinks, a handsome man approached her and asked her to dance. When the waitress appeared with the glasses, Cida and her partner came to the table and he ordered whiskey.

A tall, full-figured man approached me and asked if I wanted to dance with him. When the song ended, I thanked him and went back to my seat. Cida danced with the same partner, and he looked happy. When they returned to our table, he ordered another glass of whiskey. As I was dancing with an older man who sported a mustache, I caught a glimpse of Cida and her partner on the dance floor, with him holding a drink.

Toward midnight we were ready to go home. Cida's dance partner for the evening joined us staggering, and left the club with us.

"Come on, I'll take you home," he mumbled, grabbing Cida's arm.

"He's completely drunk," I whispered to her, "it's crazy to ride with him. He can't possibly drive."

Cida tried to refuse politely, but he insisted.

"You have nothing to worry about," he declared and dragged her toward his car, which was parked next to us. "Come on, come with me."

Cida gave in and stood next to the vehicle. Afraid to leave her alone, I joined them. I sat in the back. Cida was in the front seat, with the man's hand resting on her knee. He drove slowly and said suddenly:

"We will drive to my place first, and then I'll take you home."

"It's getting really late," I tried to object, "we need you to take us home." He didn't answer and drove into a neighborhood of private houses. As soon as we got out of the car, he put his arms around Cida—or actually, more like leaned on her, otherwise he would have fallen over from drunkenness. He opened the door to one of the houses and we went in. As soon as we were inside, he changed completely. He grabbed Cida with force and tried to grope her against her will. When she pushed him away, he tried to pull me into his arms too. I angrily told him to stop. I gave him a hard shove and he fell on the sofa. I told Cida we should go.

She followed him with her eyes, unsure of what to do. He stood up and opened the door of the liquor cabinet in the living room. He poured himself a glass of whiskey and without any warning, pulled out a gun which he probably kept in the closet, and waved it at us.

"Nobody gets out of here!" he shouted, pointing the gun at the couch, ordering us to sit down. Cida started to cry and he shouted again, "Shut up!"

Calmly he downed all the whiskey in the glass, placed it on the sideboard next to him and poured himself some more. At that point he started to cough. He made a stumbling dash for the bathroom, leaving us alone in the room. We heard him retching and throwing up. I quietly pulled Cida toward the door, we opened it, and ran for our lives. We raced through the empty streets until we reached a main road, where we hailed a taxi. That was the last time I went out with Cida to a club.

Cida sometimes worked on Saturdays as a private night nurse. When she got more than one assignment or was otherwise busy, she would refer the job to me, so I could make some extra income.

One Saturday, Cida told me that she was asked to take care of a seriously ill person at his home that night, but she couldn't make it, and asked if I was interested. I said yes. I took two buses to get to the patient's house, which was located in a respectable neighborhood, far from where we lived. I rang the bell next to a tall, wide oak door. A woman in nice clothes, with graying hair and a worried look, opened the door for me.

"Hello, are you Nurse Catarina?" She attempted a smile.

"Yes, that's me," I answered and stepped inside. "Where is the patient?"

"Come with me."

We crossed a wide living room with a wooden floor covered in Persian carpets. Several family members were sitting on a couch talking to each other. They waved to me. I greeted them and followed the lady of the house into a corridor with doors on both sides. She opened the first door. In a wide bed with headboards made of carved wood lay a man with his eyes closed. His face was yellow and sunken and his emaciated body barely made a mark under the blanket. The IV bag hanging on a post next to him was slowly dripping a clear liquid. On the dresser next to the bed were rows of medicine bottles.

"The doctor asked that you administer him a morphine injection." She then addressed me asking, "Would you like anything to drink?"

"Some water, please."

She left the room amid the sound of tapping heels and I walked up to the bed.

I sat on the edge of a large brown leather armchair next to the bed. I looked at the man close up. It was not the first time I had to care for a terminally ill person, but it was always in the hospital, surrounded by doctors and professional staff. Here I was alone, in a strange place, with a patient who could die any moment. The lady came in bringing a tray of cookies and water and placed them on the chest of drawers against the wall. She spun around on her high heels and said: "If you need anything else, just call me. I'm in the living room with the kids." I nodded.

She took a few steps toward the door and grabbed the handle. She hesitated for a moment and then turned to me and said quietly, "Catarina, don't let him suffer," and left. I got up and drank the water. I looked on the dresser for a vial of morphine and a syringe and injected the substance into the IV line. I then turned off the ceiling lamp, leaving only the dim light of the reading lamp on the night table. I returned to the armchair and watched my patient, until I heard his faint breathing.

I opened the book I had brought with me, knowing it would be a rough night.

About two hours later, at 10 p.m., the woman and her son came into the room. I put the book down on my bag and stood up for them. They asked me how he was and told them he was asleep. The lady sat down on the armchair, next to her husband, and her son brought a chair and sat next to her. She asked if I had given him a painkiller shot and I said I had.

"Mother, you can see he is sleeping deeply and is not in pain," said the son. They sat by his side, talking in whispers. Suddenly the patient opened his eyes and looked at them as if he wished to say something. His wife took his hand in hers and leaned toward him, but he closed his eyes again without uttering a sound.

His wife and son stared at his still face, waiting. He opened his eyes again and slowly, with great effort lifted the hand that his wife was holding. He didn't say anything this time either. His eyes closed and his hand dropped to his side, on the sheet. There was a moment of silence and then the woman screamed:

"No, please, don't leave me!" The son held her tightly while she sobbed in his arms. I stood on the side, my legs heavy, as if I were in a bad dream, hoping to wake up.

The rest of the family entered the room crying, hugging and trying to comfort each other. I saw the older son standing apart from the rest.

I asked him for the doctor's phone number so I could tell him to come and certify the death. The son left the room and when he returned, he announced that the doctor would arrive within half an hour.

One of the girls lit a memorial candle and placed it on the dresser, next to the deceased. I waited with the grieving family for the doctor, sitting awkwardly next to the body. Another daughter sobbed in an armchair next to him. The older son stood next to his mother, comforting her. She wiped her red eyes, blew her nose and left the room. I heard her doing the dishes in the kitchen. Her quiet sadness pierced my heart.

The doctor arrived an hour later. He filled out the death certificate and handed it to the son, who took over the formalities. He then turned to me: "You can prepare the deceased now," he said. I was not prepared to hear that sentence. I had never prepared a dead person, and I only knew what to do in theory. The mother brought me clean clothes to dress her husband in, and then I was left alone with the body. I took a tampon, wrapped it in gauze and with trembling hands slipped it into one of the deceased's nostrils. I did this to all the openings in the body, so that the fluids would not leak out. He was so thin, the poor thing, literally only skin and bones, and there didn't seem to be any substance in him at all. I sealed everything as best I could.

I hoped with all my heart that I had done a good job and that the body wouldn't smell bad. I began dressing him. I was able to insert his legs into the pants but there was no way I could lift his back. Although it was almost skeletal, it was still too heavy. I opened the door and apologetically asked for help. At 1 a.m. the dead man was ready for his funeral, and I was free to leave. The family thanked me. The widow handed me a wad of bills, more than I thought I deserved, and escorted me to the door. I left them behind, sad, waiting for the casket.

The streets were lit by street lamps. On the way I passed beautiful houses with well-kept gardens. The bus arrived immediately, completely empty. I sat down on the last row and closed my eyes. Inside my head lay the dead man, thin and pale. I saw the doctor telling me to prepare the body. I could hear the woman's strangled cries and the daughter's sobs. It was so oppressive, so heavy and despairing. Tears flowed down my cheeks, refusing to be contained.

A male voice startled me out of my thoughts: "Young lady, this is the final station. I opened my eyes, muttered a "thank you" to the driver who was standing above me and hurried to get off.

"Are there still buses to the train station?" I asked him before he disappeared inside the bus. He answered there were, but they were rare. The central station was deserted at that hour, and every little rustle scared me. Fear crept into me. I started to walk. Walking was scary too, but less so. I walked hoping to catch a bus on the way. A taxi was too expensive, so it was out of the question. I knew these neglected streets, but only in daylight. At night they were more threatening.

I recognized the famous São João Avenue, São Paulo's dubious night entertainment area. I had never been there at night, but I had heard stories. Both sides of the wide avenue were lined with bars, loud music and red lights, snooker clubs and nightclubs. A group of men came out of one of them, swaying and laughing loudly. I increased my pace to a jog and left the avenue as fast as I could. My place was not that far away. I arrived in the neighborhood around the train station, with the women in black mesh pantyhose patrolling the sidewalks.

My building stood there, tall and narrow, with walls that looked like they were covered in soot. I prayed that the elevator would work and that I wouldn't have to walk up twelve floors. When I got out of the elevator, I felt a little safer. I turned the key in the lock and opened the door.

The apartment was quiet and empty, except for the silhouettes of the few pieces of furniture it contained. I boiled water for coffee. I stood in front of the window, looking at the sky that was turning a brighter hue. Below, far down the street, there were people walking on the sidewalks. Trains chugged in and out of the station non-stop, to and from all corners of Brazil. That was the station at which I had arrived as a child, when Claudia's brother took me back to my parents in Sorocaba. That memory gave me the chills. I felt like I wasn't strong enough yet. I needed to get out of that dark zone before I got sucked into it. What was I doing there alone, in dangerous São Paulo? In an area ruled by the underworld, drugs and prostitutes? I took a sip of the coffee, which was already cold. I remembered my promise to myself, when I left Claudia. I was keeping it step by step, but I still had a long way to go without falling down in the middle.

The city lights began to go out one by one. The night was over, I thought sadly, but I was immediately comforted by the fact that it was Sunday, and I could sleep late.

Working at the Laboratory

I had been working for a year in São Paulo as an auxiliary nurse in an operating room when the person in charge of the external laboratory that provided services to the hospital approached me and asked if I would replace her. She had to move with her husband to another city and thought I was perfectly capable of filling her position. The hospital administration gave me its blessing, and I went to work at the lab. For the first month I was an apprentice, and within two months I became a lab technician in charge.

In the mornings I would come to the hospital and draw blood samples from interned patients and outpatients who came for treatments and tests. Around eleven I would take a taxi with the blood samples I collected to the main laboratory, where I helped conduct the tests. I learned to separate the serum using a centrifuge and sort the samples into types in order to distribute them among the departments according to their specialization.

On Sundays I was sometimes on duty at the main lab. I would go to the hospital to take blood from patients who needed urgent tests, and bring it to the lab. On the way I would usually stop and buy fresh, warm bread rolls for breakfast.

"Oh, Catarina, what a wonderful smell you brought with you," exclaimed Miguel, one of the regulars on weekend duty. The second one was Rodrigo, who had a master's degree and was an expert in the field of hematology. I would give them the urgent tests first, and while they performed the analysis, I helped with the administrative work and record keeping. On quiet Sundays we could sit and eat together while the tests were incubating, a process that required some time.

This was my chance to ask questions and Rodrigo would explain to me with patience and at length. "In a blood count, we check the amount of red blood cells, white blood cells and platelets per unit volume of blood. This is an initial test we perform to get a general picture of the patient's condition. Here is a pen and paper. Take some notes: Red blood cells - their role is to carry oxygen from the lungs to all the cells in the body, and carbon dioxide from the cells back to the lungs. The norm is 2.4 - 6.5 million cells per microliter. Now write this down: White blood cells..." He went on like that until suddenly he said, "I barely got any sleep last night. I'm really tired. Hold on a second. He returned with the clinical hematology book and handed it to me. "Read this at home, and I'll explain to you whatever you don't understand. Once you get the basics, I'll teach you how the tests are done, and you can be my assistant. And now good night, I'm off to sleep."

I was highly enthusiastic about the new world that was revealed to me and felt a strong desire to continue studying. But first I had to get a high school diploma.[22] That was why I signed up for an evening course, from seven to eleven at night, hoping to complete the exams within two years.

I loved working at the hospital. Every morning I enjoyed picking out a nice outfit. We were not required to wear specific uniforms, as long as we wore white. Every day I felt I was learning and making progress. I became an expert in drawing blood from arteries, which is more complicated. Doctors called me when they needed artery blood for some special test, or when the patient's veins were hard from chemotherapy and could no longer be punctured. One morning I examined in the mirror, with satisfaction, the white envelope skirt that ended in a rounded hem in the middle of my knee. I turned to leave for work when the door opened and Cida walked in, looking very unhappy. Her mother had fallen ill and she was called to take care of her. No one else in her family could take on the task. She was forced to leave São Paulo. We only had two weeks to arrange things. Cida had to change her whole life, while I had to change my place of residence—I couldn't afford the rent of that apartment by myself.

I thought it might be a good opportunity to look for a better place.

Two weeks later with great sorrow I said goodbye to Cida.

---

22 The last three years of studies were called "college" in Brazil, and upon their successful completion, a matriculation certificate was awarded.

Marcus

I moved into an apartment I rented with two other girls, whom I first met at the boarding house I stayed in upon my arrival in São Paulo, and who became close friends. Cristina, a smart, amiable girl, worked at an architecture firm, while Lourdes, a widow a little older than us, managed a café. She had three children who lived in a neighborhood far from the center, and her sister took care of them for her. The apartment was in a good area, close to the hospital, with an intercom and a guard at the entrance. My salary had increased since I started working in the lab so I could afford a third of the rent in a place like that. Lourdes and I shared the bedroom. Cristina slept in the living room. On Saturday evening Lourdes suggested we go out rather than staying home. She was going to visit a friend who had just given birth and thought we could go together.

I went with her, and afterwards we sat down in a café. Leaning back comfortably in her chair, Lourdes said: "What a cute baby... so small... I've forgotten how tiny they are when they are born." She sighed, "I really miss my children... I have to see them... I will go next week. You should come with me sometime and meet them."

"Gladly," I replied. I told her how much I loved Madalena's children when I was their nanny.

"Did you notice the guy sitting at the table next to us?" Lourdes said as she stirred her coffee with a spoon. "Seems quite nice, and won't stop looking in your direction." I restrained myself for a full minute and then turned to glance at him. Our eyes met, and I immediately turned away. As far as I could gather in the split second I saw him, he was a nice-looking young Japanese man with straight spiky hair. Out of the corner of my eye I saw him get up and head for our table.

"Hi," he said. Overcoming my embarrassment, I answered him. Smiling, Lourdes asked him if he was in the habit of having coffee alone. "It's my friend's fault. He stood me up," he said in mock regret.

"Come, join us," Lourdes said.

Facing me, he introduced himself: "My name is Marcus Takahashi."

"I'm Catarina," I answered with a smile. He was tall and well built.

"Can I sit down with you?" he asked

"Please do." And I couldn't come up with any other words to say. He sat down across from me and began to go through the menu, allowing me to examine him without feeling uncomfortable. He looked very young, about my age. He had a round face and a cleft lip that had been surgically repaired leaving barely a mark. He had a beautiful neck and muscular shoulders. As soon as he raised his eyes, I looked away.

"How cool to be on this side of a café—as a customer," Lourdes remarked. "I run one of these, and it's not that easy... What do you do, Marcus?"

"I'm studying at the Sports Academy College. My father would have preferred me to choose something else, but I like sports. Especially basketball and volleyball. And you, Catarina, what do you do?"

"I work in a hospital laboratory and I'm studying to get my high school diploma," I answered. I saw a question in his eyes, or maybe several, but he was polite and said nothing. When we got up to leave, he asked for my phone number. I gave him the number of the lab and he wrote down his number on a paper napkin. Before I went to sleep, I carefully unfolded the wrinkles of the paper napkin and memorized the number.

Marcus I sang in my heart. I loved that name. Life suddenly seemed simple. He was single, about my age, he was interested in me, and I found him charming. Sigh! I wished he would call, and that he would really like me and I him. He was real and he seemed honest and open. Maybe I would finally have a love story with a happy ending. I folded the precious napkin carefully and kept it safely in my wallet. Marcus called the next day.

He identified himself shily, hesitantly wondering if I remembered him, not sure if I was happy to hear from him. I tried to sound aloof but the giggles of joy I let out every now and then, despite myself, gave me away. That week we spoke almost every day and agreed to have dinner on the weekend.

On Saturday at six in the evening I went in to take a shower, tried on three different dresses before settling on one of them, spent a long time doing my hair, and sprinkled a little perfume behind my ears, like

Manuela had taught me. He was going to pick me up at seven. Exactly at seven the intercom rang and the guard informed me that a man named Marcus was in the elevator on his way to our apartment. Oh, my heart was beating loudly. Why didn't the guard inform me before letting him up? I heard the elevator stop at our floor. As soon as the bell rang, I went to open the door. I saw a huge bouquet of red roses, practically hiding Marcus from view. I was flushed with excitement.

"What beautiful flowers!" I said, taking the bouquet from his hands.

"Not as beautiful as you," he said. From his mouth the phrase sounded sincere, making me feel truly beautiful.

"Thank you," I answered, and proceeded to arrange the flowers in a vase.

He opened the car door for me. He drove a banana-colored Volkswagen Passat. He also opened the door to the respectable Italian restaurant we arrived at. The tables were covered with red tablecloths, the light of the candles on each one creating a cozy atmosphere. Despite his young age and shyness, he was very relaxed, and it was evident that he was no stranger to restaurants. While we waited for our food, he told me he was twenty-one years old and was born in Brazil. He asked me my age and place of birth. I said that I was his age, that I spent my early childhood in a village and then we moved to Sorocaba.

"How is it that you are only now studying for your matriculation? You seem like a serious girl, who likes to study."

"We just met and you already know me… Anyway, it's a long story." I said cutely.

The waiter brought the wine. Marcus tasted it and nodded. The dishes we ordered arrived too.

Marcus handled the cutlery with grace and skill. Retrieving from my memory all the table manners I had learned from Claudia, I chose the right knife and fork, and cut the thin slice of meat on the plate in front of me. Marcus spoke about himself and asked me about my life.

I learned that his grandfather had immigrated from Japan in the thirties and that his father owned a business importing spare parts for cars. He had an older sister, a pediatrician. I told him about the hospital and my great desire to study pathology, as soon as I got my high school diploma. He listened attentively and said in the end:

"Kudos to you for having the willpower and energy. I personally don't have that much patience for studies. I have ants in my pants and it's hard for me to sit for more than half an hour straight. My father isn't at all happy with what I do. He thinks that sports are not a serious profession. He would rather I studied business administration and came to work with him in the company…"

"At least my parents don't interfere in my academic choices."

I grinned and sipped some wine. Little by little I revealed parts of my story. By the end of the evening, Marcus knew a lot about me: that I came from a family of hard-working villagers, that my mother was illiterate, that I had been married before, and that I once had a daughter named Rebeca.

I learned he had undergone many surgeries as a child to repair his upper lip, that he loved cars and owned a motorcycle, and also that he had an understanding heart and a gentle soul.

We left the restaurant and walked side by side across the parking lot to the car. I liked his height—he was a full head taller than me. I liked that he walked next to me openly, without worrying about us being seen by anyone he knew.

As he stopped by the car and grabbed the handle to open the door for me, he stood so close to me I could feel his breath. We sat next to each other while he drove, a palpable awkwardness filling the space between us. Neither of us spoke the entire way, each immersed deep in their own thoughts.

He stopped the car outside my building and turned to face me. "I had a very interesting evening," he said.

"Me too," I replied, "Thank you very much for the meal and the wonderful evening."

"I'd like to get to know you better," he said, taking my hand in his. I felt the blood flowing to my face and nodded. "I was really looking forward to meeting you today. Since I saw you for the first time, you've been on my mind."

"I was waiting to see you too," I said, "really."

"Can I see you again tomorrow?"

"Of course."

"And the day after tomorrow, and next week too?"

I nodded, chuckling. He slowly brought his face closer to mine and I brought mine closer to his, until our lips gently met. We kissed tenderly and then passionately, with our arms wrapped around each other, our bodies pressed together. We parted panting, reminding each other that we would meet again the next day.

As I walked up the stairs, all soaked in Marcus, I remembered Carlos fondly. *Thank you, Carlos,* I thought. He appeared in my life at the right time and gave me so much. But now I could have a boyfriend all to myself. I didn't have to share him with anyone, nor did I have to hide in dark corners to avoid being seen.

The next morning, at the arranged time, the guard announced to me that Marcus was waiting downstairs. I found him sitting on a large motorcycle, with a wide grin.

"How do I get on this thing?"

Laughing, I climbed on behind him, my wide skirt gliding down behind me. He turned to hand me a helmet and helped me fasten it. I grabbed on tightly to his waist and we took off. I felt like I was flying, my skirt billowing behind me and the wind strong on my face. I clung to him, burrowing my head in his back, as a shield. Marcus accelerated.

"Where are we going?" I asked with a laugh, when I got off the bike, while also trying to fix my disheveled hair.

"You'll find out soon."

He smiled and took my hand. We strolled hand in hand on the grass, through a green park. The trees had started to grow new, late winter leaves. A group of children played ball on a piece of sloping lawn nearby, and a family laid blankets and a tablecloth on the grass, preparing for their Sunday picnic. I was as happy as the birds chirping in the trees around us. We crossed the park and arrived at the gate of a zoo.

"Are you taking me to the zoo?" I asked, a bit surprised.

"Yes. Shouldn't I be?" he asked as he handed a bill to the cashier at the entrance.

"You totally should," I said, beaming, and tightening my grip on his hand. "I love coming here," he said. "It's much more fun in the middle of the week, when it's empty… Everything is so calm and you can hear every squeak, every roar, even from a distance. But it's cool now too. It's still early, and there aren't many people."

We stopped in front of the monkeys' cage, standing close to each other.

"So cute..." I said, looking at a baby monkey clinging to its mom. Marcus smiled and put his arm on my shoulder.

"The baboons are my favorites," he said, "and I also like watching the lions, giraffes and elephants... Oh, and I forgot the parrots, and also the bats... And a few more." He kissed me lightly on the lips and went on, "But today I like being here much more, because you are with me."

When we reached the elephants, he told me about his latest argument with his father, once again about his career. By the crocodiles, I told him briefly about my time at Claudia's, and how I swore to myself that I would get out of the life I had and build one like Claudia's. I talked about my work, about how I felt I was learning and making progress, about the immunology course I planned to take the year after. I saw him gazing at me with appreciation.

"I know you'll make it," he declared, pulling me into his arms.

After a few weekends of going on excursions, dining at restaurants and kissing passionately in the car or in some secluded corner, a panting Marcus whispered in my ear:

"Maybe we could go someplace where we can be alone?"

At the time we had no possibility of privacy. We went to a roadside motel on the outskirts of the city and checked into a room.

Marcus was a shy lover. Obviously, I was the more experienced of the two, as I had been married before. If only he knew that what I had learned was not from my husband. I never told him. We cuddled in bed until dawn, then rushed to our homes so his parents would find him in his room when they woke up on Sunday.

Two weeks later, he invited me to visit his house. He came to pick me up on Saturday night after dinner, this time in his car. We turned into a beautiful street in one of the top neighborhoods of São Paulo. He stopped by one of the houses and pointed a remote control at a white metal garage door, which rolled up. We drove slowly into a spacious garage that housed two other vehicles. A shelving unit by the wall displayed a tool box and cans of paint arranged in a neat line.

We went up a few steps, passed a short path outside between flower beds and Marcus opened a wide glass door. "Hello, we're home," he announced, letting me go ahead in front of him. Taking a deep breath, I stepped inside.

His parents sat watching TV in the living room. His mother turned to greet me with a smile. She was a thin, delicate woman with a pleasant demeanor, like Marcus.

"This is Catarina," he said, and she extended her hand to me warmly. His father stood up from the armchair in my honor, shook my hand with an expressionless face and said: "Nice to meet you."

We sat on the sofa next to his mother and watched the news. The screen showed crowds demonstrating against wage freezes and the rising costs of basic products—nothing new. Marcus's father grumbled.

"Figueiredo and his plans! With such high inflation no *abertura*—liberalization—will help. How will there be democracy in the middle of an economic crisis of this magnitude?"[23]

"Want some coffee?" Marcus asked me. His mother said a few words to him in Japanese and he replied, "Okay, we'll get cookies from the pantry."

The kitchen was large, with a modern oven and a hood above the stove. A small television attached to the wall with an arm, was tuned to the same channel we had left behind us in the living room. Figueiredo addressed the nation and said that only through restraint and hard work would it be possible to reduce the national debt and revive the economy.

"Shall we go?" Marcus asked after we finished drinking. I emptied the two coffee mugs into the white ceramic sink, which was very clean, and washed them. "You really don't have to, you're a guest. He hugged me from behind and glanced anxiously toward the door to check that no one had come in. We crossed the living room again and he announced that we were going to the movies. Then he said a sentence in Japanese, probably some parting words.

My life was intense. I finished my high school courses and did well on the finals. I enrolled in clinical pathology studies and struggled with the material, which was harder than anything I had known before. I asked everyone I could for help, but there weren't many options. Sometimes

---

23 Between the years 1964-1985, Brazil was ruled by a military regime. João Batista de Oliveira Figueiredo was the last military president. He continued the trend of his predecessor by releasing the pressure of the regime – with the Abertura, to prepare the country for democracy. The global economic crisis at that time and the political liberalization led to an acute economic crisis in Brazil.

lab workers who were on duty on Sundays, whenever they weren't dozing off, and Marcus only occasionally, because I preferred to do other things in the precious time I had with him.

We met almost exclusively on weekends and sailed on his massive motorcycle. We rode for miles along the streets of São Paulo without any particular destination, and finally we stopped at a park and went for a walk. Sometimes we drove as far as the Universitaria Cidade, USP, a university city with a spacious campus and wonderful gardens. We visited the nearby Butantan Reptile Research Institute, which had laboratories for the production of venom antiserum and also an exhibition of specimens for the general public. We toured among the glass cages containing writhing live snakes. Other boxes displayed scorpions and spiders—over sixty different species and types.

Marcus loved animals, even the scary, repulsive ones that lived in aquariums. He enthusiastically told me about venomous spiders that paralyzed their prey with poison. He then explained to me that he had read in the encyclopedia how to make venom antiserum by injecting a measured dose into a goat, for example, whose blood would develop antibodies. The plasma containing the antibodies could be isolated and the serum extracted from it. I listened to him, fascinated, understanding most of what he said and thinking with pride of what a knowledgeable boyfriend I had. We walked hand in hand through a beautiful avenue lined by rare tree varieties and read the inscriptions on the little copper plates attached to them with the name of the tree and its origin.

On Saturday nights, Marcus parked his motorcycle on the sidewalk, among dozens of other motorcycles, and we went to our regular pub. We sat, talked and drank cocktails, sometimes alone and sometimes with a friend or two who joined us, until the small hours of the morning. Marcus would bring me home and come to see me the next day at lunchtime.

"What's wrong?" I asked as we held each other next to his motorcycle on a Sunday morning. From the moment I came out of the building to greet him, he seemed to me disturbed. "Nothing new," he shrugged, "my Dad, as usual."

He kissed me and handed me the helmet. After being together for almost a year, I had become highly skillful at jumping on the motorcycle behind him. We raced through the streets of São Paulo and a sign with a plane icon flew past us. Eventually we came to a stop at the Congonhas airport.

"Are we flying?" I joked. "Maybe someday," he said, smiling, and pulled me after him, up to the second floor, where we went out to a huge balcony that overlooked the runway. "Look," he said, pointing to a large airplane making its way to the runway. "Such beauty! All that power!" Wrapping his arms around me he said quietly, "I like watching planes take off. It makes me feel good. It's relaxing, you know…"

The plane stopped for a moment at the end of the runway and then taxied at increasing speed, gaining momentum. It had almost reached the end when at the last moment it detached from the ground. "It's a shame we can't hear the engines up close," said Marcus, "so as to feel this tremendous technology. What an invention an airplane is! Just awesome…" His voice faded, drowned by the roar of the engines. We both followed the plane taking off until it disappeared over the horizon.

"Have you ever flown?" I asked.

"No," he said, "but I'd love to… I will fly one day!"

"So will I," I said, with passion. "I also want to see the world. Get to know new places. I will do it. I have to! I will fly!"

A new plane rolled slowly to the beginning of the runway. "I'm sure you will," Marcus murmured into my hair, "you achieve anything you set your mind to." We remained silent for a few minutes and then he said, "My father! I can't take it anymore! He thinks he is the supreme authority. He knows everything best and thinks he can make all the decisions for everyone. What right does he have to tell me what to do! His disdain for choices is killing me. Who does he think he is anyway! Do you know that my mother found out a few years ago that he had a lover? He broke her heart, the idiot! To this day she has not recovered! And he… he dares tell me how to live!" Marcus's voice choked off with pain and I pressed my face to his neck. It's easier to bear anger in twos, I thought. I also thought I must never tell him that I once was *the other woman*, that I too had been the lover of a married man…

"Our parents are only human, you know. They're not perfect," I said quietly. The vein throbbing in his neck calmed down a bit.

"When will I meet your parents?" he asked, suddenly. I had told him briefly about my parents.

"We'll go sometime," I answered, "I hardly visit them myself. I haven't been to see them for almost a month... And you know my parents are very different from yours," I reminded him, "really different."

We stayed that way, standing in a close embrace, together, watching one plane take off after the other. In those moments I loved Marcus so much.

Prof. Rosenberg

In the oncology wing where I worked, there was a department for rheumatological-immunological diseases, under the direction of Prof. Rosenberg. He was a very tall and broad-bodied Jew, a well-known scientist in his field. He walked the halls of the hospital, usually surrounded by students or doctors seeking his advice.

Sometimes I would pass him when he walked alone, on his huge feet, a long white robe reaching below his knees, and his thoughts floating in some remote realm of science. He never greeted me. It was as if he didn't see at all, nor anything else around him for that matter. I used to think to myself how strange a person he was, and wonder how on earth he managed to find shoes large enough to fit his huge feet.

One day, after I had finished taking blood and was busy arranging the samples in the special insulated leather bag I used to carry them in to the central laboratory, I heard a knock on the door. "The lab is already closed," I said, and picked up the phone to call a cab. The door opened, and to my surprise Prof. Rosenberg entered the room.

"I apologize," he said, addressing me for the first time ever, "but I need your help." I looked at him in amazement while he began to explain, "I have a patient hospitalized here in the ward and we were not able to draw blood from him. Could you try?"

The famous Prof. Rosenberg needs my help, I thought excitedly. I could postpone delivering the blood collections to the lab for a bit.

"What test do you need me to do, sir?" I asked while picking a tray for the necessary equipment.

"I need an arterial blood gas analysis," he replied.

"No problem," I said, preparing the appropriate test tube and syringes. Together, we went up to the third floor and walked into one of the rooms.

"Thank God, you found her! She's good," the patient smiled with relief, and I greeted him with a smile of my own. He was a kind, middle-aged man whom I knew from previous hospitalizations.

He held out his arm, which had already been pierced over several failed attempts. I put my fingers on it and felt for the arterial pulse. Expectations of me were high, and I simply could not disappoint. I located the right spot and stabbed. The blood surged up with pressure and quickly filled the syringe.

"Excellent, thank you," said the professor and left the room.

I didn't hear from him again for two months until one day, while on my way to the central laboratory, our paths crossed at the entrance to the hospital. He looked at me remembering and said: "Hello, Catarina. I wanted to talk to you. How about coming to my clinic tomorrow around five in the afternoon?"

"Sure, Prof. Rosenberg," I replied.

That day I was in a whirlwind of excitement. Prof. Rosenberg didn't call anyone in for a meeting just like that, just to ask them to take some blood sample. It must be something important. What could it be? The next morning, I woke up very early. More careful about my appearance than ever, I chose white clothes with a flattering cut, a pair of pearl earrings, and dabbed on some subtle make-up. I took with me the books and notebooks I would need for my evening class and left the house for a long working day, which would end only at night.

The morning started off great, because Marcus called as soon as I arrived. We talked for a few minutes before the lab opened for the public. At five in the evening, I was in Prof. Rosenberg's crowded waiting room. I waited patiently for a patient to come out of his office. Before the next patient could go in, I knocked on the door and opened it.

"Professor Rosenberg, good afternoon," I said. Without looking up from the paper he was writing on he said: "Catarina, could you please go up to the lab and wait for me there until I'm done?"

When I entered the laboratory, Fernanda, the nutritionist, peeked at me over the centrifuge and asked kindly if I needed anything. She worked for the professor in research and was responsible for putting together the diets recommended for the patients under his care. I replied that I had been asked to wait for the professor.

"I wonder what Professor Rosenberg wants from me," I said as I stirred three teaspoons of sugar into the coffee she had made me.

"I have no clue," she replied.

I waited for an hour and a quarter until he appeared. When I finally sat down across from him, he began by saying:

"I was very impressed with your skills when you took my patient's blood a few weeks ago. My dear friend Dr. Angelo, the director of the laboratory, is also very happy with your work. *He had actually been asking around about me*, I thought in bewilderment. "I have a proposition for you. He brought his hands together and twisted his wedding ring on his finger."The workload in my lab has increased. We've started conducting tests for bone marrow transplants and I need a good, skilled laboratory technician. We often need to draw blood samples from problematic patients, especially children, and you seem well able to do so. What do you say?"

I couldn't say anything. My head was spinning with the compliments and I felt flushed and confused. It took me a few seconds to organize my thoughts into the words I wanted to say.

"Prof. Rosenberg, there are a few issues here," I answered, watching him slip the ring off his finger and push it back in place.

"Such as?"

"First of all, I've never worked in an immunology lab and I've never done transplant tests before. I have no experience whatsoever in the area of transplants. Secondly, I live alone in São Paulo and I have to pay my rent and tuition. I need a stable job. I wouldn't want to find myself fired in a few months. It is very important for me to be able to pay for my studies until the end. And lastly, there is my manager. I don't know what to tell him. I don't like leaving him just like that, after all the support and the trust he placed in me…"

"Okay," said the professor. He stopped playing with his ring and a slight smile, part mocking and part forgiving, appeared at the corner of his lips. "Regarding the tests—before you start working, you will attend a course and receive formal training. Apart from that, we hold lectures here every Thursday, very interesting ones, by the way. I think you would find them helpful. I understand that your studies are in the field of medicine, in clinical pathology. Regarding your terms of employment—talk to the accountant, he is in charge of such matters. I can reassure you that your salary will be enough to pay for your apartment and studies. As for your manager, I don't think there will be a problem." He then fell silent as if waiting for an answer.

"I need a few days to think it over," I said, calculating in my head that if I didn't get out of there within five minutes, I would be late for class. He looked at me for a moment and said,

"I need an answer urgently."

I replied that I was aware of that and would try to give him an answer in a day or two.

A cool evening breeze soothed my hot face as I walked to the college, ten minutes away. Deep down inside I knew I would accept the offer, with all the risks involved. I had to make that bet because it was a rare opportunity to move ahead. But I was afraid. I was afraid of failing. I was afraid of the controversial challenge named Prof. Rosenberg, who was much spoken about in the medical community, and not an easy person to get along with.

I was about to leave a rather interesting job in which I was my own master, and walk into the unknown, to work with a difficult person. He was a world-renowned physician, very smart, highly demanding, and there was no certainty at all that I would survive. I could find myself a few months later in utter despair, having failed in my new job and lost the previous one. During class, my mind was constantly running away, preoccupied with what answer to give Prof. Rosenberg. I had to chase after it and bring it back into the classroom. Even during the break, I talked about my dilemma with a classmate who shared a desk with me.

When the lesson was over, Marcus was waiting for me outside the college, next to the banana car. I saw his smile from afar and rushed to him. He wrapped me in a big hug and we kissed ignoring the passers-by. Of course, on the way home I told him about Prof. Rosenberg's proposal. He listened with close attention.

"Catarina, I think this is a great opportunity!" He said as he parked near my house. "I don't understand why you're worried. I'm sure you'll do well. This job is cut out for you. Think how nice it will be to no longer have to work weekend shifts."

We stayed in the car for a few more minutes, our arms around each other.

It was almost midnight and Marcus never came up to me at such hours, because I had a roommate. When I got home, I still carried his warmth inside me. The confidence he gave me calmed me down, and the idea of accepting the job offer began to take shape.

Lourdes announced that she was going away for the weekend to visit her children.

"I'm also planning to see my mother this week," Cristina said. "I'm only coming back on Sunday."

"Oh, Catarina," Lourdes said with a mischievous look, "we're leaving you the love nest free for the weekend…"

The three of us laughed, me with some embarrassment. Inside, my heart skipped a beat and I told myself that I had to make those days unforgettable. In our traditional morning call, I excitedly informed Marcus that on that coming Saturday I was inviting him to a celebratory dinner at my place.

Every Saturday morning a farmer's market was held in a square near my building. Dozens of vendors opened stalls with colorful mountains of fresh fruits and vegetables, straight from the field. That morning I took time off and went out early to pick groceries for our meal. I came back loaded with beautiful fruit, a pineapple, three mangoes and also a bouquet of flowers. My roommates were already at the doorway with their handbags and said goodbye to me with a wink.

I tidied up the flat with extra care. I spent an hour in the kitchen making shrimps cooked in cream, white rice, a colorful leaf salad with mango cubes and a rich dressing. I set the table with a white tablecloth, plates, tumbler glasses, and wine glasses, as I had learned from Claudia. On the sideboard next to the wall, I placed a vase with a bouquet of red roses mixed with delicate baby breath blossoms.

At exactly seven o'clock the guard rang me on the intercom to let me know Marcus was coming up. I ran to the record player and put on an album with love songs. I heard soft knocks on the door and hurried to open it. Marcus stood there smiling. He handed me a bottle of wine wrapped in silver paper and tied with a ribbon. We hugged tightly and I solemnly led him to the table.

"How beautiful," he said, "like an exclusive restaurant." Glancing at the kitchen he added, "Smells great too. He went over to the pot that was on the stove. "Can I take a peek?" he asked, lifting the lid.

"Dinner will be served in five minutes," I said, laughing. He opened the drawer, found a corkscrew and fiddled with the bottle for a few seconds. He poured wine into two glasses he took from the table, while I turned down the heat. He raised his glass and said:

"Cheers. Cheers to the interesting week we had. Cheers to your new job! Good luck."

"Thank you, my dear," I said, "to our lives."

"This is excellent," he marveled when we finally sat down to eat. "You really are an expert cook." He took another helping of shrimp and rice, refilled our glasses and we clinked. "To our love life." I laughed, flushed with excitement and love. "May it go on for many more years!" he declared. "Forever!"

He then pulled his chair closer to mine and put his arm around me. I put my wine glass down and hugged him with both arms. We kissed. I felt so good to be in the privacy of my apartment and so close to him. "Tell me, Catarina," he whispered, "I want to know everything about you. He pulled me closer and kissed me. "How was life with your first husband? Tell me about your little daughter…"

I wanted to open my heart to him, but instead I was flooded with tears. "It's hard for me," I replied, crying softly, "it's terribly hard for me to talk about her…"

"I'm sorry," Marcus said with apprehension, "I didn't mean to hurt you." He gently kissed my cheek, wiped my tears with his lips and then kissed my eyelids. I clung to him for dear life and we kissed like we never had before. We felt close, as if our souls could touch.

We got up from our seats. I changed the record that had finished playing to one of Stevie Wonder's and hurried back into Marcus's arms. He unbuttoned my dress and we found ourselves wrapped around each other on the living room carpet. We were giddy with wine and passion.

We had never made love like that night, so completely, with such devotion. All night we stayed close, in the same spot, dozing, until dawn came. We woke up at first light with my head on his shoulder, his arm around me, and the creaking of the record still spinning softly in the background.

Working with Prof. Rosenberg was not easy. I was required to work overtime often and sometimes I would leave at the last minute before school started, having to run almost all the way there. I tried to delve in deeper and learn the meaning of the tests I conducted. I read articles and medical literature, even if I couldn't always fully grasp everything. At every opportunity I directed questions to the doctors and residents who visited the laboratory. In the morning, before they started their patient rounds, they came by the lab. I made sure that the coffee in the percolator was always hot and fresh. While they sat down to drink at leisure, I would find out whatever had eluded me from the books.

I was just collecting the empty coffee cups left by my guests, who had scattered to go on their rounds, when I heard a knock at the door. A woman stood there with her two small children and told me they had come for a bone marrow transplant test. I smiled at the little ones and asked:

"Who's the donor and who's the recipient?"

"I'm the donor," tweeted the little boy, who seemed to me to be six at the most. I invited him to the chair first, and he hurried to sit down. Poor little guy, I thought, he doesn't even know what a test for a bone marrow donation is. My heart shrank when I realized the innocence of the mother and her sick son. They had no idea what the words they had just uttered really meant. They were not aware of the long period of suffering and pain still ahead of them, with a completely uncertain outcome.

The younger brother sat calmly and looked around with curiosity. I prepared a set of test tubes to fill with blood for the various tests I would need to perform, then picked up the large syringe that would contain all the required blood. When the boy saw the syringe, his confidence disappeared and his eyes widened in fear. At that moment, the image of Rebeca, my little daughter, popped up, looking at me with her big black eyes wide open. I lay next to her in bed, my face close to hers, and she raised her small hand to my cheek to touch it, as if she wanted to give me strength.

I turned my back to the boy on the chair and fiddled with the test tubes for a few minutes. When I calmed down a bit, I turned to him and said with reassurance: "Don't be afraid, honey. I will try very hard not to hurt you. I'll do it so gently you won't even feel it. And at the end I will give you some candy. Three pieces, OK, dear?"

He held out his arm to me bravely and didn't move a bit until I had finished. After taking blood from his older brother as well, I gave each of them some candy and a lollipop. I put stickers with the word "Hero" on their shirts and told them the results would be ready in a week's time.

I looked at the three of them walking away into the unknown, and I could barely hold back a tear. I too, like this mother, did not understand anything. I didn't know what tests were being done on my daughter. I had no idea what the doctors knew and what still awaited the two of us. What blissful ignorance—such extreme naïveté!

I sat alone in the lab, with tears slowly rolling down my cheeks. In the end I got up and washed my face. I had to control myself. I could not get emotionally involved every time a sick child showed up, or let the memories overwhelm me. I needed to do my job in the best, most professional way I could, and set some limits for myself.

The commotion in the hallway caught my attention. I left the lab to see several of the staff gathered around the small television set in the corner of the corridor, listening to a spokesperson announcing in a stern voice that Tancredo Neves, the president-elect, had died that day in the hospital. After twenty years of military dictatorship, democratic elections were held for the first time in January 1985 and Tancredo had won.

Two weeks later he fell ill and did not even live long enough to be sworn in for the presidency. His funeral was broadcast the next day. Crowds filled the streets and streams of people followed the coffin. The atmosphere was heavy. Besides the sadness over the death of a revered man, the uncertainty about the future of our new democracy was oppressive. I stood in front of the small television in the corner, mourning for a few minutes together with a group of nurses and doctors, then I hurried to the laboratory, to the blood tests that were waiting for me.

The Visit

Sitting with Marcus in a café, I looked at him and thought that we had been together for almost two years and maybe it was time.

"Would you like to come to meet my parents next weekend?" I asked. He smiled in surprise.

"I thought this invitation would never come! Of course, I'd love to go with you. While we held each other in the car, he kissed my head and I tried to explain.

"I already told you that my family is very different from yours. I myself am very different from them. I left home at a very young age and I don't really feel I belong with them. Sometimes, when I go to visit and spend time with them, I feel like a complete stranger. They're not part of my life at all..."

"I understand," he replied, brushing his lips against my hair.

"I don't know if you can understand," I sighed. "Your family is so wonderful, and you can be proud of them. They are caring and protective of you... My family was never warm to me, they never hugged me. Maybe that's why we don't have that kind of connection..." I put my head on his shoulder and tried to relax, but I couldn't let go. "I know I have no one else. After all, they are my family, and it is what it is... There's nothing I can do to change that." We sat in silence for a few moments, then I added, "I'm glad I was able to get out of there. I work and study and do everything I can to achieve a respectable life, unlike theirs. But we are different, you and I."

He brought my face closer to his and said to me quietly, looking into my eyes: "Catarina, I love you, and nothing else matters. I know your life hasn't been easy, but you've overcome the obstacles all on your own, and I'm very proud of you. I'm in love with you and I want us to stay together for the rest of my life."

On Sunday, Marcus showed up at my place wearing jeans and a dress shirt. He seemed very calm, as opposed to me. Before we left, we had some coffee, and he asked why I was so agitated.

"I couldn't reach my mother on the phone at work, so she doesn't know we're coming," I said.

"So what? It'll be a nice surprise for her when we get there. Don't worry about it…" he reassured me with a smile.

Picturing my parents' house, with the mattresses all over the living room and the kitchen full of dirty dishes, I couldn't smile back.

The trip was uneventful. Marcus talked about work at the sports club where he was a coach and I listened. "Do you remember Ricardo? I told you about him. What a kid! So mature for his age. He scored five baskets in the last game. He is making such good progress. He simply listens and gets what he's told. It is a pleasure to coach the kid. I enjoyed watching him so delighted after the game. He came running to hug me."

"You'll make a great dad," I said, resting my hand on his arm.

"You'll be a great mom too," he said, bringing my hand to his mouth for a kiss. He sneaked a smile at me and went back to looking at the road. "We will have the most adorable children in the world," he added. I tightened my clasp on his arm and told him he made me feel happy.

Meanwhile, we were slowly approaching Itú, the city where my parents lived. As we entered, I asked Marcus to stop by a cart loaded with fruit, and we got off to buy some for my parents. The seller promoted his fresh produce with enthusiasm.

"Look, my dear, what a beautiful pineapple, fresh and juicy. Hey bro, how about that watermelon? It's red and sweet and if you carry it for her, she'll be so grateful." He meant me, of course. We nodded in agreement and he weighed the pineapple, watermelon and also a cantaloupe and tangerines for us. Marcus whispered to me that we had probably made his day. We must have been his first customers and really good ones at that. The vendor grinned cheerfully and at that moment a gust of wind blew his straw hat away. Marcus went chasing after the hat and brought it back to its owner. The man thanked him and they both proceeded to load the fruit into the trunk.

We got into the car and drove away, leaving the vendor next to the cart, watching us. He held his hat with one hand and waved goodbye to us with the other. We waved back like he was an old friend and laughed, until we reached my parents' neighborhood.

The affordable housing project had been built four years earlier. The modest homes were allocated by lottery, and my mother was among the lucky ones who won. The road was not yet paved and the sidewalks were paths of dirt. Children were playing barefoot in the street with balls made from socks. Occasionally one could see more expensive houses, whose owners had added rooms on their own, but the general atmosphere was one of misery and danger. I sat uncomfortably next to Marcus, who said nothing. I would rather have followed suit, but I had to point him toward the house. His silence weighed on me. We drove to the last house on the cul-de-sac, and stopped there. The door was open, as usual, and I discerned the silhouettes on the living room sofas. We stopped by the fence and got out of the car.

Recognizing me from a distance, my siblings came to greet me, followed by friends who wanted to take a closer look at the guest. Ivone cried: "Catarina is here!" And my parents emerged through the doorway.

My mother was wearing a dark dress with light flowers and a white headscarf. I made the due introductions, and Marcus warmly shook hands with my family members. My mother apologized for the mess, because she didn't know we were coming, and Marcus reassured her. "Dona Teresa, it's perfectly fine. Don't feel bad," he said.

We went inside. Dirty dishes were indeed scattered in the living room and kitchen, chickens and dogs scurried in and out freely and no one gave it a second thought. My father sat next to Marcus on the couch and talked to him. When they got up and went for a walk outside, Mother took me aside and quietly asked if we were staying for lunch.

"I think so," I replied, "why?"

"Because I have nothing with which to prepare a meal," she answered sincerely. I took some money out of my bag and handed it to her. "Do you think this will be enough?" I asked, and she nodded. Lowering her gaze, she took the money and thanked me. She called Carlinho and Ivone, and whispered a shopping list to them.

I joined my father and Marcus in the yard. Father was in the middle of an impassioned speech: "We were the last ones left! They had allocated all the houses except one. Teresa had already said to me that that was it, that we had missed our chance on that round, when all of a sudden, the man who read out the names pronounced ours! We couldn't believe it! Teresa began to cry and couldn't stop."

He smiled to himself and some of the old excitement appeared in his expression again, as he pulled a pack of cigarettes out of his pocket.

He picked one, lit it, took a deep puff and slowly blew the smoke out of his nose and mouth. Marcus and I took advantage of his moment of happiness to go get the crate of fruits from the car and carry it together into the kitchen. Mother, who was collecting dishes from every corner of the house and washing them, smiled and said: "What gorgeous fruits."

At that moment the children returned with the shopping. She took the bags and emptied them of groceries. "I just started to work for a new company," she told us, while arranging the ingredients for the meal. "Jacuzzi, do you know it? I'm in charge of the kitchen and we cook for two hundred people every day. Every day a different menu. Marcus smiled and said:

"So we're having a professional cook our meal today."

"Not just a professional," I added, "a real chef!" And we all laughed.

Mother cut pieces of beef ribs and at the same time kept an eye on the spaghetti boiling in the pot. Father came into the kitchen and poured himself a glass of Cachaça. Mother looked at him and said quietly:

"This is his third glass today."

I arranged the slices of pineapple and watermelon on a plate and put them in the refrigerator. Marcus chatted with Ivone. She told him about the Coca Cola company sponsoring her and paying for her sports training, because she excelled at the 100-meter dash and high jump.

"Yes, instead of working and earning some money she wastes her time on nonsense," my mother grumbled, while pouring the contents of the spaghetti pot onto the colander.

My father laughed out loud. He wasn't drunk yet, but the Cachaça had already sent his spirits soaring. The ribs roasting in the oven gave off a pleasant smell. Soon the meal would be ready and we would sit down to eat. The heat outside seeped in through the open door and thin walls. A black-and-white dog, probably the family's, lay motionless in a basket, in the shade, near the entrance.

Children passed by him, flies buzzed around him, yet he did not move. Mother finally took the beef out of the oven and meted out portions of meat and spaghetti in sauce onto the plates. Each of us took theirs and sat down in one of the empty chairs. Marcus joined in and ate heartily. He said the food was excellent, and it was indeed. At the end of the meal, I served the chilled fruits, which provided some relief from the heat. By then, the house was unbearably hot. Father dragged himself to bed while Mother sat down on the sofa and lit a cigarette. Ivone, Marcus and I washed the dishes and tidied up the kitchen. Then we took chairs outside, under a canopy, to find refuge from the suffocating weather. The dog looked like he had passed out in the basket, with flies flying over his nose and ears. We were not spared either. I saw that Marcus was having a hard time swatting away the annoying insects and wiping the sweat off his red face.

I poured cold lemonade for all of us, which refreshed us a bit. At four in the afternoon, we decided it was time to go home. Mother got up from the sofa and announced that she was boiling water for coffee, and before Marcus could react, the kettle was already on the stove. Father came in from the room, stretching.

"Coffee is good," he said, "isn't it, Marcus?"

"That's right, Mr. Alemão."

We stayed for another hour, said warm goodbyes to everyone and got into the car. My family lined up on the sidewalk, watching us until we turned into another street.

Marcus looked tired and sweaty. I directed him to an ice cream parlor in the city center. We ordered the flavor we both liked, tropical fruit. Marcus held his cup with reverence, eating his ice cream slowly and with concentration, savoring every bite.

"Ivone needs to continue with her training. She sounds like she's really talented," he said. "I don't understand why people don't value sports. I gathered that Dona Teresa disapproves of what she's doing."

"My mother disapproves of a lot of things," I sighed. "She doesn't understand that one must invest in the future. She thinks her children should work, do any job, as long as they earn money. As far as she's concerned, they can work all their lives in cleaning or construction, provided they start contributing to their livelihood as soon as possible."

"You're lucky you left home early," he said, looking at me with tenderness. "There was no other way you could have left that life. You are so different from everyone else there. I'm so proud of you."

On the way back we hardly spoke, just listened to music. Marcus stopped the car near my apartment.

"What are you doing tomorrow?" he asked. We talked a bit about our plans for that week and then Marcus said, "Okay, I'm going home now. I'm tired and dying to get some sleep. I'll call you tomorrow. We kissed goodbye and I got out of the car. "It was very interesting meeting your family," he said through the window, as I smiled at him for a final goodbye. I don't know if it was fatigue or some other reason, but there was something different about him, maybe more distant.

"Hi, Catarina," Lourdes said when I walked into the apartment, "how did it go with your family?"

"OK. Hot and tiring. Itú is a hot little town. I think Marcus perhaps got heatstroke," I said, chuckling.

I went to bed early. Despite being exhausted, I couldn't fall asleep. My parents' house kept floating before my eyes in all its misery. My mother, lowering her gaze when she took money from me for groceries. How did they stay stuck in the same situation for so many years? Without any hope, making no attempt to move ahead. Fortunately for them, they were used to a life of hardship. They knew no other, not even one like mine. They simply survived from one day to the next, without any aspirations, without even a spark of curiosity to see something new.

That was the source of the great chasm between us: The desire for change. They didn't care, while I fought tooth and nail to move upwards. I was different from them, that was true, but I couldn't break away from them completely, because I came from them and they were a part of me, forever. I felt it when I brought home someone like Marcus. Beyond his praise and words of encouragement, I watched him take one step back, and maybe there would be more. What was he thinking when he met my parents? Had he imagined them sitting at the same table set with china and crystal as his well-bred family?

Was his love big enough to ignore this awkward onus that was my family, and stick with me? I was not convinced. Or maybe I was the problem? Maybe I hadn't grown enough yet to see myself as his equal? Maybe I was imagining feelings he didn't have because of some complex I still carried with me? I tossed and turned in bed almost until dawn, and only then fell asleep.

After the Visit

The week went by as usual, but something had changed. The phone calls with Marcus seemed less fluid, more restrained. And if that weren't enough, our landlord called on Friday morning to announce that our lease was about to expire and he was only willing to renew it for a higher rent. I replied that I would consult with my roommates and give him an answer within a week.

In the evening, when I spoke to both of them, Cristina immediately announced she was leaving.

She was planning to move back in with her mother and her daughter. Her daughter? I didn't even know she had one! I lived with her for a year and knew nothing about the girl. How depressing. I looked at Lourdes, who looked back at me apologetically.

"I can't afford to pay half," she said. "The owner of the restaurant I run offered me a room in her backyard a few days ago. She also wants to open a catering business, and she'd like me to live close to her. I told her I would think about it. I'm going to accept the offer. I'm sorry, Catarina."

"That's OK. Good luck to you," I said feeling abandoned.

Marcus came to pick me up. He looked great in jeans and a branded sports shirt. The smell of his fine aftershave made me dizzy.

"I missed you terribly," he whispered to me, "I've been thinking about you all week. I dreamed of you at night."

The agony of the last few days faded and I clung to him passionately. We couldn't wait to get to the motel and be alone at last, just the two of us. "How was your week?" he asked as we cuddled and relaxed, two hours later.

"Well, you know… Where to start… from the end?"

"What's wrong? That doesn't sound good."

I told him about the lease being up, and my roommates leaving me, each going their own way.

"This is really hard for me. I feel hurt, like they're betraying me."

"That's really wrong of them. They're supposed to be your friends. What are you going to do now?" He said, gently running his fingers through my hair.

"It's a problem. I need to find an apartment by myself. It's not easy, but I'll manage." After a few seconds of silence, he said:

"I will help you with whatever you may need."

"Thank you," I answered, crestfallen. Feeling disappointed, I realized that deep down inside I was hoping Marcus might propose marriage. I would have been happy to just move in with him, but I knew that in his family's eyes that would not be acceptable.

We had been together for almost two years. We were already twenty-three years old, what was he waiting for? Didn't he see our relationship as a serious one? I always believed it was. He talked about the children we would have, about wanting to stay with me for life, and now nothing. I wanted to get up and leave.

The Valero Family

On Monday morning, Dr. Daniel, one of the senior physicians in the department, approached me and asked if I remembered a lady named Clara Weiss, from whom I had taken blood a few weeks earlier. Yes, I did remember her clearly. A noble elderly woman, who came to the hospital accompanied by her daughter.

"Mrs. Weiss is a relative of mine," he said, "and she needs close monitoring and blood tests every other week. Can you go to her home and take blood from her? She lives very close."

Dr. Daniel cultivated relationships with relatives and other members of the upper class and they, in turn, supported the research conducted at the hospital. I willingly agreed and he wrote down for me the phone number of Mrs. Weiss, who lived with her daughter and her family.

The next day, at the appointed time, I rang the doorbell. A young girl in a work coat and apron opened the door and led me into the living room. From the depths of the armchair I sank into, I looked around the huge room, at the thick carpets and the furniture made of rich, dark oak. Heavy curtains hung from the high ceiling, hiding the windows. One curtain was drawn open and the wide window behind it was the only source of light. In one corner stood a grand piano and at the other end a very long dining table, surrounded by matching chairs with high backrests.

The center of the table was marked by a large porcelain urn, decorated in colorful relief. Mrs. Clara and her daughter entered the living room.

"Hello, Catarina," the daughter greeted me, holding out her hand to me, "I'm Stella Valero."

Stella was a confident woman of about forty. She smiled and thanked me for agreeing to come to their home, but through the smile I could feel her stern nature. She seemed like a person who knew exactly what she wanted. I asked Mrs. Clara to take a seat in the armchair I had been occupying and extend her arm on the armrest. I asked permission to bring one of the dining chairs closer to her. Clara rolled up her sleeve to reveal a pale, thin arm. She was a gentle person, unlike her daughter.

"That's it," I said, as I untied the elastic strap.

"Is it over? I didn't really feel anything. Kudos to you," Mrs. Clara said, smiling in relief.

"You have good veins," I answered amiably, arranging the sample tubes in the compartments of the box I used to carry them in. At that moment the maid walked in, bringing a tray with coffee and cookies.

"Catarina, come have some coffee with us. I know you don't have much time, but still, sit with us for a few minutes," Mrs. Clara said. Stella had already poured some and handed me a mug.

"How long have you been working with Dr. Daniel?" Stella asked. I started to tell her about Prof. Rosenberg when a seventeen-year-old girl entered the room. She had large light blue eyes and lush blonde hair. She smiled, and her full pink lips revealed pearly teeth.

"Charlotte, come, meet Catarina. She works at the hospital with Dr. Daniel," Clara said. I couldn't stop looking at Charlotte. She had the skin of an angel and was so beautiful. She flashed her bright smile in all directions and a few minutes later, disappeared into the house with her mother. "That is my granddaughter," Clara smiled, sitting back in the armchair. "She is going to England. She will study English for six months and then travel across Europe. When she comes back, she will begin her studies at the university."

"You have a very beautiful granddaughter," I said.

When I brought them the test results in person, Stella received me and again sat me down in the living room. Expressing an interest, she asked me about my family, whether I had a boyfriend and what he did in life.

Mrs. Clara and her family occupied a place in my thoughts. I told Marcus about them while we lounged at my place with the weekend newspapers. We were going through the rental ads, trying to find a small apartment for me only.

It wasn't easy to find an apartment that was not too far away, at a price I could afford. We saw an ad for a property outside the center, with suitable terms. When we went to see it, we discovered an apartment building built on a sloped plot of land. From the entrance we followed the landlady two floors down the stairs. We reached a small apartment, with a tiny bedroom and a living room opening onto a small, private garden. I felt like I was inside a doll house and I liked it. We agreed on the terms on the spot. It was our last week together, the girls' and mine. Cristina left a few days before us and Lourdes and I were left alone, packing up our things slowly, feeling the upcoming parting. During one of my lunch breaks I bought a small table and four wooden chairs for my new apartment. Marcus said he would help me move. On Saturday morning the movers arrived. Lourdes and I waited for them at the doorway, with suitcases leaning against the wall. They loaded the refrigerator and the few pieces of furniture and proceeded slowly and heavily down the stairs. We wandered through the empty rooms, making sure that nothing was left behind. We looked at each other teary eyed and hugged tightly. We promised to keep in touch and not lose each other.

"Where's Marcus?" Lourdes asked. "Didn't he say he would come help you?"

"He must have overslept," I said, in a tone of justification. We went down together. I asked the movers to wait a few minutes and ran to a public phone. Marcus's mother answered and said he was still sleeping. I asked her to tell him that I was already in the new apartment. Lourdes' taxi arrived and the driver placed her luggage in the trunk. We hugged for the last time and headed for our new homes.

The movers put the electrical appliances in place and assembled the closet and the bed. I dragged the suitcases and unpacked the dishes from the boxes. The movers finished their job, and I was left alone. I filled the kettle with water and put it on the gas stove. I walked around my private apartment, which was only mine, opening the windows and the door to the small garden. I felt free in my bright kingdom. Slowly, I had my first coffee in my new home, gazing at the blue sky that peaked at me through the door. I thought only the sky was the limit, that anything was possible, and that all I ever wanted could be achieved. I took out my clothes and put them away in the closet.

A white plastic bag had been left lying on the floor, and I couldn't remember what was in it. Inside was a folded cotton cloth. When I picked it up, a small album came tumbling down and a picture fell out of it. A picture of Rebeca. I picked it up gently and flipped through the album so I could put the photograph back in place. There weren't many pages, maybe ten in all. The last page had a death notice pasted on it, next to which was attached a tiny gold ring I bought for her when she turned one. I looked at the faces in the pictures, softly running my fingers over them. I closed the album, returned it to the white plastic bag and buried it in the depths of the closet.

I extended the cotton fabric and recognized the curtain I had received from a friend when Rebeca was born. It could well cover the bedroom window. I climbed up on a chair and hung the curtain.

Marcus finally showed up in the afternoon. He walked through the door clutching a television set.

"I hardly ever use it," he said. "I brought it so you could use it for now."

The remnants of the disappointment I felt toward him dissolved.

"Where do you want it?" he asked, leaning it on the dining table.

"Marcus, thank you, really," I said, quickly bringing a chest from the bedroom and pushing it against the living room wall. He set the TV down on it, plugged it in, and adjusted the antenna until the picture was neat enough.

"Everything is almost in order," he remarked admiringly as he toured the apartment. "I forgot something in the car," he said, striding out and returning a minute later with a McDonald's paper bag.

When he put it on the kitchen table I clung to his back and hugged him from behind. He turned around to face me and carried me in his arms to the bedroom. He peeled off my sweat-soaked t-shirt. That day we did nothing but be together.

We bathed together and ate cold hamburgers together in front of the TV. It was a wonderful Sunday in my new apartment. At four in the morning, he got out of bed to go home. I hated that we had to part in the middle of the night so as not to offend his family's conservative code, but there was nothing I could do.

In the morning I continued to unpack my belongings and tidy up the house. One of the carton boxes contained a few small items wrapped in newspaper. I took them out one by one. I washed and put glass cups in the kitchen cupboard, and a bottle of perfume in my bedroom. I opened another small paper package and inside I found an olive-colored porcelain dog. It was an item dear to my heart, a souvenir from Carlos. I stroked it gently and decided to find a special spot for it. I walked around the small apartment, devoid of shelves, and I couldn't find one.

At half past eight in the morning, I rang the doorbell of Mrs. Clara's house. She greeted me, well dressed and delicately made up. Smiling, she sat down with elegance in the armchair. While I was preparing the instruments for the test, I told her I had moved to a new apartment. She smiled with satisfaction.

"How's Charlotte? How's her trip going?" I kept the conversation going while tying the elastic strip around her upper arm. The smile disappeared from Clara's face. "Things are not working out so well," she sighed.

"Did anything happen to her?" I asked.

"Charlotte is giving us trouble. She has met someone in England."

I couldn't see what was so terrible about that. Clara explained that he was not Jewish. Among the Jews, it was very important to marry a member of the same religion, in order to preserve the tradition. It was not acceptable to marry a non-Jewish man. Maurice, her son-in-law, was very upset and had gone to England to see what could be done. I said I was very sorry to hear that, and wished things would work out the way they wanted. Charlotte was young and would probably forget the man soon.

I devoted the evening hours to my new apartment. A week later I passed by Stella's house on my way to the hospital and personally delivered the test results. Seeing Stella upset, I concluded that Charlotte's issue had not yet been resolved. I handed her the lab papers, remarking that the results were not that good.

"Of course!" Stella shouted, "Charlotte is killing us! Especially her grandmother. The girl has crossed every line. Her father went to bring her back and she adamantly refused to return with him. She is already living with the guy! Isn't that absurd!? She is only seventeen. Her father is losing his mind... Who does she think she is!" With growing anger, she continued, "We will close her bank account and then she'll have no choice but to return to Brazil! She has it all, this girl! What does she lack here?"

I didn't know what to do with myself. Clara sat in the armchair, not uttering a word, and I wished I could disappear. I waited quietly for a few minutes until Stella calmed down and hurried to say goodbye.

At the door she put an envelope in my pocket, as she sometimes did.

"This is for you, for the new apartment." Once I reached the lab, I opened the envelope. Despite her embarrassing outburst, she was generous to me and had given me a higher amount than the one she gave me from time to time.

End of an Era

I went down to call Marcus from the pay phone. We hadn't seen each other the day before because I had gone to visit my parents.

"How was it?" he asked.

"It was good! The Mendes family came to visit us, I mean Monica, Manuela and their mother. We hadn't seen each other in a while, and they saw my family's house for the first time. It was great to get together. How was your day?"

"It was nice, but I missed you. I'm dying to see you already. I'll come over in the evening, and I also have something to tell you."

"What is it?"

"I'll tell you in the evening."

When we met that evening, he hugged me and planted several kisses on my face. "I missed you so much…"

"Me too," I laughed, holding him close to me. "Now tell me."

"OK," he said cheerfully, lifting me up in his arms for a few seconds. "I'm flying to Japan with my basketball team in a month from now," he said, his eyes sparkling.

"You're Flying! Oh... How cool!" So that was the surprise, I thought, trying very hard to be happy for him. "How long are you going to be away for?"

"Two months." I almost choked, spilling the coffee grounds in the spoon I was holding all over the table.

"Two months! Good for you …" I said.

That month went by way too fast. Marcus was busy with preparations, and I, as usual, with work and studies. I was in constant contact with Mrs. Clara's family. She herself had to undergo a mastectomy, but wanted to wait for her precious granddaughter to return from abroad. On the day of the trip to Japan, I joined Marcus' mother and sister to say goodbye to him at the airport. Marcus arrived on the bus, with the rest of the team.

He was excited. He hugged me and introduced me to his friends, but he wasn't really with me. The place, full of families and friends who had come to say goodbye, resembled a beehive. I watched him walking away toward the gate, eager for the days to come. My heavy heart already began to feel the loneliness and longing I feared so much.

The first few days were very difficult for me. Every morning, when I got to work, I looked at the phone, with a knot in my stomach reminding me that I had no one to call or wait for on weekends.

After three days I called his mother to ask how he was doing. She told me that he was fine and that the flight had been very long and tiring. We exchanged a few polite sentences, I thanked her and hung up. Well, if she's so up to date, that means he was able to call. Surely in a few days he would call me too. Several days went by and I got no sign of life from him.

I went to visit Clara at the hospital where she had the surgery. I slowly and quietly opened the door to her private room. Clara was sleeping and Charlotte was sitting next to her reading a book. She stood up to greet me with a smile.

"I'm so happy to see you!" I told her. "How are you? How's your grandma?"

"The doctors say everything is fine," she whispered. "Let's talk outside so we don't wake her up."

We sat on a sofa in the ward's sitting room and chatted like close friends. She told me how great it had been in London and her eyes lit up for a moment, but immediately went out when she talked about her family.

"I only came home for Grandma, but I intend to return to London. There's nothing they can do about it," she affirmed.

"You must be missing your boyfriend a lot," I said. "I understand you so much. My boyfriend went to Japan for two months and it's really hard for me."

When we parted, we hugged like sisters in distress.

After Clara returned home, I saw Charlotte almost every week, whenever I went to collect blood from her grandmother. She looked nervous and upset. More than once I heard loud arguments between her and her mother from the other end of the corridor.

After almost two months, a postcard arrived from Marcus. He himself was supposed to land in Brazil a few days later, in the middle of the night. I didn't go to meet him at the airport. I waited until morning to talk to him. I couldn't stop myself from crying on the phone with excitement.

"I didn't have time for anything," he apologized, "we were constantly traveling, training and playing. It was very intense and tiring. It's great that tomorrow is Saturday. I will come to see you early tomorrow. I miss you so much, sweetie. He arrived early in the morning, with a bag in his hand. He hugged me tightly and I felt his longing mixed with mine. My resentment slowly disappeared, especially after he opened the bag and took out a delicate wristwatch, two Japanese dolls, a fan, small paper umbrellas to decorate drinks and a box of chocolates—all for me. I melted in his arms, and was flooded with love.

We had a wonderful day. With great enthusiasm he spoke about the beautiful places he saw, uncles and aunts he met for the first time, and the advanced technology. He bought himself a sophisticated camera with a professional lens and an excellent diving watch. He talked with emotion about how he experienced things without me, about the landscapes I didn't see with him, about the family I didn't meet. A sad little voice inside me whispered that he would probably have more trips I would not be a part of.

In the evening we went out to a restaurant, with our arms around each other. We raised a glass of wine to our lives and once again I felt that Marcus and I were a couple, together forever.

"Sweetheart," he said casually, "tomorrow we won't be able to get together, unfortunately, because we have a party to celebrate the trip. We the basketball team, I mean."

A stab in the heart again, as had happened several times lately. We returned to the car without speaking, but the anger and resentments that surfaced and subsided again and again, had been piling up in the basement. Now they were climbing up inside me again, and in full force. How could he be leaving me after not seeing each other for two months? Why didn't he ask me to come with him? Was he ashamed of me? We hardly ever went out in company. I had met a few of his friends from college, the ones I met in the beginning, but ever since he had been keeping me away from them. I wasn't really part of his life.

"What happened in the two months you were in Japan?" I asked suddenly.

"What do you mean? Nothing happened…"

"Nothing happened?" I was angry and hurt. "For two months you didn't pick up the phone to call me even once. Now that you're back, you'd rather hang out with your friends on our first weekend than be with me. What am I to you, really? We've been together for almost three years!"

"Honey, calm down. I explained to you that I couldn't call because I wasn't alone for a moment. And tomorrow isn't up to me, it's a team party. It's a one-off, really…"

I didn't want to hear anymore. Anger throbbing in my temples, I opened the door of the car that was already parked near my house and closed it firmly behind me. I disappeared with quick steps up the stairs of my building, because I didn't want Marcus to see me cry. Alone in bed, I cried my broken heart out. How does the person I love the most disappoint me and hurt me and I forgive him and love him again, every time? The facts presented themselves to me, stood in front of me, and I had to examine them with open eyes.

Something had changed between Marcus and me, and not just since the trip. We had slowly drifted apart, and I was not sure when it happened. Maybe it started when we went to meet my parents and maybe not.

The fact was that Marcus did not see me as a worthy partner. I could feel it, and it made me sick. It was important that he recognize me. I was so proud at the airport, when he introduced me as his girlfriend to the other players in the team. I wouldn't be able to live with him if I felt he was hiding me. I guess my humble origin got in the way, and was causing a rift between us. We had no future together.

And what would happen when I met someone new, an educated and cultured young man with the qualities I was looking for in my future husband? Wouldn't the story repeat itself when he met my family? What did I expect would happen as long as I lived in Brazil? My family was a burden, and I wanted to cut off any ties I had with them.

It wouldn't matter how far I went, even if I went to the other end of the country, an invisible force would bring me back to see what was going on with them, how they were managing, how I could help. Enough, the burden was too heavy for me. I wanted to leave, to forget them, and be free for good.

I spent all of Sunday with my eyes swollen from crying and lack of sleep, trying to concentrate and study for the upcoming exams. My studies were the most important thing to me, after Marcus.

It was ten o'clock at night when I heard two knocks on the door, like Marcus always knocked. He immediately told me he couldn't go through another night like the previous one without talking to me. He hugged me tightly and said he was sorry for hurting me and that he loved me very much. All the strength I had mustered to suppress my emotions and concentrate on the math exercises dissolved into sobs. I cried in his arms.

During my weekly visits to Clara, I learned that the situation with Charlotte wasn't good. She didn't talk much, only sighed with melancholy whenever I asked how her granddaughter was doing. Only once did she provide details, telling me about the scandal that broke out the day before between Charlotte and her parents, that the girl was in a difficult emotional state and that she was very worried.

I was sitting with Stella in the living room talking about the improvement evident in her mother's tests when Charlotte came into the living room, as beautiful and cheerful as the first time I saw her. She smiled at me and apologized for not being able to stay because she was on her way out. Indeed, the family's private driver appeared at the door, wearing a white shirt and a visor, waiting for her to come outside.

"Charlotte looks great," I marveled as she disappeared up the stairs.

"Yes," Stella agreed contentedly. "I think she has finally come to her senses, after the madness that took hold of her. She listens to us and she now understands that her future is not in London. She even started talking about Israel. She may go there for a while."

"How wonderful! How lucky she is to be able to travel. I wish I could get away from here too... My father's parents left Ukraine for Palestine, but ended up in Brazil instead."

Stella was curious. She didn't know about my Jewish roots. I could not expand much on the subject, because my father spoke very little about my grandparents. I only knew that they got married on a ship and arrived in Brazil, because they did not have a visa for Palestine. "I think it's exciting to leave the place where you were born for a few years, or even start over in a new place," I concluded.

"Would you really be willing to leave Brazil for a while? And what's the story with your boyfriend? You've been together for a long time, no wedding plans?"

"I don't think there will be a wedding." I poured my heart out to her. I told her about our relationship, which had been weakened since Marcus returned from Japan, about the thoughts that had recently begun to preoccupy me, about the differences in our backgrounds. "He is an educated young man from a well-established family, and I am not. Now I've begun to feel the class gap between us. Maybe I was too much in love before... Now it has started to bother me. I think that if we got married, he would feel he was doing me a favor, and I don't want that. I don't want to feel inferior to him, and that only thanks to him I got a good life. I can achieve a good life on my own, and I want to feel equal to my husband."

A glance at the clock on the wall showed me how late it was, and that classes would start in thirty minutes. I got up and said I was sorry to leave in such a rush. Stella gave me a hug and said she enjoyed talking to me.

I walked to the college in the sweltering heat with big strides. My openness surprised me. How had Stella and I become so involved in each other's lives? Yes, she knew my present pretty well, but she knew nothing about my past, my time at Claudia's, my marriage, or Rebeca. But what did the past matter? The main thing was the future.

In an hour I would have a math test, and I didn't have time to study. I barely knew the material. What would I do? During the first lesson, I secretly went over my math notes. During the test I stared at the sheet in front of me. The individual exercises were familiar to me. I solved two to the best of my ability and the third I couldn't do at all. I looked around in despair. The guy sitting next to me wrote furiously. I knew he had a deep understanding of the subject. While peeking at his page I tried to find some hint to the answer, but soon realized that our forms were different. I looked up and saw the teacher's gaze fixed on me. I wanted to bury myself. Of course I would fail, but being caught copying was terrible. I was standing at the bus stop feeling devastated.

And there, standing next to me was the Creative Writing teacher.

"Hello, Catarina," he said, "how are you? I was very impressed with the essay you submitted to me in our last class. I was very excited to read it."

"Thank you," I replied with a weak smile, praying the bus would arrive quickly. It was a compliment, wasn't it, and it should have made me happy; But I wasn't in the right mood to start a conversation about what I wrote.

"Is that a true story?" he asked.

I waited desperately for the bus, until finally I saw it coming from the other end of the street.

"No," I replied, "it's fiction."

I quickly got on the almost empty bus. I sat down on one of the benches and thought about the essay I had submitted. It was about a little baby girl who was born from pain, and got to live a few months until she got sick. I wrote about the fight against the disease, about the grandmother who refused to give her a little milk, about the pictures that her mother could not afford to buy, and about her death on a stormy night that had left the blue mark of a failed resuscitation attempt above the heart.

I got off the bus and the air was still oppressive, without even a slight breeze, despite the late hour. When I entered my little home, I felt relieved. It had a pleasant coolness and a smell of cleanliness. In the past few months, I had allowed myself to hire a cleaner once a week. Mrs. Anna had been there on that day, scrubbed the house until it shone and also put three pots on the stove. I ate some meat with rice and beans, took a quick shower and went to bed. At night it rained, and in the morning, when I opened the door to the courtyard, a cool, fresh air drifted inside. The sun that started to shine illuminated a vase I bought and a flower in the corner of the room.

Brazil's climate is as fickle as my life: Hours of unbearable heat and then the rain comes and washes away the haze, making the world clear again.

Pendulum

On Saturday, Marcus arrived and took me with him on the motorcycle to a wonderful place called Pico do Jaragua. I held tightly on to his broad back, with the wind blowing in my face. We drove through a nature reserve dense with tall trees and sunlight peeking between them, until we stopped by the observatory.

We were on top of the world, with all of São Paulo extending out at our feet. We kissed a lot, lost in our love, and nothing else existed at that moment. We watched the sunset together and the world was beautiful. In the evening, when he brought me home, he said he wouldn't be able to come the next day because he had to prepare for exams. All the happiness accumulated on that wonderful day evaporated. I slept badly and the next day I was restless, unable to find peace. This pendulum of emotions began to exhaust me.

I called Stella, as I did from time to time, to ask how Clara was doing and to set the date of the next blood test. Sounding glad, she told me that Charlotte left with her father to Israel. He was helping her get things organized during her first days there. She felt well and had enrolled in a university. In the meantime, she was learning Hebrew. They had a rented apartment in Tel Aviv they used when they went there, twice a year. Stella herself was planning a trip to England for two weeks, and would be very happy if I could stay in regular contact with Clara. Could I come by to see her?

I called Clara every day and dropped by every other day, before school. In the evenings and on weekends, I spent most of my time studying for the exams and hardly saw Marcus, who was studying too. It was a rough time for me.

One morning the phone rang in the office. "Catarina, could you come by this afternoon? I returned yesterday and I have some interesting news for you," Stella said. And this was the news I received once I was seated in her living room—one of her English friends was looking for a private nurse to take care of her elderly mother.

"How would you like to live in England for a year?"

"In England for a year?" I said in surprise. "I'd love to. I have three months left to finish my studies. Then I have to do a one-year internship, but I can postpone it. If it's okay for me to travel in another three months, then yes, I'm very interested. Thanks so much for thinking of me."

All the way to college I thought about the transformation that was about to take place in my life. I had to tell Marcus first. I wondered how he would react. This would be the true test of our love. Besides him, I wouldn't tell anyone for now, until the deal became final.

During the day I functioned as usual, but at night my thoughts kept me awake. What would become of me in three months? Where would I be? On Saturday afternoon I wore the light blue dress Marcus liked, and I waited for him. He suggested that we go to Ibirapuera Park. I thought it was a great place to have a serious conversation. There were hardly any people, and one could sit in the shade by the lake without being disturbed.

We walked in the park with our arms around each other, until I saw a bench under a tree. "Let's sit down," I said, "I have something to tell you." He sat close to me and listened with attention. I told him about Stella's offer. "I haven't given her an answer yet. What do you think? Should I go to England for a year?" He thought for a brief moment and replied: "What do I think? I say that's great. An opportunity like this doesn't come up twice!"

When I digested his words, my heart broke. I realized that up to that moment I was hoping he would say with ardor: "Catarina, you can't go away! I can't live without you for a whole year. Let's move in together. Let's get married..." Or at least something along those lines. I looked at his moving lips but no longer heard the words that came out of his mouth.

I began to cry, and slowly his voice came back. "Why are you crying?" he asked. I could barely utter an answer.

"I thought you wouldn't want to let me go."

"What? No way!" he protested, "I would never stop you. Besides, you're only going for a year. It'll go by fast, you know."

I didn't answer. We walked for a little while longer, and I didn't say anything else. We returned home without me mentioning the subject again. We ate together and went to bed. Lying peacefully in his arms, I realized that I had him now on borrowed time, but we had no future together. Salty tears ran down my cheeks. Marcus held me until I fell asleep.

The waves in the mattress and the dim light on his side of the bed woke me up. I saw him sitting on the edge, putting on his shoes. It was four in the morning. I did not move. He kissed me goodbye and I asked him to close the door after him when he left. The little lamp stayed on. I lay in bed for a few more minutes, staring at the ceiling. Just a few months ago, Marcus had carried me in his arms to the bed and stripped me of my sweaty tank top. How much love and passion there was between us.

God, what would become of us? I got out of bed and went to the kitchen. I made myself coffee and began to put my thoughts in order. At that exact moment I made a decision not to cry for him anymore. I had given him my all. I had loved him with all my heart and he'd broken it. He had let me down time and time again. The magic between us was extinguished, and that was the end of the matter. I would give up and not try to rekindle it. It was hard, but it was a good thing that the nature of our relationship had become clear. I would be strong. I would concentrate on my trip to England. Stella could not have found me the job at a more appropriate time. I was free. Nothing was keeping me in São Paulo. I had nothing further to do there. I already lost the closest thing to me once, Rebeca, and managed to get back on my feet all by myself. If I survived that, I was sure I'd make it now too. I needed to fly out of there as soon as possible. The next day I would set the final date with Stella and then speak to my supervisors.

I arrived at the hospital very early. At the main entrance to the building stood a tall young man in a guard's uniform.

"Hello," I greeted him, "where is Mr. Guido?"

"He has left. I am now in his place."

"Left!? Why?"

"I've no idea."

Mr. Guido had left? How did he leave without saying goodbye? We were good friends, he and I. I loved talking to him, and now he was gone without any notice. I must have been too busy with myself and my problems to sense that something was the matter with him. On my way to the lab, I passed by the office and asked for Guido's address.

While I was waiting for the results of some tests, I called Stella and we arranged for me to come by her place that afternoon. We sat in the kitchen while Clara made soup for dinner. I told them I was determined to leave as soon as I finished school. What did I need to do in order to expedite the process? I preferred to make all the arrangements in advance, so as to avoid delays. Stella examined me with her blue eyes and asked:

"Have you talked to Marcus? What did he say?"

"It doesn't matter. Marcus no longer has anything to do with my decisions."

"OK… I will talk to my friend again about your starting date. How's your English?"

"I speak a little. But don't worry, I will learn. I have three months."

As I left the Valero home, I felt the die had been cast. My trip was a done deal. I was leaving and it was not clear whether I would return or when. For some reason, tears flowed silently from my eyes, and I couldn't help it.

Stop it, I thought, feeling mad at myself. This is your chance to leave. That's what you wanted all along, isn't it? Think with your head. Stop this stupid sentimentality. Free yourself once and for all from the shackles of your family. They only weigh you down and give you nothing but pain. Stop thinking about them. Take care of yourself. Forget about them and Marcus. Start over. You'll make it, have no doubt.

A friend from college recommended to me an English teacher who gave private lessons. In our first lesson she gave me two textbooks and a workbook. My busy schedule now included learning English.

I went to Clara's personally to deliver her the blood test results which showed some improvement. I sat next to her in the kitchen while she kneaded breadcrumbs and spices with minced meat and shaped it all into large meatballs. She told me about Charlotte having trouble adjusting to Israel, a foreign country where she didn't know anyone.

"All beginnings are hard," I replied. "She will adapt eventually. She'll meet new people and have a good time."

Clara agreed with me and then told me that Stella had spoken to her friend in England, but she didn't know what they had agreed on.

Marcus came over on the weekend, and we went to the movies. We saw *Flashdance*, where Alex, a girl living in a tough neighborhood, achieves success against all odds, realizing her dream of becoming a dancer. Then we sat in a cafe and had ice cream. Images from the movie were still running through my mind, and the ending lifted up my spirits.

"I started taking English lessons," I said. "Next week I'm going to get a passport."

"Really? So soon? You don't even have a travel date yet."

"True, but it will happen in about three months and I need to be ready. I can't leave everything to the last minute. He didn't look very happy, and I celebrated a small, private victory. It was good that he was surprised by my determination. It was just dawning on him that I was serious, and really leaving.

My pain no longer felt the same either. My great love for him was starting to fade. I didn't even hate him. I might have been angry—after all, I loved him very much and he broke my heart—but little by little he became less important. I would leave Brazil with my head held high, without regrets, and who knew if I would ever return at all. This ice cream was delicious.

One morning Stella called and asked me to come see her, because she wanted us to talk. When she invited me to the living room, I had a hunch that it was not going to be a regular conversation. She sat down on the couch fiddling with the cord of her reading glasses, while Clara sat up in the wide queen armchair. Stella seemed to be at a loss for words.

"I asked you to come see us because I have a request."

"Please go ahead," I replied politely, bracing myself. At that moment the maid came in with a tray and Stella made some remarks about Clara's health, until the girl left the room.

"Yesterday I spoke with Charlotte and she sends you warm regards," she said as she picked a cube of brown sugar with a pair of tongs, and dropped it in her coffee.

"Thanks. How is she doing?"

"Not too well. She feels very lonely. I am worried... The mentality in Israel is different, and she finds it hard to make friends. I thought I'd ask you... Propose that... maybe instead of going to England, you'd go to Israel. You would have a place to live and I know many people there who could help you find a job. I'm sure you and Charlotte will get along well. Besides, my friend from England hasn't called in over a month. She might not be that interested after all."

I was so stunned I didn't know what to say. Stella placed her reading glasses on the table in front of her and fixed her eyes on me. She pushed the inside of her left cheek out with her tongue—a clear sign that she was under stress. I glanced at Clara, who was looking for something on the floor with great intent.

"This is very um... I was not expecting... I've never thought about living in Israel..." I stammered. "It's a crazy idea... interesting... it's strange that I'm sitting and talking to you about the possibility of traveling to Israel in such a natural way, and my father's parents met on a ship to Palestine and got married on it. I think I told you once, didn't I? They didn't let the ship enter Palestine, so they continued on to Brazil." I fell silent, pondering the idea for a few seconds before going on, "I think fate might be leading me to Israel and that's great. Fine, I'll go." I saw relief on Clara's face, and Stella's mouth relaxed into a wide smile.

"You may start packing," she declared with satisfaction.

On the way to college, I thought it was funny how my life was turned upside down in a few minutes, and how one can't plan anything. Something inside me told me that I had made the right decision. Israel would be the next place for me, and I would do whatever it took to manage there.

During the break I told one of my classmates that I was going to Israel. "Really?" she said. "I was there many years ago, in a kibbutz, and I hated it. I'm never going back."

"Where are you going to live?" asked another friend, who joined the conversation. I told her that in Tel Aviv. "Oh, Tel Aviv isn't a kibbutz! It's something else completely. It's a lot of fun there and you'll have a great time." She explained that Tel Aviv was a major and very interesting city, while a kibbutz is a closed farming commune. "If you need help with anything, information, or an address, let me know."

Well, I thought, Israel could not be the end of the world if both of them had been there, right? Did the fact that they had been to Israel imply that they were Jewish? I had never attached any importance to who was or wasn't Jewish. Everyone knew that São Paulo had a large Jewish community, but they did not stick out or look in any way different from the rest of the population. Soon I would go to Israel myself.

I was graduating in December. I would celebrate my last Christmas in Brazil and then leave for Israel. I had many arrangements to make and so many people to say goodbye to.

Separations

When I arrived at Mr. Guido's house, the door was opened by a man in his thirties—his son, it turned out. Seated at the kitchen table, Guido leaned over to see who had arrived.

"Oh, Catarina!" he exclaimed. "What a surprise!" He got up to welcome me.

"Mr. Guido," I greeted him, holding out my hands, which he squeezed warmly. "I had to see you again. You disappeared from the hospital without any notice, and I couldn't let you go like that. I had to bid you a proper farewell…"

"You're right," he answered, moved. "I left without saying goodbye. It was wrong of me. I was just so tired of doing this job, year after year. All those hours standing at the gate, meeting nervous, angry people who sometimes treated me in a hurtful way, with such disdain. I just decided to retire. It was so nice of you to come all the way here to see me. Will you have some coffee?"

"With pleasure, thank you very much." I sat down at the kitchen table and watched him fill a *coador de pano*,[24] set it down over a small kettle and pour boiling water into it. "It's no problem for me to come here at all, it's my pleasure," I said. "You helped me out when I was in need, and I will never forget that. In all my years at the hospital you always listened to my problems and gave me your support. You were a true friend."

Guido handed me a cup of coffee with his hands shaking with emotion. "Thank you," he mumbled. He added I was exaggerating, his eyes glistening.

Friends who wanted to say goodbye and wish me a good trip invited me to celebrate Christmas Eve with them. I chose to do so with Marcus's family. I planned to spend the holiday itself with my parents and tell them that I was going overseas.

The large Christmas tree at the center of the living room in Marcus's house was decorated with strings of light and hanging glass ornaments. Beneath it was a pile of gifts wrapped in colorful paper and ribbons, among which I placed a box with the aftershave I bought for Marcus.

The house looked festive and wonderfully pretty. I handed his mother a basket full of sweets and a Panettone cake.[25] She thanked me, hugged me tightly and said: "Catarina, we heard some interesting news about you. How is it going? It must not be easy for you to just go and leave everything behind. How are all the preparations coming along? Marcus can help with whatever you need."

"I'm fine. really," I said, shaking her hand, "I'm not going away for two months, you know, which means I have to manage on my own. I'm selling everything anyway, so I have nothing much to arrange for. I'm traveling light."

Marcus hugged me, and I felt his heart crumpling together with mine. The whole family, including Marcus' grandmother and older sister were

---

24 Coador de Pano - a kind of strainer made of cotton cloth, shaped a bit like a butterfly net. It's used by placing it over the rim of a mug, filling the bag with coffee grinds, and then pouring boiling water on so the liquid coffee is filtered through the fabric and drips into the mug.
25 Panettone is a traditional holiday cake made of compressed dough filled with pieces of dried fruit peel.

seated around the table. The atmosphere was happy and there was much laughter. Afterwards we exchanged presents. I got a bottle of perfume from Marcus and a beautiful blouse from his mother. After midnight he drove me home as I had to get up a few hours later to go visit my parents. The familiar views flashed by the bus window. I recorded everything in my mind, detail by detail. Who knew how many more times I would get a chance to travel this road and who knew if I would come back and drive through it again. As we entered the city, I saw the old fruit cart. The young salesman was standing on the side of the road, and the wind raised by the passing bus ruffled the brim of his straw hat. This time the hat was tied with a string and didn't fly anywhere. How happy I had been on the day we visited my parents for the first time. How the passage of time changed everything. The image of the man chasing the hat came to my mind, and I bit my lip to keep from crying.

We arrived slowly. The streets, decked with ribbons and flags, looked cheerful, which gave me some relief. I brought a holiday basket for my parents too, like the one I got for Marcus's family, only bigger and fuller. They received it and me with great joy. The wretched Christmas tree in the corner of the room had barely been decorated, and there was nothing under it. I opened the large bag I had brought with me and pulled out the boxes of chocolate, body lotion and scented soap I had received from patients. I also pulled out the tiny figures, pens and sketchbook I got from my Secret Santa, in the game the staff organized at the hospital. I laid it all out on the table for my brothers and sisters. The children enthusiastically opened the packages I had rewrapped for them, and soon the floor was covered with paper in classic Christmas patterns.

My father sat on the armchair, looking content and at ease. Even my mother seemed to approve. The scent of good quality meat came from the kitchen. As she grated Parmesan cheese over the tomato sauce on the pasta, she lifted the lid of the pot, and said with satisfaction that the roasted chicken looked excellent. The atmosphere was perfect and I didn't want to spoil it by breaking the news that I was leaving Brazil. I decided to postpone it for a bit.

The meal was rich and delicious. There was even smoked pork shoulder on the menu. At the end of the meal, when we were having coffee, I said: "Father, I didn't see you having anything to drink." He replied that he had been suffering from pain in his abdomen, and the doctor advised him not to drink while on medication. Mother nodded in agreement.

I couldn't delay informing them any longer. "I'm leaving," I announced.

"Already?" Mother exclaimed. "We just finished eating. It's still early! I thought you were staying over tonight."

"I'm going abroad. To Israel. In about two months. For a year, maybe more."

"With Marcus?" Father asked.

"No," I answered, "on my own. I got a proposition from a family I've known for a few years now."

I told them about Charlotte who was alone in Israel, and about the idea of me living with her. Father lit a cigarette and said thoughtfully:

"Catarina, Israel is very far away."

"And what about Marcus?" Mother asked. "He loves you. Why don't you get married? I thought you would end up marrying him."

"I thought so too," I said, "but apparently we're not ready to take that step." Dad was silent for a few minutes, then took a sip of the coffee and said slowly: "I hope you'll be alright there." He got up and went outside. I saw his figure standing at the gate, with his back to us.

Mother didn't say anything.

Ivone, who had been sitting quietly the entire time, suddenly said: "I might get married before you go."

"You?" I asked, surprised. "Since when do you have a boyfriend?" And that's how I learned that Ivone had been seeing a man named George, fifteen years her senior, a sports teacher, for several months.

How was it, I thought, that I didn't know anything about my sister, but the way things worked in the neighborhood, everyone else already knew Ivone was engaged. By that evening, the whole street also learned that I was going to Israel. People I barely knew came in through the open door to tell me how exciting it was that I was traveling so far, and wish me a good trip.

George came with Ivone, and I was glad to meet him. He was handsome, intelligent and in love with my sister. It reassured me to know that my little sister was someone I no longer had to worry about.

The next day I dropped by the Mendes family home. After the hugs and animated questions, we sat down and ate baked rice[26] that no one could make like Mrs. Mendes. The entire Mendes family was present that Sunday, in full force. There were seven of us women around the table, talking loudly, crossing stories and laughing the whole time. How I would miss their friendship.

Marcus and I saw each other every day, as if we could build up reserves of love by spending time together to make up for the days we would be apart. We sat on the couch in front of the TV, an English textbook on my lap. The announcer talked about the difficult economic situation in Brazil, the huge national debt and rampant inflation. Unemployment was on the rise. How great, how convenient it was to keep ourselves busy making costumes for the carnival and forget about hunger and poverty, added the narrator. And yet he would not recommend walking alone in the streets of São Paulo at night, because some desperate people who are not distracted by the carnival will rob us without a second thought.

Marcus watched me memorizing sentences in English while sneaking a peak at the news and smiled. Hugging me he whispered: "I will have a hard time being without you."

"So will I," I replied.

During the carnival, I used the days I had off work to study English more intensively, get a passport, collect my college diploma and transcripts, as well as run all sorts of small, annoying errands necessary before such a long trip. It turned out that my English teacher knew a few sentences in Hebrew, for some unknown reason, and that's how I learned how to say "Hello" "How are you?" and "Everything is fine."

I spoke with Stella every day, and we even set a date for the trip—March 26, less than a month away. I could no longer postpone my conversation with Prof. Rosenberg. I had to see him and let him know I was leaving.

I called him and asked for an appointment. He invited me to his office in the laboratory at half past eleven. He walked in just in time, wearing

---

26 Rice in the oven - Arroz de Forno - a casserole dish baked in the oven made of a layer of rice, topped with a layer of yellow cheese, topped with vegetables such as peas, carrots and zucchini, and finally an egg topped with grated Parmesan cheese.

a knee-length white robe over his normal clothes. He sat in his armchair and I sat in the chair across from him, just like I had done two and a half years earlier, when he hired me. This time he looked at me with suspicion, probably thinking I had come to ask for a raise.

"Prof. Rosenberg," I began, "I wanted to let you know that I'm leaving in two weeks."

"I see," he said, "and who are you going to be working for?"

"No one. I'm leaving Brazil. I am going to Israel."

He gathered his thoughts for a moment, slipping the wedding band up and down his finger, a habit that seemed to help him concentrate.

"What will you do in Israel? Are you perhaps Jewish?"

I told him I was not. Officially I was a Catholic, although at home religion was somewhat vague—our customs were a mixture of Christianity and African beliefs, as was prevalent in Brazil. I told him about Stella's proposition.

"My ticket is for a year," I explained, "but I might stay longer." His expression showed he was still surprised, as I went on to list my requests—whether he could please take care of my severance pay in the coming days, because I had to pay for my ticket, and write me a letter of recommendation in English. The trip was three weeks away.

"I hope you know what you're doing," he said, pushing the ring back into place.

"It'll be fine," I said to him in Hebrew, and he smiled.

"Well," he said, "we'll take care of everything you asked for."

"Thanks, I truly appreciate this," I said with emotion.

He nodded, got up, and left the room.

I spent the afternoon running between Stella and a friend who allowed me to call from her phone, to advertise the furniture I wanted to sell. Marcus was going to pick me up from there. I saw him waiting for me outside the car wearing a blue sweatshirt with his team's logo. To me, he was the handsomest, most attractive man I knew, and my heart went out to him. We embraced tightly, as we always did. I told him I had resigned and placed an ad to sell the contents of my apartment. His face took on a serious expression.

"Sell the TV too," he finally said.

"No, why? It's yours and I'll return it to you," I said, kissing him.

Once at home we spoke a little English, just to practice, and laughed at my mistakes.

Things could have been so good between us. How could he not see how great we were together? But enough. That was behind me. I was leaving in less than a month. Marcus would disappear like all the others, and that was it.

In the following days, the young doctors who smelled of aftershave and had coffee with me at the lab every morning, came to say goodbye to me one by one. They wished me luck, shook my hand and admired my courage. Dr. Rodrigues made sure to stay last in the lab. He was a vascular specialist, handsome and tanned, and loved the company of women. He took my hands and looked into my eyes.

"Catarina," he said, "I've known you for years. You have become a very beautiful, attractive young woman. I don't understand how Marcus is willing to let you." I smiled, feeling awkward.

"Dr. Rodrigues, thank you. But it was my decision."

On Friday afternoon I managed to buy a piece of thin gray woolen fabric and some beige linen, which I took to the seamstress. We chose a pattern for two suits.

It was important to me to arrive in Israel looking respectable. I sold most of the contents of the apartment to a young couple who were renting a flat together. They had no furniture yet and were interested in everything else I might have left too. It gave me some pleasure to think that the towels and bedding I loved would not go to waste but rather would belong to such nice people. They left the house happy, with their arms around each other. It was beautiful watching them. Both beautiful and sad.

Marcus came to help me pack, bringing several cartons with him. When I took down the curtains and folded them into the box, I told him that Ivone was getting married that coming Saturday and had asked me to be a witness. She emphatically said she'd like him to attend and I would be very happy if he came with me. He willingly agreed.

Ivone looked stunning in her white wedding dress and tulle veil, which flowed down to the floor. Her updo made her look like a princess. I hugged her tightly but gently, so I wouldn't ruin anything. My parents arrived a little after us, looking respectable. This time my father wore a suit and my mother did not have a scarf on her head. Her hair was well coiffed, straight and short. It was odd for me to see her like that. She looked like someone else, unfamiliar and older. I actually liked her headscarves. I could still feel the soft bounce of her hair under the fabric, whenever I touched it with my little hands, ages ago. We all gathered in the foyer at the entrance to the hall.

Before the ceremony, my mother and I waited standing next to the groom at the foot of the altar, while Marcus joined my brothers in the front pews. The wedding ceremony began. The groom was waiting for Ivone next to his parents and she began her slow march in his direction, walking slowly, arm in arm with my father. I saw them approach ceremoniously and I thought back for a moment to my wedding. My father didn't drink like he used to anymore, thank God. He looked much better. Things could improve, after all, I thought. Suddenly I felt a pinch on my arm. I turned my head to my mother, who was scolding me with her eyes. It turned out my cheeks were wet with tears, and I hadn't even realized it. I quickly wiped my face and looked for Marcus with my eyes. He followed the small procession with interest, then met my gaze and smiled.

We didn't stay in Itú for too long. After the ceremony we all went to the home of the groom's parents, who prepared a fancy meal for the guests. My mother couldn't find her place between the matching porcelain plates and the different pieces of cutlery. We ate quickly and returned to São Paulo.

Stella told me that the ticket was waiting for me at the travel agency and asked if I had the six hundred dollars to pay for it. I said I did, of course, and immediately notified the accounting department that I needed my severance pay as soon as possible. As I waited for the clerk who made me sign the forms releasing the amount to my bank account, I asked him to calculate the sum in dollars.

"The dollar exchange rate is very high today," he lamented, quickly clicking on his calculator. "Five hundred and twenty dollars."

"That's all?" I said, puzzled. "Maybe you made some mistake?" He shook his head and confirmed the number was accurate. I prayed that I had enough money in the bank to cover the cost of the ticket. I went to the bank in the afternoon, to exchange all my money into dollars and close the account. Luckily there were six hundred and fifty dollars there, and that was all I had. The few Cruzeiros I would receive for the furniture I sold were intended for current expenses and the seamstress. The next day I left work for a few hours and drove with Maurice, Clara's son-in-law, to the travel agency. The agent handed me the ticket and counted the money I gave her.

"You were lucky to get a seat," she said with a smile, "the flight is completely full. People reserve months in advance, because it is cheap. But nobody can disappoint Stella Valero."

Maurice smiled with satisfaction. When we were leaving the office, he asked how many dollars I wanted to buy. I replied that I had enough Cruzeiros for fifty dollars.

"Well," he said, "here's what we'll do: I'll sell you fifty dollars." He handed me the dollars and I paid for them with the balance of the allowance I had. He looked at me and added another fifteen dollars. I told him I had no more Cruzeiros left, but he replied that it was a gift.

"Now we will go buy foreign currency," he said, explaining to me that travelers were entitled to buy a certain amount. He wanted me to go with him to buy foreign currency using my ticket. I followed him to an unfamiliar area, the business district of São Paulo. We arrived at a street with tall, magnificent buildings, most of which displayed the logos of international banks: CITY BANK, CREDIT SUISSE. I already felt like I was abroad. Maurice said he needed German marks and went to the Deutsche Bank building. He asked me for my passport and plane ticket. We entered a large space with a high ceiling and marble columns. I followed him, looking around in wonderment, giddy with the splendor of the place. He strode confidently into the office of the manager, who got up from his chair with a smile and shook his hand, then mine.

"How can I help you, Mr. Valero?" he asked with obvious respect.

"Catarina is going to Israel and wishes to buy 2,250 DM," he answered and looked at me.

"Please, take a seat," the manager said and disappeared for a few minutes. He returned with a brown envelope full of bills which he counted out in front of me, and handed it to Maurice. He then entered the amount of the purchase in my passport and signed it. Maurice handed him a check with his signature and passed the envelope to me. I had never held that much money in my hands all at once. When leaving the bank, I quickly gave the envelope for him to keep.

Back at the hospital I took out the plane ticket and waved it at my co-workers.

"This is it," I said with glee, "there's no turning back now. On March 26 I am flying to Israel."

That evening I emptied out the closet of the last items. The buyers would come to pick up the furniture before I left. The few precious mementos I didn't want to take with me—Rebeca's album and the dog figurine I got from Carlos safely wrapped in rice paper—I placed in a small box, labeled *Rebeca's Photos and Belongings*. I wondered how to keep it from getting lost, and decided to leave it with Lourdes, a trusted friend, until I could return to pick them up.

I lay down to sleep on the living room couch, making a mental calculation of how much money I would have left after receiving the rest of my salary and the money from the furniture. Clearly it would barely cover my rent and livelihood, and I wouldn't be able to buy any more dollars. I had to take good care of what I had left. At that moment I remembered that the ticket and cash were still in my bag. I quickly got up and looked for a safe place to put them until the trip. I stuffed the envelope deep inside the oven and went back to the couch. What if I turned on the oven by mistake? I was struck with doubt. Maybe that wasn't the safest place. What? There was no way I'd forget for a moment where I put the ticket. All I had in my mind those days was the trip, and I certainly had no intention of baking anytime soon. That was how I soothed myself to sleep.

Another week went by, and Friday arrived. At mid-morning, Prof. Rosenberg came by the laboratory to bid me farewell.

He stared at the three envelopes he held in his hand for a moment. Once again, he looked like his head was teeming with thoughts competing to get ahead of one another. After a few seconds he came back to reality and handed me the envelopes.

"Catarina," he announced, "today is your last day of work. I wrote you a letter of recommendation and added two more letters to colleagues of mine, heads of departments in hospitals in Israel. They can make it easier for you to find a job… What else can I add? I wish you lots of success, and if by any chance you don't get by there, you can come back to us. You will always have a place here."

I thanked him from the bottom of my heart, reiterating that I had learned so much thanks to him. I had met a great number of interesting people through him and also the Valero family, who were having such a huge impact on my life.

We shook hands warmly and he said: "Take good care of yourself!"

In the evening, the young couple came to pick up the furniture. I threw in, as promised, the last items I had not been able to sell and did not intend to take with me. The curtain I got from a good friend for Rebeca's birth and the tablecloth Maria had sewn for me were also among them. They paid me more than we'd agreed on.

Last Days in Brazil

The house was completely empty, except for my two suitcases in the corner and the TV standing by the wall. A sheet and blanket, a birthday present from Marcus, lay on the floor, and on them a pillow and another sheet to cover myself with. The suit I was going to wear when I left for my new life was hanging on the bedroom door. In the meantime, I had three nights left to sleep on the floor. Marcus came in the morning to drive me to the central bus station, so I could go say goodbye to my parents for the last time.

He looked around, examined the empty rooms and the bedding on the floor and said: "My mother would like invite you to stay with us. You can't really sleep like this."

I thanked him and said there was no need, that I was fine, but could he please take back the TV. "It's a shame to leave it in the apartment like that."

On the way to the station, I asked him to stop by the café where Lourdes worked. I placed my precious cardboard box in her hands and explained to her that it contained all the objects that were important to me, like pictures of Rebeca and a few others. She promised to keep it safe for me until I came back to get it.

I arrived in Itú before noon. The family slowly gathered. My mother and brother returned from work and Ivone came over in the evening with her husband George. How happy this beautiful couple made me. They were so great together. I said goodbye to them with hugs and kisses, not having the faintest idea how long it would be before I saw them again.

At night I had a hard time falling asleep. Maybe because of the strange bed or perhaps because of the excitement or distress. It wasn't the crowded quarters that bothered me. Only my little brother, who stuck to me from the moment I arrived and didn't leave by side for a moment, was sleeping with me. I woke up with a dog licking the palm of my hand. It was still early but my siblings' friends ran noisily in and out, talking loudly as if they were on the street in the middle of the day. Then I smelled my father's coffee and knew I was home.

After breakfast I told them I had to leave for São Paulo before noon, because I had arranged to meet some friends at a café to say goodbye to them too.

My mother looked at me with sad eyes and said: "What, aren't you coming by again?"

"But Mother," I said, "I'm leaving the day after tomorrow in the morning! When could I come? I still have things to sort out. I will write to you from there. Promise."

My father wrote down their exact postal address on a piece of paper and handed it to me. Then began a barrage of hugs and kisses, with my siblings dropping in, one by one, to say goodbye.

I hugged my parents and my mother blessed me, praying that God would protect me. When I left for the bus station carrying the bag of clothes I had brought with me, Aroldo joined me. He asked me if I was scared. I told him that no, I was not afraid, just a little worried and curious about seeing the Middle East. I was eager to walk down the streets of Jerusalem and Bethlehem, to see the Dead Sea and Eilat. Those were places I had only heard about, and now I would be able to visit them myself. He searched for words and finally said: "Take care of yourself. The news talks about the terrorism there. It is a dangerous place. Besides, you'll be all alone..." His concern touched me. When I saw the bus arriving, I hugged him, told him not to worry, that I wouldn't be there alone, and we parted.

In the empty apartment I went through the documents I needed to take with me, and checked for the umpteenth time that they were all there. I already had butterflies in my stomach. The date was approaching, and there was no going back.

I put on a tight-fitting white skirt with a side slit and a purple blouse. When Marcus arrived, he looked me over admiringly and complimented me. We hugged tightly and left for the café. My friends, most of them from work, came to wish me a good trip and good luck. I invited Maurice and Stella to join. Many of those present were Jewish, and were familiar with the situation in Israel. The others asked me specifically about the security issues.

On the way home, Marcus and I were both silent. I put my hand on his, saying nothing. Suddenly he asked if I wanted to be with him tonight and I answered that I would be very happy to. We both knew this would be our last night together, but neither one voiced the thought. We just talked about other things. We got a room in a motel. In the darkness, cuddled in bed, only a part of me was with him. Another part was far away and busy with thoughts that were only mine. What was the point of sharing them with someone who was no longer part of my life? Marcus fell asleep pretty fast while I watched him, wondering how he could sleep so well when I was leaving in two days.

The next morning, I went to Stella for the final arrangements before the trip. The maid led me to the living room and asked me to wait for a few minutes. Stella entered the room playing with the cord of her glasses, her tongue pressed against the inside of her cheek. I immediately knew something was wrong. She hugged me and sat down facing me.

"Catarina," she said, "something bad has happened. I received a call from my friend in Israel and it turns out that Charlotte has left. She went to England without anyone knowing, except her friend—my friend's daughter. We had been calling the apartment in Tel Aviv for two days and no one answered. This girl, her friend, this moron..." her voice rose to a shriek, "said nothing. We didn't know what to think, we were going crazy with worry, until she finally told her mother. The mother immediately called to tell us."

I felt my head spinning. My legs weighed a ton and I couldn't move. This had to be a bad dream. Soon I would wake up and everything would be fine. I could no longer hear what Stella was saying but suddenly I spoke up.

"What am I supposed to do? Everything is ready for me to go. I quit my job, and sold everything I had."

"You can fly, if you want to. It's up to you. If you want to live there alone, that's fine with us. There will be no one to meet you there, you do understand…"

"I'll manage," I replied.

"Mr. Maurice is in the bathroom now. When he comes out, he will explain to you exactly what to do when you arrive," Stella explained.

I tried to put my thoughts in order. I took a glass of water from the table and drank slowly. I didn't even notice that the maid had placed a tray with glasses and cups of coffee on the table. I relaxed a little with each sip, until Maurice entered the living room and greeted me with a weary, gloomy *good morning*.

"What do you want me to explain to Catarina?" he asked Stella impatiently.

"What do you mean what to explain? Everything. How to get from the airport to the place where she will receive the key to the apartment. You have to give her their address, and also the address of the apartment. You should also give her the names and phone numbers of our friends, so she can contact them in case she has any problem. Also tell her what she needs to watch out for. In short, all she needs to know," Stella snapped.

Maurice sat down and carried out his wife's instructions one by one. He told me that the Israeli currency had been changed a few months ago from the Lira to the Shekel. He took some bills out of his pocket and handed them to me.

"Here are a few Liras so you can pay for a taxi from the airport. You can still use the old currency, it's fine," he continued. "Just take a taxi from a taxi stand. Don't get into any cab you find on the street, and certainly don't get into any stranger's car. The situation in Israel isn't that simple. There is terrorism and kidnappings, and hitchhiking is dangerous."

Strangely, up until that moment, he had never mentioned terror or danger, neither when we went to get the tickets from the travel agency, nor when we got foreign currency at the bank. I think he was trying to scare me into giving up on the idea.

Gathering all my strength I replied: "Don't worry, Mr. Maurice, I'll be fine. He looked at me with hesitation for a moment and then made up his mind.

"If so, then fine. The key to the apartment is with my accountant. I wrote you his name and address and I will call to let him know you are coming. I also wrote you the names of two acquaintances of ours, so you can talk to them in case you have any issues." He handed me a note and I put it in my bag.

"Thank you, Mr. Maurice."

"Mr. Maurice will be in Israel in two weeks," Stella announced. "Until then you will have to manage on your own."

"I'll be ok," I assured her. Maurice got up from the armchair, shook my hand and wished me all the best. I thanked him again. He went out, and Stella followed him with her eyes.

"He's devastated," she said. "He took the whole story with Charlotte very hard. He's flying to England to convince her to come back and I really hope it won't be too late, that she doesn't do anything stupid before then."

I was getting up from my seat to say goodbye when Clara entered the room and extended a thin arm toward me.

"Catarina, I wanted to wish you a good trip," she said in her weak voice. I hugged her gently, feeling her fragility. I was thinking that might be the last time I ever saw her. I would be really sorry if we didn't meet again.

"Thank you, Mrs. Clara," I said. "Take care of yourself. Make sure you get the tests done regularly. The girl replacing me is very professional. Keep well."

Stella squeezed my hand with a worried look and said: "Come by tomorrow at noon with your baggage and we'll go to the airport together. That way we can talk on the way." I had no choice but to agree.

I was hoping to go with Marcus, but now I'd have to tell him to meet me at the airport. I called him from a payphone, and heard the disappointment in his voice. He asked if I wanted him to come to me in the evening, but I preferred to go to bed early. "See you tomorrow," I said.

Before I returned home, I stopped by a friend from college. She suggested I sleep at her place instead of on my floor. She and her father drove me to the apartment, and while they carried my suitcases to the car, I lingered for a little while to make sure I had not forgotten anything, and to lock up.

The envelope with the flight ticket and cash parted from the oven and went safely into my handbag. I stood at the doorway for the last time. I had the most amazing time of my life in that apartment. I remembered how full of hope and faith I had been when I arrived, so long ago. Some of my dreams did come true. I had happy days and nights full of love, but they were gone. I was starting a new era, once again full of hope and faith... I needed faith. Yes, I was sure that interesting times awaited me. I would learn a lot, see new things. Live. Maybe I would be happy too.

I grabbed the hanger with the suit from the bedroom, closed the front door behind me and locked up. Tomorrow I would give Marcus the key so he could return it to the landlady for me.

On my last night in Brazil, in another bed, with a friend from college, I lay awake for hours thinking about Charlotte. How could she do such a thing to me? I was so angry at her for abandoning me and forcing me to be alone in a foreign land. But really, what could she have done? She followed her heart, betrayed me for love, and there was nothing more important than love. I could justify her actions. Luckily it didn't happen when I was already there—I would have felt responsible, and Maurice and Stella might have silently blamed me.

I suddenly woke up in a panic, in a strange room full of light. Where was I? I was supposed to fly that day. Had I missed my flight? I looked at the clock, but it was only 8 a.m. The room was airy and pleasant, a late summer morning peeking through the cracks between the blinds. I got out of bed and headed toward the voices coming from the kitchen.

"Good morning!" My friend greeted me in English, while her mother laughed and asked: "How is your English? Sit down, honey, and have some breakfast."

"My English is ok," I replied in English too, smiling and grabbing a bread roll. "The teacher you recommended helped me a lot." My teacher was a friend of the mother's, and lived in the same building. "She even taught me a few words in Hebrew," I added, as I buttered the roll. I wondered how she learned her Hebrew and had wanted to ask, but I was too embarrassed.

After a long shower I put on my travel suit, which had been waiting for me on the hanger for several days. I tucked the light purple silk shirt into the waist of a pearl-gray skirt, and over it a tailored jacket matching the skirt. On the left side of the jacket sticking out of the pocket was a small triangle made from the same fabric as the shirt. The elegant look was crowned by black high-heeled pumps. After ordering a taxi, I said goodbye to my friend and her mother. The taxi stopped in front of the hospital, near Stella's house, and I got out with my two suitcases. That was roughly the spot where I had stood, years ago, when I arrived in São Paulo from Sorocaba. I looked for the last time at the impressive building of the hospital, which I learned by then had once been a monastery. I said goodbye to the high arched windows with the white stone decorations, and the turrets with the pointed roofs.

I slowly parted from the elegant red brick walls. I will miss you, glorious hospital, I told myself. I had gone through a lot between those walls and I was taking with me both beautiful and harsh memories. I had learned so much, acquired a profession. If on that day I was standing there with two suitcases and an uncertain future, yet feeling confident that things would work out for me, it was to a great extent thanks to Santa Casa de São Paulo.

I walked into the elevator that took me up to Stella's apartment. Their chauffeur took my luggage and Stella came out to greet me with a smile. I waited for her in the kitchen, together with Mrs. Clara. The cook stirred the two pots that were boiling on the gas stove. Clara sat down to chat with me but every few minutes she would go over to the pots, check on the stew, and give the cook further instructions.

Stella appeared in the kitchen and announced that we were ready to leave. This was definitely the final goodbye. My heart shrunk with emotion. I hugged Clara again, said goodbye to the cook and the maid, and we left the building.

In the back seat of the car, Stella and I talked about Charlotte.

"Catarina, don't tell anyone what happened. Not even the friends whose numbers Mr. Maurice gave you. Be extra careful with Patricia, she likes to gossip."

"But I don't speak Hebrew, and barely any English," I reassured her. "I can't tell anyone anything."

"Patricia speaks Portuguese," Stella said. "Actually, you have to be careful with everyone." She warned me again, going on and on about the shame their daughter had brought upon them, until I could no longer listen.

With great relief I saw the airport in the distance. We entered the hall with me pushing a cart with both suitcases on it. I recognized Marcus from a distance, standing tall and handsome, in a tight t-shirt.

My stomach was gripped with pain. He crossed the hall toward me in quick strides. He hugged me without any embarrassment and held me close for a long time, our hearts beating against each other, as if we were alone. We forgot everyone around us. When I moved my head away from his chest for a moment, I noticed Stella out of the corner of my eye, standing and smiling over my shoulder, her tongue pressing into her left cheek.

I slowly broke away from Marcus as two friends who came to say goodbye to me approached us. After a few final hugs, Stella said there was no point in her keeping me any longer. I was supposed to go to the departures area anyway, and she and the girls left.

Marcus bought us drinks and we sat down in a quiet corner. I handed him an envelope for the landlady, with the key and the balance of the rent I owed, and asked him to deliver it to her as soon as possible.

"I have something for you too," he said, giving me an envelope. "Please don't read this now. Open the letter only when you arrive in Israel," he said, his voice breaking. His eyes were full of tears that rolled down his cheeks. I leaned over to him and kissed his moist face.

We kissed gently until I got up and said quietly that I had to go. He escorted me to the gate. I told him there was a layover in Brasilia and I would call him from there. The glass door opened for me and closed behind me. I didn't look back and the tears I was holding inside came gushing out. I cried in the passport control line. I cried while I walked in the duty-free zone. I cried, feeling angry with myself. Why was I crying anyway? After all, I wanted to go abroad.

I went to the bathroom and washed my face. I put on makeup and felt better. At the duty-free shops people were pushing loaded carts or juggling cigarette cartons and bottles of alcohol. I headed to the perfume section, and went through all the tester bottles. I picked up a Chanel 5 perfume and sprayed a little on my wrist. The smell was exquisite—the expensive fragrance of beautiful women like Marilyn Monroe. I sprayed a little behind my ear too and left the store.

I then went to stand in front of a large glass window that overlooked the aircraft tarmac and the runways. It was a huge area, much larger than the one Marcus and I used to go to sometimes, so long ago.

The Trip

I heard the announcement about my flight starting to board over the loudspeakers and rushed to the gate. It was really happening, there was no going back. I was getting on a plane for the first time in my life. My feet tapped on the linoleum floor of the sleeve that led to the plane, and my heart pounded in my chest. I found my seat. The plane was not full. I got a window seat with no one next to me. I looked out at the setting sun.

A cute flight attendant stood in the aisle, demonstrating to the passengers how to fasten their seat belts and put on the life jacket in an emergency, before inflating it. I struggled for a few minutes with the buckle until I was able to figure out how it worked, then felt the plane taking off at last.

It glided slowly along the tarmac, coming to a near stop by the runway, and then it began to taxi. The fast acceleration pushed me backwards until l was almost glued to the backrest of my seat. Suddenly I felt very heavy, watching the ground tilting toward me like a postcard. I closed my eyes in fear but opened them immediately again, to make sure I didn't miss anything. The earth disappeared and from my window I saw only the sky. The plane gradually stabilized and the distant towns shrank to the size of toys. The lights went on and within minutes, all I could see was a dense carpet of twinkling stars below me.

"What would you like to drink?" a pleasant voice asked me. A smiling flight attendant stood in the aisle with a drinks cart. I asked for water and she handed me a full glass, with an ice cube clinking against the edge. "You may unbuckle your seatbelt now," she said in a friendly tone. I thanked her and took a sip of the water. It slid down my throat, cool and soothing, and I was able to relax into my seat. I looked at the TV screen, following with interest the tiny moving plane marking our route on the world map. A few hours later, the pilot announced he was preparing to land, and that those passengers continuing to Israel had to wait in Brasilia for a few hours. The landing was smooth and I was hardly afraid. Most of the passengers who, like me, were on their way to Israel, were transferred to the transit lounge. I looked for a pay phone to call Marcus like I promised, but couldn't see one anywhere. A member of the airport staff pointed to a far corner of the hall. I quickly went there and picked up the phone, then remembered I had no tokens, so I placed a collect call through the operator.

Marcus picked up immediately, with a strangled hello.

"Marcus! Are you crying?"

"I can't stop... I've been crying from the moment you left. Come home, please."

"I no longer have a home."

"Come back to me! I love you. I can't live without you. Come back to me and we'll get married."

Those words, which I had wanted to hear so badly, he only now remembered to say them?

I listened to him in silence, letting it all sink in.

"Marcus, I can't go back. We were together for three years and every day I waited to hear this from you, and now that I hear you say it, I'm not sure it's what I really want..." I replied, ultimately, overcome with a sense of failure. What would I give to turn back the clock and hear these words a few months ago. And what if I take a flight back to him now?

Will my story really have a happy ending? No... it is no longer possible to fix what's broken. Even if we try, it won't be the same. I have to put my emotions aside and think with my head.

Maybe his resolve will weaken by the time I return? I certainly won't force marriage on him, and I don't have a house to live in. What am I going to do, move in with my family? That's impossible. How can he be putting me in this situation? Why is he doing this to me? Do I even want to be his wife? What if he feels in the future that he did me a favor? I don't want to feel like I owe him. I want to succeed on my own merits. I must continue on the path I have chosen. I'm not going back.

"Marcus, I'm sorry. I love you, but I'm not coming back. It's too late."

The words coming out of his mouth were slurred from the crying and I could barely understand what he was saying. "I love you too. I'll be waiting for you."

"Marcus, you are free."

"No. I can't be. I love you."

"I have to hang up now, Marcus. Goodbye."

I placed the handset back on the hook, and couldn't move. I stood stunned, frozen, trying to collect myself and my emotions. I walked on shaky legs to a nearby bench and sat down heavily. I stayed there without moving, feeling drained, waiting for my strength to return.

Deep down I knew I had made the right choice. I was already a different Catarina from the one who had been deeply in love with Marcus. Going back to him now wouldn't work. I had invested everything I had into this journey toward the unknown, and I wouldn't get another chance. Who knew what awaited me on the other side of the ocean? When the speaker announced we were boarding, I automatically walked to my seat. The plane was full, and I wasn't sitting alone. This time I didn't close my eyes when we took off. I looked at the distant land of Brazil and knew that now I was really on my way to Israel.

The scent of warm food reminded me that I hadn't eaten since the morning. At last, the serving cart reached my row too and the flight attendant handed me a tray with salad, roasted meat, and fruit compote in small containers wrapped in foil. I also chose a small bottle of wine. I ate almost everything, and by the last sip of the wine, I felt dizzy.

I smiled at the lady sitting next to me and she asked whether that was my first time traveling to Israel. It turns out that she had been there several times already. She had a daughter who worked at the embassy of Brazil, which made me very happy. I'd have some kind of a lifeline, someone to turn to if I needed. The lady, whose name was Celina, went on to tell me her daughter had married a religious man and wasn't living happily, unfortunately. She sighed, and then asked me where I was planning to live.

"Good for you, Tel Aviv is a great city!" she said, confirming enthusiastically what I had already heard.

The screen in the front began to display the titles of the featured film, and the lights on the plane dimmed. I took off my high-heeled pumps, reclined the backrest, and began to watch the movie.

The next thing I saw was Celina returning to her seat next to me, and putting a toothbrush back in her bag.

"You were sound asleep," she said to me, kindly. "Don't you want to freshen up a bit? Breakfast will be served soon…" When I returned to my seat, Celina said beaming, "My daughter will be waiting for me at the arrival hall. Will anyone be waiting for you?"

"No. I need to call someone and let them know I arrived before going to get the key to the apartment. I hope they understand me."

"No problem, my dear. My daughter speaks several languages and she will call on your behalf. Don't worry. We will go out together, so as not to lose each other. In the meantime, note down the phone numbers of the Brazilian embassy and my daughter's private number. You can always call her if you need anything."

I carefully wrote down her daughter's phone numbers and even her address. I felt grateful and much more at ease. I also gave her the phone number of Maurice and Stella's apartment, where I would be staying.

The air inside the cabin became stuffy, with heavy, suffocating waves coming from the smoking area in the back of the plane. The day crawled slowly by. I alternated between looking out the window and at the movie screen. Celina told me we were scheduled to land at eight in the evening. Toward six the sun began to set. I felt a flutter in my stomach. We'd be arriving soon. My great adventure was about to begin. And again, the tiny plane appeared on the screen, this time flying across the Mediterranean Sea.

"This is it. We're in Israeli airspace," Celina said when the plane reached the coast. There was a rumble of excitement along the whole plane, as the loudspeaker announced in three languages that we had to fasten our seat belts, because we would soon be landing at the airport. Fields of lights stretched out below us. The plane began its descent, and as soon as its wheels touched the ground, the passengers burst into applause and singing. Today I know they sang *Heveinu Shalom Aleichen*— We have brought peace upon you, but at the time I thought it was the most surprising and touching thing I had ever experienced.

I was pushed out with the streams of people exiting the plane, afraid of losing Celina. I followed her onto the bus that took us to a stone building with the sign that said *Welcome to Ben Gurion Airport*. Immediately upon entering the terminal I found myself standing in the crowded passport control lines. All around us were armed soldiers in military uniforms. I felt they were watching me and my heart began to pound.

Did I look suspicious to them? I didn't notice that the official at the window, also in uniform, was asking me to approach. The person behind me signaled me to move ahead. I rushed to the window, feeling nervous under the man's serious gaze. He looked at me sternly and asked me something in Hebrew. Celina was nowhere to be seen and I didn't understand a word of what he was saying. What did he want from me anyway?

He repeated a question in Hebrew.

"I don't speak Hebrew," I stammered in English.

"Where are you going to be staying?" he asked in English.

"Tel Aviv," I answered, confused.

"The address? What is the address of the place you'll be staying at?" he repeated in English.

"Ah… Rachel Street 3." He examined me impassively, signed my passport, and handed it back to me. Relieved, I took it and rushed past his booth. My eyes searched for Celina but I could not find her. I followed everyone to the baggage claim and suddenly saw her there, waving at me and calling my name. I dragged my two suitcases feeling lighthearted, heading outside beside her. We passed the last gate to freedom and went through to all the people waiting in the arrival hall for their dear ones. A young woman ran up to Celina with a cry of enthusiasm. They stood for a long time, hugging and kissing. They took out their handkerchiefs, wiped away some tears and hugged again. I waited quietly on the side until they regained their composure, and Celina introduced me to her daughter, Roberta. Together we looked for a public phone. Roberta dialed the number I gave her, explained that I, Catarina, had landed and that I was coming to get the key. After hanging up, she confirmed that all was fine and that they were expecting me. The two women shook my hand and said goodbye to me. I saw them walking away, together, and I was left alone.

First Days in Israel

Lots of people I don't know. Not even the ones on my flight. Strangers I had never seen before, who found each other, hugged and walked out together. I picked up my luggage and strode toward the exit. People around me spoke loudly in all kinds of languages that I didn't understand, both in the hall and out on the street. Suddenly someone called out to me:

"Taxi to Tel Aviv? Taxi to Jerusalem?"

"Taxi to Tel Aviv," I said. "How much?"

"Twenty-five."

"Lira?"

"No, no Lira. Dollars. Lira no good."

"OK."

The driver swung my suitcases up to the roof rack of the taxi, then secured them with an elastic strap. I opened my notebook and showed him the address of the accountant who was waiting for me with the key. He glanced at it and said:

"Yes, yes, it will be fine."

"I got into the car, picked up one of the folding seats in the middle row and sat down. I waited for the driver to get in on his side, but he was in no hurry to do so. To my surprise, two other men got in and sat in the back seat. Not a few minutes passed and two more crowded onto the folding seat next to mine. The driver started the car and we set off. God, *who are these people?* I thought I had gotten into a taxi, but apparently, I hadn't. Maybe it was just someone's private car? Maurice warned me not to hitchhike. Maybe they were even terrorists? I sat frozen in my seat, praying silently. What else could I do?

The passengers talked to each other animatedly, in a strange language, laughing and shouting. The car got on a dark highway, while I cowered in my corner, dying with fear. I glanced at my wristwatch, but it wasn't set to the local time. I remembered that we landed at eight in the evening. The clock in the car showed half past nine. The road seemed endless to me. We drove on and on, but when I looked at the clock again, only three minutes had elapsed. The spirits in the car calmed down and everyone fell silent. In the surrounding darkness I suddenly saw distant lights and on the sign on the side of the road something was written in Hebrew and in English. I read *TEL AVIV*, and felt much better.

We arrived in the city. One of the passengers turned to the driver and spoke to him while pointing in a general direction ahead. A few minutes later, the driver stopped to let the passenger out. The next stop was the Carlton Hotel, where three other passengers got off.

The driver turned to me and said in English:

"Now I'm taking you where you need to go. What's the address?" He looked at the note I handed him: "Reines Street 30. We will be there in five minutes. I relaxed in my seat and breathed a sigh of relief.

"Where are you from?" he asked me. "Oh, Brazil! Football... Pelé!" He went on speaking in English, enthusiastically and a lot. I couldn't follow. I barely understood a word here and a word there. "Samba... Carnival..." Eventually, we arrived. At long last.

I got out of the taxi and the driver took the luggage off the roof. I pulled my skirt down and adjusted my jacket. The driver put the luggage next to me and waited. Of course. I had to pay him. I quickly opened the bag and handed him a bill, as we had agreed. He smiled and said, "Pelé... Pelé... Football... Brazil..." and then he said goodbye to me.

I was alone with the two suitcases in front of the building. There were no doors at the entrance, no guard and no intercom. The note read: *The Mizrahi family, 1st floor, apartment 4.* There was no elevator either. I took the suitcases, one in each hand, and went up a step to the first floor.

I bitterly regretted having worn high heels. I got to the door, arranged the handkerchief in the left pocket of my suit, combed my hair with my fingers, and rang the bell. The door opened immediately and a man of about forty greeted me with a smile on his face.

"Welcome to Israel, Catarina." I smiled awkwardly and shook Mr. Mizrahi's hand. He helped me carry the suitcases inside and immediately two small children and their mother appeared. She offered me a drink in English.

"Water, please," I said.

Mrs. Mizrahi poured me mineral water and put on a kettle to make coffee. I said I was very grateful but there was really no need. Mr. Mizrahi insisted.

"Yes, yes, coffee, then I'll take you to the apartment," he said in a language that resembled Spanish. The coffee tasted awful, like black water, but I said in English:

"Thank you. It is very good." We talked a little, he in his strange Spanish and I, in stammering English. "Maurice sends his regards," I added.

"And how is Charlotte? She left suddenly and didn't even say goodbye." I answered that she was perfectly fine.

A little while later he got up and returned with two keys, which he hid in his pocket, and within a few minutes we were already on our way to the apartment that would be mine for the next few months, each of us carrying a suitcase. Before we turned left, he pointed to where the street continued and explained: "Here, farther ahead, is Arlozorov Street, which is the main street. It has many important things, such as a bank, supermarket and bus stations." He also mentioned Dizengoff Street, where people went for entertainment. He listed a few more useful places, all in his peculiar Spanish. I still didn't know that it was Ladino, the ancient language that the Jews from Spain spoke among themselves. I was trying very hard to understand him.

We crossed to the other side and entered a small dead-end street. "We're almost there." Mr. Mizrahi pointed to a nearby building. We stopped in front of it and set down the suitcases. He patted his pockets, rummaging through them. He finally announced: "I found them," and pulled out the keys. He opened the main door and went up the two stairs that led to a small, narrow elevator that took us up to the third floor. There was a sign in Hebrew on the apartment door. I wanted to know what it said and he answered, *The Valero Family*. He pushed the suitcases inside and said, "Well, I'm leaving now. If you need anything, please call me. Boa noite," he added in heavily accented Portuguese.

"Boa noite, Mr. Mizrachi, and thank you very much." I waited for him to get in the elevator before closing and locking the front door.

At that precise moment, the phone rang. I looked for it, but couldn't see it anywhere. Where the hell was it, I thought, walking in circles in the hall while the phone kept ringing. I finally found it on a small table that was right in front of my eyes. I recognized Stella's voice, weak and distant.

"Catarina! How are you? Is everything okay? I called several times but there was no answer."

"I just arrived this second."

"Great, the main thing is that you arrived well. We will speak again soon. Good night," she said and hung up.

As soon as I hung up, the phone rang again immediately.

I quickly picked up and said:

"Yes, Mrs. Stella," but it wasn't her. Marcus's concerned voice came through: "Hi, Catarina. I was very, very worried. It's very late and you didn't answer. I tried several times."

"I literally just walked in."

"Is everything okay?" He spoke fast and I felt he was trying to end the conversation.

"You sound stressed. Is anything wrong?" I asked.

"Calls to Israel are very expensive. I will talk to you soon. Love ya."

I was left holding a mute handset for the second time.

I entered the living room and turned on the light. Blinded for a moment, I closed my eyes. When I opened them, I couldn't believe what I saw. A large crystal chandelier with golden arms dangled from the ceiling. The antique style furniture was heavy, with rich wood moldings, and upholstered in a thick embroidered tapestry fabric. The walls were covered in light pink wallpaper. On the marble surface of the living room table was a painted Chinese vase, looking totally out of place. The paintings on the walls had wide, gilded frames. Everything glittered and shone. I couldn't figure out what all this had to do with the Valero family's elegant home in São Paulo. The rest of the apartment looked more normal.

There were two bedrooms with empty closets, except for bed linen. I chose the room with the double bed and put on the bedding. I sat on it and opened my bag to check how much money I had left, thinking I would have to go to the bank and convert it to Israeli money. I noticed a white envelope and remembered that it was the letter Marcus had given me, the letter he asked me to open once my plane took off.

I debated whether to leave the envelope sealed until morning: I was dead tired. But I couldn't help myself.

"Dear Catarina," it read. "It's 2:30 a.m. and I can't fall asleep. I still can't digest the fact that you are leaving today. You are the most significant person in my life. With you I felt complete and spent the most beautiful moments I've had in my life. I will miss your love very much and you will always remain in my heart. I tried to give you peace and tranquility by my side, but you were determined to travel to the end of the world following your dreams. I understand you. You are a lovely person and you should not change. Stay the way you are, wherever you are…"

I continued to read the letters that were blurred by the tears filling my eyes, until I couldn't take it anymore. My heart ached with yearning and sorrow. His words touched me because I felt he understood me. It was a pity that he didn't know how to love me enough. I sobbed into the pillow. When I opened my eyes again, I was in bed, with all my clothes on, the sun shining through the spaces between the slats of the blinds.

It was ten thirty and I knew the banks were only open until twelve. I didn't have time to make myself coffee. I filled a glass of water from the tap and took a big gulp. I felt the taste of salt in my mouth and spat it out immediately. I emptied the glass, rinsed it well and filled it again with water. I sipped carefully, but couldn't swallow. I would have to get some bottled water.

I took the small elevator down and went out into the street. The sun was bright and dazzling. I was not used to it shining so brightly. A young girl directed me to the nearest bank. I walked briskly, looking at the streets of Tel Aviv. Three-story houses, all built in a uniform style, all kind of off-white, all similar. Many trees were planted along the sidewalks—and I thought Israel was a desert. The streets were so different from what I imagined, different from how they looked at night, and much more beautiful. I almost missed the small branch of one of the banks, but I spotted it at the last minute. I approached a clerk at one of the counters and asked where I could exchange dollars. She directed me to a colleague, who welcomed me with a broad smile and invited me to sit down. He asked how many dollars I wanted to change.

"Fifty." His smile disappeared. He piled some bills in front of me and gave me back my passport.

I examined the foreign bills and put them in my wallet. On my way home I stopped at a supermarket. It was not big, but it was orderly and clean. There was a warm smell of baked goods in the air and I felt my stomach rumble. I walked along the shelves looking for the products I needed. An older woman saw me going through the aisles checking the packaging. She addressed me in English and kindly asked me where I was from and if she could help me.

"Thank you, sincerely. I am from Brazil. I don't know Hebrew at all and my English isn't very good either, as you can see, so it's hard for me to find what I'm looking for," I answered as best I could.

"From Brazil?" she said, "Then we can understand each other. I speak a little Spanish."

She helped me find the rice and oil as well as bread, butter, and mineral water.

I added up the prices in my head and allowed myself the luxury of buying half a chicken. I had to carefully calculate my expenses until Mr. Maurice arrived and helped me find a job. When I got home, I made myself coffee using mineral water. I pulled back the heavy curtains and opened the living room windows. A pleasant March sun shone on me, warming up the apartment. I opened the sideboard, and as expected there was a stereo. I pressed some buttons but the radio refused to work.

I stretched out a little on the couch, and woke up at midnight. I dragged myself to bed, changed clothes and fell asleep again. I woke up to a loud ringing. A glance at the clock showed it was two in the afternoon. I got up and staggered to the living room.

"Who is it?" I asked in Portuguese, and then in English.

"Charlotte, is that you?" answered someone from right outside the door.

"Charlotte isn't home. Who are you?"

"It's Joe, the owner of the apartment. Is Maurice around?" Well, I thought, he did know Maurice and Charlotte, so he probably was not a stranger. And it even made sense for him to be the owner of the apartment, as he claimed. I opened the door carefully and saw a man about forty years old, of average height, with curly hair and a wide grin. "Hello," he said, "I know Charlotte left, so when I saw the open windows, I got worried. Who are you, please?"

I said, as I opened the door wide, that I was Catarina, a relative, that Maurice was not yet in Israel, and that he would arrive in ten days or so. He kindly asked, in the same strange Spanish I had already heard from Mr. Mizrahi, if I needed anything, and if he could help me in any way. I hesitated for a moment and answered in Portuguese:

"The truth is, yes you could. The radio isn't working."

"I'll take care of that right away. He stepped confidently inside, went toward the sideboard, and leaned over the device. That confirmed he was who he said he was. He definitely knew the place. I hid a yawn, and then another.

"Forgive me," I apologized awkwardly, "I'm going to make myself some coffee. Can I make some for you too?"

He said yes. I went to the kitchen to put on the kettle. At that moment I noticed that I was in my nightgown, and hurried to the bedroom to change into proper clothes. Meanwhile, Joe tuned the radio to some station, but I didn't understand a word. He continued to scan stations until he heard a well-known song in English.

"Is this OK?"

"Yes, thanks. Nice song."

I came back from the kitchen with two cups of coffee.

"There is also an air conditioner and a TV," Joe said, "but the TV has only one channel in Hebrew and two in Arabic—from Jordan and Lebanon."

"That's fine. I'll make do with the radio." He sat down in the armchair next to the small table on which I had set the coffee cups.

"Excellent coffee," he said, taking a sip. "From Brazil?"

"Yes, Charlotte left it in the cupboard."

"It would have been funny if she had taken it back with her to Brazil."

So, he didn't know the truth about Charlotte, I thought, but didn't say anything.

"Are there other stations on the radio besides this one?"

"Yes, but only in Hebrew and Arabic. There is one station in particular, called *Kol HaShalom*—The Voice of Peace. It was founded by a man named Abie Nathan, and he broadcasts from a ship. He plays music from all over the world, and talks about peace."

Joe also explained some other things that I didn't quite understand, but the songs were very beautiful. When he finished his coffee and got up, I walked him to the door. He stopped in the small hallway, tore a page out of a notepad that was lying by the phone, took the pencil next to it and wrote down a number. "Here's my phone, just in case."

For two days now I had hardly eaten, only slept. No wonder I was so hungry. I cooked a large pot of chicken and rice, the scents mingling with the pleasant sounds of the Kol HaShalom station. I ate a large portion, and saved the rest in the freezer.

I felt wonderfully calm and full of energy. I knew I was ready for a new life.

Sitting in the dining room late into the night, I wrote long letters to Marcus, my family, and my friends. In the morning I went out with determination to look for a post office, to mail the whole pile. I walked toward Arlozorov Street and turned west toward the sea, until I reached Dizengoff Street. In the corner was a large, modern shop with framed photographs in the shop window. I went inside and walked around a bit, like in a gallery, looking at artistic portraits and landscapes under the sign *Faraj*.

Dizengoff Street was crowded. Fashion stores, cafés full of people, including many my age, talking and laughing. On the sidewalk I saw a group of young men in black leather jackets and boots, with punk haircuts. I did not expect people to be so modern and bold in the Holy Land. Still looking for the post office, I finally asked a man who was walking in front of me. He answered me loudly and with wide hand gestures. Thinking he was about to hit me, I turned quickly away from him. I tried again and approached a young woman, who said in English that the post office was located at the square with the large, colorful spinning fountain. I walked a long way until I saw the fountain above the square. People sat on benches around it and watched the play of colors, which changed as the fountain turned. Streams of water rose and faded to the rhythm of a classical melody. Small children ran among pigeons pecking at the ground. I found the post office, mailed the letters, and bought a pack of ten aerograms that could be sent from any mailbox, without requiring stamps.

On my way home I ran into the woman who had helped me at the supermarket.

"Hello, how are you? How are you managing?" she asked.

"Fine, thank you."

"Great. I see you are walking alone. Have you been to beach yet?" I answered I hadn't.

"Then come with me. I'm going for a walk by the sea this afternoon. Shall we meet outside Faraj at four?

At four on the dot, I was standing near Faraj, which was probably a popular Tel Aviv meeting point, and I saw Mrs. Hannah coming toward me with athletic lightness, even though she must have been over the age of fifty. She showed me the way to the seashore. We climbed up Independence Garden and looked out at the sea from the top of the cliff. The sun shone bright.

The blue sky and water met on the horizon, blending into each other. I stood in awe of the blue breathtaking beauty. In the distance I saw a ship that looked like it was stranded.

"Is that ship over there heading ashore?" I asked. "Is there a port in Tel Aviv?"

"That's Abie Nathan's ship. It doesn't go anywhere. It simply floats far from the coast, outside Israel's territorial waters, and broadcasts as a pirate radio station." Mrs. Hannah told me about herself and many other people like her, who were tired of wars, who did not want to send their children to the army at the age of eighteen and admired people like Abie Nathan, who devoted all their efforts to bringing peace. Yes, I too saw young men and women, almost children, wearing uniforms, passing by me on the street.

We walked down the hill, and continued along HaYarkon Street, where I saw a strange building, all white moldings, that looked like some weird combination of lace and whipped cream. We sat down on the matching bench on the sidewalk. Mrs. Hannah said that according to rumors, a very rich man had his architect-lover design a building to her liking, and this was the result. There were many opinions about this building as well, she added, and she herself had not yet decided whether she liked it or not.

I sat there, marveling on a white sculpted bench, in a wonderful land I had arrived in just days ago. I used to think it was all holiness and desert, and here I discovered an endless blue sea, child soldiers, and people who dedicated their lives to peace. I found a country full of contrasts and disputes, and warm people who opened their hearts to newcomers like me. While these reflections were passing through my mind, my soul began to become attached to this land. Before we parted with a hug, Mrs. Hannah gave me a piece of paper with the address of the Brazil-Israel Center. She said I could go there if I needed anything, or just wanted to hear some Portuguese.

The next morning was completely different. The sky was cloudy, with cold winds blowing. I looked for busy Dizengoff Street with its throngs of people, down which I had strolled just the day before, but it was quiet. Most of the shops were closed and few people were out walking. I returned home on a street without any traffic. No buses drove by. I walked around the apartment and then sat down in front of the TV. The picture was clear only on the Hebrew-speaking channel.

The phone rang, and Stella was on the line, asking how I was doing. I told her about the empty streets and how strange it was. She laughed and said that was because it was Saturday, the Sabbath in Israel. People rested and the city was quiet. She called to let me know that Mr. Maurice was in England and would be arriving next Thursday. I asked how Charlotte was and she said briefly that Maurice would tell me. I asked about Mrs. Clara's health and then ended the conversation.

That night my sleep was restless. On the one hand, I was waiting for Mr. Maurice to come and help me get my life started, but I also found it disturbing to share an apartment with a man I didn't actually know. I checked the cleaning supplies in the kitchen cupboard. Fortunately, the labels were also in English, and I could understand what each product was for. I scrubbed the toilets and bathrooms, cleaned the floor thoroughly and dusted the shelves in all the rooms. I vacuumed the furniture and the Persian carpets in the living room, and their color turned from dull to lively.

When cleaning the kitchen cupboards, I discovered some canned food and a bottle of olive oil. The days went by. I wrote letters. I missed Marcus. One day I visited the Brazil-Israel Center. A kind receptionist welcomed me cheerfully. Not many people seemed to frequent the place. It was good to hear my mother tongue.

That day Joe took me for a walk on the beach. I walked barefoot on the waterfront while the cold waves caressed my feet. I felt free and laughed out loud. Joe looked at me and smiled. He treated me to Turkish coffee and baklava.

He was nice, and spoke about his wife and daughters. I liked having him as a friend.

On Thursday, after cooking rice soup[27] and tidying up the house, I waited in the living room impatiently. At eight o'clock in the evening I heard a rustle from the stairwell. Someone was outside the front door, fumbling with the lock. The door opened and I got up. Maurice, bending toward the lock, was pulling out the key. His disheveled hair revealed a growing bald spot. I was thrilled to see him. He raised his head and looked at me tiredly with his pale blue eyes almost gray now. He was unshaven.

"Hello, Catarina," he said, straightening up. He looked a decade older than when I last saw him. Despite wearing a dark blue tailored suit with golden buttons, he still looked sad.

"Are you okay?" I asked.

"Yes, yes. Just a bit tired. After a shower I will probably feel better. How have you been?"

"Great. I made canja de arroz."

"Nice. Thanks. Well, I'm going to take a shower and then we'll talk." He returned to the kitchen after showering and putting on clean clothes. He asked if there was any water and I poured him some mineral water.

"The water here is salty, isn't it?" I smiled, and he nodded in acknowledgment. I couldn't help but notice the tear in his undershirt, which was showing under his unbuttoned shirt. I could try to sew it for him.

"Mr. Maurice, your undershirt is torn!" I pointed out.

---

27 Rice soup - Canja de arroz - is a typical Brazilian dish made with chicken breast, vegetables and rice.

He did not answer. He looked out the open kitchen window, as if searching for words. It was dark outside. In the building opposite us, a man was out in the balcony, leaning on the railing. The lanterns in the distant street were already on, and the trees below us looked like a dark mass.

"I know," he finally answered, scratching his forehead. "This is the custom with us, the Jews. When someone close to us dies we tear a garment and mourn for seven days."

Oh my God, had something happened to Mrs. Clara? I was deeply worried.

"Who died, Mr. Maurice?" I asked fearfully.

"Charlotte... My daughter," he sighed. "She went off and married a gentile. To me she is dead." The words erupted from deep inside his heart, heavy and grave. "She ran away from here to England, against our will. She fooled us. She left Israel without us knowing and married him even though we, her mother and father, did not agree to this marriage."

She married a non-Jew, therefore she no longer existed. For a long time, I didn't know what to say. Finally, I asked:

"What does Mrs. Stella think about this?"

"It's hard for her too, but she's stronger than me. She is upset, of course. She is also angry with me for behaving like this," he said, and left the kitchen.

I did everything I could to comfort him. I set the table with a white tablecloth, bowls, and cutlery, while I heated up the soup. His sorrow touched me. I felt more at ease with him after he opened his heart to me. He was no longer Mr. Maurice Valero, the aloof businessman, but almost a friend.

My fear of his presence in the apartment disappeared. During the meal I avoided mentioning Charlotte. He said that Mrs. Clara had recovered and was feeling great, and that maybe she would be coming to Israel with Stella. The fact that I was here created an opportunity, because I could be with her some of the time. She had not been to Israel in many years, since she joined Stella and him in Brazil.

He asked how I was managing with the money I had and I answered that it was fine but that it was running out. I gave him back the Liras he gave me in Brazil, because they were no longer valid.

On Friday, Maurice and I went to the supermarket together. It was a wonderful experience to be pushing a cart overflowing with groceries without me having to constantly calculate whether there was enough money for everything. In the evening he informed me that the next day, Saturday, we would go for a walk in Jerusalem. Jerusalem! I couldn't believe it.

The anticipation did not let me sleep. I would finally go to the Holy of Holies. I would walk the Via Dolorosa. I would see the Western Wall. I could insert a little note between the ancient stones! I would be able to thank God for bringing me to the Terra Santa and also ask him to take care of my family and my friends, as I promised I would.

Now it was really happening.

The next day I stood facing the open wardrobe. I needed something dignified and modest yet festive, suitable for a visit to the Holy City. It was a sunny, light-blue spring morning.

I studied the short-sleeved blouses and chose a very light purple one and a narrow, white skirt. Maurice ditched his blazer and appeared in a summer dress shirt. I put on sunglasses, feeling like I was on a vacation. We took a *Sherut* minibus, the only kind available on the Sabbath, to the central bus station and another one from there to Jerusalem. The winding road led us up the hills, between groves of trees and bushes. And I thought Israel was yellow and sandy! The views surprised me again. Suddenly, in the middle of the green, a scrap of a car, strange and out of place, appeared on the side of the road. Behind it was the rusty skeleton of a truck, and right after that a burnt jeep. I turned to Maurice with a questioning look.

"These are monuments," he said. "They are the remains of vehicles from the War of Independence and were left here on purpose, as a reminder. Since then, there have been more wars, two major ones, and some smaller ones called operations. Everyone here knows someone who has lost a loved one in the war." Suddenly, in a strange way, I felt that I was not alone, that I was part of a whole community of bereaved parents. I am like these people, who bury their dead and their pain, and go on living. I felt so close to this country.

The Paineira Tree (The Final Chapter)

I stayed in Israel for four consecutive years. Every three months I traveled abroad in order to renew my residence permit. That's how I visited Portugal, Egypt, Italy, and Spain. I worked caring for adults and children, and found an unpaid job during my free time, as a part-time assistant, in a medical laboratory. I stayed in touch with Marcus until he told me he had met someone else and got married. In 1988 I returned to Brazil. I had to decide whether I belonged there or not. I made a stopover in Greece, because I had never been there before. I toured around alone, feeling lonely and filled with longing. When I discovered which place I really missed, I realized where my home was.

As soon as I arrived in Brazil, I began to arrange my return trip to Israel. With the help and guidance of Prof. Rosenberg, I contacted the Jewish Agency who directed me to a Reform rabbi. For six months I learned how to become a Jew. At the end of my conversion process, I submitted my request to immigrate, and in 1989 I made Aliyah, officially becoming an Israeli. With documents at hand and a new letter of recommendation, I was offered a permanent position in a laboratory.

I maintained a loose connection with my biological family, but over the years I created a new family of close friends in Israel. In 1993, while living with a roommate in Tel Aviv, I received an ominous telegram from my sister Ivone, asking me to call her, which was not a simple procedure. By that time Ivone was already divorced with two children and could not afford her own telephone line. I had to coordinate in advance with her ex-mother-in-law, who had a device at home. That's how I learned that my mother, who suffered from high blood pressure, had a stroke while sitting on the sofa applying nail polish.

"At least she didn't suffer… At least she died well-groomed."

Ivone chuckled bitterly. After the conversation ended, I sat in my kitchen, stunned. Why should it make any difference to me? After all,

I didn't miss my mother. So many times over the years bitter memories and feelings of anger and resentment would surface. How could you? I used to ask. How could a mother be so hard on her daughter? And then I would cry alone, bitterly, feeling sorry for the lonely girl I had once been, and I couldn't forgive her.

But behind the sadness and anger I had dreamed that one day we would talk, she and I, and she would explain. I would understand her and she would understand me. Maybe, just maybe she'd even say she was sorry, and we would hug and cry on each other's shoulders, for the first time in my life. And then my constant pain would disappear once and for all. Now, that was never going to happen! Never, ever! I was left with questions and unresolved grief. How does one go on from here?

Two years elapsed since my mother's death, during which time I made many friends, including Uri, a good friend of my roommate. I also had partners, but had not been able to build a stable relationship with either one of them.

I decided to take a two-month break, and fly to Brazil again. On that trip, in a moment of closeness with my father, I asked him:

"Father, tell me the truth. Was Mother my real mother, or was I an abandoned child she adopted? Maybe I'm your daughter from a previous relationship?"

"Of course not, Catarina," Father answered, taken aback, "of course you are Mother's daughter. Hers and mine. I remember when you were born. Mother brought you home and you were almost as small as a puppy. Why are you asking me such a question?"

"You know why." I said quietly, "Mother treated me differently from the others. She was so hard on me. She was very demanding with me. She was never protective of me at all. She refused to help me when I needed it most."

Father sighed, shook his head and said slowly: "It was because she trusted you so much. She knew you were strong. She always used to say, 'Catarina knows what she wants, and she'll get it. She knows how to manage...' Mother loved you and thought about you a lot." He fell silent, and then continued, "A few months before she died, she asked Aroldo to take her to the sea. She had never been to sea before. When they returned, Aroldo told me that when they were at the beach, she saw a plane flying in the sky. She looked at it and said, as if talking to herself, 'Maybe it's flying to Israel, to the Holy Land, where Catarina is…' You were always in her thoughts."

On that same trip I also saw Mrs. Mendes, whom I once, for a long time, considered my second mother. She was moved to the core when she saw me. After a long hug, we sat on the sofa with her five daughters and tried to cram a six-year separation into an hour. Before we parted, she took my hand and held it for a moment.

"I miss your mother," she said. "What a strong woman she was. A true heroine. She fought for her children every day. All the burden fell on her shoulders. She did not have it easy. Many times she would say: 'It's good I have Catarina, she helps me carry the load of this family.' Especially during the period you worked in São Paulo, in that house. I once asked your mother: 'Donna Teresa, Catarina is so young, and she is so far from here. Isn't there a place for her that's closer?' But your mother said that in São Paulo you earned well and you wouldn't get that kind of salary in a nearby town, and that anyway there was no room in the house for nine people and one more on the way."

Yes, I thought, clearly remembering the warehouse where I visited my mother with her bulging belly, during the time I worked for Claudia. "After you came to visit, I asked your mother what you had said about the family you worked for, and your mother admitted that she had not asked, that you two barely spoke, because she was afraid you would say that you were unhappy there and that you wanted to come back home."

My journey ended in Bahia, where I strolled along the ancient alleys, sat at the beach alone, and pondered. I tried to understand my mother's behavior toward me, to put myself in her place. There were times when I almost managed, but then I remembered the hair she stole without asking me, the milk she refused to give Rebeca, and I thought: How could a mother do such a thing to her daughter.

The conversation I had with my father helped to soften something in me. I thought of that woman who fought all her life to bring bread to her children, who could not read or write, and who only saw the sea at the age of sixty. In her childish innocence, whenever she looked at a plane in the sky, she thought that of all the countries in the world, maybe it was flying to a small and forgotten country, where her daughter was.

Did I have a place in your heart, Mother, even though you never showed it? Maybe. I think that now I can put the past behind me. One chapter is over, and there is nothing that binds me to this place anymore. I need to build a new life in a new country. I need to start my own family.

I returned to Israel with the certainty that this was where I belonged. I wanted a partner and children. My relationship with Uri soon turned from one of friendship into flourishing romantic love. Shortly after I became pregnant, we got married, and Noa was born. My renewed motherhood revived in me the most difficult time in my life, the illness and loss of Rebeca, who left just like she had appeared, as a surprise. She passed through my life like a shooting star, as if she had a role to play, and then it was over, and she disappeared. I can't define for what exact purpose she was given to me, but when I look back at my life after her, I think of how strong I am.

If at the age of eighteen I was able to climb out of the abyss I was thrown into, grab life, and hold on to it, that means I am really strong. That I can handle anything without breaking. Thanks to Rebeca I left Nezinho. If she hadn't disappeared, I would still be living in a miserable house, struggling every day in an existence of poverty and ignorance.

There is no doubt that had I been able to choose, I would have chosen for her to live. But I also know that would have forced me to stay. I was not given a choice. That was the path life took me on, and I walked it to the best of my ability. I can only be grateful for the wisdom and deep emotional charge it gave me.

When I looked at Noa, washed and well-fed, in the cute little cot we bought at baby supply store *Shilav*, I thought of my first daughter, crying from hunger on her makeshift bed between two chairs. In the midst of the happiness and love that filled my heart, there was a stabbing pain, and under it, were hidden doubt and guilt. Had I done enough? Maybe I could have done more to save her? Sometimes, when Noa got fussy and raised a fever, as crazy as it was, I'd wrap her up in a blanket, put her in the car seat and drive her to the emergency room for tests, so I could sleep at ease.

Then Jonathan was born. The children grew up and reached the age when I could remember myself. With each passing day I was amazed at how big the gap was between their childhood and mine. As my experience of motherhood extended over the years, I understood my mother less. Logic could explain away her harshness toward me—the poverty, the great burden that fell on her. But my heart did not understand. I wanted to put my thoughts in order, to tell people about the girl I was, about the life I had then. Maybe one day I would tell my children too.

The story of my life was kept hidden inside me for many years, and I didn't share it with anyone. I didn't feel like I had anything to be proud of, and too many things hurt me when I brought them to my consciousness. One day, when I was talking to a close friend, I accidentally blurted out, in a moment of openness, that I had fought tooth and nail to study and that I didn't get any help from my parents, except for three pencils, a notebook, and an eraser.

Suddenly, the dark little secret from my store of secrets became words and soared out of me into the world. This story wasn't just mine anymore, and suddenly it didn't weigh on me. It looked less dark and threatening once it was out in the open. That day I took a pad and a pen and started to write. But I didn't last long. It was not easy for me, and I constantly escaped to my daily chores.

When Jonathan turned four, I took my new family to meet my old family in Brazil. We started in the city of Itú where my father and brother live. The taxi stopped in front of the house. I pushed the rusty gate and through the open door to the house, I saw my father smoking on the sofa in the living room. When he noticed our arrival, he got up. Dropping his cigarette on the floor, he crushed it with the sole of his shoe, and came out to greet us. The yard was infested with weeds and the pungent smell of the chicken coop floated in the air. I held on to Noa and Jonathan, as if drawing strength from them, and we walked the short distance to the door of the house, where my father awaited. I glanced at Uri, who was walking behind me with an impassive face. My father wore a wrinkled white shirt, and trousers. He had aged since I last saw him. He stretched out his arms and called out choking with emotion:

"Catarina, your children are so big! I can't believe it!"

He held me tightly to him, his body smelling of sweat. Taking a handkerchief out of his pocket, he wiped his eyes and nose. The children came closer and hugged him too. He kissed them on the head and again wiped his eyes with the handkerchief.

After I introduced Uri to him, we went inside. A ten-year-old girl was sitting on the living room sofa. I knew it was Carla, the daughter of my little brother Reginaldo, who died at the age of thirty-two. He and her mother were drug addicts and were unable to take care of her, so my father was raising her. Between her skinny knees a yellowish piece of sponge peeked out from the torn upholstery. Father invited us to make ourselves at home.

Uri examined with suspicion the seat of the chair offered to him before sitting down. Through the open door, a chicken suddenly came flying in, landed in the center of the living room, and then strutted around, pecking at the crumbs scattered on the floor. I discerned droppings in one of the corners.

Examining the inside of the house, I saw the walls were built of red bricks, typical of the region, badly plastered. Whoever had placed the window frame in the wall and slapped coarse cement to affix it, did a sloppy job of sealing all the perimeter, because there were slivers of light peeking through the spaces. A broken door had been designated to lean against the wall opposite me. The apartment looked like a collection of scrap that was disposed of, and then collected by an amateur builder to become a house. Everything looked so shabby. I didn't remember it being that bad. The children looked around in shock and said nothing. I asked them to sit on the sofa, next to their new cousin and my father. Uri's face was still expressionless.

Hearing Ivone washing the dishes in the kitchen, I got up to help her. The kitchen was large and empty. A small fridge, a table, and an oven. The table was covered with dirty dishes and so was the sink. Ivone was soaping glasses with a frown.

Once the sink was empty, I saw that the bottom was some shade of yellow-brown, like rust. I poured us juice and coffee. Ivone arranged some rolls she baked herself and brought with her from home in a bowl. When she joined us, she angrily remarked to Father that the least he could have done was to prepare properly in our honor. He could have tidied up the house or dressed more appropriately.

Noa asked to use the bathroom, and I went with her. Seeing the stained slab and the yellowing toilet, I asked her to try not to sit down.

The neighbors who heard about the expected guests from Israel, slowly filled the house, dragging with them benches from the yard or chairs from their homes. Crowds of children surrounded Noah and Jonathan, asking them questions. I translated from Portuguese to Hebrew and from Hebrew to Portuguese. They wanted to see what Hebrew writing looked like and were fascinated by the strange characters written from right to left. I pulled out the chocolate bars I had brought from Israel and offered them to the little guests who crowded into the room. They looked at the chocolate as if it were a rare wonder. The cubes quickly disappeared into their mouths. They smiled at me happily, the whites of their eyes standing out against their brown faces and chocolate-stained white teeth. After an hour I became redundant. They no longer needed my translation and all the children, including mine, went out to play in the yard. We stayed at my father's place until the evening.

The next day I went to see him again, with a suitcase full of clothes. The house was relatively tidy. He was wearing clean clothes and smelled of soap and aftershave. I looked at Ivone, who was already there, questioningly. When we were alone, she explained to me that she asked Aroldo's wife to clean the house in our honor and paid her.

Aroldo, his wife, and their three children lived in a small, modest, but clean house, which bordered my father's yard. He worked as a plasterer and painter and she worked in housekeeping.

"She cleans well," Ivone added. "She does a great job when she comes to my place."

"Is she your housekeeper? How? She's your sister-in-law!"

"So what?" Ivone shrugged. "If she didn't clean at my place, she would be cleaning somewhere else. I always pay her on time and treat her well. What's wrong with that?"

I distributed the clothes we brought. The children's clothes that did not fit Carla or Aroldo's boys went to the neighbors. Uri's old clothes made my father happy, because they were both the same size. I handed him an envelope with some money I had prepared for him. He refused, saying he was fine, but in the end, I convinced him by saying it was easier for me to give them money than to buy them unnecessary gifts no one would use.

I wanted to cram all my past into one trip, and after two days in Itú, we took a taxi to Sorocaba. At the entrance to the city, the monumental paineira tree, over one hundred and fifty years old, was still there. It made me feel happy, like seeing an old acquaintance, confirming I had returned home. We asked the driver to stop for a moment and got off to give my old friend the honor of a visit. It was already half dry. Its splitting trunk had been filled with concrete to stop the decay. A few thick branches still covered with leaves insisted on surviving, as the last signs of life. Hardship had not been able to defeat it, I thought and was filled with appreciation. We stayed for some time on the narrow green strip that divided the boulevard, caressing the mighty trunk and circling around it.

Long trains of low houses stretched along the sidewalks, like in the past. Most of them were residential houses, but there were also warehouses and workshops. The city had not changed much. We continued our ride and the driver slowed down at the first stop on my list of sites. It was a magnificent building in Sorocaba terms: the church. A tall light-yellow building, with brown stripes around the windows and door cornices. Above the main door, in the front, was a large, colorful porcelain image depicting a saint holding baby Jesus in his arms. I looked at the high spires and the cross that topped the dome, remembering with silent respect the construction worker who was killed with a tremendous thud right before my eyes.

'Let's go in. It's beautiful inside, and also cool." In the pleasant dimness of the great hall, I recognized the long wooden pews, the platform on which the priest stood, where I waited for the bread handout. That was where I saw my beloved Raphael for the first time, and it was also where I said goodbye to him. Here we met as children and here I accompanied him on his last journey.

Pointing to the colorful stained-glass windows, Jonathan cried:
"Wow, cool windows!"
"Shhh... You're not allowed to talk so loudly here, right, Mom?" Noa admonished right away.

I pulled my children toward me and held them close.
"Do you remember I told you about my life in Brazil, before I met Dad? So, a long, long time ago, this is where I got married for the first time."

We left the church, got back in the taxi and I guided it through the alleys to each of the many houses I lived in as a child. We started on Benjamin dos Santos Street, in a house where mother burned the wood shavings and blackened the walls. My new family and I stood before the wall that surrounded it and peered through the bars of the gate. The small yard was paved with concrete, like in all the other houses.

It looked exactly as it did back then, when I was eight years old. I suddenly returned to that day, when we arrived in Sorocaba. After the beautiful house father built for us in Jacarezinho, we found ourselves, all six of us, in a single room with a tiny kitchenette, one bed, and two mattresses shoved against the wall.

We then drove slowly down the street, in the direction of the hair salon where my mother sold my hair. At one of the street corners, a forgotten memory suddenly came back to my mind. I had gone shopping with my mother. My hair was still long and flowing shiny over my shoulders. A foreign woman, with white skin and nice clothes, approached my mother and asked: "Excuse me, do you maybe have any free days during the week? I have a daughter about the same age," she said, pointing at me. "Maybe you could work for me too?" Mother answered a firm no, grabbed my hand and dragged me after her.

"Stupid woman," she muttered angrily to herself. "How dare she think I'm the nanny. So what if my skin is darker? So stupid!"

We arrived at Villa Gutierres. The neighborhood had grown, and was impossible to recognize. I wasn't able to locate the house that Carlinho's godfather so generously lent us. Only the mental institution was still there, and now nothing about it seemed scary to me. The last stop was the house in Alsindo Guanabara, where Nezinho carried me over the threshold on our wedding day.

On the tombstone covered with light brown ceramic tiles only two names were engraved—those of Nezinho's parents. My Rebeca's was not mentioned, but I knew she was there. I also knew that her father had joined them eight years earlier. My brother told me about Nezinho's passing. He was now closer to his daughter than he had ever been in life.

The four of us stood in silence by the grave. I took out a picture of Rebeca from the bag and the children bent down to look at it. A tear rolled down Noa's cheek. I held her close to me and for the first time in my life I was by Rebeca's grave and did not cry.

"She would have been seventeen by now," I said, thinking out loud. Near the exit, a concrete structure made of four pillars and a roof, with a tin table inside, housed multiple puddles of clotted wax with a smoking candle stick stuck to it. I took out some remembrance candles I had prepared in advance from my bag, and each one of us lit a candle for my Rebeca and all her ancestors.

In the following days we went on a journey across the sites of my childhood, the Paraná region.

Breakfast at the hotel was served on a huge table full of locally baked breads and cakes, fresh cheeses, and homemade jams. The glass of milk I poured smelled just like it used to when my father filled up a tin mug straight out of the cow's udders.

Outside, the taxi driver we had ordered was waiting, wearing a respectable shirt and pressed trousers, wiping the car's windows. We drove through green pastures, corn and bean fields, and coffee plantations. Herds of cows and horses calmly grazed in the vast open spaces.

The children, who were glued to the car windows, asked to get off for a moment, to look at the cows up close, and pet the little calf by the fence. In the end we stopped by a coffee plantation where they got off to look at the trees and take pictures next to them. Noa picked green, yellow, and red pods that were not yet ripe. She kept them for a long time after we returned to Israel in a drawer next to her bed.

We arrived in Jacarezinho thirty-five years after I left the place, and I didn't recognize anything. I didn't know how to find the Matias family's fazenda either.

I was so hoping to see Seu Nestor Matias again. He had a special place in my heart, where I kept people who were dear to me, and some moments of kindness. For a moment I thought I had lost the trail that could lead me to him, and then I remembered the Jacarezinho hospital. Everyone had to go through it at some point, at least once. They must have patient records and addresses. Following the signs, we reached the hospital. The office attendant was kind.

"I'm looking for a man named Nestor Matias. He owned a fazenda in Jacarezinho. We live in Israel, in the Middle East," I explained to her. "We came here specially to look for him. Could you give me his address, please?" The clerk listened to me attentively and finally said that she was very sorry, but she was not allowed to give out people's personal information. I wasn't going to give up easily, really not. I tried to think of reasons and moving words to convince her, but right at that moment someone addressed me:

"Ma'am, I think I know whom you are looking for," said a man who was waiting for his appointment. "He has two sons, doesn't he? Well, he lives nearby. Right at the exit from Jacarezinho. I can tell you how to get there."

The driver followed my instructions, and stopped near a large house in an old neighborhood. I got out of the car alone and went to the gate. I clapped my hands and called: "Ode casa?" Anybody home? as we used to do in the village back then. My voice was filled with emotion.

A dark-skinned young woman came out to meet me. I assumed she was the housekeeper. I explained to her that I was looking for Seu Nestor Matias, and she asked me to wait a moment. A well-groomed woman, a little over sixty, her hairdo fixed with hairspray, came out the door. I assumed she was his wife, but I remembered her beautiful and regal, whereas now she looked like any ordinary woman.

"Mrs. Matias," I smiled excitedly, "my name is Catarina Granater. I am the daughter of Alemão, who used to work for you thirty-five years ago. I don't know if you remember me. I was eight years old when we left."

Her facial expression suddenly changed, from puzzlement to surprise, and then broke into a broad grin.

"Catarina! I remember you as a little girl. Six years old, maybe! I can't believe it's you! Of course I remember your father, the whole family. Come on in."

She was surprised again when I introduced Uri, Noa and Jonathan to her.

You have children who are older than you were then! Such lovely kids... Take a seat, please, I will get Nestor right away." She disappeared in the direction of the kitchen and then came out again and called aloud, "Nestor, come. Come look who's here!" The maid walked in with a tray and a pitcher of fresh lemonade. Mrs. Matias was pouring cold lemonade into glasses when her husband entered the room. I saw a thin elderly man, walking slowly on unstable legs. He was wearing a cowboy hat, like my Seu Matias, but he was much shorter. I eyed him carefully and slowly discovered, in his features, the Seu Nestor I knew. He looked at us perplexed. "Nestor, this is Catrina, Alemão Granater's daughter. The little girl who played with our Nei, remember?" his wife explained. Recognition flashed in his eyes.

"Seu Nestor," I said, moving closer to him, "I will never forget you. You saved us back then, when we lost everything. You helped us through the trial. You drove us early in the morning to the train. You did so much for us. I don't know what we would have done without you!" Nestor held out a trembling hand to me. He looked at me and his lips quivered. His eyes filled with tears and he nodded. When I hugged him, we both cried. We took the paper napkins his wife handed us and laughed as we wiped our faces.

"You've grown so much!" he said in a weak voice. He looked so old and frail, my heart ached for him. "Are these your children?" He looked at Noa and Jonathan, who were sipping lemonade and following, embarrassed, the little drama unfolding before their eyes. He approached Noa, and she politely put the glass down and stood up for him. He hugged her, and she hugged him back. Jonathan did the same. He shook Uri's hand and slowly sat down on the couch. I told them about our family's saga in brief. I said that my father lived in Itú, and that Ivone, who arrived in Jacarezinho as a baby, was now the mother of two sons. Seu Matias told us they had sold the fazenda, and his sons were taking care of the remaining farming business. On that day, Nei was in Londrina, at a cattle fair, meeting some customers from Canada.

I told them we were in Jacarezinho and I didn't recognize anything. That I had no idea how to find the place where we lived. Nestor's wife offered to show us around.

After eating a typical Brazilian meal with seasoned cuts of meat, white beans, and fresh vegetables, we drove to the fazenda. It extended out before me, old and neglected. The fishpond was empty of water. There were new tenants living in it now. We also found the school. It remained as it was, only smaller, and one corner of the roof had collapsed. It looked like it was waiting for my visit before crumbling down completely. A new church, built of stone, rose up right next door.

We returned to the village and Mrs. Matias showed us the way to my lost paradise. The stream was hidden by the tall grass, the fruit trees were gone, and so was the bridge. The railroad had been shut down and the rails dismantled. We toured the area for a while. The green fields stretched out wide and bright, just as they did in the memories I carried. My children, drunk with all that open space, ran around in the grass that reached up to their knees. In my mind's eye, they became Catarina and Aroldo running to the stream, back then, thirty-five years ago.

On our return to Israel, something changed in me. I felt that something was bothering me, and I could not pinpoint what it was. A kind of invisible wall arose between Uri and me. A few days later, he handed me a large green hardcover notebook and said briefly:

"This is for you. It's time you started writing down the story of your life." That was it. It dawned on me that we hadn't talked at all about everything I experienced on this long journey.

He did not mention the encounter with my family at all. I thought it would have been appropriate for him to say something, to ask... He could have said, for example, "It's unbelievable that this is your family and that they still live like this." or "Lucky you left Brazil. Kudos to you for being able to break away and make so much progress." Or he could have asked, "How do you feel after returning to the sites of your childhood?" "Do the memories weigh you down?" "How do you feel when you see your family living in such conditions?" During the whole month we spent in Brazil he didn't say a word. I had told him my story before we got married, and now, after being there and seeing it with his own eyes, he didn't have a single question to ask? After all, he hadn't been able to hide his initial shock. I think I overheard a conversation he had with his mother on the phone: "You can't imagine how they live here," he said.

Could it be that he suddenly saw the great gulf that existed between us? Was it possible that he valued me less now, after seeing where I came from? Or maybe the problem was with me? Maybe my old complex floated up to the surface from the recesses of my soul, and that's why I needed so much support from the man I was with? But if I really needed support and wasn't getting it, then we had a problem. Maybe that is where the relationship between Uri and me started to unravel, maybe not. Maybe there were completely different reasons that kept us apart, as happens with many couples that eventually break up. Our marriage did not survive, and three years later we got divorced.

I returned to writing my story, this time together with my best friend.

One day I took Noa to a swimming lesson and sat down at the shaded café, in the patio by the pool. Noa was already twelve years old, around the age I was when I lived in Claudia's house. I plunged into my memories, and became the thin eleven-year-old girl again, in the big house, scrubbing the marble floor and sweeping the water in the patio with my feet frozen. I saw myself eating all alone in the laundry room and peering over the wall at the neighbors' TV.

Suddenly, out of nowhere, a familiar voice asked me:

"Mom, why are you crying?" My thoughts quickly scrolled back up the present, and I saw Noa, wrapped in a towel, staring at me. I hastened to answer:

"It's nothing, Noa. Just tears of emotion, you know. Do you need anything?"

"Do you have two shekels for a popsicle?" she asked. I gave her the coins and watched her baffled. How? How was it that my daughter, exactly the same age I was when I worked so hard in a strange house, was now swimming in the pool and buying herself ice cream, just like that? Who would have believed then, thirty years ago, that that is how my life would unfold? I looked at Noa, popsicle in hand, running on the grass toward a jubilant group of children her age, and I stared in wonderment.

One day I remembered the great telenovela, *Jungle of Stone*. Maybe I could find a synopsis of the story on the Internet, because I no longer remembered even the little I was able to gather from watching the neighbors' TV. That evening I sat down at the computer, and was surprised to find that not only did the synopsis exist, but I could watch entire episodes. Thrilled with my discovery I chose one. And here, from a distance of thirty years and thousands of miles, Regina Duarte and Francisco Cuoco were pulled out and appeared in front of me in black and white. I loaded episode after episode. The vague elements of the plot that I recalled were completely unraveled and woven into another story. The cave, which I clearly remembered as the place where

Fernanda was imprisoned, turned out to be an abandoned house. I stayed by the computer screen until the wee hours of the night.

I finally got to watch all the episodes of the telenovela in order, until the last one.

It's never too late.

Glossary

Agrião – Arugula-like green leaves

A sua abença mãe – Bless me, mother.

Bauru – pastrami and yellow cheese sautéed in a pan, topped with tomato slices and dips.

Bornal – a rucksack or shoulder bag made of cloth.

Caipirinha – a cocktail made with pinga, lemon, and sugar

Calabresa – a kind of sausage - Calabresa fried with onion rings is a typical Portuguese dish

Candomblé – a religion brought to Brazil by African slaves

Coxinha de Galinha – a dish made with shredded chicken breast, mixed with sauce and wrapped in dough cooked in water. The dough is shaped as a chicken leg, dipped in breadcrumbs and fried. When the shank is still warm, a toothpick is stuck to its narrow end to get the effect of a drumstick.

Curandera – a healer or medicine woman who uses herbs, plants, magic, and spiritualism to treat illness

Empanadas - a typical Brazilian dish of fried dough filled with meat or vegetables

Faixa de Umbigo – a wide umbilical band used to wrap a newborn baby

Fazenda – a farm

Feijoada – a stew made with black beans and several types of meat

Guaraná – a mildly carbonated Brazilian drink

Guarapá – the sweet nectar of squeezed sugar cane

Havaianas – a well-known brand of flip flops or toe sandals

Jabuticaba – a fruit tree whose small, black, sweet fruits grow on its trunk

Moringa – a large clay pot with a handle and two openings for drinking that keeps the water cold.

Nossa Senhora Aparecida – a version of the black Holy Mary, dressed in a magnificent blue robe and a gold crown on her head; Her figurines and pictures were very much loved and venerated by the Catholic public in Brazil.

Pamonha – a batter made with grated corn kernels mixed with milk and sugar, all wrapped in corn leaves and boiled

Panettone – a traditional Christmas cake, made mostly with dried fruits

Pingado e Pão com Manteiga – coffee and buttered bread

Pinga or Cachaça – a distilled spirit made by fermenting sugar cane juice

Quentaō – a hot wine with ginger and sometimes cinnamon

Terra da Garoa – the land of the drizzle

Umbanda – An offshoot of the Candomblé religion, which was brought to Brazil by African slaves

Venda – a grocery store

My mother

My father in his youth

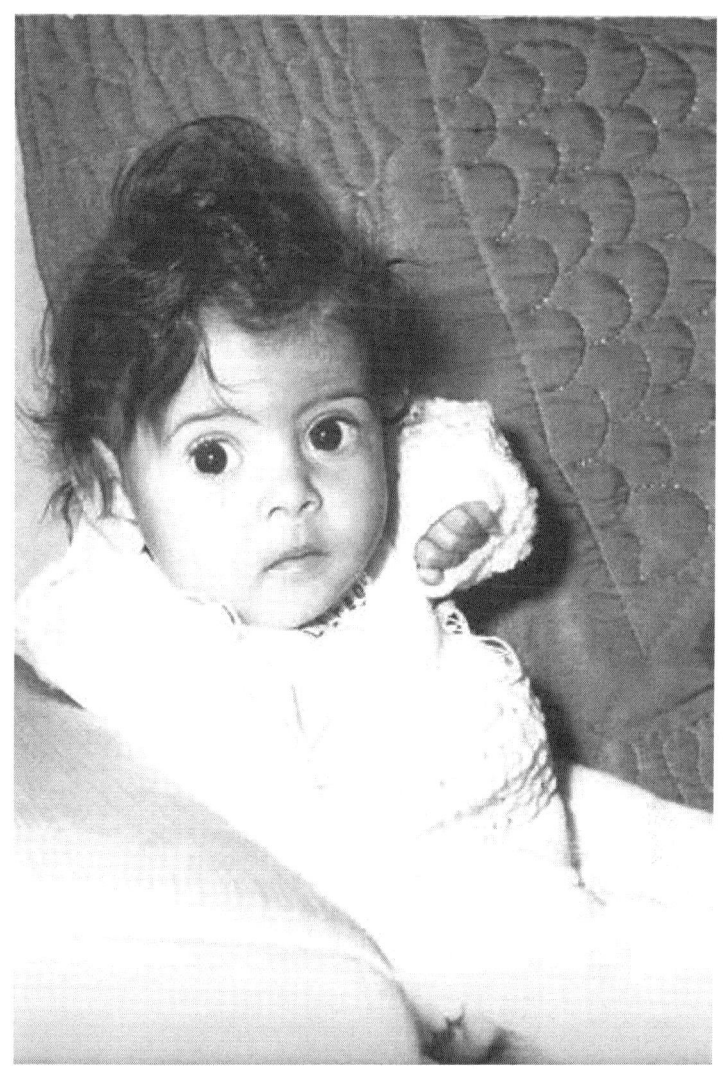

Rebeca

The Paineira tree at the entrance to Sorocaba

I, Catarina, at the age of 28

Made in the USA
Middletown, DE
22 November 2025

22816023R00215